Acid Track

Detective Mahoney Series

Julie Hiner

Killers and Demons

Damage Done by Acid Track

"Of corpse I had to read Demon Julie's new story that opens all doors to horrifying acts of preserving doll-eyed innocence. In Acid Track, she plumbs the depths of a depraved mind while planting plenty of intriguing clues along the way."

Cami Schulte – Stark raving fan of crime novels, reading safely from her home since the 70s.

"Wow! The second in the Detective Mahoney page turning, mind numbing series did not disappoint. It is crafted with a perfect balance of criminal detective know how and deep dark psychological horror. I can hardly wait to see where Demon Julie takes us next!"

Rhonda Francis – Book Connoisseur & Disruptive Neighbour

"I was hooked from the first page. Just like in Final Track, Julie transports you to the glamour of the 80s, frantically following Detective Mahoney to some of the darkest places your mind can imagine. Every glam rock lover needs this in their collection."

Holly Marinelli – Book Lover & Head Banger Extraordinaire

To all the lost souls
Taken from earth
Far too soon

To all those
Left behind

Contents

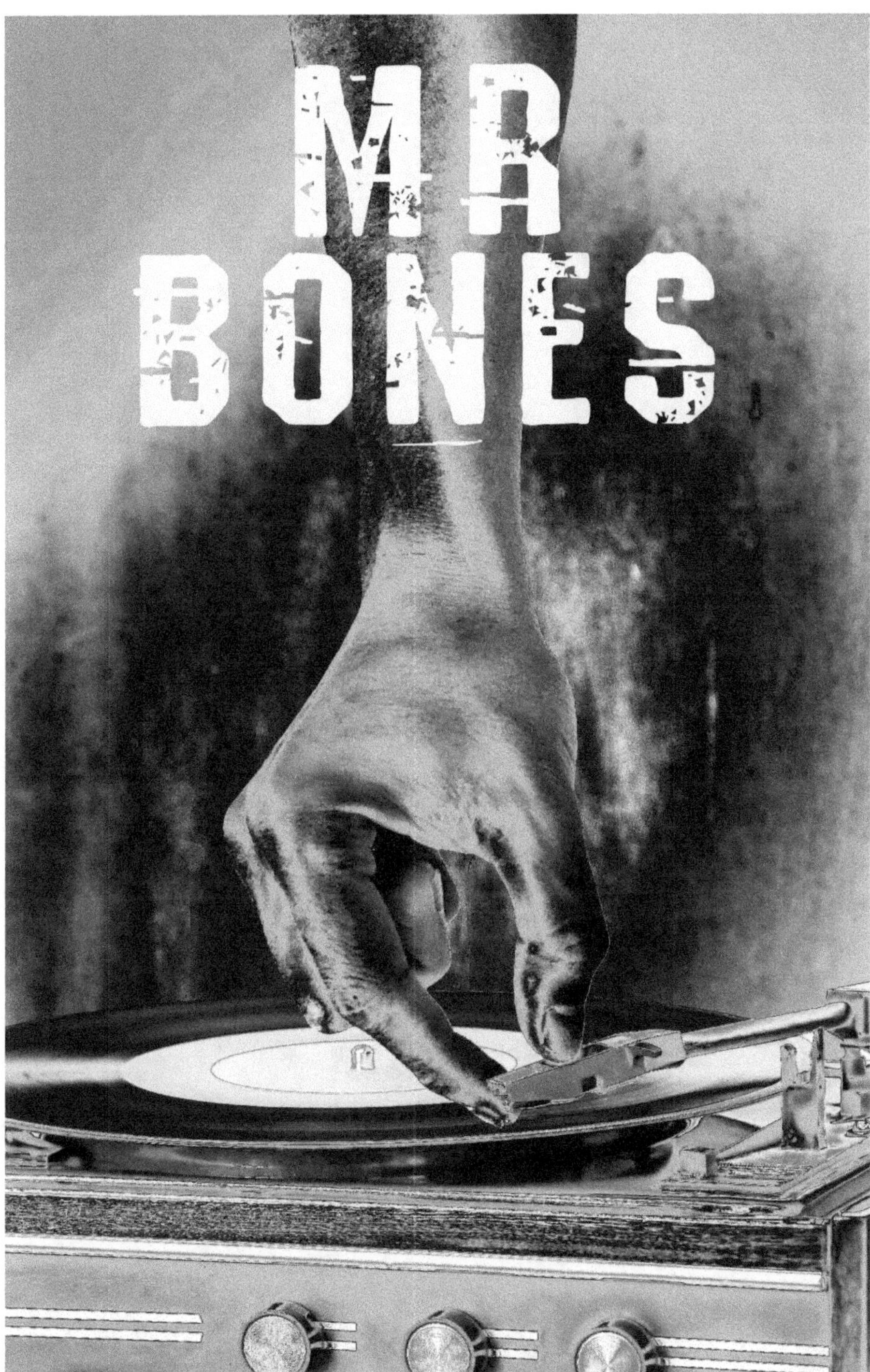

MR
BONES

Chapter One

Cave and Coffin

Detective Mahoney stared at the small corpse. White lengths of cloth wrapped the body, concealing any identity. Mahoney was sure it was a kid.

The body was tucked away in a coffin-like structure at the back of a cave near Wash-A-Way Point. No one knew how long it had been here.

The cave closed in around Mahoney, stifling his breathing. He lifted his gloved hand. A silver chain hung from his pointer and middle fingers. An oval-shaped, arctic ocean pendant swayed back and forth. He swore on his life it was identical to the one left on the first victim in his last case. *What did Seth have to do with this small mummy in the back of a cave?* He'd hoped to say goodbye to the sadistic monster. Leave him behind bars for someone else to deal with.

He'd barely slammed the door on the Glam Boys murder case, catching the first serial killer to reach gruesome fingers over his hometown. At least, during *his* twenty-year watch. He'd read about the serial killers lurching down south all across the states. This breed had now surfaced further north, here in Canada, in his beloved city of Calgary, Alberta.

The scent of lavender seeped up behind him. Medical Examiner Terra Blackwood approached. "Medical team has arrived. We'll lift the body out of the hole, get it to the morgue. The crime scene techs will deal with the coffin."

Clasping the rim of his tattered, grey derby with his pointer and thumb, Mahoney looked up over his broad shoulder. "Sounds good. I'll check in on your...processing...on my way back to HQ."

Blackwood nodded. The single silver streak in her dark hair slid over her shoulder. As she walked away, the lavender cloud departed with her.

Mahoney returned his attention to the small, lifeless figure.

He pulled his tweed coat tight around his chest. The cave loomed, suffocating him. Visions from recent murder scenes muddled his mind. Corpses of college boys painted up like rock gods whirled around his head. A barrage of images followed. Purple vials of poison poured through his thoughts, sadistic messages carved into flesh bled down dead torsos, shimmering black tassels flapped, pale skin stretched over brutally branded necks. Had Seth, the psycho he'd locked away, resurfaced into his life?

Chapter Two

The Killer that Won't Go Away

The rusty orange door on his '69 Pony creaked as Mahoney slammed it shut. The murder scene he'd just walked away from replayed through his mind like a movie reel stuck on a frame. A dark cave, a small body wrapped like a mummy, a concrete coffin—the images refused to leave him alone. Tossing his tattered, grey derby onto the passenger's seat, he looked down at it. *Poor old hat. Really took a beating on that last case.*

The four doors of his old car closed in on him. He pulled his heavy eyelids open and looked at his unshaven face in the rearview mirror. Dark shadowy rings wound around his eyes. *You need some sleep, old man.*

He scanned the pile of cassettes on the passenger seat. A flash of white poked out from underneath his derby, catching his eye. Mahoney slid the hat aside and stared down at the plane ticket.

He was supposed to go to the Sunshine Coast for some good ol' rest and relaxation. He snickered. What did he know about relaxing? He was supposed to go see his family...or at least the remnants of it. His wife had added the prefix 'ex' to her title years ago. He used to call her Bea, a pet name that had surfaced on their honeymoon. That was off limits now. Letting go of the idea that she'd be his again was still a struggle. He had hope that his daughter, Stella, wouldn't kick him out of her life too. At ten years old, she was still a little girl in his eyes. Yet, she conveyed the sense of awareness of a young woman when her eyes narrowed as she analyzed his explanations. Soon she'd be blazing through her teenage years, and he didn't know how much longer she'd put up with his excuses.

He looked at the ticket that secured his spot on a flight leaving at six o'clock in the morning. *Dammit.* How many times could he choose a case over his daughter? How much more patience would she have for him?

He rested his heavy head against the driver's seat and closed his eyes. Taking a couple of deep breaths, he relaxed his shoulders, willing calming energy through his body.

Old memories resurfaced. A sandy, brown beach floated into his mind. The warm sun bathed him. The beach stretched miles in both directions. Cheerful giggling rung out against the crashing of the waves. "Daddy, Daddy, watch me swim." Blonde curls bouncing, his little girl ran toward him, arms stretched out. His bare feet sank into the soft, warm sand, the granules grinding gently around his toes. Little birds ran at the speed of light along the surf, frantically thrusting their long beaks into the wet sand between thunderous crashes of surf. Seagulls squealed, sweeping along the surface of the water.

A cloud of floral forest permeated his nose. There she was, still vivid in his memory. Bea, the one woman he had opened himself up to. Blue scarves swirled around her beautiful figure. Long, sandy locks touched with strawberry fell around her shoulders. She had given him everything—her love, her trust, their daughter. Warmth tingled through his insides. His heart pulsed. Stepping a bare foot over the sand, he walked toward them.

Two steps in, a mummy-carcass flung itself in his path. An ice wave sliced through him, from heart to stomach. His eyes popped open. *I can't turn my back on the cave case.* Someone left that small figure wrapped in the coffin. He needed to find out who. He shook his head hard.

Turning the key in the ignition, he sighed. *C'mon Bug. You're not done yet.*

Sifting through the pile of cassettes, he halted when a man with hypnotizing eyes looked back at him, wild curls framing his face. Jim Morrison. A dark poet turned rock god. New to Mahoney's tape collection, the cassette reminded him of his younger, cooler days when he spent hours listening to his stack of LPs. He opened the case, pulled the tape out, and slid it into the tape deck. An eerie riff vibrated through the car.

Backing out of the gravel lot, he cruised down the highway. The sun hung low in the sky, an orange bulb lined in a blood-red hue. *A good blues riff and an open road. Should clear my mind.* He stared hard down the long road ahead. The deep voice wafting from the small black speakers spoke of a river of blood, thigh high, following him.

He focused on the violent ruby sunset glowing on the horizon.

Kid mummy. Coffin. This isn't the work of a one-time killer.

The beat pounding from the little black speakers thumped faster, the riff grew edgy, the raspy voice sung of rivers of blood and sadness. Mahoney felt himself drowning in his own destructive river. He could see the sadness wash over Stella's face when he didn't walk off that plane tomorrow.

He took a deep breath and gripped the steering wheel.

Can my team handle this?

Gut tightening, he shook his head.

Can I?

His mind toggled between images. Bit by bit, the new case took over his dreams of seeing Stella. Wife and daughter, hand in hand, walked away along the beach in his mind, dissolving behind a carcass crawling over the sand. A young boy's ghastly face forced out the blonde curls. The boy's screams stifled trickling giggles. Mahoney's heart clung to his past. The large cavern within him opened wider every time he saw the vacant remains of a young being. His heart would have to wait. He knew this case would call him. It already had. He wondered if it would be too late to salvage his past after he caught one more monster.

It's out of my jurisdiction.

Maybe his heart wouldn't have to wait.

They called you, Bug. You, the fancy-pants profiling guy.

The cave and coffin had their claws in him. He knew it. The past his heart clung to slipped through his fingers as he drove into his own river of blood.

Chapter Three

Garden Chameleon

The tall glass doors slid open. Cool air rushed across Jud's face as he entered the high-ceilinged, bright space. His heavy works boots thud against the polished floor as he bee-lined for the greenhouse section. He needed a new tree. Now. The culmination of the years of hard labour he'd spent building the perfect garden, the ultimate sanctuary, was finally here. Tree number forty-two would soon be at the apex of his creation.

Trickling sung through his ears as he passed the makeshift waterfall on the far-righthand side of the store. He took a deep breath and relaxed his shoulders. Patience would pay off. He'd been waiting to plant the last tree for so long. And for the friend that would go along with it.

"Good morning," a teenaged girl greeted him. A red apron with Bob's Greenery painted brightly down the front clung to her boney thighs. Her bright-red lips shone under the fluorescent lights.

He forced a smile. "Good morning." *Slut. Probably use those whore lips on the entire staff.* He kept walking, eager to get to the greenhouse.

"Good morning, sir." A man with slicked-back hair, donning the same red apron, tipped his head.

"Good morning." A waft of spicy cologne stung Jud's nostrils as he walked past the man. The odour flung him back to a dark alley. He shook away the unwanted memory. *Sick son of a bitch. Who do you lust after in your free time?*

He reached another sliding door and stepped through. A warmth pillowed around him. He ran his fingers through his long hair, pulling the sandy-blond locks away from his eyes. A delightful concoction of fresh greenery, rich earth, and fruity blossoms plumed around him and seeped into his nose. His mind cleared of the bothersome distractions by the incompetent staff.

"Jud. How's the garden?" Kent set down a potted plant and scurried over. His wiry frame reminded Jud of a younger version of himself, before hours of digging holes and moving trees had chiselled his arms and torso.

Good. Kent's here. I'm nice to him, he gets me specialty items. "Garden is great." Kent always worked on Sunday mornings. Jud counted on it. But the small chance that something would prevent Kent from being here for Jud nicked away at the back of his mind. Kent always found the item that Jud asked for, no matter where he had to order it from. The rest of the staff was useless in comparison.

"You didn't come in last week. Avoiding the crowds?"

"Yeah. That time year. Everyone thinks they're a gardener." *Stinking wanna be gardeners and their stupid chatter.*

"True. First timers tend to think gardening is easy. They don't appreciate the time it takes to build up real skill."

Jud nodded. He enjoyed Kent's appreciation of an experienced gardener.

"It's good you came in now, beat the crowds that trickle in when the morning service ends at St. Francis down the street." Kent wiped his soiled hands on his jeans.

Jud stifled a snort. *Church. Idiots thinking their tainted souls can be saved by some all-knowing being. If they hadn't preserved their innocence as a child, it was too late.*

"Trees are doing well?"

Oh Kent, you always seem genuinely interested. "Spectacular. The Crab Apple is still blooming like it did its first year. It's flourished better than I could have hoped for." *And so has Timmy. They make a good pair.* "And that Honeycrisp I put in last year, it's showing promise. I think it might be an early bloomer." *Johnny's settled in well.*

"You've got it down. I put in a couple of new trees myself this year. I can't imagine having a garden as extensive as yours. I think I can manage even a half-dozen nice trees..."

Jud's mind wandered. He continued to smile and nod, looking Kent right in the eye. *Yeah, yeah. I need my tree. I need to get back to my garden.*

"Anyways. I'm hoping to do well with these two this year, and then expand it next year."

"Wonderful."

"Looking for something specific today?"

"Yes. Do you carry the Bubblegum Plum?"

"Hmmm. I don't think we would have any of them in stock. But for a customer like you, we could definitely order one in."

"How long would that take?"

"Oh, I can put a rush order on it. Maybe a week at the most."

Jud bit his lower lip and furrowed his brow. Snapping the smile back on his face, he washed away the hint of worry. A week on order through Kent would be the fastest way to get the tree. "Of course. That would be fine."

"All right. Let's just step over to the counter here and we'll get that order done up."

"Great. You're a star." Jud looked into Kent's eyes and smiled wide.

"Oh, just doing my job." Kent's cheeks flushed and he waved a hand at Jud.

You're an easy friend to make, Kent. I can put the sugar on for you. Anything to get this tree in my garden.

Chapter Four

No Time For Sunny-Side Ups

Mahoney took a long, slow sip of coffee from his bright-blue mug. Setting it down, he looked at the summer-yellow words staring back at him. "Best Dad." Tingling sprinkled around his heart. Warmth rushed through him. His mind buzzed. A shot of cold seized his insides. *Lies.* He stared at the mug, looking at the words that were a blatant reminder of his biggest failure. Two sunny-side ups sizzled in a pan, snatching his attention. Grease flying, engulfing the air in his tiny kitchen, he nestled his cheek against his soft, white robe. *The simple things, Bug. It's all you get.*

A buzzing jolted him back to reality. Staring at the phone vibrating on the small kitchen table, he hesitated. *Damn phone.* He'd just been decked out with an upgrade. This one was lighter than the hunky brick he'd been lugging around. He still missed his tiny beeper.

Taking a few steps over to the table, he picked up the phone, flipped it open and pulled up the antenna. "Detective Mahoney." His voice exuded alertness. Even if he wasn't ready to conquer the next evil predator invading his city, he could sound like he was.

"Bug. It's Peggy."

"Pegs." He pictured her blonde bob and full, red lips. If she didn't have a teenaged son, he'd swear she was in her early thirties.

"Sarge needs you in right away."

Had Blackwood made progress on the mummy? Had the argument over jurisdictional rights been resolved? He'd cancelled his flight after leaving the scene at the cave. Sarge wanted him on hand, ready to go. He'd slipped back into the long hours that were a comfort to him, trying to close out his last case. He could still hear the sadness in Stella's voice when he'd called her and told her he wasn't coming. "What's going on, Pegs?"

"Well, it's that case you were called out to at the beach in K-Country. The one with the really old remains. Ugh. I shudder every time I think about it."

Chuckling, he said, "Actually, finding bones was much less disgusting than finding rotting flesh."

"Oh, my. I can't even imagine. I don't know what's happening to Calgary. It wasn't that long ago it still felt like a town here. We're still processing files on our last case, and it was...gory."

He could picture her biting her bottom lip. "I know."

"Anyways, Sergeant wants to round up the team. He wants a full debrief on the scene."

"When is the big party happening?"

"Well, you know, soon."

"You mean soon as in now, five minutes ago?"

"Yes, you know him."

"It's been sitting, what, two weeks?" *While I work on files and dream of rescheduling my flight.* "What changed?"

"The medical examiner has an ID. Kid lived in our jurisdiction – solidifies our involvement. Sergeant wants you to go see her then get over here."

"I'm on it." He could swear a cloud of lavender wafted over the greasy eggs.

"Were you cooking breakfast?"

He looked longingly at the yellow yolks. "Yeah, I was. You know me too well."

"You should take a few minutes and eat. You might be here awhile. Looks like it's not just your team that was called in for the briefing."

"Really? What's going on?"

"Well, there's chatter, you know, about why he wants a debrief."

She grew quiet. He suspected she was contorting her pretty smile into a worried frown, like she did when she was debating something. "Don't hold out. It's me."

"I know, Bug. It's just. Well, I know you were hoping to reschedule that flight to go see your daughter."

"Pegs, spit it out."

"There's talk the RCMP want collaboration on the case. That they aren't equipped to deal with the scene they uncovered. The pendant you found insinuates linkage to your last case, and, well, the crime scene was rather serious. Beyond the capabilities and resources they have," She said, spurting out the information in a vocal burst. "And there's talk the team you formed, for your last case, well, that it's the best equipped for this kind of thing."

Turning the stove off, he slid the pan to the back burner. "Tell Sarge I'll be there, pronto. And, Pegs, don't worry about me."

"OK. I'll tell him. But I can't promise anything about not worrying."

"Agreed. Thanks."

Snapping the phone shut, he set it on the counter. He stared at it, debating whether or not to call Stella and tell her there was no rescheduling his trip in sight. The sound of her voice when he'd told her about his cancelled flight still stung his ears. She knew then, that he wouldn't be coming anytime soon. He snapped his attention from the phone. Looking at the eggs, he moved to action. "Eggs, looks like you're going with me." Plucking two pieces of browned sourdough from the shiny silver toaster, he laid them on a cracked, wooden cutting board. Sliding the sunny-side ups onto a slice of toast, he closed them in with the second slice. Wrapping a paper towel around his homemade breakfast-to-go, he slipped into his bedroom. Moments later, egg sandwich in one hand, tattered brown briefcase in the other, he locked the apartment door behind him.

As he walked along the hallway, he wolfed down a bite and tried to fight off the visions of corpse faces blurring his mind from the last case. If he couldn't clear his head, how would he deal with a new barrage of images? He swallowed hard against the half-chewed bite of breakfast-to-go laced with a shot of fear and drowned in doubt.

Chapter Five

The Bone Story

Mahoney pushed against the heavy morgue door. A rush of cold met him as he moved into the quiet room. Medical Examiner Blackwood, engrossed in her work, peered into a microscope. Most of her face was hidden by a pair of large, plastic goggles and her long, dark hair. The collar of her army green turtleneck peeked over the top button of a full length, white lab coat. His heartbeat quickened.

"Blackwood."

She looked up from her examination. The single silver strand in her dark hair caught a glimmer off the fluorescent lighting as it slipped behind her shoulder. "Mahoney. Heard you'd be coming by."

"You did?" His heart thumped. He willed it to ease up. He couldn't go down that road—mixing murder with love.

"Your sergeant's got his fingers deep in this one."

"Yeah. I guess so. Seems we've been pulled in. I was told to come by here and check in, then get my ass over to HQ, pronto."

"Well, take a look." She motioned toward a shiny steel slab. "Then I'll pump your head full of chemical-related facts."

He turned to the steel bed, approaching the small, motionless figure lying atop. The horror of the remnants sprung to life under the bright lumens bathing over the dead child. Mahoney scanned the corpse up and down. It was nothing but a skeletal frame, covered in a reddish-brown, paper-thin layer of decayed flesh. A layer of pallid skin moulded the skull, folding into contours reminiscent of the features that once composed the child's face. Sunken holes of nothing, where eyes had once been, stared back at him gauntly.

He swallowed. A tingling sprung across his neck, migrating down his arms. "Geez. Nothing but skin and bones. How can we get anything from this?"

Blackwood slid up next to him. "Don't despair. There is some skin tissue. And bones can tell us a lot. I know it looks bleak, but don't give up before Mr. Bones here has a chance to tell us his story."

"How long does it take remains to turn into a skeleton?"

"Well, Mr. Bones here isn't quite a skeleton. And he didn't follow the usual path of decomposition. We've already obtained a slew of data."

Mahoney slipped his notepad from his pocket, flipping it open to a fresh page. "Shoot."

"Thanks to the forensic anthropologist, we have an ID."

"Really?"

"Yeah. She's meticulous." Blackwood picked up a notebook and flipped the pages. "Here. Caleb Johnson. Twelve years old. Went missing May 6, 1977."

"How did you determine the ID?"

"Like I said, it was thanks to our forensic anthropologist. She'll do a better job at explaining. She should be here for morning rounds any minute now. Before she gets here, you have to see this." Turning, she plucked two black spheres from a table next to the silver slab. Her gloved hands hovered over the cracked, white face, placing the glass balls into the empty sockets. The void eyes stared back at him. A chill crept down his back.

Blackwood's voice broke the eery quiet. "Fake eyes. They were placed just like that, in the empty sockets."

"Are you serious?" Mahoney rubbed the back of his neck.

"You know I am. I'm sure you've noticed the difference in colour between what's left of the skin on the body and the skin on the face. There was more skin on the face."

Rubbing the bristle on his chin, Mahoney looked at the gaunt face with fake eyes. "This kid was made up, like a doll?" A flash of a dead face, painted up like a glam rocker, flashed through his mind. Was he dealing with another killer that saw his victims as dolls?

"I'll leave that guess work up to you. You ready for the facts pertaining to the preparation of the body for its long rest?"

"Yeah." Mahoney stifled a smile. *She sounds like a professor.*

"The body's decay was halted by a number of things. The concrete box was air tight, keeping it dry. The cave was cold. Most importantly, the corpse was prepared. According to the stages of decomposition, the remains are literally stuck in the mummification stage. A body prepared like this can be preserved for hundreds, even thousands, of years." Turning toward him, she lowered her plastic lab glasses, releasing them to dangle from a dark cord around her neck. "I hope you're ready for this."

"Of course." Flushing his voice with confidence, his thoughts dived in the opposite direction. *I was going to start fixing things I've broken.* His daughter's face flashed through his mind. His heart seized. With jurisdictional confusion and no identification of the victim, he almost had real hope he'd be able to reschedule his flight. *Guess that's on hold.* His heart plunged toward his stomach.

"There were traces of methanol, glutaraldehyde, and CH20, otherwise known as formaldehyde, in both the skin and the bones. These are the ingredients used in the embalming process to disinfect and preserve. Essentially, this concoction prevents putrescence. It slows rotting."

"He wanted this kid preserved. Why?"

Ignoring his question, she stuck to her citation of facts. "Traces of Natron were also found. Natron is a salt with drying properties. It's used to dry the skin. Removing moisture further feeds preservation."

"I see. He was keeping this kid. But for what?"

"Then, there's the cherry on top. You notice how sunken the remains are? Like you said, just a skeleton with a bit of skin. Most of the organs were removed." She moved over to the adjacent table. "You see these?" She ran her gloved hand along a row of elaborately engraved jars. "They were hidden in the floor of the coffin. In each of these jars, an organ was contained. The kid's stomach, liver, lungs and intestines were all removed and left in separate jars. Removing the organs removes moisture and substance that will readily decay. Another step that further facilitates preservation. The only organ left inside the kid was the heart."

Mahoney scribbled wildly down the white page of his notebook. Hand halting, he looked up. "The heart. Why would he leave the heart?"

"That's your realm. There's more."

He followed her lead over to a microscope.

"When you came in, I was using this electron microscope to examine some of the strips of cloth the body was wrapped in. I've made out what appears to be writing. Even with the electron beam and fluorescent screen, I can't tell what it says. I'm going to send all of it over to be X-rayed. I think we need a thorough examination under higher-power magnification."

"Messages? Why do these guys insist on leaving us messages?"

"I don't know. Take a look at this." She motioned over to the microscope.

He leaned over and peered into the eyepiece. Blurred, curved lines wound round, creating fuzzy intertwined circles. He lifted his head. "Some sort of symbol?"

"Yeah. I'll get it magnified and cleaned up. But I thought it was weird."

"Yeah. Weird." The blurred circles wound through his head, forming a swirling vortex.

"Let's move on to the final bit here. The pendant you found at the scene, since it was reminiscent of the pendant on the first victim in our last case, I made it a priority item. It was clean, nothing on it."

"The gem looked the same as the pendant we found on our first Glam Rock boy. It was hard to track down. I visited every store we could find during that last investigation. Only one place sold this rock, and it had to be special ordered. We suspected Seth made up the fake name on the sales record. What are the chances of the same stone being in the cave with a young boy wrapped up like a mummy and placed in a concrete coffin?"

"Not high." Her purple tinted eyes bore into his.

Whoosh. They both turned their heads as the morgue door opened. A woman in a lab coat walked through, the collar of her black turtleneck reaching toward her chin. Her long brown hair fell around her shoulders. Tortoiseshell glasses framed her face.

"Detective Mahoney, I presume. I'm Doctor Sherice Sabin." She extended her hand toward him.

He returned the introduction. "Nice to meet you, Doctor Sabin."

Doctor Sabin turned to Blackwood. "Terra, don't let me interrupt."

Blackwood smiled. "Not at all. Your timing is impeccable. We just broached the topic of determining ID. You'd be better at explaining the details." Her cheeks flushed pink.

Is it hot in here? Mahoney felt the chill of the room clinging to his skin. "Blackwood tells me bones can tell us a lot."

Doctor Sabin said, "Yes. Examining the evidence in a skeleton is like reading a book. There's a full story, if you know what to look for."

Mahoney flipped his notebook to a fresh page. "I'm all yours."

Doctor Sabin pushed her glasses up the bridge of her nose. She perused her notebook, flipping through the pages. "For starters, it was clear, from the stages of growth in the bones and teeth, we were dealing with a child. A male child. I launched a full chemical analysis of the bones. Calcium levels are a biochemical marker. Along with others, they can provide us with a time of death window. This is an indicator of the minimum time for which the victim has been deceased. It seems our boy here has been dead for at least ten years. Give or take a year."

Mahoney looked up from his ferocious scribbling. "Ten years?"

Blackwood interjected, "Seth would have been...what, twelve?"

"Yeah." Mahoney rubbed the bristle on his chin.

Doctor Sabin continued, "We used ten as a starting point. We looked for missing children—boys—in our timeframe. Simultaneously, we proceeded with a facial reconstruction, which wasn't too hard given the amount of skin remaining on the face. We also superimposed photos of the skull on the photos of the missing kids. Bones are like a time capsule. They led us to Caleb."

Mahoney nodded. "I'm impressed with how much you can get from these remains."

"I leave no bone unturned. Especially in cases like this." Her lips pursed into a straight line.

Blackwood chimed in, "So, we're back to Seth's pre-teen years."

Mahoney responded, "Just a kid. What's the likelihood of him conducting murder?"

"My thoughts exactly."

"Doesn't seem possible. A child killing a child. Even if he did, how would a kid get both the body and the concrete coffin all the way into that cave?"

"Yeah. The coffin was at the very back of the cave, all the way across the beach. Getting into the cave wasn't easy. I guess he could have moved it in when the water levels were lower. But, still, do we honestly believe a twelve-year-old could drag the weight of the concrete box all that way?"

"Look at you, asking questions like a detective."

"Whatever." Blackwood smirked.

"You have a point. And do we believe a kid committed murder?"

Blackwood's smirk turned down. "Well, before I came up north, I worked on cases where that happened. Not as young as twelve. There was a guy who killed his grandparents at fifteen. Another one who gutted his friend with a knife in the woods at sixteen. Both had their slates wiped clean, only to become serial killers in adulthood."

Mahoney shook his head. "It's possible, then. But something doesn't add up here." Snapping his notebook shut, he straightened his stance.

Doctor Sabin interrupted, "One more bone-related fact for you, on the skull."

"The skull?"

"Yes."

Blackwood removed the glassy black eyes, placing them gently back in the container on the silver-topped table.

Doctor Sabin said, "Look at how sunken and black the gaps for the eye sockets are."

"That isn't typical?" A cold trickled down Mahoney's neck.

"Not to this degree. There was actually a build up of a black substance caked onto the bone. To the extent it was merged with the bone."

"So what's the black stuff?"

"Blackened, dead eye tissue, indicating a chemical burn."

Blackwood said, "Traces of Alkali were found around the eye sockets, mixed with the dead skin and eye tissue."

"Detective, it appears the eyes were chemically burned," Doctor Sabin said. "How severe, it's near impossible to tell."

"How the eyes were removed, well, we're working on it, but I'm not sure there's enough here to see a full picture," Blackwood said.

"What the hell?"

Doctor Sabin concluded, "The way the black residue was melded with the bone, the chemical compound had come into contact with the skin. Chemicals from living flesh were melted into the disintegration agent which then merged with the bone."

"What? You're saying Caleb had his eyes burned to nothing, in their sockets, while he was still alive?"

Blackwood said, "The skin tissue was living when it was burned with the black chemical. The child *could* have still been alive. We aren't one hundred percent sure. The eyes may or may not have been removed prior. We're still working on this."

Mahoney's mind spun. "Got it." A prickle shot through his brain, reaching his neck, causing the hairs to protrude wildly. The prickle made its way slowly down his spine, vertebrae by vertebrae. The tingling sensation crippling his mobility, he stood frozen, staring at the empty eye sockets.S

He forced his eyes away from the caverns in the skull. "Anything else for me?"

Blackwood and Doctor Sabin shook their heads in unison.

He snapped his notebook shut. "You've given me a lot to process here."

"We'll keep you updated," Blackwood said.

"I know you will." He nodded, turned, and headed for the door. His mind rushed over the slew of bone-related facts. *Dead ten years. Preserved. Eyes burned out.* How did the murder in his life keep getting weirder? To top it off, the monster he'd just put away seemed to have resurfaced.

Chapter Six

Detectives vs Red-Coats

Mahoney strode across the parking lot of Homicide headquarters. The sun peeked over the horizon, creating a soft pink filter over the cloud line. He thought about the two sunny-side ups he had tossed between his toast, wrapped in a paper towel, and wolfed down on the way to see Blackwood. The breakfast-to-go stirred in his stomach. He hated eating fast. Eating was one thing you should have time for. *Perks of the job, Bug.* He chuckled, shaking his head. He walked through the main doors and down a long corridor toward a cluster of cubicles.

"They're gathering in the war room." Peggy shot a full red lipped smile at him. Stray strands from her blonde bob danced over the tiny wrinkles around her eyes. "I put a fresh pot on for you."

"Awful nice of you." He strode past the front desk toward the cubicles huddled in the back against the window. Tossing his tweed coat over the back of his chair, he settled his derby onto his desk. He eyeballed the pile of files still in the queue for processing from the last case. *Glam Boys will have to wait.*

Heading down the hallway, he looked at the door leading into the war room. The tiny, hot space had caged him and his team for days on end. He was sick of being cooped up. *Maybe we're just here to go over the scene. The Horsemen might take this one. It was on their turf.* Despite the logic of his thoughts, an instinct crawled through his gut, telling him that he would be the one hunting the killer.

Approaching the door, he paused. Voices broke through from the other side, some of them familiar, others foreign to his ears. Multiple conversations fought over each other. Random words reached into his eardrums. *Jurisdiction. Scene. Body. Our turf. Serial. Mummy.*

Rolling his shoulders a couple times to shake off the tingles crawling over his arms, he steadied his mind and looked at the door. *OK, Bug. Get on with it.*

He swung the door open. A rush of hot air suffocated him. The room was packed full. He smiled as he caught a glimpse of Sutton and Hayes tucked into the corner. Sutton, eating a greasy-looking breakfast sandwich out of a Styrofoam box, his brown curls bobbing around his shoulders. The familiar green rabbit foot, Sutton's lucky charm, hung from his belt. Hayes drinking one of his healthy breakfast smoothies, his buzzcut as short as ever. *My boys. Still eager from the last case.*

His shoulders relaxed as he eyeballed Dara in her pristine navy suit, perched beside the little round table at the back. Her typewriter sat ready for her quick fingers. *My favourite analyst.* In the opposite corner, three Royal Canadian Mounted Police dressed in spiffy long red coats with wide shiny black belts stood deep in conversation. *Horsemen.* The tallest RCMP talked down to the other two, his wiry moustache twitching erratically. *Williams? Yeah. Williams. Greeted us at the cave.*

A hand touched his shoulder. "Mahoney. Thanks for the rush on this. It's getting restless in here."

Mahoney turned to face the familiar voice. Sergeant Jackson was standing behind him, blocking out a chunk of wall. At five-foot-five, the Sergeant was built like a square brick. He lowered his glasses, revealing the wrinkles etching the years of experience over his face.

"Sarge. Of course. Have we established our involvement here?" Mahoney's eyes darted to the red-coats in the corner.

"Body was on their turf. The boy the ME identified lived on our turf. Not sure how this will proceed."

His gut tingled. "You sure about that? Feels like we're gonna be running this thing." He glanced at Sutton and Hayes. "I finally listen to you, make plans..."

"I know. You were going to see your daughter. You just came off a real doozy of a case. You did a stand-up job. Wish I could give you a break."

"Yeah." Mahoney sighed.

"But you saw the scene out in K-Country. Complex. Like what you and your boys just finished dealing with. The Mounties aren't equipped for this."

"Right." *Red-coats riding on horses in the mountains all day.*

"And there's the possibility of linkage to your last case."

The tingling grew in his gut, spreading through his stomach. "The pendant."

"Yeah. I'll drive, get things started. But I need you to lead this."

"Got it, Sarge." Eggs and sourdough swam against a current of stomach acid. He inhaled deeply and walked over to the corner of the room, next to Dara.

Dara glanced up at him. "No rest for this team."

"Suspect we're gonna need your super analytic powers more than ever." Mahoney glanced at the pot of coffee perched on the table.

"Peggy just put that pot on. She thought you'd want a fresh cup."

Choosing a chipped sickly-green mug from the less-than-impressive selection, he poured himself a cup. Sergeant Jackson slipped to the front of the room. Clearing his throat loudly, he put the buzzing conversations to a sudden halt. "Gentlemen, let's get started. I realize this is unchartered territory for us all. This level of collaboration isn't normally required. I think you'll all agree, we need a fresh approach here."

The sergeant paused, scanning the room. "For starters, let's get to know each other." Turning to the long red coats, he nodded. "Sergeant Williams, thank you for joining us. Sergeant Williams and his team, Constables Roberts and Rudson, were the first on the crime scene."

Glimmers of fluorescent lighting shot off the black belts as the officers turned around the room, nodding their hellos. Williams' red coat curved over his belly.

"Dara Deschutes is our best analyst. She's been with our department a long time. She's a computer wiz. Her analyst skills are some of the best in Canada."

The sergeant waved a hand to the back of the room. Dara's cheeks flushed. She nodded.

"Detectives Sutton and Hayes are the core Homicide detectives working with our Prime Investigator, Detective Mahoney."

Sergeant Jackson nodded at the Homicide team. Sutton, mouth stuffed in mid-chew, set his to-go box aside and nodded. Hayes lowered his shake and waved.

Sergeant Jackson moved up to the cream-coloured wall spanning the left side of the room. He pointed at the collage of photos laid out along the chipped paint, held in place with brightly coloured plastic tacks. "You're all familiar with the scene. The victim was buried in a rectangular plot dug several feet into the ground. Found by a couple of teenagers poking around in the back of the cave. The body was wrapped like a mummy and placed in a concrete coffin-like structure. We suspect the high water levels this year washed away enough sand to expose the concrete structure."

He paused, scanning the photos.

"This is old news to everyone in this room. Now for the new information. The victim has been identified as twelve-year-old Caleb Johnson. He lived in the city here, with his parents. He went missing one night after playing in the park with his friends. Everyone in the neighbourhood knew each other. Kids always played together. The park was only a block from his house. Parents have been notified. We've given them time to process. It's a lot to take. Their kid was missing for over ten years. We'll need to interview them further when they are able."

The room stirred.

Williams' moustache twitched. "Then the investigation is yours, Sergeant."

Sergeant Jackson raised his voice. "Technically, yes. And the body, found in K-Country, is yours. Technically."

Williams' cheeks flushed pink. He nodded.

"I'll ask Detective Mahoney to join in at this point. He can give us an update on the medical examination."

Mahoney made his way to the front of the room, his mind swirling in hazy circles. Chatter hummed through the room. Setting the puke-green mug down on the table beneath the crime scene collage, he looked at the photo of twelve-year-old Caleb. Tousled blond hair. Bright-blue eyes. A smear of dirt on his cheek and the sideways stance of his collar indicated some rough play right before the class picture was taken.

Why? Why this kid? And why do I have to look at another young face? His limbs heavy, he stared into Caleb's eyes. An inkling crawled through his stomach. *Williams doesn't want this. My team is all this kid has.* No one else would be looking for the killer. Not after all this time. *All right, kid. I've got you.*

His sergeant patted his shoulder. "Whenever you're ready."

Mahoney watched Sergeant Jackson head toward the back corner and settle himself in beside Dara. *OK, Bug, get moving.*

Clearing his throat, he strode to the centre of the room and faced his audience. Pulling at his dwindling energy, he gathered it into a ball and forced it into his voice. "OK. Let's keep moving, folks." The room settled. Mahoney pulled at his collar, the hot air closing in around him. "As Sergeant Jackson indicated, I was able to stop in and get an update on the progress of the medical examination. Cause of death is still to be determined." Mahoney sipped from the mug, the lukewarm liquid sliding down his parched throat.

"Detective, the boy's been deceased for over ten years. How can it possibly be determined when or how he died?" Red-coated Constable Rudson inquired from the corner.

"Good question. I myself was amazed at how much can be determined from skin and bones. A forensic anthropologist has been assigned to the case. She's the one that determined the ID, through facial reconstruction, and chemical analysis of the bones."

Rudson nodded.

Mahoney continued, "When the body was unwrapped, it became apparent it had been well preserved. Chemicals that are used to embalm were found. The skin had been dried with a salt used to assist in preservation of remains. There was a series of jars found underneath a panel in the concrete box. Each of them holds an internal organ. The size of the organs, and the fact the body was missing all of them, indicates they likely belong to the victim."

Pausing, he tipped the mug to his lips, attempting to soothe the dryness scratching his throat.

"A set of fake eyeballs were inserted into the victim's eye sockets," Mahoney said. "The kid's real eyes appear to have been either removed or chemically burned, disintegrated. Possibly while the kid was still alive."

He scanned the faces looking back at him. The frown on Williams' face deepened, pulling the strands of his moustache into an abstract shape. Rudson swallowed hard, looking down at his shoes. Roberts shifted back and forth on his feet. Sutton sucked on the red straw protruding from his Big Gulp. Hayes leaned against the wall, arms crossed.

"Burning eyes from sockets. This isn't your typical kill," Mahoney said. "This isn't a rash response to an emotional situation. This is planned, calculated."

"You think the killer planned out what he did to this young child?" Williams' face was flushed.

"Yes. The level of organization of this guy is high. Can you imagine what it would take to obtain this concrete box and get it into the cave? As well, the elaborate preparation of the body before it was buried."

Rudson's eyes widened.

Mahoney continued, "He's got a plan, he's prepared. He executes a carefully written script to live out his fantasy."

Williams shook his head. "You are suggesting the man who did this *fantasized* about killing a young boy and…well, torturing him and mummifying him? What the hell are you talking about here?"

Constable Roberts shook his head and crossed his arms.

"Yes, I am." Mahoney shot a glance to the back of the room. Sutton stifled a smirk with a long swig from his Big Gulp. Hayes looked at the ground.

We don't have time for this. Need to get them on our wavelength.

"Look, all I'm saying is this guy is evolved beyond what we are used to seeing around here. He's different than the type of killer we are used to catching. He isn't driven by a spontaneous emotion in response to a bad situation. His behaviour is different than the *normal* killer. And he is meticulous. He won't leave us a trail. We need to *understand* him in order to find him."

"Understand him?" Williams' moustache twitched over his red face. "What kind of voodoo are you guys into out here?"

"Yeah, I agree. How can we waste time understanding a guy like this? We need to focus on the evidence, catch this guy," Rudson said.

Williams glared at Rudson. Rudson backed into the corner. Williams' red face glistened with sweat. His moustache pulsed. "We may not get murders out in the mountains like you get here in the big city. But this isn't our first pancake breakfast. What this needs is processing, filing and a ticket to cold case."

A fire surged in Mahoney's belly. *What the fuck was this twitchy-moustached red-coat talking about? Cold case, my ass.*

Williams turned to his constables, barking words at them. Mahoney scanned the perimeter of the room. Sutton and Hayes chattered at each other. Voices rumbling through the room, the hot air closed in on Mahoney. He opened his top button, stretching his collar away from his sticky neck. He looked across the room. The back wall seemed to be moving away from him, the space between him and his team opening up into a vacant gorge. He found Dara's eyes. She met his gaze and smiled at him, giving him a single nod. Grinding his teeth, he took a long sip of cold brew, put the ghastly green mug down with a plunk, and stood up tall.

"Hey. Settle down," Mahoney's voice cut through the mess of chatter.

Like a series of meerkats, faces shot toward the front of the room.

"Cold case isn't an option here." Mahoney shot a stern gaze to Williams.

Williams' pink, puffy cheeks jiggled. "The boy's been buried over ten years. Whoever did this is long gone."

"That's only speculation," Sutton said.

Roberts glared across the room. "My sergeant's right. No way we'll solve this now."

"We don't know that." Sutton took several long steps toward the red-coated corner.

"Be reasonable." Constable Roberts stepped up, meeting Sutton in the middle of the room.

"*You* be reasonable. Have you ever *been* on a murder case?" Sutton's face flamed. Spit flew from his mouth. His beefy stature loomed over the red-coated constable.

"My track record is none of your business," Roberts replied, launching his face at Sutton.

"Riding horses in the mountains all day isn't a *track record*." Sutton raised his arm and the lid popped off his Big Gulp, bright-orange pop spilling over his hand. The green rabbit foot dangling from his belt swung wildly back and forth.

Hayes jumped across the room, lodging himself between Sutton and Roberts.

Mahoney glared at Williams. Williams' tomato face gleamed under the bright lights.

Sergeant Jackson strode to the head of the room, waving his hands. "Enough! All of you. Settle down."

Heads turned. Voices quieted. Sutton walked to the back of the room, plunking his Big Gulp into the waste basket, shaking off the sticky pop. Roberts backed up into the front corner beside Williams. Hayes rejoined Sutton. Sutton looked at the ground. Roberts looked sheepishly at Williams.

Sergeant Jackson continued, his voice remaining at a high decibel level, "If we are to accomplish anything here, we all need to work together. Sergeant Williams, the body was found in your jurisdiction. You own the scene. The boy lived in our jurisdiction. My team owns the investigation. Whether we like it or not, those are the facts." He paused, scanning the room. "We need to find some way to work together to move this forward. You all have valid points here. Yeah—the kid has been dead for a long time. It is our *duty* to pursue all possible paths to try and solve this thing." He rescanned the faces around the perimeter of the room. "Look at this." He walked up to the cream-coloured wall and threw his pointer finger aggressively at the photo of the dead boy. "What happened to this kid is horrific. The murder case Detective Mahoney just closed is the closest thing to *this* any of *us* have ever seen. That is why I was contacted. That is why my team is here. This is a complex situation. We're in this together, like it or not." The sergeant's eyes were wide as he glared around the room.

The temperature shot up several degrees. No one spoke or stirred. Williams' face was stern, his moustache still. Sutton stood, arms crossed, mouth in a tight line. Roberts, tucked into the red-coat corner, frowned, nodding his acknowledgement.

"Detective, could you please continue." Sergeant Jackson motioned to Mahoney.

Mahoney faced the imploring stares in the room. "I understand what you are all saying here. Trust me. When we started dealing with our last case, we had a hard time wrapping our heads around the idea of looking at behaviour. We didn't *replace* traditional methods of investigation, we simply added to them. The combination of the two is what led us to find our guy. This case we are now dealing with, it's going to require the same approach. We don't have to figure that out right now. Why don't we start by divvying tasks."

Williams' moustache pulled into a thin, wiry line. "How can my team help?"

"I think another scan of the scene should be done. We used this approach on the last case, and going back to scenes uncovered important details. Sergeant Williams, can you and your team assist in ensuring the security of the area, and searching it again? Take your time. Look for the smallest details."

Williams said, "Consider it done."

"Hayes, join Sergeant Williams and his team. Share your knowledge of processing a murder scene—by the book."

"Got it, boss." Hayes nodded.

"You'll need to follow up with those teenagers. Make sure they've told you everything about how they found the coffin. And find out anything you can on anyone who might have seen something. I know it's a long shot."

Hayes tipped his pen, then scribbled in his notebook.

"The boy's parents need to be interviewed. Sutton, stick with me and we'll tackle that one together. I'll need you to help me out with other interviews in the neighbourhood. We also need to visit the park where the kid was last seen."

Sutton tipped two fingers in acknowledgement.

"Dara, I'm going to need your computer skills. I need a search on the process of preserving a body. A detailed one."

"Of course, Bug." She slipped her glasses down her nose, releasing them to dangle from a string of sparkling beads.

"I'm also going to need about a million other searches. We'll start by trying to figure out where he was able to obtain all these supplies."

Dara nodded.

"OK, everyone. Let's get on it. We'll meet back here tonight. Let's make it nineteen-hundred. Give us some time for our hefty tasks."

Finding Sergeant Jackson's gaze, he was met with a firm nod.

He watched everyone filter out of the room, the buzz of chatter leaving with them. The quiet of the room soothed him. He took a deep breath, ran his fingers through his hair, then walked up to the photo of Caleb. *We're all you got, kid. Let's just hope we can do you some justice.*

Chapter Seven

Morning Paper

Jud sipped his morning coffee from a chipped brown mug. Plunking the mug onto the faded cherry-wood table, he scowled. *Stupid mug. Who paints something the colour of shit?* As he sat back against the chair, a piece of wood snapped. He leaned forward and cranked his neck. A spindle, reduced to two jagged splinters, clung to the chair frame.

"Dammit." Turning back to face the table, his eye caught the faded cabinets and rusted sink. He frowned at the general dismay of the kitchen. He knew he should make some time to give it a makeover. But that would dig into his time in his garden. *Yes, the garden.* A smile replaced his scowl as bright-green cacti in full bloom took over his mind.

Can't wait to get up there today.

He picked up the wrinkled newspaper. His scowl returned and deepened. *Goddamn paperboy.* He unrolled the paper, spread it out on the wooden table, and smoothed it with his calloused palms.

Jud scanned the Calgary Chronicle front page for the top news stories. *Pathetic city. More like a town pretending to be big time.* A smile pulled at the sides of his mouth as he thought of how long it had been since he had been back. *Suckers still living in the cold winter up there. Ha. I've been basking in this golden sunshine year-round for years now.* Taking a swig of coffee, he turned back to the wrinkled Chronicle.

He blinked his eyes rapidly. Setting the coffee mug down with a loud plunk, a splash of hot black trickled down his hand. "Goddammit." Tossing the paper onto the table, he bolted out of the chair. Shaking the hot coffee off his hand, he pulled the paper toward him and stared at the headline.

"Boy-Mummy Found Buried in Cave"

What? What the hell is this?

Wiping his hand on the back of his jeans, Jud sat back down on the chair with a thud. Holding the paper up with both hands, he grabbed for his reading glasses as he squinted at the small print. Pushing his glasses against his face, the print came into focus.

"The body of a 12-year-old boy was found Saturday, May 9, outside the city limits in Kananaskis Country. The state of the body was well preserved, having been sealed by an advanced mummification process. The remains of the boy-mummy were further preserved in a sealed concrete box, which was buried several feet into the sand at the back of a cave. The coffin-like structure was discovered by two teenagers near Wash-A-Way Point. The Royal Canadian Mounted Police, first on the scene, suspect the higher-than-usual water levels washed away the sand covering the concrete box, revealing it. It has not yet been determined how long the boy-mummy has been buried in the back of the cave."

Jud slapped the paper on the table. A single bead of sweat crawled down the back of his neck. *Well, I'll be damned. Even the best hidden treasures aren't safe.*

Jud's eyes darted across the rest of the article, plucking out the critical pieces with an imaginary highlighter.

"...body deemed the child-mummy...skeletal remains may leave little for police to work with... Local Homicide Detective Mahoney, AKA 'Bug'—the squasher of perps..."

Jud snapped his gaze to a halt.

"...the squasher of perps, known for his high success rate in solving local murders. Detective Mahoney was the Prime Investigator on the Glam Boy murders. The door has barely been locked on the suspect arrested for this series of murders, and charges are still pending due to an extensive mental assessment ordered by the court and currently underway. An oval shaped arctic pendant, found at the scene of the child-mummy, has a striking resemblance to one found at the first scene of the Glam Boy case. This leads the question—is the scene in the cave the work of the Glam Boy killer?"

Jud re-read the last sentence several times. Heat flushed his face. *The mummy is mine. That little freak—he couldn't accomplish what I have. He better not talk about me.* Jud continued reading.

"During the Glam Boy case, Detective Mahoney implemented criminal profiling techniques in collaboration with the FBI's behavioural analysis unit.

Some members of the local Homicide department deemed these techniques to be 'New Age Hocus-Pocus.', creating doubt in Det. Mahoney's ability to keep his city safe. According to Det. Mahoney himself, this killer is no match for his advanced investigative techniques."

No match? I'm no match for some Bug? Jud skipped over the rest of the article, resting his eyes on the last sentence.

"The child-mummy case is the second high profile murder case to hit Calgary this year."

Jud tore his attention from the article and raised the shit-brown mug to his lips. Taking a sip of coffee, a white chip in the porcelain sliced his lower lip. *Damn mug.* He slammed the mug onto the table, coffee sloshing over his hand. *Dammit.* He stood up, walked over to the sink, and turned on the tap. The cold water soothing his hand, he looked up at the tattered cabinets. *I should really get around to re-staining these.* His gaze wandered through the window over the expanse of land. Focusing on the pathway, his eyes stepped along the red bricks, finding their way to the garden entranceway. *Never enough time. The garden always comes first.* His shoulders relaxed. *My garden. My sanctuary. It must come first.* Licking the fresh blood trickling down the side of his mouth, he narrowed his gaze.

So, someone's tampering with treasures that don't belong to them, huh?

He stared at the fuzzy end of the brick path, imaging the entranceway to his sanctuary. *My friends are safe in their sanctuary. But my friends of the past, that's another story.*

He clenched his teeth, turned off the tap, and walked back over to the newspaper.

Looks like I got a double mission. I got a freak to shut-up. And, I got a 'Bug' in my midst. Got some squashing of my own to do.

Chapter Eight

Caleb's Friend

Mahoney sunk into the plush, pleather couch. It was soft and comfortable—unlike the tattered cavern worn into the sofa in his bare apartment. Warm rays of sunshine filtered through a large window, casting a vibrant glow over the spacious living room. Large ferns lined the walls, making the space feel fresh. Joseph, who'd been with Caleb that day at the park, walked across the polished hardwood floor and handed Mahoney a cup of coffee. Mahoney reached for it.

"Thank you." The spicy aroma prickled Mahoney's nose.

"My pleasure." Joseph sat down in a chair that matched the couch.

Sutton popped open his notebook.

Mahoney asked, "What do you remember about the last time you saw Caleb?"

Joseph took a sip of coffee. Thin blonde-white hair scattered over his head, dancing over wire-framed glasses. Eyebrows, even thinner than his hair, turned in toward his light blue eyes. "To be honest, I've pushed it from my mind. I didn't want to remember. I mean...Caleb...he was there one day, and gone the next. I was eleven. I wasn't ready to lose a friend."

Mahoney said, "Take your time. I know it's been a long time, but anything you can remember might be able to help us."

"Say, why are you looking into this now, after so much time?"

Mahoney's gaze flicked to Sutton. "We found Caleb."

"What?" Sweat sprouted across Joseph's brow.

Mahoney said, "We have his body. Which means we have evidence. We might be able to find out who did this."

"But what good would it do now?" Joseph's knee shook.

Sutton said, "The evidence indicates that whoever did this could kill again."

Joseph steadied his knee and took a gulp of coffee. "I see. Well, I wouldn't want anyone else to have to deal with this. I mean, Caleb's parents...they were never the same." He stared into the mug gripped in his hands, long, delicate fingers wrapping around both sides. "They know? That you found him?"

Mahoney said, "Yes."

Joseph sighed. "OK. Let me think. I don't know how much I can remember."

Sutton said, "Take your time. Close your eyes if you want. Think back to that day. What you did. What the weather was like. Anything that will take you back there."

"OK." Joseph placed his mug on a clear, glass coffee table. He sat back into his chair, closed his eyes and took a deep breath. "There were probably six of us, including Caleb. Same kids who were often in the park. It was a warm day. My mom didn't make me take a jacket." Joseph smiled.

Mahoney said, "Good. What did you do in the park?"

"Same stuff as usual. We would have swinging contests, see who could get the highest." Calm washed over Joseph's face.

Sutton jotted down notes.

Joseph said, "When I left, Caleb was still there. He lived closer. I had to get home for dinner." Joseph's eyes darted underneath his eyelids.

Mahoney waited a few moments. "Did you see something unusual?"

Joseph's eyes popped open. "A man." His lips tightened into a thin line.

Sutton said, "I don't recall that from your statement."

"I didn't tell anyone. I told the police officers I hadn't seen anything." Beads of sweat drizzled down Joseph's left cheek. "I wanted to. But I was too scared. After a few days, I knew I should, but I was afraid all the parents would blame me for not speaking up right away." Joseph grabbed the mug and took a long gulp. The mug clinked against the glass table as he set it back down. He wiped his brow with the back of his sleeve. "I'm sorry." He wiped his cheek. "It nagged at me. I pushed it away. I hadn't thought about it in so long. I guess I told myself to move on."

Mahoney said, "You were a kid. You can help now. What did this man look like?"

Joseph took in a deep breath, then exhaled. He wiped his palms along his legs. "He had long, reddish-blond hair. He was wearing jeans and a plaid work shirt. I remember, cause we were all in t-shirts. I wondered why he wasn't hot."

Joseph swallowed. "He had on these big work boots. I didn't usually see anyone wearing those. Our parents were all office workers." He shook his head, then met Mahoney's gaze. "He stood out. Our street was quiet. We didn't often see someone we didn't recognize." Joseph's shoulders shuddered. He started to speak, then stopped.

Mahoney asked, "Is there something else?"

"I always cut through the alley behind the park. My house was on the next street over. The man was there, in the alley, tucked behind the corner of a fence. It looked liked he was carving something into the wood. He stopped when he saw me. I think he shoved some sort of switch blade into his pocket, but I'm not sure. It all happened so fast. He came up to me. My arms tingled. He talked to me." Joseph stopped and looked straight at Mahoney, the shaking in his knee resurging.

Mahoney said, "What did he say?"

"His voice, it was deep...and eerie. Geez, I sound cuckoo." He shook his head.

Sutton said, "Not at all. Please, go on."

"He said it was a real nice day out for us kids to be able to play in the park. He said I wouldn't want to ruin it by telling people that there was a visitor, now would I?" Joseph narrowed his eyes. "I know, it was a long time ago, but now that I think back, the memory is vivid in my mind. I had such a feeling, in my gut." Joseph licked his lips. "He reached out and took my hand. His hand was rough. It scraped my skin. And..." Joseph clenched his jaw.

Mahoney said, "What?"

"There was a small picture of a tree with hanging fruit, drawn, on the inside of his wrist. I guess it was a tattoo. He caught me staring at it. His eyes...it's like he was staring right into my soul." Joseph scuttled to the edge of his seat. "I felt cold. It was a hot day, but I had goosebumps up my arms."

"What happened next?" Mahoney asked.

"He dropped my hand and walked away. It was a few moments before I could move again. Then...the next day, everyone was looking for Caleb."

Chapter Nine

The Park

Placing his grey derby atop his head, Detective Mahoney scanned the park. Tucked away at the end of a cul-de-sac, nestled between two houses, and opening onto an alleyway, it was the perfect little refuge for children to play and still hear mom calling when dinner was ready. The park where Caleb had played, over ten years ago, every day after school. Until the day he didn't come home.

Sinking his hiking boots into the green grass, Mahoney ventured toward the shiny silver slide. He pictured young faces filled with excitement and little fingers wrapping tightly around the rungs as children climbed to the top. Turning toward the merry-go-round, little faces blurred as the wheel spun faster and faster. Giggles of delight echoed through the air. This park had once been a place of merriment.

Caleb's parents still lived on this street, a few doors down. Mahoney pictured Caleb's mother. Her tired, pale face riddled with permanent wrinkles of worry, lines of anxiety and doubt forever etched into the blank canvas that had once been painted in warm tones of happiness. Caleb's mother said none of the children would go near the park for weeks after Caleb's vanishing act. They were all afraid. After a few months, the occasional sighting of a young person in the park occurred. Over time, the street changed. The kids had all grown up and moved away. A fresh wave of children took over the park. Caleb's parents were only shells of who they had once been. They looked far older than they were as they clung to a haunted past.

Scanning the alleyway bordering the back of the park, Mahoney looked into the backyards of a row of houses. His eyes settling on an overgrown lawn, he perused the broken, abandoned toys scattered about. The creaking of a swing, swaying slightly in the breeze, grabbed his attention. He jaunted over to the swing set in the middle of the park, next to the merry-go-round, and stood staring at a single swing, swaying back and forth.

He saw Caleb's face, the sun's glow beating off rosy cheeks, blue eyes sparkling. Caleb bent his knees, straightened his legs, bent his knees, straightened his legs…on and on, willing the swing into motion. The swing gained momentum, Caleb's legs slicing through the warm summer air, pumping his little body higher and higher, his red running shoes reaching for the blue sky. The image of Caleb vanished. Mahoney stared at the swing, swaying, creaking, empty.

All right, Bug, why are you here?

Straightening his derby, he walked over to the back-right corner of the park. He turned, scanning the entirety of the children's playground. *Think. Where would someone be able to hide? To linger?*

Mahoney scanned the park again, then looked at the end of the cul-de-sac where the park opened up onto the street.. *Too open. Doubt he would have strolled in that way.* He pictured the kitchen in Caleb's house, opening up onto the front main room, the large bay window providing a full view of the street. *Getting close to dinner time. Dad sitting in the front room with a beer. Mom in the kitchen cooking. He could have been seen. A stranger walking up the street toward the park where the kids were would have caught someone's attention.*

Mahoney looked along the alleyway bordering the back of the park. *Joseph saw him strolling down the alley.* A row of houses lined the opposite side of the alleyway. He walked up to the closest fence, housing the backyard of the first house along the row. The fence was a good foot taller than him. The openings between wood planks were thin.

Someone in the yard may see a figure, but unlikely they'd be able to identify him. He would have been able to stay under the radar back here. Mahoney bolted his gaze from one end of the park to the other. *Two potential entranceways.* Mahoney walked over to the corner of the house bordering the left side of the park. He tucked himself behind the corner of the backyard fence of the house, on the edge of the park and the alleyway. Peering at the park, he could see the entire span of the children's space. *Concealed, with a perfect view.*

A slight pulse grew in his gut. He turned his head toward the back fence. Neurons firing, brain tingling, he halted. His hand shot to his derby, pushing it against the top of his head. His eyes convulsed. A symbol, carved into the top of a wooden plank at the corner of the fence, stared back at him.

Grabbing his phone from his belt, he flipped it open and pushed the buttons. His eyes never left the symbol carved into the fence. "Sutton. Grab the camera from the car. Meet me over at the park."

He pushed the off button, abruptly ending the call. He briskly pushed in another series of numbers and held the phone up to his ear. His eyes still fixated on the symbol. Its curves wound artistically into the wood. *Nice clean cuts. Must have been done with a freshly sharpened knife. Thin knife.*

"Medical Examiner Blackwood."

"Blackwood. It's Mahoney."

"Mahoney. Pleasant surprise."

His heart fluttered. The pulsing in his gut grew stronger, snapping his attention back to the symbol. "Did you get anything back on those messages yet? The ones on the cloths?"

"Not yet. Can you hang on for a second?"

"Yeah."

"I'll give the lab a call."

Mahoney waited, phone pressed against his ear, eyes glued to the symbol. The curves wound round and round, twisting into a mesmerizing spiral. Something about it pulled him in. He couldn't move his eyes away. Did it match the blurred spiral he'd stared at under Blackwood's microscope?

"Mahoney."

He jumped. "Yeah."

"Lab is just wrapping up their analysis. They found a message, written repeatedly on several of the cloths. 'I have committed no murder.'"

His neck tingled. The tingle migrated down his back as he stared at the fence. The carved circles swirled, intertwining. Like a vortex. "Did they get a better image of the spiral?"

"Yes. Analyst said it's some sort of symbol—a series of circular swirls, intertwined. It made him think of a swirling vortex."

The tingling crept back up his spine, vertebrae by vertebrae. A cold chill rushed through him.

"You think I can get a copy of those sent to HQ before the end of the day?"

He could see her smirk. "I might be able to help with that."

"Thanks." He snapped his phone shut, pushed in the antenna, and looked across the park. Sutton tromped through the grass, camera in hand.

I have committed no murder. What the hell does that mean? You murdered this kid, sicko. He looked back at the symbol. The skin around his skull seized, resisting the pull of the vortex.

Chapter Ten

Rose Quartz

Taking cautious steps down the creaky wooden stairs, Detective Mahoney squinted at the blue door at the bottom of the ancient staircase. His teeth unclenched as his foot steadied onto the floor. Turning the golden knob, the door squeaked as he pushed it open. Welcomed by mountains of polished stones every colour of the rainbow, glints from the overhead lights bounced off sparkly gems.

He stepped into the room cluttered with chunks of polished rock. A warmth washed over him. The last time he came into this shop, he was overwhelmed. Shocked so many treasures could be housed in one room. He dug his hand into his coat pocket. Running his fingers over the polished oval hiding away snug in its permanent home, a tingling rush of heat washed through him from his crown, through his heart, down to his stomach.

A clinking noise jerked his eyes to the back of the room. A woman, her figure lost in long flowing material, her dress like a thousand scarves woven together with magic air, floated across the floor on invisible feet.

"Hello. Welcome." Her smile wide and inviting as she greeted him, she glowed with warm energy.

His body swelled with warmth, as if he were bathed in a ray of sunshine. "Hello, ma'am. I'm Detective Mahoney."

"Yes. I know you. You were here a while back, asking about a rare gem."

"Yes. I was."

"Well. Let's have a look at you." The woman stood back, running her eyes all over him. "Well now. Seems like that rose quartz is taking to you. You're starting to believe in this strong sense of intuition you have."

Mahoney couldn't help but smile. This foreign world of gems seemed so comforting to him. "Yes."

"Well. Why don't you come over here to the counter. I have just the thing for you."

Mahoney followed the flowing streams of colour up to the glass counter. He watched as the woman turned to the back of the room, opening an old wooden cupboard. Returning to him, she shuffled a deck of large, ornately decorated cards in her gem-dotted hands. Spreading the mysterious cards out on the glass counter, her intense eyes peered at him.

"Close your eyes. Feel your inner being. Let it guide your hand to a card."

Mahoney did as he was told. Closing his eyes, he took a deep breath. Warmth vibrated through his heart, down his insides. Reaching out his hand, he let go of all control. His hand floated over the cards, halted, and landed on the chosen one.

He opened his eyes. The woman looked at the card marked by his fingertips.

"Well now, that's interesting." She reached out, plucked the card from his fingers, and turned it over. "The dolphin. A very special one, indeed. Do you know the significance of this spirit animal?"

Spirit animal? "No. I do not."

"The dolphin symbolizes breath. When it makes an appearance on your journey, it is a reminder to check your life's blueprint." Her voice was like clear water trickling over a pebbly stream. "You may be holding your breath in times of stress and anxiety. You may need to still your inner chatter and self-doubt. A meditative journey can help. Now, that would be fitting, given your current, shall we say, scavenger hunt, wouldn't it?" Her right eyebrow slanted, reaching up her forehead. Her hand provided a rest for her chin, her pointer finger covering her mouth, a shiny, black stone concealing half her finger.

Scavenger hunt? Could she be referring to my case? Her wisdom-infused words stimulated his brain. His body tingled. His internal organs pulsated a warm, soothing vibration. *First the rose quartz, now a spirit animal?* What was happening to him?

"That was, uh, very insightful."

Sliding the cards together in a quick shot, she looked at him. "Well now, that isn't why you came here, is it? You're looking for something specific, aren't you?"

"The last time I came here I inquired about a pendant and the blue-coloured stone it was made of."

"Yes, I recall. Arctic topaz. A gem that doesn't get asked for much."

"You had provided me with the record of sales for the months prior to my visit. We've found another pendant, very similar." Reaching into his pocket, he retrieved a photo and slid it across the glass counter.

The woman peered at the photo. "I see."

"Turns out, this pendant could have been lying in the vicinity of where we found it for a good ten years. Would you have sales records that far back?"

"Oh my. That's a good question. Let me have a look." Turning, she peered up at several crooked shelves housing a series of old books. "Well now, ten years ago, that would have to be the top shelf." Pulling a stepladder over to the shelves, she ascended and reached. Her gem-adorned finger moved along the old hardcovers.

Mahoney watched in silence, pushing the building list of tasks from his mind. He had to be here. This place, this woman, they were the key to finding how this arctic ocean stone got into the wrong hands. And whose hands those even were.

"Here we go." Scarf-dress woman pulled a book from a shelf and stepped down to the floor.

Thumping the book onto the countertop, she wiped thick dust away with her hand. "This one hasn't been opened in a while." Opening the front cover of the book, the binding crackled. Her finger ran down the first page. A magenta stone shimmered against the fluorescent lighting bathing her hand. "Oh dear, the print is rather worn. I *think* this says seventy-four...and that might be seventy-eight...or is that a nine?" She turned the book toward him.

He squinted at the faded print. "Can't say. Half the numbers are worn away. I'm looking for seventy-seven."

She turned the book back toward her. "Let's take a look." Running her pointer down the gold edges of the stack of pages, she stopped about two thirds of the way in. Slipping her thumb into the book, she flipped the stack of pages over. She stared at the page. "Do you have any idea of what month you are looking for?"

Good question. Getting that concrete box into that cave would have been near impossible in the winter. He flipped his notebook open. May 6. The date Caleb went missing. "Let's start with May."

Flipping further through the pages, she hummed. She stopped and ran her finger down a yellowing page covered in fancy black handwriting. She flipped another page and ran her finger down its length. After turning several more pages, she looked at Mahoney. "Patience will lead us to what we seek." She looked back down at the book and continued.

Mahoney leaned against the counter. His shoulders heavy, he shoved the growing list of to-do items from his mind. He imagined his bed.

She shook her head and looked at him. "I'm sorry. These entries, the dates are all over the place." She paused. "Recordkeeping isn't in my realm of talents. I had to learn over the years."

He leaned into the counter, sliding a palm over the glass. "We need to find any records of sales you have for seventy-seven." He looked up at the shelf. "Even if I have to search all those books myself."

She closed the book, closed her eyes, and took a deep breath. She opened her eyes and looked at him, covering his hand with her gem-speckled fingers. A sparkle lit up her eyes. "I have a better idea." She slid her hand into the waves of scarves flowing around her body and pulled out a long chain. A six-sided clear crystal hung from the end, spinning, catching the sunlight streaming in the window and shooting rays of blue, purple, and orange in all directions.

His shoulders clenched. *What the heck is this?*

The crystal moved back and forth hypnotically. She stilled it with her hand, closed her eyes and hummed softly. Eyes shut, she reached out, finding the countertop with her hand. Her fingers grazed the photo of the pendant. Her eyes popped open. She stared at the crystal. "Show me yes."

The crystal jerked once to the right.

"Show me no."

The crystal twitched to the left.

"Is the gem in this photo arctic topaz?"

Who's she talking to? The crystal? Mahoney rubbed the bristle on his chin.

The crystal moved right. She smiled. "Was this gem purchased here, in my store?" The crystal made a second move to the right. Her smile widened. "Was this gem purchased in May of 1977?" A third jump of the crystal to the right. "Was I the first owner of this store?" The crystal made a sharp move to the left. Her humming resurfaced.

Mahoney stifled the urge to speak. He wanted to know what the heck was going on. He wanted proof Seth had been in this store in 1977.

"I remember him. He was a special boy with a tortured soul."

He looked at the woman, blinking hard. "According to what? This crystal?" He pointed at the dangling clear stone.

She smiled. "Yes. According to my crystal. It's provided me answers many times over the years. This crystal is calibrated. Left, my left, means yes. The gem is arctic topaz. It became a gift for a special boy who was in need."

What is this? The rose quartz he had bought into. For some reason it calmed him. He didn't want to believe in the spirit animal, but what she said about the one card that he somehow picked with his eyes closed was dead on. He exhaled. He knew he had to play the crystal game to guarantee her easy co-operation. "You gave the gem away? It wasn't a purchase?"

"No. We can look through every one of those books, Detective, and you won't find any record of it. It was a gift. This boy, he came in here, and there was a deep sadness washing through him. There was fear and torture in his soul. His eyes looked vacant. He wandered around the store, aimlessly. I approached him. I looked into his eyes. I knew he needed this gem. He needed his own rebirth before it was too late. When I slipped the gem into his hand, his energy changed." She paused, resting her elbows on the counter and looking skyward.

He looked at her. He looked at the crystal. "I'd like to confirm. I need to look through your books."

"Of course. I can help you. But I assure you, you won't find anything."

He sighed, shook his head and flipped his notebook open. "Do you remember what this boy looked like?"

"Yes. He had long, dark hair—in a ponytail. He was a rather wiry little thing, but he was tall."

Mahoney looked back at the crystal. "You don't know his name?"

"No. He was rather secretive."

"Do you have any idea how old this kid was?"

"He wasn't quite a teenager. He was on the verge, but he still had such a childlike quality." Her eyes drifted with her thoughts. She snapped her hand on the countertop and looked right at Mahoney. "There was one thing."

"What's that?"

"When I gave him the gem, I hoped it wasn't too late for him to turn his path. When he left, I had such a feeling inside of me, I was afraid it was already too late to save him from the darkness he was clouded in."

A pang shot through his gut. *Black ponytail. Skinny. Tall. Pre-teen. Down a dark path. Tortured. Sounds like Seth. But how can I jump to that conclusion? Nothing concrete here.* "I see. Can you think of anything else at all?"

Her lips pursed. She ran the magenta-stoned finger along her chin. "No. His energy was consuming."

Mahoney stood up from the counter. "Fine. Let's get going on those books." He snapped his notebook shut, slipped it into his pocket and walked around to the other side of the counter.

"The crystal already gave us the answers we need," she said.

"Sure. But I need to be thorough." He looked into her eyes. "This is a Homicide investigation. I need to follow protocol."

She nodded. "Of course."

"I'll get them down. Is there any way to divide and conquer this?"

"We should start with the top shelf. That's where the older books are."

He stepped up the ladder and pulled out a book. The weight of it heavy against his hands, dust fluttered into his eyes. He turned and passed the book down to her.

Taking the book, she smiled. "You keep that rose quartz with you. It will guide you on this hunt, just as it did on that last one. You will find your way."

His cheeks burned. His heart swelled. "Will do." He turned and grabbed another dust-coated book, wondering how long it would take to look through them all. He could call for backup, but that would derail the other paths of investigation. Walking out of here now, without concrete proof would leave him relying on psycho Seth to tell him the truth. No. He wanted to look in the eyes of that sicko, holding solid proof in his hand, and pressure him to tell the truth about what had happened in that cave. He pulled out another book, hoping he wouldn't walk out of here putting his faith in a dangling crystal.

Chapter Eleven

Black Cat and Old Spice

Jud placed the stack of books on the shiny counter with a thud.

"Hello Jud." Miss Dalmasno smiled from across the counter.

He smiled back and handed her his library card.

She paused before scanning it. "Judson. What a lovely name." She pushed her thick black glasses with her pointer finger.

Judson. He hated his full name. It reminded him of the woman who gave it to him. Suppressing a scowl, he smiled. "My mother's idea. I go by Jud now."

The scanner blipped as she passed it over the card. She handed it back to him. "Sorry, I shouldn't pry. I've noticed it before, and I just thought it was a lovely name." Looking at the stack of books, she nodded. "You've picked out a great selection here. Malice Aforethought—a forgotten classic. Wolf Hall. Now that's an old one. I don't usually see that one checked out. You are not the typical reader I see around here." She plucked a book off the top of the pile. The scanner bleeped as she ran it along the spine of the book.

"I like an intellectual read." His stomach churned as he forced the smile to remain glued to his face. Miss Dalmasno's pink lipstick glared at him like a neon sign.

"Isn't this interesting." She picked up the next book in the pile and examined the title. "Fundamentals of Organic Chemistry?" She raised an eyebrow and looked at him, curiosity washing over her face.

She had a good brain on her. She always inquired about what he was reading. Even the more scholastic topics. "Yes. I have a rather extensive garden. It is somewhat of a passion of mine. Chemistry basics can be applied to the preservation of trees, lengthening their lifespan."

"Well, that's fascinating." She looked straight at him.

It's too bad she had glaring, pink lips. And of course, she was a woman. Every woman had a rotten core. Although, hers didn't show. Yet.

Resisting the scowl his eyebrows longed for, he focused his mind on the chemical facts darting through his mind. "Yes, it is. For example, a subset of the chemical compounds used in the embalming process are extremely effective in prolonging the life of most fruit trees. The concoction has to be slightly altered, of course, to avoid damage. By replacing the harsher chemicals with less toxic ones, the tree is encouraged to flourish without damage." A natural smile took over his face.

With hazy eyes, Miss Dalmasno rested her chin on the top of her hand. "Truly fascinating. I had no idea."

Charming too. Maybe she was a good one. Was that possible? "Yes. Well. There's a wealth of information out there, for those willing to put in the effort to absorb it."

"Yes. I do agree. That's one of the reasons I love the library so much." Her eyes wandered over the tall bookshelves at the back of the room. Jud turned and scanned the rows and rows of books. A wave of calm washed through him. The smell of dust and old soothed him. The sight of thick, bound books bulging with information calmed his core. Miss Dalmasno's sweet voice plucked him out of his reverie.

"Oh, I'm taking up your time." She picked up the next book. The scanner blipped.

"It's not a worry. I love being in the library."

She placed the last book on top of the stack, pressed the bridge of the thick, black frames with her pointer and met his gaze. "It's my favourite place. I think we all have a favourite place."

"Yes. We all do." A vision of his garden materialized in his mind.

She slid the stack of books toward him. He set his bookbag down on the counter and put the books inside. Hoisting the bag over his shoulder, he turned to leave.

He walked over to the massive library doors and pushed the ornate golden handle. Walking down the concrete staircase, his work boots plunked onto each stair. The sun, high in the blue sky, stung his eyes. Fishing his sunglasses from the back pocket of his jeans, he slid them onto the bridge of his nose.

He walked briskly along a pathway, weaving through a manicured park. The mid-afternoon heat hit him fast. Sweat sprouted across his forehead, trickling down the sides of his face. Running his hands through his damp hair, he pulled it back, securing it with an elastic into a ponytail. Hoisting the bookbag higher up on his shoulder, he quickened his pace. *Can't wait to get back to the cool shade of my sanctuary.*

Something brushed against his leg, vibrating through his jeans like a small motor. Halting, he looked down into a pair of emerald eyes gleaming from a furry, midnight-black face.

"Scat," Jud snarled.

The cat brushed harder against Jud's leg.

"Scat!" Jud pulled his leg away. He stared at the cat. A flash of déjà vu washed over him. Narrowing his eyes, he searched his mind for a clue. "Wait a second. You're the pussy that stared me down in that dark alley, aren't ya? Ghost cat."

The black feline strutted away, tail pointing skyward, ass exposed. Turning, the cat sat on the pavement, tail wrapping around its black body, green eyes staring at Jud.

Jud swore he caught a whiff of Old Spice. The same odour seeping from the pores of his mother's clientele. *Disgusting wastes of flesh.* The same scent that followed him down that dark alleyway that night, years ago. It was all he could smell for weeks after that old sicko bent him over that dumpster like a piece of trash. The first time he'd been invaded, exposing a service he didn't know he had. One that could buy him anything he needed on the streets.

Jud snapped his attention back at the cat. "Don't stare at me. Freakin' ghost cat. Scat!"

He waved his arms toward the cat. It didn't move.

"You are a ghost cat, aren't you?" He stared into the same green eyes that had pierced into his soul that night in the dark alley.

Jud took a big step with his left foot, swinging his right leg back, preparing to send the cat flying away with one hard steel-toed boot to his black, fuzzy ass. Jud's leg swung forth with full force. He stumbled, nearly falling flat on his back. After several awkward steps, he caught his balance. Jud adjusted his heavy bookbag. He looked around. No more cat. He turned in a full circle, scanning the entire walkway.

No more cat. Vanished into thin air.
Stupid ghost cat.

Chapter Twelve

Mummification Ritual

Mahoney thumped down into the chair next to Dara and stared at neon-green letters zipping across the black computer screen. Her teacup clicked as she set it on the floral-patterned saucer. Sliding the cup and saucer toward the teapot perched on the far end of her neatly organized desk, she turned her attention to the data churning on her computer screen.

"Bug, look at this." Her eyes ran at light speed down the screen. "I did a combined search to include organs in jars, embalming, and Natron. Most of the search results point to the Egyptian process of mummification."

Mahoney stared at the screen. *How is she deciphering this?*

Her eyes glued to the cryptic language, she continued translating, "The process involves five main steps. Embalming, brain extraction, removal of internal organs, drying out, and wrapping. Seems like the process applied to the young boy was very close. The brain extraction is missing, but everything else seems to have been followed."

"I wonder if the brain removal was too complicated. What does it say about the procedure?"

She clicked at the keys. "They are pulled out through the nostrils. Hmmm...sounds complex. But, if the brain isn't removed, appears it would dry up on its own. So, there might not be any impact to the preservation of the body."

"It wasn't necessary. Does it say more about the organ removal?"

Her fingers moved over the keyboard. She paused, watching the screen. "Yes. They are removed through a small incision in the left side of the abdomen. They are stored in what are known as canopic jars, and buried with the body."

"Canopic jars?"

"Yes. Special, engraved jars. Usually made of limestone or pottery."

"Anything else? Anything about the heart?"

Clicking at the keys, Dara entered another search. "Let's see here." She eyeballed the green text flashing down the screen. "The heart was left in the body. It was viewed as the centre of a person's being." A quizzical look washed down her face.

"So, despite what he's done to this boy, the killer still viewed him as a being? This doesn't add up. He treated him as an object." Mahoney shook his head. "What can you tell me about the embalming?"

"I'll go back to that." Dara tapped at a key several times. "A chemical composition is injected into the arterial network. As Blackwood indicated, the composition includes formaldehyde, glutaraldehyde, and methanol. Professionals who perform this are usually experts in anatomy, thanatology, and chemistry."

"Thana...what?"

"Thanatology. Uck. Says here it's also known as the scientific study of death. A deep dive into the bodily changes postmortem. There's more here. Gives me chills." She pulled up her floral, silky sleeve, exposing creamy skin peppered in goosebumps.

"I wonder if he was schooled on any of this. Given the nature of what he did, my bet is on thanatology." Rubbing the bristle on his chin, he looked at Dara. "I also wonder about that injection—is it easy to do?"

"After we finish with this, I'll search—find out how someone gains knowledge on Thanatology. I'll also dig into the procedure itself with some more thorough searches. The initial sets of parameters I've used are only scratching the surface on this data mine."

"You still have all that extra power Quesnel hooked you up with?"

She smiled. "Yes. She left the access in place. She even sent over a minor release update on the automatic text retriever."

He chuckled. "Any details on the wrapping?"

"Long strips of linen are used. A coating of warm resin is used between wrappings."

"Blackwood sent the cloths for further processing. I'll check in with her, see if anything more was found."

"Oh, and Bug, it says here magical words are written on the strips of linen, and amulets are attached for protection."

"Blackwood had the strips of cloth analyzed. There was a message written multiple times—'I have committed no murder.' This guy didn't just preserve this boy. This is part of his ritual. At least, that's what Agent Quesnel would say."

"Bug, speaking of ritual, looks like there is a final procession after the last step of mummification. Now that sounds ritualistic. I'll do some more digging into this."

Dara turned in her chair and rested her hands in her lap. "Will Agent Quesnel be involved with this?"

"Nothing official has been said. But this looks like her area of expertise, doesn't it?"

"It most certainly does. I wouldn't object to having her brainpower on this." Dara alternated between hitting the enter key and scanning the screen. "I don't see anything else here, Bug. I'll need to dig deeper into this final procession."

Flipping his notebook open, Mahoney scanned a few pages. "Does it say anything about inserting fake eyes?"

Dara continued scrolling through the neon data. "No, Bug. That's it. Hang on." Her fingers danced over the keys. The screen lit up again, letters of green flashing in strings. The movement on the black screen halted. She leaned in toward it. "No. Nothing like that. I'll keep searching."

"Sounds good. I should get moving."

"What additional searches should we add?" She turned to her teapot and poured herself another cup. Orange blossom wafted through the stuffy office air.

"I'd like to know where someone can get their hands-on embalming fluids. And white wraps. And these canopic jars. These things can't be simple household items."

Dara jotted down in a notebook, pink feathers bouncing in the air from the end of her pen.

Mahoney stifled a smile. "Where the hell does someone buy glass eyes?" He flipped through his notebook.

"Anything else?"

"Let's see. The salt. Natron. Is that a typical item? I don't know. And Alkali. The chemical they found in the eye sockets. Geez."

"All right." Her pen bobbed, pink feathers floating.

"I also want to know about this concrete coffin."

"I got the results from the crime lab. Composition of the concrete was standard. Could be a dead end."

"OK. Focus on the searches that might yield something."

"Got it."

Standing, he rolled the chair back to the desk he stole it from. "Thanks, Dara. You're a computer wiz. Don't know what I'd do without you."

She tipped her teacup toward him.

Mahoney spun on his heel, walking away and perusing his notes. Slipping through the war room door, he switched on the lights. A humming sound emanated through the room, the fluorescent tubes coming to life. He sat down at the long centre table, reached out, and pulled out his notepad. He looked up at the cream-coloured wall and carefully examined the photos of Caleb. The clock ticked loudly, staring its white face down at him. *Team will be back soon. What are you missing, Bug?*

Chapter Thirteen

War Room Recap

A mix of voices rumbled through the stuffy room. Mahoney pulled at his collar. Rubbing the back of his sticky neck, he snapped a file folder onto the table. The noise echoed through the room. Heads turned. A series of eyes stared at him.

"Let's get rolling. None of us want to be here all night."

Mahoney walked to the front of the room. He looked at Officer Williams, huddled in the front corner with Rudson and Roberts.

"Officer Williams, we normally do a round-table. Could we start with you?"

"Of course." Standing up straight, Officer Williams looked around the room. "We spent the day back at the scene in K-Country. Detective Hayes was a great help. We did a thorough scan of the entire area—the beach, the cave, everything. We couldn't find a single thing."

"Not surprising. This guy is organized. It's unlikely he would leave something that would help us. And it's been ten years."

"Really? So why did we spend all day there?" Williams' cheeks blazed.

"We had to be sure. If there was anything at all, we didn't want to miss it. We have to take detail to the extreme here."

Williams' mouth straightened into an annoyed pout.

"Dara has been deep in computer searches. Turns out the Egyptian mummification process is a mirror of what was done to this kid. Except for removal of the brain, it seems our guy followed it precisely."

"If he is so organized, as you say, then why would he skip a step?" Roberts asked.

"The brain dries up on its own. Given the complexity of removing it, and the lack of impact to the preservation of the body, it was an unnecessary step."

Roberts raised an eyebrow, then nodded at Mahoney.

"In addition to the embalming, drying, and wrapping, there seems to be a ritualistic aspect to the mummification process. A final procession. Dara, can you give as an update on this?"

Slipping her black glasses down her nose, she looked up from her typing. "Yes. The people proceed with the mummified body down the main street of the town. They walk and they cry. The amount of crying is representative of how much the person was loved. When a child has passed, a high display of emotion would be encouraged to better prepare the soul for the afterlife."

"The supplies he would need, to embalm, to dry?" Mahoney prodded.

"Yes. Natron, the salt found on the boy, doesn't appear difficult to obtain. The embalming chemicals, however, are more difficult to get. These substances are normally purchased by funeral homes and morgues. A licence is required to purchase these. Legally, that is." Dara dropped her glasses, letting them hang from the string of sparkly beads around her neck. "The wrappings appear to be common cloth. The jars—they seem to be difficult to find. I am still working on this."

"Good. We'll need a list of funeral homes and morgues. And more details on how to get the licence to purchase embalming fluids. Our killer may not have had a licence. We'll need to poke around at these places and find out anything we can. What about the fake eyes?"

"It appears making dolls is a widespread hobby. Finding the fake eyes is quite easy." She scanned her notes. "I do have a list of local stores. That's all I have for you now. I'll keep on looking."

"Great. Detective Sutton accompanied me to the park where the kid was last seen. We were able to interview the parents, several other parents who still live on the street, and the five kids with Caleb that day." Mahoney opened his notebook and flipped through the pages. "When Caleb disappeared, none of the kids saw anything. Or they had said so at the time. One of the kids, Joseph, was able to share some information he was too scared to divulge during the initial investigation. He saw a man. The man talked to him when he was leaving the park. The man scared him into keeping his mouth shut. Really creeped him out. At the time, Joseph was only eleven years old. Now, as an adult, the fear is gone, for the most part. He gave us a description."

"How will that help, all this time later?" Roberts asked.

Sutton glared at Roberts. "It won't at this very second. As we develop leads, it will help us filter."

Mahoney continued, "Interviewing the parents, we got a good look at the street from inside the houses. A stranger would have been noticeable. I think he approached the park from the back alley. And we found this." Pulling a photo from a file folder, Mahoney walked up to the crime scene wall, picked up a tack, and added the photo to the collage of Caleb. "This symbol was carved into the fence bordering a backyard, at the edge of the park and the alleyway. This symbol matches one of the markings Blackwood has been able to retrieve from the cloths wrapped around Caleb."

Williams' eyes bulged. The other two red-coats were silent. Sutton and Hayes focused on the tacked-up photo.

"Appears our guy was indeed at the park where Caleb was last seen," Mahoney said. "The same symbol carved into the fence also appearing on the cloths wrapped around Caleb indicates the ritualistic component to what the killer has done."

"This is some really strange stuff here," Williams said.

"It is. We have to push this. We have to keep moving. The killer could still be out there. He could still be doing this."

"But the body is over a decade old," Rudson said. "Do you really think this guy is still out there, committing murder?"

"With a high probability."

"But wouldn't he have stopped by now? So he wouldn't get caught?" Roberts asked.

"No," Sutton said.

"Why not?" Roberts shifted from one foot to the other.

"Because." Mahoney looked directly at Roberts, then at Sutton. "He won't. He can't."

"What are you talking about here?" Williams' moustache bobbed up and down.

"The killer has a compulsion that is out his control."

Williams wrinkled his nose and narrowed his eyes.

"A killer like this, he can't stop." Mahoney shook his head. "This type of killer—they *need* it. Kemper claimed killing stopped his blackouts. Rissell said it was the only way to stop his *inhibitions*. Bundy stayed away from his fiancée when he felt his *sickness* coming on. After a spree in a sorority, he called her pleading for help—saying he couldn't stop." Mahoney glared around the room, startled at the facts he'd gathered since Agent Quesnel came into his world.

Williams pursed his lips, backing up into the corner. Silence settled over the room.

"We're not getting in another argument. The point is, we have to stop him." Mahoney paused, flipping through the files in the folder. "Let's get on with it. The pendant we found in the cave. The gem is the same as the one we found on our first body in our last case. This stone is hard to find. I went back to the store where we located the purchase in the last case. Unfortunately, the recordkeeping was less than organized ten years ago." Mahoney rubbed the back of his neck. "Store owner claims to recall giving the gem to a kid who came in. The kid fits the description of the man we locked up in the last case. Seth Henderson. But we weren't able to find any records confirming this for certain."

Dara stopped typing. Sutton took a long sip of Big Gulp. Hayes stared across the room.

"Seth wasn't even a teenager when Caleb was murdered. But he may have been in that cave," Mahoney said.

"How do we find out?" Rudson asked.

Sutton slipped the red straw from his lips. "We have to talk to Seth."

Mahoney nodded. The room remained still. "To fill in those who weren't on our last case, I've been paying regular visits to the killer, Seth. He's currently being held in a high security psychiatric institution. He's under assessment, as ordered by the court. After his arrest, I was able to get him to open up about his victims. At least somewhat. There is a possibility a number of bodies are still out there. I've been continuing to interview him, in an attempt to find these other victims. Since I have an ongoing...shall we call it, *rapport* with him, I'll pay him a visit tonight. See what I can find out about this pendant, the cave, and the man at the park."

Sutton and Hayes exchanged a glance. A sudden chill made Mahoney shudder. He shook it off. "Where does that leave us? Next steps. Dara, you have a slew of searches to continue with. We need a list of funeral homes and morgues, and the details on getting a licence to purchase embalming supplies. Also, we need to know more about the expertise required for the preservation process. Whether anyone can do this, or certain knowledge and skills are required. And you'll keep digging on where to get the supplies."

"On it." Dara nodded, her fingers never leaving her typewriter.

"Somehow we need to figure out what this symbol means. And the message. Blackwood found out the same message was written repeatedly on the cloths that wrapped Caleb. 'I have committed no murder.'"

Sutton looked at him quizzically. "So the guy who murdered a young boy wrapped him up in cloths on which he wrote the message 'I have committed no murder.'"

"Yeah. Doesn't click. But if we learned anything from our last case, the message is important. There is a reason he left it. It may not be what it seems."

Williams shook his head. "This guy sounds cuckoo."

Hayes nodded. "A piece of the puzzle."

"Puzzle? He sounds insane. You can't possibly think the message means anything." Williams' moustache twitched.

"With high probability, it does," Mahoney said. "We just came off a case that left us a trail of bodies with messages carved into the flesh."

Williams' face paled.

"Turns out, the messages gave us big clues to how to find the guy."

Williams remained silent.

"Dara. I'll add that to your searches. But we'll also have to think about other ways to tackle this piece. The message and the symbol—there might not be a record of these in any computer database. Sutton, stay behind after we convene. Everyone else, we'll start fresh in the morning."

Williams said, "Do we really need to be here again tomorrow?"

Mahoney stood tall. "Yes. The scene is still yours, Sergeant. For the time being, we need the whole team, all of us, to stay on the same page. We may have new information from the medical examination. We may have more from our interviews tonight. We'll need to review our strategy for the day, in fresh light. We need to stay on top of every tiny piece we uncover, no matter how small. And we need to work together, as a team. We can't afford to waste our efforts, miss anything, or redo each other's work."

Williams pursed his lips. "All right. See you in the morning." He tipped his hat and led his officers toward the door.

"And Sergeant Williams..."

Williams halted. "Yes?"

"Technically, your team owns the scene. It wouldn't hurt to continue rescanning the scene for a few more days, maybe widen the search. Perhaps at first light. I'm sure you'd like to process the scene you own as thoroughly as possible." Mahoney shot a stern gaze at Williams.

Williams narrowed his eyes. "Fine."

Chapter Fourteen

Toxins and Gems

Mahoney watched the attendant swing the silver door open.

"Detective, please proceed. The door will be locked behind you. The interview will be monitored. At any sign of trouble, we will interrupt." The attendant glanced into the room.

"Thank you. I'm fine," Mahoney said.

Mahoney entered the room. Cold rushed over him. He looked at the man sitting at a rectangular, silver table. The man's arms rested on the table in front of him, his hands cuffed. His long, dark hair hung in ragged strands, hiding his face. His head was titled down. Underneath the table, his ankles were chained together.

"Seth."

Seth didn't move.

Mahoney walked a few steps toward him. "Seth. It's Detective Mahoney. Can I speak to you for a few minutes?"

Seth slowly raised his head, looking straight at the wall of bars on the far side of his cage.

Moving toward the table, Mahoney slid the chair opposite from Seth away from the table, and sat. Removing his derby, he eased it onto the table, to his right. Intertwining his fingers, he placed his hands on the table in front of him, and looked directly at Seth. Seth stared right past him, as if he wasn't even there.

"Do you remember our last meeting?"

Seth's eyes drifted eerily, landing in a direct, piercing gaze. "Yes, Detective. Of course I remember. You made promises you didn't keep. Why should I talk to you?" Seth's voice hissed across the small space between them.

Small spatters of spit landing on Mahoney's face, he held Seth's gaze, forcing his face to remain still despite the temptation to flinch against the wet spray. "I realize you are less than happy with your current circumstances. I understand."

Silence emanated through the room as Seth stared right at him.

Mahoney waited, hands perched on the table, his stare meeting Seth's.

Seth jolted to standing. "Understand? You understand? You don't know what it's like. You have no idea what this is like." Seth raised his fists, his wrists pressing hard against the metal rings holding him captive.

The door opened. "Detective, is everything all right?" The attendant leaned into the room.

Mahoney turned his face to the door, his hands and body unmoving. "Yes, we are fine. Perhaps something to drink would help us relax." Looking up at Seth towering over him, he leaned back in his chair and relaxed his shoulders. "Seth, would you like a cold drink?"

Seth's eyes bulging, his nostrils flaring as he panted, he eased into his seat. Dark stands of hair sticking to the sides of his face, he leaned back against the chair. "Something cold would be nice. And how about a cigarette?"

Mahoney looked back at the attendant. "Could we please have a cold drink and a couple cigarettes."

The attendant closed the door without a word.

"You think they will actually bring me a smoke?" Seth, almost smirking, relaxed deeper against the back of the chair.

"If I have anything to say about it, then yes, they will."

Seth grunted. "You've broken your promises before."

"I understand your frustration. I know you wanted your dolls. You're an intelligent man. You must understand your request wasn't possible. Your dolls, you know they were people, real people."

Seth stared at him, his mouth turned into a grisly frown.

Mahoney leaned in closer. "Seth, they were gone. Decomposed. Disintegrating. You know that. It's time to move on." Heat flushed his neck. *Don't lose it. Play his game.*

Seth looked down at the table.

The door opened again. The attendant walked in silence toward them and placed a can of Tab on the table, along with three cigarettes, a lighter, and an ashtray next to the can.

Seth's mouth turned into a sick smile. He looked at Mahoney. "Well, well. Look at this."

Mahoney nodded his head toward the pile of treats. "Go ahead. It's all yours."

Seth reached for the can, clamping his hands around it, sliding it across the table. He pulled the small silver tab. The pop hissed. Raising the can between his hands toward his lips, he took a long sip. Setting the can back onto the table, he looked up at the ceiling. "Oh, yeah. Cold. Sweet. That's good."

Looking over at the cigarettes, he reached his hands over to the ashtray, pulling it toward him. Lifting a cigarette to his lips, he snapped the small wheel on the lighter, a flame sparking. Inhaling long and deep, he breathed the toxic fumes in, closing his eyes. Exhaling a slow puff of smoke, he opened his eyes again and stared back at Mahoney.

"OK, Detective. I'll forget about my dolls for the moment. Why are you here?"

"OK, Seth. I'll be straight with you. We found something you may know about."

"Oh yeah? What would that be?" Taking another long drag off the quickly dwindling cigarette, his eyes locked on Mahoney. Seth's gaze pierced into him, digging deep inside, searching.

"A body was found. A young boy. He was wrapped up like a mummy and buried in a concrete box."

Seth's upper body snapped forward. His hands plunked onto the table. His eyes glazed over.

"Seth. What do you know about this?"

Seth froze.

Mahoney gritted his teeth. He resisted the urge to lunge over the table and force the information out of this sicko. "The body had been there for at least ten years. I know you didn't have anything to do with what happened to that boy. I found something there, something that may belong to you." Leaning over, he pulled a photo from the inside pocket of his tweed coat. Sliding the photo across the table, he set it in front of Seth.

Seth's eyes came into focus. He looked down at the photo. His hands shaking, he took a final drag of the tiny remains of the cigarette, then pushed it down into the ashtray. He stared at the photo, the corners of his eyes moistening.

"Do you know anything about what happened? Did you see anything?"

Seth tore his eyes from the photo, sitting back against the chair, his shoulders slumping. The handcuffs around his wrists rattled against the table as his hands shook. He looked at Mahoney. "Sid."

"Sid?"

"My mom's disgusting boyfriend."

"Did Sid live with you? In your mother's house?"

"Yes. Sid." Tears ran down his cheeks. His jaw clenching, he spat out the words, "Sick fucker. He did things. I saw him do things." Moaning loudly, he banged his forehead against the table.

The door opened abruptly. "Seth, are you OK?"

Mahoney stifled a sigh. *Tell her you're fine, sicko.*

Seth stilled. His head rested against the table, his body slumped. "I'm fine."

"Are you sure? Do you want to go back to your room?"

"No. I'm fine. Leave us."

Slowly raising himself from the table, he looked at Mahoney. Helping himself to another cigarette, he sparked it to life with the lighter, breathing in long and hard.

A cold calm washed over Seth. His face took on a vacant stare. He smoked, and he stared at Mahoney.

"What can you tell me about Sid and this kid?"

Exhaling a cloud of smoke, Seth stared back at Mahoney. "He did things to that kid. I saw him. I hid, on the stairs, where I wasn't supposed to be. He did things. The same things he did to me."

Seth went silent. He took several long drags from the cigarette, staring past Mahoney.

"OK, Seth. What can you tell me about the cave?"

His voice monotone, his stare vacant, Seth said, "I followed him. I saw him take that kid out of the basement. I saw him put that kid in his truck. I saw. I snuck in the back of the cab when he went into the basement. I hid under the pile of shit he always had thrown back there. I was real quiet. Like a good boy. When the truck stopped, I waited. It was real dark. I watched him carry that kid across a beach. I watched him wheel the coffin into a cave. He had this crazy contraption, with a motor. When he turned it on, I panicked. I crouched behind a stack of wool blankets in the corner of the truck bed. This contraption—it lowered the coffin onto a trolley with studded wheels. I could only see part of it, from under the blankets." Taking another drag, Seth stared straight ahead, looking at nothing. His face moist with tears and sweat, his hair stuck to his cheeks and his neck.

So he knows where the body was. "Did you go in that cave?"

Seth's voice was a mere whisper, the words leaving his mouth in a robotic voice as he said, "Yeah. I went in the cave. Wanted to see."

"Was the pendant yours?"

"Yeah. My special pendant. A nice lady in a gem store gave it to me."

"How did it get into the cave?"

"He saw me. That look. He saw me. I thought I was done for. I dropped my special gem. Thought it was the end for me. That look." Seth stared at nothing. His lower lip trembled. The cigarette shook between his fingers.

"Seth, are you still with me?"

No response.

"Seth?"

No response.

The door opened. The attendant walked over. "Detective, I'm afraid your interview is over. He gets like this, during his therapy sessions. Usually when they talk about Sid. He'll probably be in his own world for a few hours now."

Another attendant joined them, pushing a wheelchair. The two attendants helped Seth into the wheelchair. Seth remained catatonic, his only movements in response to the prompts given to his limbs.

Mahoney watched as they wheeled Seth out the door. *Pendant was his. The way he reacted—his fear seems genuine. And he knew the body was left in a cave by the water. I think he's telling me the truth. I need to figure out who this Sid is. Doris, I hope you're home.* He picked up his briefcase and derby, and headed for the door.

Messy Doris

He rolled his rusty orange car up to the curb, put it in park and stared at the rotting house. The last time Mahoney was here, he took down a monster and put him away. Seth, the tortured soul he visited regularly. Week after week, Mahoney listened to the emotional outpours as Seth talked about his dolls and how they were safely hidden. His human dolls. The corpses of college kids he'd painted up like Glam Rock Gods and disposed of in elaborate displays in parks across the city, and on the outskirts of its borders. Mahoney put on a face of empathy and spent hours pretending to care in hope he would receive a useful tidbit. Seth continued to claim that the investigation had only uncovered a portion of his human dolls. If there were more, Mahoney wanted to know. He wanted to give closure to their families.

He grabbed his derby, opened the car door with a creak and stood tall. It was time to pay a visit to the mother of psycho Seth, to find out what she knew about this Sid. Was Sid the one who killed the boy wrapped like a mummy and hidden in the back of a cave? Were Seth's accounts of his torture at the hands of Sid true? Where was Sid now?

Mahoney strode up the cracked, crooked concrete steps, eyeballing the erratic sprouts of brown grass. He knocked on the door and waited for a response.

"Whooo'sss thhhere?" a raspy voice pierced the door.

"Detective Mahoney. I need to talk to you, Doris."

The door flung open. Doris stood in all her glory, an old bathrobe wrapped tightly around her sagging body. "What *you* want?" She teetered like a round weeble.

Her breath stung his nose. "Let me in. We need to talk."

She raised her hands. "Eck. Don't care." She turned and shuffled away. Weaving from side to side, she knocked over a coffee table. A bowl spun out of control and chips flew through the air, landing all over the floor. The chips crunched as she walked over them, shattering them into little pieces. She reached an oversized chair and plunked down into it, pulled a lever, and flung herself back.

Mahoney shut the door. It wouldn't close. He nudged it hard. It shut with a thud. He turned and walked over to where Doris was sprawled out. A bottle of Jim Beam perched on a small table next to the chair. A glass full to the brim sat next to the almost empty bottle. *Dammit, Doris. Guess I'm not getting much out of you.*

He sat on the edge of the couch across from the chair, avoiding the spring sticking out of the frame. "Doris, do you know a Sid?"

Doris leaned forward, picked up the brimming glass, and took several gulps. She plunked the glass back onto the table, liquor spilling over her hand. The sweetness of the liquid floated over to him, teasing Mahoney's nostrils.

She laid her head back into the chair and closed her eyes. "I...I...don't know nobody." Her words slurred. "They all hate me."

"Who hates you?"

"All of 'em. Slooopppy fuckers." Drool slid down the side of her chin.

"I need to talk to you about Sid."

Doris' mouth gaped open. A loud snore grumbled.

"Good idea, Doris. You sleep off that Jim Beam." He stood, grabbed the bottle, walked over to the kitchen and poured the last bit down the sink.

He walked over to the door and looked at Doris. "I sure hope you're not the best lead I've got." He forced the tight door open and headed back to his car.

Chapter Sixteen

Dive Bar

The neon-blue light pulsated, printing the words *Live Wire* onto the pavement over and over. Mahoney looked down at his shiny black dress shoes. *What was I thinking?* He looked at the black door. He thought about the Stepping Stone Pub and the seat up at the bar that had been his for years. Simon's face appeared, his lips moving, offering him a drink. Wrenching the black door open, he stepped into the joint before he could change his mind.

Scattered with few patrons, the place was quiet. Looking over to the bar, he saw long blonde curls and tight pleather. *Good. She's here.* All he wanted was a no-fuss bite and drink before he called it a night. Finding a new bartender was a hassle he didn't want.

Walking up to the long, shiny slab dotted with high-top stools, he perched atop one of the circular cushions.

Turning to face him, her blonde curls slid over her shoulders. Tossing a white rag into the sink, she placed her hands on her hips. "Heya, sweetie. Here for a night cap?" Her candy-floss lips stretched across clean, white teeth. Her eyes left the rag, finding his face. "Hey wait, I know you. You're the detective." She slid up to the bar, leaning onto her elbows, her ample breasts pushing against the top of her black corset. A floral-fruity concoction wafted over him.

Mahoney pulled his eyes from the circular brown dot marking the curve of her left breast. "Yes, miss. I was here a while back, on a case."

"Yeah. And I told you before, it's *Sasha*." A whiff of bubblegum escaped from her mouth.

"Right. Sasha."

"You were here asking questions about those murders."

"I was. The Seth Henderson case."

Her smile straightening, her eyes glistened as she stood up. "Yeah. Right. That was awful. I mean, I just can't believe Seth had anything to do with…what happened."

Shifting his weight, Mahoney removed his derby, placing it on the bar. "Yeah. I understand. There were people in his life who, well, knew a different side of him." An image of Simon, his friendly neighbourhood bartender, popped into his mind. He still couldn't believe Seth, the killer he had hunted down, and Simon, his nightly bartender, were the same person. Anger swelled in his belly. He pushed it away and looked at Sasha.

"You got that right. He was the sweetest thing when he came in here." Shaking her head, she looked at the counter. Snapping her gaze back his way, she slapped her forehead with her palm. "Where are my manners? What can I get ya?"

"Ginger ale, please. And do you serve food here?"

"Oh yeah, you're the ginger ale guy. I remember." Her smile returned. "Yeah, we got a kitchen. Not too shabby either." Sliding him a plastic menu, she dug a glass into a pile of ice. Pushing against a tap with the glass, she looked at him. "I know you'll think I'm crazy, but, well, I actually felt bad for Seth. Like I said, he was real sweet. He came in here a lot during the day, when it was quiet. All he wanted was to chill out and watch some TV. I guess I'm stupid to feel bad for him, but I think he had a rough time at home." She slid him a tall glass, looking down at the counter. Tapping her pink-polished nail on the counter, she pursed her lips.

Taking a sip of sweet pop, Mahoney cleared his throat. "You aren't stupid. Trust me, he had a side to him some people were exposed to. If that's all you knew of him, well, then it would be easy to think he was a different person than the one who killed those college boys."

She looked at him. "Yeah, I guess you're right. Do you think how he was treated at home had anything to do with, well, how he became?"

"I don't know if that can be conclusively determined. He will be under professional assessment for some time. What did he tell you about his home life?"

"Well, I think he lived with his mom. And I think she was pretty awful. Seth didn't say a lot. Sometimes he would come in here with cuts and bruises. I don't know. I wondered if they were from his mom, or if they were self-inflicted. It just seemed bad. I didn't pry. This was his safe place." She leaned against the back of the bar, crossing her milky-white arms. Her breasts bulged against shiny black pleather. The brown dot pulled at his gaze. He forced himself to look into her eyes.

"Don't let this worry you too much."

"Awww. Aren't you sweet? I knew it the minute I saw you." The candy-floss smile returned.

Heat aroused his cheeks. He cleared his throat and pointed at the menu. "Well then, what do you recommend?"

"Oh, well, the pizza's pretty good. Burger ain't too bad either."

"You got pepperoni?"

"Yeah."

"That'll do."

Locking his gaze, she nodded. Turning, she slipped away. He stared down at his glass. *This place ain't so bad. Not when she's here.* The heat flared up in his cheeks again. He shook his head, looking down at his glass. The cold bubbles prickled his face.

"Your order's in. Say, you never came in before just to hang out."

"No. I, uh, used to go to another place. For a bite before heading home. But, it, well, it doesn't work for me anymore."

"Huh. So, maybe you'll stop in here sometimes?" Arms stretched out, her pink-polished fingers tapped the shiny black bar.

"Yeah, maybe." He took a long sip of bubbles.

"You know, if you ever wanna hang out, well, I do get a day off once in a while. I'm actually gettin' one this Thursday. I'll be over at a place called The Roxy. It's, well, it's a nice break from this place."

The fire returned, flushing his entire face. "I'm not good at promising anything. My work schedule dictates my plans."

"Not a problem. I'll be there anyways. You feel up to it, you can stop by."

"Sasha! Order up!" a deep voice shattered the moment.

"Your dinner's ready. Be right back."

He watched her bounce over to the kitchen. Rubbing the back of his neck, his scalp tightened around his head. *Bug. What are you doing?* Looking into the tall glass, he watched the bubbles rising to the top. *She's young. She's just playing with you. Just a fun distraction. Or, she's just being nice. Maybe she feels sorry for you, old man.*

Breaking his thoughts, she slid a piping-hot, cheesy pizza his way. "There ya go. Fast and hot." She leaned back against a silver sink, crossing her arms. Pink nails tapping her creamy skin, she scanned him up and down. "You look like you work hard. You could probably use a break. I meant it. I'll be at The Roxy, Thursday. I could use some good company." Smacking her gum, she shot him another wide smile. Her pink lips glistened. Sweet strawberry wafted over the greasy pepperoni smell.

He looked at her. *I bet you taste real nice. Like a fresh berry.* She seemed easy going, fun, light. Like she just wanted to let off a little steam. His gut rebelled against the thought. He'd misjudged before, leaving a wake of hurt.

Pulling a piece of pizza from the pie, he paused and looked up at her. "Like I said, case load dictates my schedule." Ignoring the droplet of sweat crawling down the back of his neck, he dug into the hot slice.

"Sasha! Order up," the voice from the kitchen boomed again.

"You enjoy your dinner. I'll be back in a flash."

Gooey cheese sliding down his throat toward his grumbling stomach, he watched her blonde curls bounce away. Maybe finding another bartender wasn't so hard after all.

FRESH
ONE

Chapter Seventeen

Open Road

The long dirt road snaked through the empty desert. The occasional makeshift trailer-trash town popped up. Most of the time it was just Jud and his trusty truck. Yup. He bought his truck way back in '69, and it still purred like a happy cat full from its last kill. He did all the work himself. No need for those useless auto shop liars who would take the clothes off your back if they could.

A clutter of trailers, their walls barely hanging on for dear life, huddled together at the crest of a hill ahead. It looked deserted, except for the tattered clothes hanging from wooden pegs fluttering in the breeze. *What do they do out here in the middle of bumblefuck? Gotta be survival of the strongest. Bet if I set my lawn chair out on the side of the road here and opened a can of Bud, I'd be ringside at a show of critters trying to survive at sundown.*

One hand resting easy on the steering wheel, Jud reached over to the passenger side and lifted the lid of a small cooler. He picked up a cold can of Dr. Pepper and slapped the cooler shut. No need to expose his lovely picnic to the clinging humidity. He pulled the silver tab and the pop hissed. He took a long sip. The cold bubbles tickled their way down his parched throat. He took another sip, then placed the can in the centre cup holder. He stared ahead at the long, open road with no end in sight.

It was going to be a long drive. But he had an important message to send to a creepy crawler. There wouldn't be much scenery either, but these backroads were less travelled. And they headed right for the Big Beaver border crossing where he could slip under the radar. Jud shot a glance into the truck bed, reassuring himself he hadn't forgotten anything. Taking a mental inventory, he saw the red gas cans, makeshift pump, wool blankets, flares and a Coleman lantern.

He looked back at the road. His mind drifted. A dark alley snaked its way through his thoughts. A shiver slithered down his spine. Despite the heavy heat of mid-afternoon in the open desert, a chill washed over him. For a brief moment, he was in the corner of that dark alley, huddled against the cold of the concrete wall. Pain throbbed in his empty belly. The stench of piss stung his nostrils. The *clank-clank, clank-clank, clank-clank* of a bottle pierced the quiet as it rolled across the pavement, alerting him that he was never alone.

Jud shook his head and refocused on the road. The dark alley was forever etched into his mind. At times it loomed, but it was a good reminder of what he could survive. And now, he didn't need anybody.

He checked the gas gauge. The needle bounced around the quarter-tank mark. Peering into the rearview mirror, he could no longer see the pile of trashy trailers. He scanned the horizon. Nothing in sight. This would be a good place to fuel up. He pulled over into the ditch and turned the engine off. The quiet of the open desert engulfed him.

The door creaked as he pushed it open. He stepped a boot onto the silver panel then jumped to the ground with a thud. Dust clouds scattered around him in a haze. He walked to the truck bed and pulled out a red gas can, a long clear tube, and his homemade pump. He snapped the little door to the gas tank open and turned the cap with a click. The tube slid easily into the tank opening. He secured the homemade pump to the end of the tube and the gas can. The viscous, brown fluid oozed through the tube into the gas tank as he repeatedly pumped his arm. He smiled. *I've come a long way since my first night in that dark alley.*

When he felt resistance against the pumping, he removed the tubing and shook out the remnants of the gas. Noxious fumes stung his nose as a few thick droplets hit the dusty ground. He put his supplies back into the truck bed and walked around to the other side of the truck. He unzipped his jeans. A sour smell stung the stagnant air as a bright-yellow, rainbow-shaped stream shot through the air, creating a small, rancid pool in the dry, brown earth. Shaking himself clean, he zipped his jeans shut and walked back to the road. Launching himself off the silver platform with his right boot, he settled into the driver's seat.

Pulling back onto the road, he switched on the tape deck and cranked the volume. The dark, dreamy voice of the Lizard King seeped through the truck cab. A dark poet turned rock god. Jud's own desert king—at least in his mind. The voice sung haunting lyrics of streets of blood, and the fragility of a child's mind—like an eggshell. The words soothing him, Jud sank back against the seat and took a long swig of sweet pop.

No unnecessary stops. No time. He needed to get back to his sanctuary and his new plan for the Bubblegum Plum. This *Bug* was just a glitch to be ironed out.

Jud shifted his left foot, resting his boot against the corner of the floor mat. His shoulders sunk into the soft plush seat. He sung along with the poet, losing himself in the droning lines of a dark tale.

Chapter Eighteen

Small Town Hunt

Jud sat in his truck, the engine rumbling as it idled. Ringing raindrops echoed through the small black speakers. His face was hot. His shoulders were tight. The deep voice of his desert king sung of a toad dead on the road. *I'm the stupid toad cooking on the side of the road.* Gazing across the street, he scanned the spattering of children running erratically across the playground. The pickings were slim. They all looked homeless, in tattered hand-me-down clothes and shoes riddled with holes.

What kind of shit town is this? It's worse than where I escaped from. I need to choose. I don't have time.

His right eye twitched. He blinked hard and shook his head. *Dammit.* He hated rushing. Deviating from his normal script had not been in his plan. But he needed to cage this *Bug. This Bug wants to take my special friend? I'll give him his own special friend. He thinks he can take me down? I'll cage him. Make him think I'm in his stupid city. But I'll be long gone.* And he had to do it fast, before the critter crawled too far into territory he didn't belong in.

His eye twitched again. He slapped his palm against it and rubbed hard. *Damn eye.* It hadn't twitched in a long time. Not since...well, not since he'd left, migrated down south, and retreated into his sanctuary. He'd made some stops along the way. It had taken him many test locations before he found the right one. It still bothered him that he'd had to leave his special friends behind, along the way.

Get on with it. He had to settle for this poor-quality hunting ground. It was the only way to get the message signed, sealed, and delivered before sunrise tomorrow. If he waited until he got to his destination, all the schools and playgrounds would be empty. This would have to do.

He picked up a pair of binoculars from the passenger seat and peered over the children again. A flash of shiny red locks caught his eye. He jolted the binoculars in the direction of the strawberry curls. *Clean hair.* He tilted his gaze down the boy's body, then back up again. *Clothes don't look too shabby. He may be the cream of the crop in this tainted litter.* Homing in on the boy's face, he smiled. *Clean skin. Pure. Unblemished.* He licked his lips. His internals tingled. *Looks like I got one.*

Placing the binoculars back on the passenger side, he settled in against the driver's seat. He picked up the copy of *The Perfect Gardener* he had just borrowed from the library back home. The final bell of the day wasn't for a couple hours. He had some time to kill before the litter of kids would be released into the wild. And he would be there, waiting for his pick of the lot.

He opened the book to the page with the corner turned down.

"Caring for Your Bubblegum Tree."

"The Bubblegum is a special tree. It needs extra care, and requires more attention than other plum trees—and most other fruit trees, for that matter. Be prepared to commit to a strict, daily schedule of care and maintenance. Your efforts will be rewarded. The shape of the tree itself is unusual. The trunk will grow into an upright vase shape. The blossoms are a creamy white. The tree will yield fruit sometimes within the first year. The fruit is a deep-red colour and tastes of sweet bubblegum."

Placing his pointer finger between the pages, he rested the book on his lap. *Strawberry curls. Not my usual choice. Might be nice.*

He turned the page corner back down, placed the book in his lap, and reached for his notepad. Flipping it open to the last used page, he scanned his notes.

Lunch Bell start: 12:00

Lunch Bell end: 12:45

End of Day Bell: 2:45

He looked at the clock beside the tape deck. 12:34. *Two hours.* He tossed the notebook aside and picked up the hardcover book from his lap. *I'll be a Bubblegum tree expert by the time the school bell rings.*

Chapter Nineteen

Reddy

Jud turned the key and the engine went silent. He opened the door of his truck and jumped to the ground, his heavy work boots hitting the pavement with a thud. He walked to the side of the truck bed and looked at the carefully wrapped package. *Time for processing. Gotta be quiet, don't want to wake up that obnoxious bitch.*

Jud hoisted the small body, wrapped in a blue tarp, over his shoulder. He grabbed his black duffel, sliding the strap over his other shoulder. Turning away from the truck bed, he walked cautiously up the back pathway, toward the rotting house.

He paused, glancing from corner to corner of the backyard, surveying the garden he had harvested with his own two hands. The once carefully tended trees were limp with rotten fruit and brown leaves. Not a single blossom bloomed. A small snort rumbled his nose. *Stupid bitch. She let my creations rot along with her.* Shaking his head, he turned and trudged toward the house.

When he reached the back porch, he moved a cracked flower pot with the toe of his boot. Concrete scraped across concrete, sending a chill down his back. *Better fuckin' be here.*

A flash of silver under the moonlight, his shoulders relaxed. He set the duffel bag down on the porch. Slowly bending his knees, he crouched while balancing the body against his chest and over his shoulder. He picked up the silver key. He stood up, slowly, and shimmied the key into the lock. He turned it. It clicked. A wave of relief flooded his insides.

Slipping the key into the back pocket of his jeans, he applied the slightest amount of pressure with his fingertips to the old door. Clenching his teeth, he willed the old hinges to stay quiet.

He applied a consistent amount of pressure to the door until it had opened just enough for him to slip through. He picked up the duffel bag and stepped into the house. He closed the door quietly behind him. Lifting one foot, he placed it down onto the floor with the utmost caution. One step at a time, he made his way across the rotting floorboards in an attempted silence. He took several steps.

A creak jolted him into a frozen stance. After several moments without a scuffle or thump from upstairs, he continued. Sweat beads burst across his forehead. His arms clenched the tarp. Reaching the staircase, he clicked the door behind him and exhaled the cloud of air pressing against his chest.

One work boot against one wooden stair at a time, he descended into the dark basement. Counting down the steps, he reached the concrete floor at the bottom. Clinging to the tarp with one arm, he reached his other hand toward the wall, grappling for the switch. The room buzzed as fluorescent lights stung his eyes.

Diamonds bounced off the concrete walls. His eyes snapped to a disco ball swinging from the centre of the room. Purple velour and hot pink radiated from beneath the dazzling ball. *What is this? The little fairy added his own touch.*

He turned his head toward the back wall and scanned a series of posters, plastered to the concrete. Tight-panted freaks stared him down with wild eyes, muscles rippling against bright pleather. *Yeah, his own feminine touch.* Something tugged at Jud's heart. *I did love that boy. Seth. He was so pure.* His gaze drifted to the back corner of the room. His old tape deck was nowhere to be found. A large ghetto blaster stood in its place.

He walked over to the centre of the room. He set the duffel bag on the floor and placed the body on a steel-slab table.

"I'll be with you in a minute. Don't move now, you hear?" He smirked. He crouched and shuffled through the open duffel bag, searching for the one item that he would leave behind. The fur of the plush toy was soft against his rough hands. As he pulled the treasure from the bag, he stared down at the brown bear with broken eyes. The right one was cracked. The left one had fallen out and had been replaced by two purple band-aids, forming an X. He turned on his heels and slid open the silver door underneath the steel slab bed. The bear stared back at him as he perched it inside. *Here's to you, Seth. Doris will find this. She'll know I've been here. She'll think I'm watching—that'll shut her up. I'm sure she'll pass the message on, and that little freak will shut his mouth too.*

Walking over to the boom box, he scanned the rows of cassettes. A jolt buzzed through him as his eyes fixated on titles. Titles that belonged to him. His collection hadn't been cleared out when he left. *Well, what do ya know? That little freak liked my music.* A pile of cassettes, his cassettes, still sat stacked upon one another. Several more stacks had been added, plastered with band names and album titles he had never heard of.

A dramatic face caught his attention. The man on the cover poised his lips as if to speak, his eyes pierced through anyone who stared, and his fire hair flew around his head, dancing on his shoulders. The Lizard King. A dark poet turned rock god. A survivor of the belly of the desert. In Jud's mind, he was the king of the desert.

A warmth surged through Jud. He remembered this tape from way back when he taught Seth all about his special friends. He plucked it from the pile, opened the plastic case, and slipped the cassette into the boom box. He hesitated. *Can't wake Doris.* He scanned the table. Spotting a bright yellow Walkman, he grabbed it and transferred the cassette. He hooked the Walkman to his belt, pressed play, and placed a set of attached earphones over his head.

A bluesy riff meandered in the background. A dark voice seeped from the music machine. A poet of darkness, sending his eerie vibe into the ether, speaking of a severed garden and the plowing of plants. Jud closed his eyes and drank in the words. His mind slipped away to another time. A time when he built his first garden, here in this place. A time with his most special, young, unblemished friend.

A dark ponytail slipped through his mind. A straitjacket trailed along. A white, pure face, dark eyes looking back at him. Jud could smell that fresh, clean kids' shampoo Doris used to buy for Seth, her only son. A wave of longing thrust through Jud, jolting him back to a time when he lived in this house and played with Seth, down here in this dark basement.

The voice vibrating through his ears suddenly belted into the headphones, speaking of angels finding their way through death. Jud's memory was jolted forward to the time when he left this cold, empty town, severing the dream for the garden in his mind.

Jud snapped his eyes open. He took several long strides back over to the steel table. There was work to do. Unzipping the duffel bag, he dug inside, pulled out a pair of latex gloves, and snapped one over each hand. He unwrapped the tarp and posed the young, redheaded boy on the silver slab.

He caressed the boy's cheek with his plastic-covered fingertips. "Wish I could take my time with you, Reddy."

Hoisting the duffel bag onto a small, square table, he dug around inside, retrieving multiple items. He placed the items in a neat row on the table, fussing with each of them until they were perfectly lined up.

He looked at the boy. "No time...you're just a message. Can't keep you."

A list flashed into his mind like a neon sign, brighter each time it buzzed on.

1. Save Innocence

2. Preserve Vessel

3. Remove Internals

4. Dry Vessel

5. Wrap Vessel

6. Save Soul

His palms slapped against the steel. He leaned toward Reddy. His nostrils flared and he caught a whiff of clean kids' shampoo. Slamming his eyes shut, his brain hummed, the neon list buzzing on, *bzzzz*, off, *bzzzz*, on, *bzzzz*, off, *bzzzz*, on, *bzzzz*. His eye convulsed three times. He slapped his palm against his eyelid and rubbed hard, plastic sticking to thin skin.

He slapped his palm against the steel again, shaking his head. *Get yourself together. This is a rookie move. No time. Just a message. Wraps and eyes.*

His gaze snapped to the boy's open eyes. *Dammit. His soul. His innocence. I'll be dammed if I let that be tarnished, message or no message.*

He turned his attention back to the bag, sifting through the contents within. He pulled out a long silver knife and held it up to the light. A glint flashed off the thin, sharp blade. *I may have to rush with you, Reddy, but I won't let your innocence be taken.* Jud leaned over the boy and proceeded to execute the portion of his script that he simply could not skip. His eye ceased to twitch. His shoulders relaxed. Upon completion of the critical step in his process, Jud held up a jar and eyeballed the prized possession that he would take with him—the one piece of Reddy that he'd keep forever. He leaned over and placed the jar underneath the steel slab bed, beside the teddy bear. He'd clean up, then grab the jar before departing.

He reached into his bag and pulled out a small vial. Settling the vial on the steel slab, he plunged his hand back into the bag, grabbing a gas mask. After securing the mask around his face, the strap winding across the back of his head, he turned his attention back to his new, special friend.

Jud lifted the vial and turned the cap. Fumes violated the stale basement air. Tilting the vial with caution, he attended to the final step to save Reddy's innocence.

Jud stood up and eyed his work, then closed the vial. He leaned over, slipped it into the bag, then rifled through the contents for his next item. He held up a bag full of black doll eyes. Shifting through the collection, he chose the perfect pair. As he placed the black, non-eyes into the empty sockets of the dead boy, his face relaxed. His eye was still.

He caressed the freckled face with his gloved hand.

"You'll never see things that will rot your core. Your innocence will never be lost."

Standing up, he admired his work. The neon blinking flashed into his mind again. *Preserve. Preserve. Preserve.*

Grinding his teeth, he shook his head and stood away from the body.

"Shouldn't rush this. I should preserve him first." His eye twitched hard. "No time. Can't."

He turned and walked quickly to the duffel bag. Clutching a roll of white cloth in his hand, his arm shook as he walked back to the boy. His arm shook harder and harder until he dropped the white roll. He bent over to pick it up. His eye twitched. Boots clunking against the floor, he forced himself back to the steel slab and unrolled the white cloth hastily. Wildly wrapping the cloth around the boy, he haphazardly covered the body.

He thought of the detective, Bug, and the newspaper article rambling on and on about how this Bug stole his mummy. His special friend. Every muscle in his body tensed. His eye twitched harder, moving into convulsions. He slammed his work boot against the concrete floor, halting the wrapping.

He stood up and took a long, deep breath. Exhaling slowly, he calmed himself.

"I have to wrap. I need to leave Reddy before sunrise. This Bug needs to think I'm here. He needs to be caged, scrambling in the limits of his city."

Unwrapping the white cloth, he re-rolled it into a tidy ball. Starting the procedure from the beginning, he began at the head of the boy, and wrapped his small body in a meticulous, mummy-like body wrap. Stifling the thoughts racking his brain, he followed his well-practised procedure of wrapping a small, still body. Words jolted through his mind. *Innocence. Vessel. Soul.* He shot them down with mental darts. Sweat poured down his forehead, over his twitching eye.

The room blurred around him as he rushed through the wrapping process. He couldn't take it anymore. If he wasn't going to execute his full script, then he needed to get out of this basement full of memories and do what he came to do. He wrapped the body back in the blue tarp. Placing it in a haste onto the concrete floor, he snatched a spray bottle and cotton cloth from his duffel bag. Wild sprays of disinfectant landed over the steel slab as he jerked the bottle across the table and wiped the surface sporadically. His head spun. The room blurred. His eye squeezed in mad twitches. The basement walls closed in on him. Pulling off the gas mask, he threw it into the bag, along with the cotton cloth, spray bottle and remaining tools. He yanked the zipper shut.

Pulling off his latex gloves, he shoved them into the outside pocket of the bag. His eye twitched again. Just once. But hard. He slung the bag over his shoulder, heaved the blue tarp-covered body over the opposite shoulder, then retreated up the wooden stair, snapping the light switch off on his way.

Chapter Twenty

Fresh One

Detective Mahoney pulled his rusting '69 Pony into a slot next to a black-and-brown Jeep Wrangler. *Blackwood's here.* The lining in his stomach blanketed his half-digested breakfast-to-go. The driver's side door creaked as he pushed it open. Snatching his battered derby from the passenger side, he rose from the car. He settled the derby onto his head, adjusted his belt and took a few long strides toward the tall trees.

He spotted the trailhead marked with police tape. An officer stood, notebook flipped open, talking to a young woman. A small pack clung to her back, a water bottle sticking out of the side. She had on bright shoes with good grips. He guessed she'd been out for a morning jaunt that led her to a gory discovery. Mahoney walked past them, nodding at the officer. A whiff of sharp citrus welcomed him as he moved into the dense forest. Trekking along the dirt trail, his hiking boots gripped the loose rocks with confidence. The dark silhouettes of tall firs loomed over him, chilling his skin. Pulling the sides of his tweed coat toward his chest, he lengthened his step. An ominous chill flushed through him.

A flash of yellow yanked his gaze toward a taped-off square section directly ahead. Bursts of sunshine clawed their way through the thick canopy of branches. A bright ray bounced off an iridescent *C* on the back of a black jacket. He counted half a dozen Crime Scene Technicians scattered around the outskirts of the neon-fenced square. *Wow. They're all in on this one.* Several uniformed officers huddled off to the side, deep in discussion.

Stooping over, he ducked under the tape fence. A gigantic fir tree stood at the far end of the square. The towering green branches stretched far into the blue sky above, the solid trunk planted into the dark earth. At the base of the tree a rectangular plot plunged several feet into the ground. Mahoney closed his eyes, inhaling the rich aroma drifting from the piles of fresh soil on either side of the plot. He knew he had to look. But he didn't want to. *Open your eyes, Bug.*

Forcing open both eyelids, he titled his head, looking down. A small figure lay in the freshly dug grave, wrapped in swaths of white dirtied with dark brown-and-green smears. His hand stroked the day-old bristle on his chin. *Can't even be five feet.* A bead of sweat trickled down his back, despite the chill hanging in the air. The body was small. Too small. A hand on his shoulder snapped him from his reverie.

"Mahoney."

He turned, seeking the source of the intrusion. Purple, almond-shaped eyes looked at him. His shoulders relaxed. "Blackwood. Glad to see you."

"Anything seem familiar to you?"

"Didn't we just unwrap a mummy? Geez."

"Well, appears the only cases you and I get are the crazy ones. I'm sure you've noticed the stature of the victim."

"Yeah." Shaking his head, he looked at the ground. "You think it's a kid?"

"Appears so. I'd rather get it to a more controlled environment before unwrapping it."

"Understood. We'll focus on the scene itself. Did the techies say how big their perimeter is?"

"I don't think they've determined that yet."

"We need it wide. Looks like the atypical is becoming the typical around here."

"I'll go check in with them."

He revelled in her lavender scent as she walked away.

Looking at the scene, he rubbed the back of his neck. *OK, Bug. Now what?* He stared down at the childlike mummy. *What happened to you, kid?* The white ghost face of a young boy flashed into his mind. He shoved it out. Pulling a pair of latex gloves from his tweed pocket, he snapped one over each hand. He crouched down beside the open excavation. His palm sunk into the soft soil as he peered inside.

A sickly stench rose from the plot, stinging his eyes and crawling down the back of this throat. The partially processed breakfast lingering in his stomach churned. Blinking hard, he willed the egg-and-cheese sandwich to stay put. Pins prickled the back of his neck. His shoulders clenched.

White-cloth wrappings wove around the body's head, concealing the face. Glassy, black spheres stared back at him from the eye sockets. The piercing stare crept through him, like a centipede inching down his insides. *Why would he place the fake eyes outside the wrappings? It's like he's forcing a link to Caleb.*

A gentle tap on his shoulder pulled him away from the hypnotizing stare of the black, void eyes.

"Mahoney, they said they're widening the perimeter."

"We need a walkthrough. If this guy left anything, we need to find it. Blackwood, the eyes...they look the same as the ones on the other body. But they're on top of the wrappings. It doesn't make any sense."

"Yeah. I noticed. I don't want to remove anything until we get the body secured. The techies completed a thorough processing of everything inside the yellow tape. The body, the tree, both were completely covered in prints."

"Prints?"

"Yeah."

"So, this guy goes through the necessary preparation, mummifies his victim, digs a grave several feet into the ground, and marks the spot. But he leaves prints everywhere?" He cocked an eyebrow.

"Yeah. Exactly my thoughts. This guy was too organized, and too careful, to be leaving prints."

"We need to run them. Pronto."

Shifting back and forth on her booted feet, Blackwood peered into the plot. "Dammit. Look at that."

Mahoney faced the hole. Several shiny burgundy beetles scurried down the dirt wall, their legs creeping over the child-mummy.

Blackwood glanced at her watch. "Medical team should be here. I'm going to check on their status. I want to get this body out of here. It's too exposed." Pulling her cell phone from an opening in her heavily pocketed pack, she turned and walked away. Dead needles scattered over the ground crunched under her sturdy boots.

Mahoney remained focused on the mummy. Gazing into the grave, he scanned the soiled lengths of cloth. He inched his focus over the head and down the body. His eyes probed for any hint of a clue. Closing his eyes he willed all thoughts from his mind.

Shiny black tassels flapped into his thoughts. The ghostly face of a young, dead man stared at him. Clenching his eyes hard, he willed it away. Files from the last case were still being processed. His mind had yet to wipe away the faces of the dead college boys left exposed in the wild.

The ghost face whispered through his mind. *Bug. Listen.* He stared at the phantom face. Fuzzy at first, it became clear, dissolving every other image. *Bug. Listen. Look inside.* He pictured the leather-bound journal in his hands. The one he had retrieved in the depths of the dungeon of the last monster he caught, the one that lay hidden beneath the steel slab where innocent victims had been tortured. Slipping a hand into his tweed coat pocket, his fingers stroked the smooth, polished surface of his hidden gem. His eyes sprung open. He stood and walked along the open grave. A crisp, sweet aroma caught his senses. It reminded him of fresh cut wood. He walked toward the tree at the head of the plot. His gaze followed the contours of the cracked bark. He narrowed his eyes. Something appeared to be carved into the bark. *Bingo.* The open plot created a barrier between him and the carving on the tree.

Waving his arm, he summoned Blackwood. She sprinted toward him.

"You got something?"

"Look." He pointed toward the mystery carving.

"Is that a carving?"

"I think so." Mahoney's feet rooted into the ground. He stood and stared.

"Here." She handed him a small pair of camouflage-patterned binoculars, *Zeiss* branded on the side.

Mahoney took the compact device and snickered. "Should've known you'd have just the tool for the job."

"Yeah. These babies have a magnification power of ten and a light gathering power rating of twenty-five. Should be adequate to identify your mystery item."

He raised the circular lenses. He homed in on the cuts in the bark, tuning the binoculars to focus. His mind wrenched. His forehead tightened. He stared at a small series of circles cut into the bark.

"Mahoney, what is it?"

Lowering the binoculars, he twisted to face her. "I think it's a swirling vortex."

"Well, that's a humdinger."

"You got that right."

Chapter Twenty-one
Fresh Carving

The parking lot was almost empty. Mahoney watched as the last black, shiny truck drove off, iridescent letters, *CST,* catching the final glimmer of sun.

He adjusted his derby and walked toward his car. Sutton shuffled up to him. "So, boss. What do you think?"

"Two isn't enough to declare a series. But, I'd say we got a series."

"Yeah." Sutton ran his hand through his brown curls. "Two bodies, with clear linkage. Looks like back-to-back serial cases."

"Serial serial killers." Mahoney smirked at his lame attempt at humour. Sutton chuckled.

At least someone finds me funny. "We need more manpower."

"Sergeant getting us some?"

"I asked. Not sure he can though. Without Hayes, you're all I've got."

"You think Hayes is OK with the red-coats?"

"Yeah. He'll keep them in line. He's good at sticking to the process."

"True. And he won't be pushed around."

"I'm counting on it." Mahoney rubbed the back of his neck. His palm sticky with wet sweat, he wiped it on his pant leg.

"There's a lot here. Where do we start?"

"We identify the weirdest clues and put pressure on them."

"Like the symbol?"

"Yeah. Did you see it? Looked like the one on the fence at the park."

Sutton shook his head. The bright-green rabbit foot dangling from his belt swayed back and forth. "Yeah. It's weird."

"You've got good instinct. Follow it."

Sutton smiled sheepishly. "OK, boss. Want me to get the photos of the tree carving to the crime lab—get them amplified?"

"Yeah. Make it top priority."

Sutton scanned the sky. "Reckon we can squeeze in a few more hours."

"My thoughts exactly. I'm gonna check in with Blackwood. See what else she might have unravelled."

"I'll give you a shout after I drop in the crime lab. That symbol is bizarre. And the eyes. They were on top this time. More noticeable."

"Yeah. Bugs me."

"I could check some of those stores Dara found—for doll eyes." Sutton twisted his wrist and looked at his watch. "Might be too late."

"Give it a try."

"Anything else?"

"Yeah. Find me a ghost."

"You mean Sid?"

"Sid."

"Maybe the symbol and the eyes will lead us to him."

"Let's hope so."

Sutton waved, walked over to his shiny blue truck, and unlocked the door. "Later, boss."

Mahoney nodded. The orange door of his Pony creaked as he opened it. He plunked down into the driver's seat and turned the key. The engine rumbled. He relaxed his shoulders against the seat and closed his eyes. An image of a dolphin floated into his mind. *What did the gem store lady call it? Spirit animal.* The dolphin swam through the ocean of thoughts drowning him. He focused on the smooth, curve of the blue fish as it plunged through the waves of ghost faces and bizarre clues, forcing them to float away and dissolve into nothing. His mind cleared. A sense of peace stilled him.

Chapter Twenty-two

Speeding Through Town

Driving fast down the main street crossing the centre of the city, Mahoney stared straight ahead. His mind raced over the images from the murder scene he had just left. A small body wrapped like a mummy nestled in a freshly dug grave. Black nothing eyes. The investigation had started with a coffin in a cave—out of his jurisdiction. But the scene in the forest, this one was smack in the middle of his territory. He shuddered, feeling the investigation grabbing him, sinking its claws into his skin.

He focused hard on each intersection he whizzed by, flashing his siren just long enough to blast through. Leaving the second murder scene behind, the glaring similarities to the coffin in the cave cluttered his mind. The massive tree looming over the plot dug into the earth cloaked his thoughts.

This one's in the dead centre of my city. My jurisdiction. He could feel the claws of this case digger deeper into him. He imagined them piercing his flesh, droplets of blood trickling down his arms. Two murder scenes, taking a strong hold on him, not letting go.

Turning a knob on the tape deck, tinkling raindrops echoed from the small, black speakers, trickling through the car. The deep voice he couldn't seem to get enough of lately sung of riding into a storm. *I'm driving straight into my own storm.* Hadn't he read somewhere that the dark poet turned rock god had a name for himself? Some sort of reptile king? He shook the thought from his mind and let the lyrics take him away, his mind drifting.

His brain went into overdrive. *The body was small. Gotta be another kid. And wrapped like a mummy, again. Why were the black eyes placed on top of the wrappings?* The similarities were too significant to ignore. But the differences between the two scenes hijacked his train of thought. *And the prints.* Why were there prints all over the scene? *And the symbol. What the hell?* He was sure it was the same as the one on the fence in the park where Caleb disappeared.

His head spinning, he blinked hard and concentrated on the road. Turning the volume back up, he tried to lose himself in the crooning of a crazy man. Not his usual blues, but he was pumped up. He needed something to match his mood. Something more aggressive. *Only a few more blocks. Blackwood might have something. Of course she will. She's good. Too good.* A slight calm trickled over the aggressive vibe pulsing through his veins. *Chill, Bug. Chill.*

Chapter Twenty-three

Unwrapping the Mummy

Pulling into the morgue parking lot, he swiftly made his way through the front door. Mahoney flashed his badge to the personnel at the front desk and hurried down a series of long hallways to Blackwood's zone. Pushing open the morgue door, he scanned the bustling room. *Lots going on for mid-week.*

Passing by a row of bodies, his eyes refused to ignore the scene. Two adults, a male and a female, lay next to each other on silver slabs. Across from them, two children, one boy and one girl, were side by side. Mahoney's eyes glued to the girl. A large, bloody gash opened her abdomen. Her closed eyes were dark with blue and black circles. One of her arms lay in a limp wreckage of deep slices. A bone pierced her skin, sticking out of her wrist.

A voice jolted him. "There was a massive car wreck last night, on the Trans Canada, just outside the city limits." Doctor Sabin shook her head, her emerald eyes peering through her tortoiseshell glasses. "Family of four was struck head on by a car that had crossed the median. Poor girl was in the front passenger seat. Last I heard, they hadn't determined the cause of the accident."

Mahoney forced out a word or two. "Wow. That's terrible. You on your way to see Blackwood?"

"Yes. Looks like she's deep in her processing routine." She looked across the room.

Following her gaze, Mahoney found Blackwood in her usual spot.

"Let's go over to the body. I'll summarize what I've found for you, and Terra can fill you in on the rest."

Mahoney followed the doctor away from the dead family. They approached a small body lying on a steel slab. The long, white cloths that had been wrapped around the body at the scene were removed. Mahoney's gaze glued to the sickly remains. The pallid skin glowed under the fluorescent lighting with a blueish hue.

Spots along the arms, legs and torso were puffed out in a ghastly display. The putrid stench had followed from the earth plot, stinging Mahoney's nostrils. His mind immediately went into action. *Why is this body so different than the first one? There should be a pattern here.*

Blackwood looked up. Big, square, plastic goggles encased her almond eyes.

Mahoney grinned. "Don't let us interrupt you."

"No problem, Mahoney. Sherice, thank you for joining us. Let's get a jump on the rundown of this boy." She moved toward the small, blue body. "We have here eight-year-old Benjamin Brown. He went missing two days ago from Morse, Saskatchewan. When we couldn't find an identification we extended our search to missing children in the surrounding provinces."

Mahoney cocked an eyebrow. "Saskatchewan?"

"Yeah. He was last seen at school. Somewhere between there and home, he vanished."

"Why would our guy grab a kid from a province over, then bring him and dump him here?"

"I can't gamble a guess on that. How about some print-related facts?"

"Of course."

"Look." Blackwood picked up Benjamin's hand, turned it over, and pointed to his fingertips. "The skin is removed from several fingers on each hand. We sent prints from the fingers that still have skin to the crime lab. The results indicate there's a high probability the prints at the scene match the major contours of Benjamin's prints. It appears it was his prints all over the scene."

"This kid was forced to leave his mark all over his own murder scene?"

"Based on the estimated time of death, it's likely the prints were made after the boy was deceased."

"He removed the skin, used it to paint up the scene. Geez." Mahoney shook his head and rubbed the back of his neck. "So we know who the kid was, we know where he came from, and the prints aren't going to give us a lead. What else can you tell me?"

Blackwood pointed at the blue boy. "You notice how different this body is from the one we found in the cave?"

"Yeah. The skin on our first victim was dry, brown, thin. The skin on this one is blue."

"It is. And you see how puffy his body is?"

Mahoney nodded.

"The body is retaining fluid and air right now. This happens a couple days postmortem. Benjamin here is at the beginning of his bloat stage. Leaking enzymes cause internal gases to build up, puffing up the skin. The bacteria produced release sulphur, making poor Benjamin blue, bloated, and smelling like rotten eggs."

"So, the body wasn't prepared at all, like the other one?"

"No. No traces of embalming chemicals or drying salt. And the organs are still in tact. No jars were left in the plot."

"He dumped this one in a hurry. No preservation. No planned future visit."

"Appears so." Blackwood pointed to a silver table adjacent to the body. "There were two pairs of black glass eyes. The ones on top of the body, at the scene. Another pair were inserted into the eye sockets. The eyes are gone."

"Why would there be a second pair of fake eyes on top of the wrapped body?"

"I don't know. But there were traces of Alkali in the eye sockets."

"He took time to chemically burn the eyes. Just like Caleb?"

"It appears so. I doubt we can determine if the eyes were removed or entirely burned."

"Why does he want these kids to have no eyes? It must be important if he took the time but rushed on other steps. Why was he in a hurry to get this kid buried? It's like he wasn't preparing him the same way. Maybe the purpose of this kill was different."

"Could be. That's for you to figure out. Let's get through the facts so you can go and ponder the meaning of the mummy."

"Yeah. Good." Mahoney rubbed the bristle on his chin with vigour, narrowing his eyes.

"Sherice, did you have an update?" Blackwood turned to face Doctor Sabin.

Doctor Sabin walked up to the small body. "Terra, I hope you don't mind, I intervened on the toxicology report, put a little pressure on them. I have the final copy here." She placed a folder on a small silver table.

Blackwood smiled, her cheeks flushed. "Not at all. Guess you're more charming than I am."

Mahoney wondered if they had known each other before this case started. "What's the conclusion?"

"COD was poisoning. The chemicals used to burn the eyes seeped through the nasal canal into the skull." Doctor Sabin shook her head. "Poor kid. I was able to take samples of residue from the eye sockets, nasal passages, and brain matter, from both victims. The chemical breakdowns show high levels of the chemical used to burn the eyes. Furthermore, the chemical analysis from these samples have a high level of correlation between victims."

"Wow. That's a new one for me. And I've seen a lot of CODs," Blackwood said.

Doctor Sabin said, "That's all I have for now."

Mahoney stared at the body. *Poisoned by eye burning.* Prickles crawled down the back of his neck.

Blackwood said, "One more thing. There appeared to be a message on one of the cloths. I've sent them all to undergo the same process as the cloths on the body from the cave."

"Eyes. Messages. Cloths. This has got to be the same guy. Why did he surface ten years after burying the boy in the cave? And why did he rush with this one?" Mahoney rubbed the bristle on his chin.

"That's your job." Blackwood smirked.

"Anything else for me?"

"Not at the moment."

"I'm heading to HQ. I'll be in touch. Thank you both." He nodded.

He spun on his heel and headed to the door. *Mummies. Eyes. Messages. Poisoned by burning eyes.* This was dark. Real dark. The claws of the case wrapped around his throat, suffocating him. From one case to the next. No break. He was in deep, and he wasn't getting out anytime soon.

So much for re-scheduling his trip to the Sunshine Coast.

Chapter Twenty-Four

Seeking Quesnel

Mahoney pushed the cell phone against his ear. He looked through the windshield, watching rows of trees race by. *Two bodies. Again.*

The phone rang. He waited.

"Behavioural Analysis Unit, FBI. Agent Quesnel."

"Quesnel. It's Mahoney."

"Mahoney," her sultry voice seeped through the phone.

"Did you get the files I had faxed over to your office?"

"I was just perusing them. What's happening to that small city of yours? Two serial killers, back to back?"

"Yeah. There's no other conclusion, is there?"

"Nope." She clicked her tongue against her cheek. "Two mummies. Fake eyes. Can't be a coincidence. You might only have two bodies, but this looks like a serial situation."

"Yeah. I know."

"And the symbol on the fence matching the one left on the cloth." She whistled. "This guy has some strange fantasy in his head."

"Dara's been digging for me. She ran me through the Egyptian mummification process. The steps are detailed, in a certain order, and, well, strange." Large pine trees dwindled as Mahoney left the park behind the morgue. As he drove through the quaint neighbourhoods between the park and the heart of the city, rows of freshly painted houses and manicured lawns swept by.

"Sounds like my kind of killer."

"Yeah. And there's a ritualistic part to it. They do this procession with the body after it's prepared. Dara's still working on her searches, but..."

"We have organization and ritual. We just need to unravel his fantasy."

"Bingo. But there are big differences between the two scenes." Picket fences dissolved into office towers looming over the downtown core. "This second one, the kid was wrapped up again, but none of the organs were removed. And the body was all bloated up. No acts were taken to preserve the kid."

"Maybe he had no intention of visiting this one."

"Yeah, that's what I thought. But there's more. There were two pairs of glass eyes. One in the eye sockets, like the first body, and a second pair on top of the wrappings."

"Hmmm. Like he was in a hurry. Or he specifically wanted you to notice them."

Herds of people in suits spilled from office buildings onto crowded sidewalks in the belly of the city. Approaching a busy intersection, Mahoney flipped his siren on, maneuvered through the lights, then flicked it off again. "You mean like he was leaving some kind of hint?"

"Yeah. He may have been leaving a message. Explicitly linking this body to the last one."

"Announcing he's still out there?"

"Or he wants credit. What else is different?"

"There were prints all over the scene. Looks like they belonged to the victim. The kid has skin missing from his fingertips."

"He's playing with you, Mahoney."

"What?"

"Yeah. No preservation, so he's not planning anything with this body. He's just leaving it. Prints to lead you off track. And he specifically wants you to notice the eyes. They are important to him, and they link the two bodies together. He only wrapped this one up to solidify that linkage. I think the purpose of this is different."

"So, like you said—he left the body as a message?" As he escaped the heart of the city, he pressed down on the gas pedal. His car sped along an open section of the main artery connecting the bustling core to the industrial outskirts.

"Yeah. He wanted it to be found. He wants it known that he's still out there, and that he was responsible for the one in the cave. He may also be trying to derail you. Was there media coverage on that cave scene?"

Mahoney sighed. "Probably. Usually can't be stopped."

"Can you find out where it reached? I think this guy saw it. The timing would be too convenient otherwise. It triggered him to leave this second one, his message."

"I'll dig into it."

"What about the pendant? The photo in the file, it looks just like the one Seth left on his first victim. Seth would have been...what...twelve?"

"Yeah. I went to see him."

She whistled low and long. "Mahoney. You've got balls."

"Yeah, well, I had to know. Besides, I've been making regular visits to him anyways. I'm still trying to find out more about his victims. I tracked down the source of the pendant. The lady running the place may have given the same type of gem to a kid fitting Seth's description, just over ten years ago. There's no proof." A burst of yellow blended into a line of soft pink as the sun touched the horizon.

"So, what did Seth say?"

"He was at the cave. Followed his mom's boyfriend. He said he saw the boyfriend do things to the boy. He watched the boyfriend move the body and the concrete coffin into the cave. He dropped the pendant while he was there. His answers to my questions were a bit cryptic. And he's still obsessed with his dolls."

"He will be, till he dies."

"Yeah, well, he was the same old Seth. Talking about his dolls and my broken promises. When I brought up the cave and showed him the picture of the pendant, he changed."

"Did you see Simon?"

Mahoney gritted his teeth. Simon. Seth's alter ego—the friendly neighbourhood bartender. "Nope. No sign of Simon. It was still Seth, but it was like he was a child. I think this boyfriend of his mom's was as bad, or worse, than he is. I think this guy messed up Seth real good."

"Well, there were references in his journal to some man-monster, remember?"

"Yeah. I need to get that journal out of evidence and take another look. I do recall the entries. Seth said this guy did things to him. He also said he saw this guy take the kid into the cave. I think he was an observer, not a participant. I think he may have gotten a bad beating for what he saw. When he talks about this man, he turns childlike. He ends up in a catatonic state."

"It's a defence mechanism. The mind doesn't want to comprehend what has happened. It shuts down. The memory is too much to process, it's too physically taxing. Sounds like Seth simply shuts down when triggered by memories of what this guy did to him."

"Yeah. They told me at the psych ward this has been happening in his sessions."

"But you got an explanation, at least. You know Seth was likely there. Explains the pendant. And you've got a prime suspect."

"Yeah, sure, an explanation from a mentally unstable murderer. Not much to rely on. And yeah, I've got a prime suspect, but he's a ghost. We don't know who this guy is."

"What do you mean?"

He pictured her red lips twisted in contemplation. "We only have a first name. Seth called him Sid. That's all we know. There's no record of anyone living with Seth's mom. Her name is the only one on the title."

"Have you talked to her?"

Drunk Doris reeking of Jim Beam popped into his mind. "I tried. She'd had a long night with Jim Beam before I arrived. I'll try again, but I'm not too hopeful. When we brought Seth in, she was furious. I doubt she'll be co-operative with us now."

"So what do you need with me?"

"Your profiling."

"Sounds like you're getting good at it yourself."

"Well, you definitely gave an old boy some new tools. But it's always best to get an expert opinion. And...well, we're collaborating out of our jurisdiction here. The first body was found outside the city limits. The Royal Canadian Mounted Police—RCMP, as we call them—own the scene."

"Let me guess, newbies to the concepts of ritual and fantasy, don't buy it." Her half snort-half snicker rippled through his phone.

"Yeah. These ideas are totally illogical to these guys. Their reactions are...well, let's just say they sound like..."

"Like you did when I started talking about fantasy in your stuffy war room?"

"Yeah." He chuckled.

"Criminal profiling is still a baby. My team is small. We don't have much reach across the United States, yet. We need to build our repertoire of real applications."

"This is the perfect real-life example for you—a real gruesome case. Plus, it would extend your reach outside the US." He paused. "And...I need your influence to smooth things over here."

"Mahoney, you asking me to come visit you?"

"Yeah. You got time?"

"For a killer who preys on children, burns their eyes out, and wraps them up like mummies? You know this is my game. I'll catch the next flight out."

"Swell."

Chapter Twenty-Five

More Manpower

Mahoney tromped through the office, weaving his way through the cubicles. Piles of files cluttered desktops, spilling over into pools of cold coffee. Chipped mugs and cracked pens. What a mess. Detectives were like pigs in a pen.

He rapped three loud knocks on Sergeant Jackson's door.

"Yeah," came a gruff voice muffled through the door.

Mahoney pushed the door open and started his rant without a hello. "Sarge, I need manpower. Now."

Sergeant Jackson leaned back in his chair and removed his glasses. He inspected Mahoney from head to toe. "You just come from the scene?"

"Yeah."

"Where'd you stop on the way?"

"Stopped at the morgue. And I chatted with Agent Quesnel on the way here."

"Your fancy FBI agent...huh. You think we can afford her?"

"Don't care. She's on her way."

"On whose dime?"

"Don't know. Maybe we can split it."

"Easy for you to say. You don't have to balance a budget."

Mahoney placed both palms on the cherry-coloured desk and leaned over it. "The bodies are linked. This is even more complicated than our Glam Boys case. I had no choice. We need to figure this out, now." Sweat sprouted across his brow. Heat swelled over his back and neck.

The sergeant placed his glasses on his desk and folded his hands. "You're gettin' hot under the collar, Mahoney. Bring it down a notch."

Mahoney backed off from the desk. He took a deep breath. "Listen, we need to stop this. It'll be even worse than last time."

"I know. I trust you. We'll work it out with your fancy FBI agent. I do believe she's a necessary asset. But you gotta give me more time on any additional detectives. We're already running thin. We may have to wait until Hayes is done helping the red-coats."

Sweat trickled down Mahoney's back.

"Why don't you sit for a minute." Sergeant Jackson motioned toward a chair.

Mahoney plunked down. He rested his elbows on his knees and rubbed his temples with his forefingers.

"See, take a minute, cool down a little."

"I hate wasting time."

"You're not wasting time. You're regrouping. You'll see, it'll clear your head. What else you got planned tonight?"

"Sutton's following up with the weirdo shit we found at the scene. I gotta go over what Blackwood gave me. And touch base with Dara." He took a deep breath. "Oh, and someone leaked to the paper. I need to get over there and find out who."

"Don't waste energy on the paper. They're not gonna spill where they got their info. Focus on the case. Then get a little shut-eye. You'll think better tomorrow."

"Yeah. Sure."

"Listen." Sergeant Jackson put his glasses back on. The small, rectangular lenses amplified the crow's feet around the corners of his eyes. "I can't produce detectives out of thin air." The sergeant's eyes pierced into him.

"Fine. Sorry. I get anxious."

"I know. You've got this. Simmer down a little."

Mahoney stood and nodded. "Fine, boss." He swept through the door and closed it with a click behind him.

Chapter Twenty-six

Newspaper Rant

Mahoney rapped hard on the office door. The gold nameplate jiggled. A clank echoed as one side of the golden plate came loose. It dangled by one end, swinging back and forth, scraping across the door.

Fuck. He stared at his path of destruction. The swinging golden plate glaring under the fluorescent lighting, the perfect print stated this was the domain of *EDITOR-IN-CHIEF — MR. HAMMINGTON* whom he had intruded and wreaked havoc upon. He rapped again, timing his knocks to avoid colliding with the swinging title.

No answer. He pressed his ear against the door. No sound from within. Maybe Mr. Hammington wasn't in. Or maybe he was avoiding the angry man with a badge storming his office. Mahoney gave up. He turned to leave. A click of a lock and the door opened. A stout man with a serious black moustache stared at him. Mahoney looked down at the man, short but thick.

"How can I help you?" The man—Mr. Hammington, presumably—looked up at him.

"Mr. Hammington?"

"Yes."

"I'm Detective Mahoney." He flashed his badge. "I need to talk to you."

"Of course, come on in." Stout Hammington motioned his welcome.

Mahoney entered the office and stood behind the two chairs facing the thick wooden desk.

"I do apologize for not answering the door sooner. I was on a call."

Mahoney glowered as Mr. Hammington made his way behind the desk and sat down in the plush-looking leather chair.

Mahoney plunked his briefcase on one of the chairs facing the desk, and pulled out a wrinkled copy of the Calgary Chronicle. He slapped it down on the desk and turned it to face Mr. Hammington.

Splashed on the front page was the headline that made Mahoney's veins seethe with hot blood.

"Boy-Mummy Found Buried in Cave"

Mahoney glared at Hammington. "I want to know who the source was on this article."

The head of the newspaper sat up straight and motioned to the chair Mahoney towered over. "Please, sit."

Mahoney ignored the gesture. "This article. It's about *me*. It reveals my private nickname. It questions my ability to conduct an investigation—my ability to keep my city safe. It reveals evidence that hasn't been made public yet. I want to know how this..." He plastered the paper with his hand and spun it around. "Mike Cunning...I want to know how he got this information. And who the fuck he thinks he is that he can pry open an investigation and plaster unofficial information all over a front-page article. He even quoted *me*. I wasn't interviewed." Heat flushed up his neck and over his face.

"Now, Detective...Mahoney, was it?"

Mahoney nodded.

"Detective Mahoney. My journalists protect the identity of their sources. If they didn't, they wouldn't be able to uncover the truth. And that's what we're after here, at the Calgary Chronicle. The truth."

"Some truths are private. And they don't impact people of the city. Your *journalist* invaded *my* privacy." Mahoney's temples bulged. Red veins popped across his forehead.

"Listen, Detective, I'll talk to Mr. Cunning. I can encourage him not to share private details that don't impact the people of our city."

"Tell him not to write articles that aren't approved by my department."

"Quite frankly, the public has a right to know what's going on. Don't you agree?"

"Sure. As long as it doesn't impact the investigation. What your *Mr. Cunning* has published here, it egged this killer on. It drove this maniac to kill again."

"There's been another murder?"

Dammit. Hell, this bloodsucker will know by sundown anyways. "Yes. I'm sure your team will have their bloodthirsty teeth sunk deep into it by day's end. The point is…what this Mr. Cunning wrote in the first article may have prompted him. Is that what your paper strives for? To incite murder?" Sweat trickled down the back of his neck. He needed some air.

Hammington's forehead wrinkled. "I assure you, Detective, that is not what my paper strives to accomplish. I also assure you none of my journalists would print something that would knowingly cause any danger to this city."

"Does your paper deliver outside the city?"

"It is possible, yes."

"I need a full record of any subscriptions, both in and out of the city limits."

"Well now, the privacy of our subscribers is of the utmost importance to us here. I can't share that information."

Dammit. Why didn't I get a warrant?

"I'll be back. With a warrant. You're just wasting time, Mr. Hammington. You could be helping. Your paper is putting this city at risk." He snatched the paper, stuffed it in his briefcase and turned to leave.

"I assure you, Detective, it is not the intention of my paper to cause this city harm. We are here to serve the people of the city. Not to harm them."

Mahoney turned and glared.

"You must understand, as a legitimate press, I must follow certain laws. Privacy of subscribers is one of them."

"Yeah. Fine. I'll be back. You'll get your bloody warrant." He walked to the door, turned the knob, then paused. "Do this city a favour—start digging into those records now." He walked out the door and slammed it behind him.

He took a deep breath, composed himself, then strode through the office. Most of the cubicles were empty, the room was dimly lit, except for a few desk lamps of those writing last-minute, earth-shattering articles for the early press.

At the edge of the room, just before the exit, he walked by a desk with a light on. The young man working at the desk looked up at him with wide eyes through circular spectacles. He wore a white, pressed shirt and navy-blue tie. He looked far too fresh to be pushing past clock-out time.

"What are you looking at?" Mahoney barked at the young man.

"Nothing, Detective." The young man swallowed. "You're looking for subscriptions?"

"You heard all that?"

"You weren't quiet." He smiled, then quickly pressed his lips into a thin line.

"Yeah. I'm looking for subscriptions. You can help me?"

"Yeah."

"Why would you? Your boss in there was clear. No info without a warrant."

"Well, I suspect you're getting that warrant right away. And, well, I'm just finishing up for the night. I don't have anything to do the rest of the evening."

Mahoney closed his eyes, took a deep breath, then looked at the young man. "That would be great. I'm not always this angry, you know."

"I doubt you are. Listen, Hammington's gonna ask me to do this anyways...once you get your paperwork. I'm the youngest of the pack. I get all the grunt jobs. I could run a search tonight, have it ready."

"That would be great, kid." He smiled. "Thanks."

"Anytime."

Mahoney slipped a card onto the young man's desk. "If you get lonely, give me a call. I'll keep anything you tell me under wraps till I have the warrant. And you'd be doing this city a service."

The young man's eyes bulged as he looked at the card. "You got it."

Mahoney walked over to the elevators, pushed the button, and adjusted his derby. He'd made one enemy and one ally. Not too bad.

Chapter Twenty-seven

Where's my Bartender?

Mahoney pushed open the black door. A cloud of warm air engulfed him. The room was buzzing. He expected it to be quieter mid-week. A three-piece ensemble of long-haired, tight-panted rock star wannabes shuffled around the stage. A voice, a subtle drumbeat, and a lazy guitar riff formed a meandering performance, fighting with the rambunctious chatter.

Mahoney almost turned to leave. Then his stomach rumbled. The empty shelves of the fridge in his apartment made an appearance in his mind. A milky-white breast marked with a subtle birthmark followed. He should stay. At least have something to eat.

He looked across the room at the bar with the shiny black countertop. There were three open seats. With a brisk stride he shot across the room and hoisted himself up onto one of the chairs. Placing his derby on the slick counter, he sat back against the chair. His thoughts scattered and his mind hummed. Closing his eyes, he willed his brain to settle.

"Can I get you a drink, sir?" a deep voice intruded on his mini-meditation.

He opened his eyes. No Sasha. He clenched his teeth. "Ginger ale, please. And a pepperoni pizza, to go."

"Right away, sir." A young man smiled at him in a black t-shirt clinging to his muscular contour.

Dammit. He was looking forward to a cotton-candy smile and whiff of fruit and flowers. He needed a distraction. Now *he'd* have to steady his mind.

Bzzzt. His phone vibrated in its holster. He grabbed it and snapped it open. "Mahoney."

"Mahoney, it's Blackwood."

The skin on the back of his neck and down his arms tingled. "You got something for me?"

"You know it. The message, on the second body, it was written repeatedly over the wrappings, just like the first one." Excitement trickled through the earpiece.

"What did it say?"

"Neither have I sinned against the God of my own town."

"What?"

"Yeah. A bit bizarre. I have committed no murder. Neither have I sinned. It feels very...anti-ten commandments."

"Biblical speak, but opposing the rules."

"Yeah. I have no idea how you figure out where this is coming from. But I knew you'd want to know right away."

"Thanks." He smiled into the phone.

"Anytime. I'm still working on this one. I'll keep you posted."

"I know you will." He snapped his phone shut and re-holstered it. *My own town. What did this mean?*

Young black shirt returned, setting a tall glass filled with ice cubes and ginger bubbles on the counter. "Your pizza will be right up, sir."

His phone buzzed again. He slid it out of the holster and snapped it open. "Mahoney."

"It's Sutton. I stopped by the crime lab. They're working on amplifying the photos of the carving."

"How long will it take?"

"They don't know. Hours. Overnight. I told them to rush it."

"Stay on it."

"All the hobby shops are closed. The eyes will have to wait till tomorrow."

"OK. See you in the morning."

"Sure thing, boss."

He snapped his phone shut, set it on the counter, then took a sip from the tall glass. The cool bubbles soothed his parched throat. He scanned the room. *Why is it so busy? And where is Sasha?* Twisting his head, he glanced at the stage. *And who the fuck are these goons?* He thought this place was known for solid acts.

He took another sip. It hit him. It was Thursday. *Double dammit.* What had she said? He pictured her pink lips talking to him. *The Roxy. My day off. This Thursday.* He could have joined her at The Roxy. Whatever that was. He waved off the thought. It was late. Besides, what was he doing chasing her? Going to a new joint and walking dangerously on the ledge of a bad choice didn't sound like the cherry on top of a murder-scene-and-morgue-filled day.

Tight shirt returned, his smile wider than before. "Here you go, sir." He placed a piping-hot box on the counter, and the bill on top. He saluted and turned to his other customers.

Tight shirt's cheeriness irritated Mahoney. He smiled anyways. Flipping open his tattered wallet, he placed a few bills on the counter. He chugged the rest of his ginger ale, slid his phone into its holster, grabbed the pizza box, and turned toward the black door.

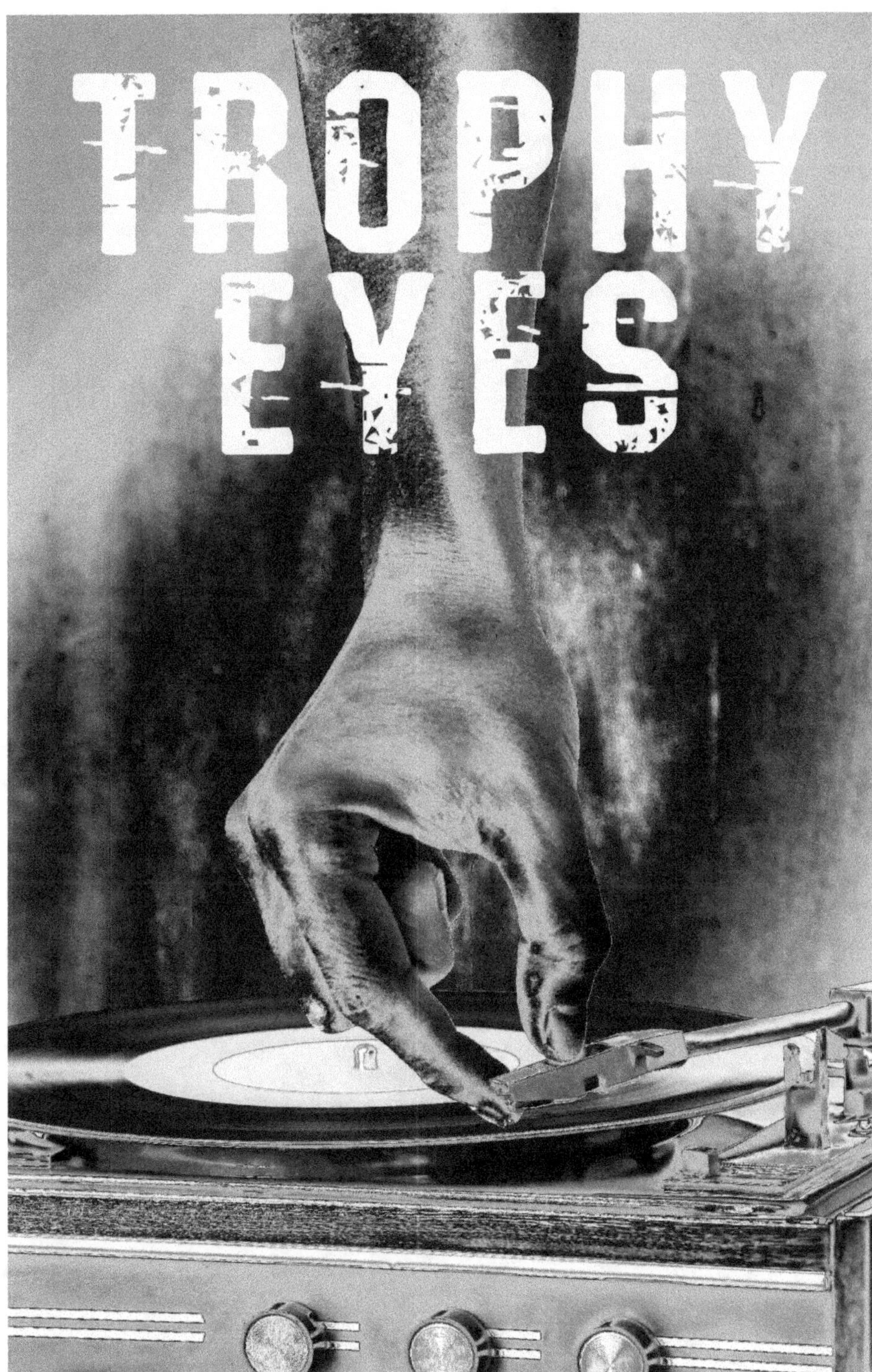

TROPHY
EYES

Chapter Twenty-eight

Paper Peruse

Mahoney stepped into the small room. The fluorescent lighting glared in his eyes. The air smelled fresh. *Dara and her mountain-air spray.* He smiled to himself.

Putting his Styrofoam cup onto the long centre table, he moved over to the cream-coloured crime scene wall. He scanned the two separate photo collages, one for Caleb and one for Benjamin. *Two bodies, again.* He sighed. *The second one, it just can't be a coincidence. But why did this killer resurface after ten years? Is Quesnel right? Is the dead boy a message? For my team? For me?*

He turned to the centre table. Taking a swig of coffee, he fished through his tattered briefcase. Pulling out the wrinkled copy of the paper, he scanned the front page of the Calgary Chronicle.

The headline hit him again.

"Boy-Mummy Found Buried in Cave"

His temples pulsed.

Words leaped off the page as he scanned the article he had read at least a dozen times.

"...remains of the boy-mummy...coffin-like structure...RCMP, first on the scene...buried in the back of the cave...child-mummy...skeletal remains...Local Homicide Detective Mahoney, AKA 'Bug'—the squasher of perps..."

He shook his head. He thought back to the first time he was called Bug, after a series of successful arrests. He had openly resisted. But they were persistent, and over time the name stuck. *It's fine when it's people I know. My team. But this, in the paper.* He rubbed the back of his neck, then wiped his moist hand on his pant leg. *If the people of my city don't trust me to keep them safe, then how can I?* Heat rushed through his neck. He loosened his collar and stared at the newspaper.

"...one of the worst killers the city has ever seen... arctic pendant..."

Dammit. How did they find out about the pendant?

Was Quesnel right? Had this killer read the article? Was he still in town? Had the article hit other cities? He hoped that kid journalist came through for him. The warrant was taking longer than he'd like.

Chapter Twenty-nine

Restless War Room

The door opened, jolting Mahoney from his morning read. Voices pierced the quiet room as a stream of bodies flooded the small space.

"Sergeant Williams, Constables. Good morning." He watched the red-coats take up their usual corner. The temperature shot up several degrees.

"Hayes. Sutton." Mahoney nodded at his boys.

Mahoney walked to the back corner of the room. Stopping at the small, circular table holding the coffee pot, he topped up his Styrofoam cup. Dara walked in and sat down at her usual perch. "Good morning, Dara. Thanks for your magic mountain-air touch this morning."

"No problem. Don't know how long it will last with all these bodies in here."

"Yeah, it's a full house again. It's going to be hard to get everyone moving in the same direction."

"You know, Bug, sometimes not everyone has to move in the same direction. Different paths can come together."

He pondered her words. "True."

Dara focused on feeding her typewriter a fresh white page.

"Dara, I'm going to need a slew of searches. Not sure we'll get to it with all these bodies to co-ordinate in here."

"Let's talk after the meeting."

"Sounds good. Better get this two-cent show going." Mahoney walked to the front of the room.

Raising his voice over the building chatter, Mahoney launched the meeting. "Good morning, everyone. Let's get started."

The volume in the room dwindled. Mahoney glanced at the clock. *Where's Quesnel? She would have touched down by now.* Shaking off the prickles running down his neck and arms, he faced the room full of faces.

"A second body was found. Derailed us yesterday."

Williams said, "We used the day to continue searching the beach, around the cave. Nothing more was found. We should wrap it up out there today."

Hayes said, "We need to do more scanning inside the cave."

Williams glared. "As I said, we should wrap it up today. There's nothing there."

Mahoney took over. "The beach has been thoroughly combed?"

"Yes." The wiry moustache bobbed.

"The inside of the cave?"

"There's nothing." The wiry moustache twitched.

"We've barely touched the inside of the cave." Hayes' red face popped out against the cream-coloured wall.

Williams continued to glare.

Mahoney said, "We'll need a couple more days to scour the inside of the cave as thoroughly as the beach. Sergeant Williams, I am sure you would agree you want this scene processed properly before you wipe your hands of it."

Williams nodded, his lips in a thin line. "Of course."

Mahoney continued, "Let's review the new scene. The more info your team has, Sergeant"—he looked at Williams—"the better equipped you'll be for your thorough search." He walked over to the photo collage of the scene in the woods and pointed at the pictures. "Both bodies were wrapped in white cloths. The boy in the cave was set in a concrete coffin. The boy in the forest was set in a freshly dug plot, but no box. Both were buried. Both had fake glass eyes. We only have two bodies, but it seems we have another serial killer in our midst."

Williams said, "Two bodies aren't enough to support that conclusion."

"Technically, yes." Mahoney met Williams' gaze. "But the similarities are too significant to deny. And, we have—"

"You don't know that," Williams said. "It could be some copy-cat thing. I've read about that." His moustache twitched. His pudgy cheeks brightened like two ripe cherries.

Mahoney said, "Let me finish. Then we can all voice our opinions."

Williams straightened his stance and raised his hands. "Proceed."

Mahoney took a gulp of cheap, lukewarm coffee. *Chill out, Bug. You don't have time to argue with a dick in a red coat.* "The new body isn't preserved at all."

Sutton asked, "So why was the victim wrapped up?"

"We think the killer made an intentional link between the two victims. To let us know he's out there."

Williams shook his head. "*We? We* haven't discussed this. And after ten years? That can't be. Whoever is responsible would be long gone by now."

Hayes said, "Then how do you explain the mummy wrappings and the eyes?" A vein in his neck throbbed.

Mahoney shot Hayes a look. "Guys. Take a step back. We'll consider *all* possibilities here. It seems *likely* the same killer committed both of these murders."

Mahoney took a sip of cold coffee. A tear split through the rim. *Cheap Styrofoam.* He plunked it down on the table. "It appears the killer was in a rush, but wanted to link the bodies. A clear attempt to get our attention."

Williams' moustache twitched erratically. "Why would a killer want to be noticed? No one who commits murder wants to be found out."

"Actually, there are known cases in which the killer wants recognition," Mahoney said. "There was..."

"Recognition?" Williams blurted. "What are you talking about here? When people commit crimes—especially *murder*—they want to get away with it."

Mahoney cleared his throat. "This type of killer is a unique brand. Someone who continues to kill, victim after victim, they see the murders as their vocation. Their life's work."

Roberts said, "I don't buy this. Why are we on this path again? Why aren't we sticking to the scenes, the facts. Why are we talking about this hocus-pocus stuff?"

Mahoney glanced at the clock. *I sound like Agent Quesnel. I didn't buy this stuff, why should they?* "Look, I didn't believe this stuff either. On our last case, I fought this train of thought. The bodies built up, fast. It became apparent we had to consider behaviour. We didn't abandon the facts. We layered on a parallel path. We merged the two."

Williams and Roberts shook their heads.

The door swung open. Agent Quesnel burst into the room. "My apologies. My flight was delayed."

Mahoney's shoulders dropped several notches. "Agent Quesnel. No apology necessary. Thank you for joining us on such short notice."

The fluorescent lights gleamed off her platinum boots as she strode to the front of the room. Her fire hair bounced off her slick, black jacket. A hum of chatter resurfaced around the room. Mahoney pulled at his collar, heat rising up his neck leaving a sticky coating of sweat.

Agent Quesnel whispered to Mahoney, "I can feel the tension in here. Restless crowd, hey?"

"Yeah. I was trying to convince them the cases are linked, that this guy wants recognition. That his kills are his life's work. They're not buying my behaviour bullshit. I think one of them actually called it hocus-pocus."

"All right." She winked at him, then spun on her heel to face the crowd.

Mahoney raised his voice as he said, "OK, everyone, let's continue. This is Agent Quesnel, from the criminal profiling division of the FBI. She helped us out on our last case and was kind enough to fly out here today to join us. As I was saying, in our last case we needed to add a behavioural component in order to catch the killer."

Rumblings echoed from the red-coat corner.

Agent Quesnel took charge. "Do we know these cases are linked? No. Not for sure. But with high probability, they are. You've seen the photos." She pointed at the crime scene wall. "The second body was wrapped, just for the sake of wrapping it. No preservation. The eyes were placed on top of the wrapping, to grab attention. Serial killers are not your typical killer. It is clear whoever committed the second murder was calling attention to these aspects of the body."

Williams said, "We don't *know* it's the same killer." His face brightened to the shade of a ripe tomato. His eyes bulged.

Agent Quesnel said, "We don't. But it's likely. And at the very least, there is a link between the two bodies. Let me ask you a question. Have you ever seen a murder scene like these two?" She pointed at the crime scene photos.

Williams swallowed. "No."

"I have. I've seen far worse than this. This type of killer, he won't stop. He can't stop. He is so immersed in the murders he commits, it consumes his entire life. It will come to the point where he has nothing else, if it hasn't already."

"This is all speculation. This whole *behaviour* thing—it isn't a tried-and-true method." Several beads of sweat trickled down Williams' red face.

Agent Quesnel walked right up to Williams and raised herself onto her the tips of her platinum boots. "Officer Williams, have you ever looked in the eyes of a sadistic psychopath who *gets off* on killing people, cutting them apart, and displaying their body parts in elaborate designs?" She glared. Her lips formed a thin, tight line. "Have you ever been told, face to face, by someone who spends all their time planning and executing murders that it is their life's work, their vocation?"

The room was silent. Williams' face froze in a blank stare.

Mahoney snuck a peek at Dara, poised behind her typewriter. She shot him a wink.

Williams stood tall and swallowed hard. His voice was meek. His face flushed a brighter shade, his pores stood out like the seeds in a strawberry. "No."

Agent Quesnel backed up a few steps and continued, "I'll give you a few real-life examples. Kemper. He called his murders *his vocation*. He needed recognition so badly he turned himself in. Green River killer—he said killing was his career. And, Bundy, well, he called his murder scenes his life's accomplishments." She stood back and licked her cherry lips. "I heard these very words come out of their mouths." She stared straight at Williams. "Are you going to ignore real experience?"

Williams stared back. Roberts shifted back and forth on his feet. Rudson focused on the mug he was holding.

Mahoney said, "Look, we're not abandoning our usual investigative strategies. But we have to consider other aspects specific to this type of killer. We were able to catch the killer on our last case because we analyzed both the facts and the killer's behaviour." He turned to the red-coat corner. "Officer Williams, your team still owns the first crime scene. The medical examination was done in my jurisdiction. My team now owns the body. I *want* to process the body with the utmost care. I *want* to execute due diligence to do all we can to find this guy. Don't you?"

Williams clenched his teeth. "Of course."

"I'm sick of arguing." Mahoney turned the Styrofoam cup, facing the tear away, and took a long swig of coffee. He walked back over to the series of pictures, displayed in two separate collages. "On our last case, we had hard pieces of evidence. One item was a straitjacket found on the third victim. Even though the jacket had a serial number, we were unable to determine where it came from.

Until we considered the behaviour of a serial killer. They tend to have a juvenile record of some sort, either in a jail or a psychiatric institution. When we dug back into the juvenile files, we found the serial number, and the owner of the jacket. We caught him in the middle of his ritual with his latest victim."

Williams' face eased to a light shade of pink. "I see."

Mahoney said, "None of us want this guy to get away with this. As Agent Quesnel has reinforced, he won't stop. We need to stop him. In order to do that, we need to work together."

Williams cleared his throat. "Detective, you say this behavioural track, it helped you solve your last case. But that was one case. How do you know it will work again?"

"I've worked on two serial cases. The one we just finished. And we got the guy. The other one—that was years ago, out east. We only stuck to what we knew. Pure evidence. But there was no physical trail. The guy was a ghost. A lot of young girls are dead. And the case went cold."

Williams' face went pale. "I see."

Silence blanketed the room. Mahoney glanced up at the clock. *What did Dara say? We don't all have to be on the same path to come together?*

"We can divide this up. We can share detective manpower. Your team can focus on the facts. I'll work with Agent Quesnel on the behavioural aspect."

Roberts and Rudson nodded at each other. "Fine," Williams agreed.

"Like I said, a thorough search inside the cave would leave you with a well-processed scene."

Williams nodded.

"Has any further searching been done underground?" Agent Quesnel said.

"Inside the cave?" Williams asked.

"Yes." Agent Quesnel nodded. "I suggest searching underground. At least within the cave."

"You can't think there's more buried in there?" Williams asked.

"He could have used the same area to dispose of multiple victims," Agent Quesnel said.

"Really?" Rudson asked. "But doesn't that increase the changes of getting caught?"

"Easier for him to revisit the bodies. He chose well—it took ten years for anything to be found."

Mahoney said, "Officer Williams. All I'm asking is for you to finish heading up a full and thorough investigation of the cave. Just a few more days."

Williams nodded. "That I can do."

"Good. I'll check in with you later. We don't have to drag you back here tonight." Mahoney turned to the back of the room. "Hayes, you stay with Williams. Sutton, you stay with me."

Heads nodded back at him around the room. The room filled with dull chatter as bodies streamed through the door. The hot air clung to Mahoney's chest. He loosened his collar more and rubbed the back of his neck. Agent Quesnel stood coolly leaning against the wall beside the crime scene photos.

"You got yourself a tough crowd here, Mahoney."

"I know. We're spinning our wheels. I thought if we all got on the same page, I don't know, they'd be more compelled to take their search seriously. And they'd have their eyes peeled for things they may not have thought of. It's a waste of time. We'll have to work separately. We need to focus and get moving."

"Splitting up the group was good. Cross-jurisdictional work isn't easy. It's not the norm down south either. It's starting to happen, but it's slow and it's difficult. The red-coat team can focus on the scene. You and I can weave in our behavioural hocus-pocus." She winked at him. Her fire hair blazed under the fluorescent lights.

Layers of tension lifted from his neck and shoulders. He wiped his forehead with his sleeve. "I could use a good dose of hocus-pocus right about now."

Chapter Thirty

Hunt For Mummies

Mahoney stared at the neon-green text flashing across the black computer screen. Taking a sip from his Styrofoam cup, he watched Dara lean in close, inspecting the search results.

"I searched the entire province. Nothing," Dara said. "There haven't been any bodies of children found who resemble the two boys."

Mahoney asked, "How far back did you search?"

"Ten years."

Agent Quesnel leaned over Dara's shoulder, her fire hair slipping over her face. "Let's go back further. The body in the cave took a lot of preparation. That was a sophisticated scene. It wasn't his first. He could have been building up to that for a long time."

"Twenty years?" Dara looked up at Agent Quesnel.

"At least. Even thirty. Or as far back as you can. I know the databases may be limited."

"Got it." Dara looked back at the computer screen, her fingers tapping away at the keys.

Mahoney rubbed his chin with his thumb and forefinger. His mind whirred. He could think much more clearly now that the team had been divided to conquer separate streams. With Dara and Quesnel speeding ahead, the tension building in every cell of his body had eased. "We need to widen the search. Maybe this wasn't the first kid he took from another province. We need to look cross-country. There has to be a reason the killer didn't pick up a local boy."

Agent Quesnel said, "I agree. I think he left the body here to create a clear linkage between him and the cave boy. But why not take a local kid then? It would have been much easier. There's something significant about Saskatchewan."

Dara typed rapidly. "OK. I'll get on this. I'll use the same criteria as before. I'll go back in time as far as the database will allow. And I'll extend the area of the search. Cross-country. Anything else?" Dara looked up at each of them, fingers perched over her keyboard.

Mahoney stared at Quesnel. "What do you think? Are we missing anything here?"

Agent Quesnel clicked her tongue, little wrinkles forming across her forehead. "I don't know. Let me chew on it."

"Quesnel, let's grab Sutton and get back to the war room. Get this investigation on track. Dara, more will come up during the briefing, I'm sure."

Dara clicked a key with her pointer finger. The black-and-green computer screen vanished, replaced by a prompt asking for a password.

Mahoney followed the two of them toward the war room. Fire hair and slick grey bun, side by side, striding toward the stuffy room with an air of confidence. His gut tingled. The tingling increased into a steady vibration, weaving up his insides and circling his brain. He slipped his hand into his pocket and slid his fingers along the smooth polished quartz. He was eager to move this investigation in the right direction. For how long, he didn't know, but he would take what he could get.

Chapter Thirty-one

Investigative Triangle

Mahoney walked to the front of the war room. Body odour clung to the stifling air, but the temperature had dropped a bit. "Let's get moving."

"One moment, Bug." Dara sprayed the room with a mountain-fresh mist, from front to back. Returning to her typewriter, she placed the spray can on the table. "There. Much better."

Sutton smiled. "Thanks, Dara. Nice to be rid of the stink of bodies."

Mahoney nodded. "Agent Quesnel, can you fill everyone in on what you told me on the phone?"

"This isn't a copy cat. He wants us to know the Cave-Mummy was his." She twisted in the cheap plastic chair and set her gaze on Mahoney. "He wants *you* to know."

Mahoney shifted from one foot to the other. *I know.*

Agent Quesnel stood up. Her platinum boots clicked across the floor. "Everything was rushed—except he took the time to burn out the eyes. They were important to him." She looked at Mahoney. "You still got that newspaper article?"

Mahoney riffled through his briefcase. Pulling out a wrinkled copy of the Calgary Chronicle, he smoothed it against the centre table.

Sutton, Quesnel and Dara formed a circle around the wrinkled article. Silence ensued for several moments.

Sutton whistled. "I gotta agree with the FBI agent on this one."

Dara looked up, eyes wide. "They even used Bug. How did they get so many details?"

Mahoney cleared his throat. "I don't know where they got this stuff from. I paid a visit to the paper last night. Didn't get any answers...yet. I demanded sources. Dead end. I also demanded subscription records. The boss over there won't budge without a warrant. One of the staff is compiling a list in anticipation of the warrant."

"Who'd you charm?" Sutton asked.

"Young journalist. I mean, what? No. I didn't *charm* him. He offered to help. Get a move on the records while we're waiting on the warrant." Mahoney shook his head.

Quesnel said, "We need to know where that paper got to. It might tell us if he's still lurking around, or if he's moved on."

Mahoney stood tall, walked to the front of the room and cleared his throat again. "New strategy. We can motor without the heavy red-coat weight."

Sutton and Quesnel took seats in the cheap plastic ensemble. Dara moved to her corner spot.

"New items. Buried under a big tree, near a well-travelled path. This further supports our suspicion the killer wanted it to be found." Mahoney walked up to the whiteboard and picked up a bright-orange marker. He drew a funnel. He scribed the word EVIDENCE at the top of the funnel and the word TRAILS at the bottom.

"Our investigative strategies focus primarily on the evidence. We scour every last piece to create trails for us to follow." Beside the funnel, he drew a triangle, pointing downwards. On the left top corner he wrote EVIDENCE, on the right top corner he wrote BEHAVIOUR, and on the bottom tip he wrote TRAILS. The cap snapped as he pushed it onto the pen. He set the pen down on the metal lip of the whiteboard with a click and walked to the centre of the room.

"We're evolving our investigative strategies. I created this the night I figured out how to identify the killer in our last case."

"Seth," Sutton whispered.

"Yes." Mahoney swallowed against the rage burning in his belly. "We had plowed through a slew of physical evidence and potential clues. We weren't getting anywhere. Our killer, Seth, kept slipping through our fingers. We had been talking about his behaviour. It helped us create new potential leads. But nothing concrete was coming of it. When I merged the two, paths opened."

Quesnel nodded, the fluorescent lighting gleaming off an orange streak in her hair.

"What do you mean, merge?" Sutton asked. His forehead wrinkled, his eyes inquisitive.

"I looked at the most glaring piece of evidence and questioned the behaviour of a serial killer in relation to it. A straitjacket, found on one of the victims. It had a serial number, but we were unable to identify it in the institution records. It hit me. Agent Quesnel had talked about how serial killers typically spend time in their teens locked up, either in prison or a medical institution. I launched a search into the juvenile records. And, bingo."

"I like where you're going, Mahoney." Fire hair swung as Agent Quesnel stood and walked to the back of the room.

Dara sat up from her typing and smiled at him.

"This will be our approach. Quesnel, you said the eyes were important to him."

Dara said, "Traces of Alkali were found on both victims. It's easy for someone to get their hands on this substance in common stores."

Sutton said, "They both had those fake glass eyes."

Dara adjusted her glasses. "I have an updated list of doll and hobby supply shops around the city. They all carry black glass eyes."

Sutton raised a hand. "I'll get on that. I wanted to check them out last night, but they were all closed."

Mahoney said, "Good. See if anyone who worked at any of these places ten years ago is still around. See if they had any repeat or bulk purchases of black eyes back then. Find out if any eye purchases have been made in the last few days. And if anyone noticed any suspicious-looking, or suspicious-acting, patrons." He paused. "What else?" He pointed at the bright-orange triangle glaring at them from the clean whiteboard.

Agent Quesnel pulled the eye thread, saying, "He didn't want these boys to have eyes. It could be his way of preventing them from seeing."

"Right. He didn't want them to see him. Or where he was taking them," Sutton said.

Agent Quesnel crossed her arms. "Good possibilities. He may have a hideout somewhere that he takes these boys to and that he doesn't want revealed. There is a chance he may not want the boys to react to the things he is doing, or he wants to hit them by surprise, heighten the reaction to the torture. But then, why not just blindfold them? Actually removing the eyes, that heightens the importance he is placing on them."

Mahoney scribed furiously on the whiteboard.

Agent Quesnel pulled the final bit of thread, unravelling the eye theme, "There is also the possibility he is keeping them."

"The eyes?" Sutton took a loud sip of Big Gulp.

"Yes. It isn't uncommon for a serial killer this involved with his victims to keep something to remind him of them. A trophy. Brudos kept feet in his freezer. He liked to display his collection of women's shoes using them. Bundy took heads. He burned one of them in his fiancée's fireplace."

Dara cringed. "Gross."

Sutton wrinkled his forehead. "Messed up."

Mahoney said, "We haven't found any eyes at either scene. Williams is on the cave. We could revisit the forest. But, if they were a prize, then he wouldn't leave them behind."

"Precisely." Agent Quesnel nodded.

"He reappears, out of nowhere. He could have been revisiting an old hideout." Mahoney rubbed the bristle on his chin. "I need to go back and see Doris. I dropped in on her last night. She was drunk and unruly. Quesnel, you join me. We've got two bodies with strong indications of murder. Seth knew about the cave near the water. I didn't tell him where the body was found. Puts him at the scene of the first murder. We need to find out if Sid exists and, if so, who he is. Our next strongest lead is Doris. She could be involved. Seth's primary residence was Doris' house. If Sid exists, appears he lived there too. Could be evidence in that house, from either of the murders. Plenty for a search warrant. I'll get a rush on it."

"Sounds good."

"Let's talk about embalming. Dara, you said a licence is required to obtain embalming chemicals?"

"Yes." Dara looked up and nodded. "I have an initial list of places that sell the chemicals."

Sutton sat up in his chair. "Killers like this, don't they blend in well?" He ran his fingers along the green rabbit foot attached to his belt. "To get what they want?"

Agent Quesnel said, "Absolutely. And they can be quite charming. It's amazing how well liked these guys can be."

The rage in Mahoney's belly burned hot as he thought of Seth. He gulped down cold coffee.

Sutton said, "So, maybe he charmed someone into selling him the chemicals. Or he knew someone who had a licence."

Mahoney scribbled orange words on the whiteboard. "Sutton, take a stab at the facilities that sell the chemicals. Ask around about regular customers, and whether or not they came in alone. It's a reach. We're looking back a decade." He shook his head. "Dara, any update on the jars?"

"Yes. Canopic jars. Usually engraved, like the ones left at the first scene. And made of limestone or pottery. I'm having a hard time nailing down where you can get these. I found one place. An Egyptian specialty store. I'll keep looking."

"Quesnel, you and I can hit the Egyptian store, after our drop-in on Doris. What else?"

Sutton said, "The heart. It was the only organ still in the victim."

Agent Quesnel said, "Yes. What does the heart symbolize? Was there a reason he left it?"

Dara said, "The heart was seen as the centre of the being."

Sutton continued, "So, the killer, he treats these young victims like, well, kind of like his objects. He takes their eyes out. He removed the organs of the first boy. He preserved the kid. Like he was going to do something with him, later. But then he leaves in the heart? It's as if he cared about him." He shook his head. "I sound cuckoo."

Quesnel marched to the front of the room. "No. Not cuckoo at all. This is good. This is exactly how you need to think. If he did have an inkling of thinking these boys were human, that tells us something about him. His personality. It could help us flesh out his past. It might give us clues to why he is doing this, and ultimately to who he is."

Mahoney nodded. He jotted more bright-orange notes. "Dara. What about the expertise needed here? What was it you said...anatomy, chemistry, and..."

"Thanatology. The scientific study of the dead."

"Any leads on where someone studies the dead?"

"No. Nothing specific came up in any of my searches. There's a lot of books that mention it."

"OK. What else?"

Sutton looked up from his notebook. "I got those amplified photos back from the crime lab. Looks like the carving on the tree matches the symbol on the fence at the park."

"The symbol was also on the cloths wrapped around Caleb." Mahoney said. "We need to make some progress on this symbol and the messages." He flipped through his notebook. "The message left on the first boy was '*I have committed no murder.*' The message on the second boy was '*Neither have I sinned against the God of my own town.*' We don't know what the symbol means. Another crazy puzzle."

Quesnel said, "They sound biblical."

Mahoney responded, "Yeah. That's what Blackwood said. And they almost sound like he's countering some sort of rules or commandments." He paused. "The part about 'my own town'—it bothers me."

Quesnel said, "Could be he's been here all along. Or he left, then came back. But he sees this place as his home."

Dara looked up from her typewriter. "I'll dig."

Mahoney shook his head. "Sutton—doll eyes and embalming chemicals. And help Dara out when you get back."

Sutton nodded and flipped his notebook closed.

"Quesnel, you and I have a date with a crazy woman and an Egyptian store."

Agent Quesnel smirked, crossed her arms and leaned back against the wall. Her rhinestone bracelet caught a glimmer off the bright lighting.

Mahoney stood tall. "Let's move. We'll touch base later if we can."

Sutton nodded and left the room. Dara followed, a stack of typewritten notes in her hand.

Quesnel stepped away from her perch against the wall and walked toward Mahoney. "Looks like you've got yourself a team of profilers. You're breaking ground up here, you know." Strands of fire hair slipped around her face.

"I don't know what I've started. But I'll be damned if another sicko thinks he can leave a trail of bodies around here. We've got a date with a woman connecting them both. Shall we?" He extended his arm toward the door.

She spun on a platinum heel and strode confidently toward the exit. He followed her, watching the slick stands of her fire hair glaring back at him. He wondered how the fire burning within her had started. He wondered if the rage burning within himself would ever subside. Maybe someday he would learn her secrets. Maybe someday he would learn to let go of his own.

Chapter Thirty-two

Trophy Eyes

The stairs creaked under Mahoney's hiking boots as he descended into the dark basement. Running his hand over the rough, cold concrete wall, he squinted into the blackness.

"Do you see a switch anywhere?" he yelled over his shoulder.

Heels clicked on the creaky stairs behind him. Agent Quesnel yelled back, "No. Nothing."

"Be careful on these stairs. I think they've been here awhile."

Looking down at his feet, he blinked hard, trying to bring the next step into focus.

The air cooled as he lowered himself down each stair. Finding the concrete floor with his foot, his shoulders relaxed. Running his hands along the contours of the cold, rough wall, his finger grazed something sticking out. He moved his hand back over to the protruding item.

Squealing pierced the silence as warmth and fur brushed against his leg. He flicked the plastic. Light flooded the room. Two mice scuttled across the concrete floor, disappearing through a hole in the corner.

"Uck," Agent Quesnel said.

"Yeah. I think one of them brushed against me." A slight tremble shook his shoulders.

"Gross. Those things are filthy. This place looks filthy too."

Mahoney scanned the basement. It was exactly the way it was the last time he had been down here.

The steel-slab bed sat in the centre of the room, bright light glaring off the shiny surface from the buzzing overhead florescent tube. A flash of a college boy's pale face covered in blood and tears appeared in Mahoney's mind. A remnant from the last case that ended right in this very spot. He could still see the trembling young man, his arms paralyzed at his sides, his eyes looking at him, past him, into nothing. The look of terror was etched into Mahoney's memory forever.

"Hey, look over here." Quesnel's voice jolted him.

He looked over to the corner of the basement where she stood, beside the escape route of the filthy, furry mice.

She pointed up at the ceiling at a large metal hook, securely attached, ready to bleed out a carcass. "That hook was here when we processed Seth's scene. Didn't we find remnants of one of the victims?"

"Yeah. We suspected he had been hung here, by the wrists. There were traces of blood on the hook that matched his type."

"Looks like something is sticking to it."

Mahoney rubbed his chin. Something red and sticky clung to the sharp point at the end of the hook. "Did we just step into a fresh crime scene?'"

She looked at him. "We might have. The hook was clean after processing when we arrested Seth. He's locked up. Couldn't have been involved in the second murder. But, Doris...has she been up to her own questionable activities? Or, is this the work of the mysterious Sid?"

"Let's replay the scenario. It's about a six-hour drive from Morse, where the kid lived and was last seen. Likely the killer would stick to the speed limits to stay under the radar."

"OK. So the killer picks up the kid, drives him here. He—or she—wants to leave a message in the same city as the cave crime scene. But the killer comes here first. The place for processing his or her victims before creating the scene. If Doris is the killer, it makes sense. She's got her own in-home dungeon for processing bodies. But, if Sid does exist, and he's the killer, why come back here?"

"Maybe this is the only place he could go. Maybe he's been away for a while. Doesn't live here anymore. He picked up the kid, what, on his way here?"

"Exactly. Then he comes here. He carries out his ritual. Preps the body for disposal."

"We need to look for traces of a fresh victim. The boy."

She pointed up at the hook. "Looks like a good start."

Mahoney pulled his cell phone from the holster on his belt. He yanked the antenna up, flipped the phone open, and punched at the numbers. "Mahoney here. I need crime scene techs. 99 Rosemont Street. Nope. No body. Blood. And perhaps some flesh."

Shoving the antenna back into the phone, he looked at Quesnel. "We're gonna have to grill Doris on our way out."

Quesnel clicked her tongue. "She wasn't thrilled to let us in. Good thing we had that warrant."

"I figured we'd need it. We left a bad taste in her mouth the last time we raided her basement."

"Yeah. And she seemed pissed that Sid took off. If he isn't real, then she's one hell of a performance artist. When you asked her about him, her face burned with rage. Assuming he exists, why would she help him now?"

"True love never dies?" He smirked.

"Very funny. I guess even though she hates Sid for leaving, she could still have a deep inner desire to help him."

Re-holstering his phone, he walked closer to the hook. "Is that skin?"

Quesnel's boots clicked on the pavement. "I think so."

"Let's leave it for the crime techs. Let's explore." He fished a pair of latex gloves from his pocket and handed them to her.

Snapping them over her hands, she wandered over to the steel slab. "Do you think the killer laid the boy here, or went right to hanging him from the hook?"

"The killer takes the boy. Boy was last seen leaving his school, around 2:45 p.m. It takes a little time to lure him away. Then a six-hour drive to get here. So, it's at least nine o'clock p.m. by then. Is the boy still alive?"

"Possibly. But it would be extremely difficult for the killer to resist going through at least a partial script of his or her fantasy. So, unless the killer had somewhere to spend time with the boy, alive, in Morse, then I peg it as a swipe and run. Bring the boy directly here. Live out a shortened fantasy, then dispose of the body."

Mahoney shuddered. "Yeah." He walked the perimeter of the steel slab, eyeballing every square inch. "I don't see anything at all. Doesn't mean there aren't traces of something."

"It's probably clean. I'm surprised there's anything on that hook."

"Me too."

Mahoney crouched down. Slowly opening the door at the base of the steel slab, a flash of a leather-bound book appeared in his mind. Opening the same door now that led him to the discovery of Seth's journal, a tingle crept through his insides. His heart drummed in his ears, pushing hard against his chest. Moisture popped across his brow. He peered into the darkness on the other side of the door. He saw a dark shape. Squinting hard, he forced the shape to come into focus. It was too hard to make out. Clipping a flashlight free from his belt, he clicked it on and pushed it into the black space behind the door. Bright light flooded the small area closed in by four steel walls.

He reported his findings, "There's a jar and a stuffed toy." He grabbed the soft bear, pulled it out and looked up at Agent Quesnel.

The brown bear was tattered. The right brown glass eye was cracked, the left eye was covered with two purple band-aids, crisscrossed in an X.

"This is weird. Why a teddy bear?"

Quesnel clicked her tongue against her cheek. "I wonder if Seth knows anything about it." She paused. "What about the jar?"

Mahoney's stomach churned. "I was hoping you wouldn't ask."

He crouched down again, and looked back into the cabinet at the jar. Reaching in, he pulled it out. His entire skull tingled while a million spider legs walked down his back. A chill swept over him. "What sweet hell is this." His lips tightened and he swallowed hard. Standing up, he held the jar around the top.

Agent Quesnel looked up. "Bloody Hell."

They both stared in silence at the jar. A pair of white spheres floated in clear liquid, bright-blue irises staring back at them.

Mahoney rubbed the back of his neck. "The trophy you were talking about."

She stared at the floating eyeballs. "If these belong to the Saskatchewan boy, then it confirms they were removed, not chemically disintegrated.

He looked at Quesnel. "Geez. That's freakin' creepy. And I thought I'd seen it all since I met you."

"It can always get worse."

"Apparently. You can add this to your list of examples."

"Yikes. The grossest one I've seen was lips. Women's lips. This guy had a whole collection of them. Displayed, you know—like you would display dead butterflies. They were framed and hanging on his wall."

"What?" Mahoney looked at her, then back at the eyes in the jar. "OK. I get the point."

"Never seen eyes, though. Why would he leave them?"

"If he was rushed, maybe he got flustered. Maybe he had to leave in a hurry." Mahoney looked around the room. "I can't hold this jar any longer. I'll leave it where we found it for now." He crouched down, and placed the jar back in the steel cabinet.

He moved his gaze around the basement. The back wall where the series of posters still hung, displaying the images that Seth's carefully groomed victims had copied. The corner, where the hook hung, and the ornately decorated silver pedestal still stood. The pedestal that had held an array of glass bottles, dark green and purple, housing toxic concoctions that were promised to take Seth into an afterlife where his deepest fantasy would come true. And the purple couch, spattered with sparkly diamonds flashing from the disco ball above. They never did figure out what happened on that couch, but Mahoney had a gut feeling that the purple velour played an important role in Seth's script.

Agent Quesnel snapped him from his memory collage. "Hey, Mahoney. You still with me?"

"Yeah. I just..."

"You saw a lot the last time you were down here."

"Yeah."

"I get it. I have a constant stream of images that won't leave me alone. I see them all day, and they form mini-movies in my dreams at night."

"What's the worst thing you ever saw?"

She sighed. Crossing her arms, she stared at him. "You really want to know?'

"Yeah. I do."

"Fine." She closed her eyes and took a deep breath. Opening her eyes, she looked right at him. "Girl. Six years old. Dressed up in a sequinned black cocktail dress and red feather boa. Makeup caked on. Scarlet lips. The colour that doesn't belong on a child. When she was found, her body was deep into the putrefaction phase. Decomposed. Maggots infested her entire insides. I never smelled anything like that in my life. Like a toilet in a homeless bathroom that had been defiled beyond comprehension." She stopped. "There was semen inside of her. It was less than twenty-four hours old."

Mahoney stared at her. A scuttling noise echoed across the quiet basement. He snapped his gaze to the corner, witnessing two furry creatures scampering across the floor. A creaking noise came from the stairs.

"They're here."

"Good. We need to get this thing moving."

"Mahoney."

"Yeah?"

"The images. They might last forever. But they do fade over time."

"Good to know."

Rotting Doris

The clicking of Quesnel's heels up the old, creaky stairs beckoned him. Mahoney followed her through the doorway, leading from the basement dungeon into the upstairs living room. Doris sat in an oversized chair, the covering torn in several spots, white stuffing poking out. The shape of her body hid under an oversized floral frock. The fading pattern of yellow flowers matched the paleness washing over her face. She sunk into the chair, quiet and rotting with the rest of the house.

Quesnel locked eyes with Mahoney. He stepped forward and led the way.

He announced his approach as he neared the tattered chair. "Doris, we need to talk to you."

Doris twisted her fleshy neck toward him. "I don't care what you do."

Mahoney sat down on a couch that had seen better days and faced Doris. "When's the last time you went down into your basement?" *Did you put those eyes there? Did you hang some kid from a hook?*

Her eyes narrowed. "Last time you were here, you took my son. Now you want to ask me about my habits in my own house?"

"Yes, we took Seth." *Play along, Bug. Pretend to care. Keep her talking.* "You know he needed help. He wasn't well."

She looked down at her coffee-stained floral frock. "Yeah. I know." A tear trickled down the side of her cheek. "I miss him." She grabbed a dirty glass off a small round table next to her chair and gulped back hazy brown liquid.

"You know, he can have visitors."

"He won't see me. He hates me." Several more tears joined the first one. She plunked the glass down, snatched a bottle of Jim Beam perched next to it and helped herself to a healthy re-pour. Sweet liquor floated through the air.

Mahoney felt an internal sigh whisper through him. *Keep playing along. Get her trust. If there is a Sid, we need bait.* "You don't know that."

Doris looked right at Mahoney. "Yes. I do. And I don't blame him. I'm a no-good mother. I should have been nicer to him. He's fragile." She pulled a balled-up tissue from somewhere inside her shapeless frock and dabbed at her eyes. "I know I'm no good. And I know Seth's broken. But it wasn't all my fault. I never should have let Sid into our house."

Quesnel shot a look at Mahoney, then looked at Doris. "Was Sid here, recently?"

Doris looked at Quesnel with wide eyes. "No. He's been gone a long time. He's not right, you know? The things he does..." She shot back another large gulp, pressing her lips together.

"Have you been down in your basement recently?" Quesnel asked.

Doris shook her head. "No. I don't go down there. Not since you people dragged Seth away. I couldn't. I didn't want to see what he'd done. Didn't want to see what Sid had made him." She sniffed loudly and rested her forehead on her palms.

You making up this Sid? Let's find out. Mahoney leaned over and placed a hand on Doris' arm. "Listen, I know it's hard. I know you miss Seth. But we think Sid has been back. And we need your help to find him."

Doris shook her head, her face flat against her palms.

Put on the sugar, Bug. Mahoney continued, "You're sad about what Sid did to Seth. You can help us find him. If we find him, we can stop him from doing things to other boys."

Doris looked up. Her faced was streaked with tears and mucus. "I can help?"

Gotcha. "Yes. You can help. You would be doing a good thing."

Contemplation washed over her face, quickly turning to suspicion as she narrowed her eyes again. "Why should I help you? You took away my son."

Mahoney sat up straight, snapping his notebook shut. *You got her where you want her.* "Listen, Doris, you *know* Seth murdered innocent college kids. You *know* he's sick and needs help. It's *his* fault that he was taken away."

She continued to glare.

Pretend you believe in Sid. "We found things in your basement. We know Sid was here. You can't tell me you didn't hear a single thing." He stared straight at Doris.

Doris' face relaxed. She wiped her face down with the disintegrating tissue.

"You *know* your treatment of Seth is under question. Since there's no *proof* other than what he wrote in his journal, you've been allowed to stay in your house. We just found evidence in *your* basement that could link you to a murder, unless we can nail it on Sid. *You* could end up in a cell."

"Fine," Doris spat. "I heard something. A couple nights ago. Downstairs." She paused, staring straight ahead at nothing.

Bingo. "What night was that?" Mahoney asked.

Doris looked at the half-empty bottle on the small table beside her chair. Wrinkles crept across her forehead. "I think it was two nights ago. Wednesday, I guess."

"Did you find out what it was?" Mahoney asked. *Eyes? Flesh on a hook?*

"Not till the next day. I couldn't get out of bed. I was terrified. I knew it had to be Sid." She stopped again.

Quesnel prodded, "You were terrified?"

"Yeah. He's not nice. I didn't want him to see me. I stayed in bed. The next morning, I didn't hear anything at all. I thought he was gone, so I went downstairs. I found...well...he left things."

Mahoney asked, "What things?"

Doris looked into Mahoney's eyes. "Eyeballs. Floating in a jar." Her arms shook.

"Where were they?"

"In a steel cabinet." She moved her gaze past Mahoney, staring into nothing. "How could I not have seen what he was? How could I have let him into this house?"

Mahoney's mind flashed back to the Stepping Stone Pub. He saw Simon, his friendly neighbourhood bartender, pouring him a drink and chatting it up with a smile. He shook his head. "Sometimes we don't see people for who they are. Some people can pretend to be entirely different than who they really are."

Doris explored Mahoney's face with her eyes. "Yeah. He was strong and fit. He grew trees. He was nice to me. I couldn't believe it. But it seemed real." She sounded like she was trying to convince herself.

"You're sure it was Sid, in the basement?" Quesnel asked.

Doris turned her head to look at Quesnel. "Yes. Only two people know where the key is. Seth and Sid. Besides, no one else comes around here."

Mahoney asked, "Did he leave anything else?"

"After finding those eyes, I got out of there."

Mahoney continued, "Why didn't you call the police?"

Doris' eyes sprung wide open. "Are you kidding? I was sure he'd come back for them. He'd *kill* me if they weren't there."

"You still think he'll come back?" Quesnel asked.

Doris nodded. "Yeah."

Time for you to be the bait, Doris. Mahoney looked at Quesnel. "We need eyes on the house when we leave. We may have already spooked him, but in case we didn't."

Quesnel nodded.

Mahoney looked back at Doris. "What does Sid look like?"

Doris cringed. "Long, sandy blond hair. Muscular. Fit. An outdoor guy."

"Does he have any distinctive markings? Anything unique?"

Doris looked at Mahoney. "Yeah. A tattoo. Of a tree. On the inside of his right wrist."

Without a pause, Mahoney continued his line of questioning. "Do you know Sid's full name?"

Doris shook her head. "No. He told me he was Sydney Smith. But I found at least half a dozen fake IDs in his drawer. I'll never know who he really is."

"Do you recall what the other names were, on those IDs?" Mahoney asked.

Doris squinted, biting her lip. "No. One of them was Mick something." She shook her head. "I'm sorry. I was shocked he wasn't who he said he was."

Quesnel crossed her arms. "Do you know where he might be?"

Doris continued shaking her head. "No. He up and left without saying goodbye. The day of Seth's twelfth birthday. I was so mad. I ruined the cake I'd baked for Seth." She looked down at her hands. "The only one I ever made for him."

Mahoney asked, "Is there anything else you can tell us about Sid?"

Doris looked at him, her eyes widening. She moved her gaze past him, looking out at nothing with a vacant stare. "Sid. He's nowhere. He's everywhere. It's like he's watching me, no matter where he is. I'll never escape."

Mahoney glanced at Quesnel. He sat back into the couch. "Doris. I need you to think. Hard. Is there anything else you can think of that might help us find Sid?"

Doris shook her head. Her eyes glazed over. It was like she was physically present, but her mind was somewhere else.

Mahoney leaned over and whispered to Quesnel, "I've seen this stare before. Seth gets this way. I don't think we're getting anything else out of her."

Quesnel nodded. "We should take her in."

"Yeah, we should." He stood and motioned Quesnel over to the corner of the room. "Either Sid exists, or Doris has some explaining to do about the eye balls and the dirty hook. Let's tell the techies to get the scene processed then get the hell out of here. I'll put a watch on the house. Doris won't be able to leave. In the off-chance Sid hasn't seen us, he might come back for those eyes. If she's not here, he'll be suspicious. If he doesn't show, we bring her in."

"Good idea."

Mahoney walked back over to Doris. "OK, Doris. We're going to leave you here, for now. When we're done with your basement, officers will set up outside. You won't see them, but trust me, they'll be here. You need to stick around. If Sid comes back, don't say anything about us."

Doris continued to stare vacantly across the room.

He crouched down and shook Doris' arm. "Doris. Do you understand me?"

She jolted. Her voice quivered as she said, "Yeah. I won't...say anything."

Mahoney whipped a card from his tweed coat pocket and snapped it on the table next to Doris. "Put this in your pocket. If Sid comes, call me immediately." He looked at Quesnel. "Let's go. We'll check back in later."

Quesnel nodded and followed him across the old kitchen and out the door.

Chapter Thirty-Four

Missing Eyes

The door slammed against the wall with a loud bang. Doris jumped in her filthy oversized chair. Jud rammed the door shut behind him and stomped across the room, his heavy work boots thumping against the old, creaky floor. He had to wait for over a half hour for the police cruiser out front to roll away. Now this.

"You devious bitch! Where did you hide it?" His throat stung as he yelled. He couldn't believe he had left his prized possession down in the basement. Stupid move. He let himself get overwhelmed with memories of Seth. Maybe he shouldn't have come back here. But he had to leave a message for the two people that could tie him to the cave-mummy boy in the newspaper. And the basement was the perfect place to carry out his script. Although it was rushed. He hated rushing. He loathed the fact that he left the one thing that he needed for his collection.

Doris cowered back into the chair, against the stuffing protruding from a large rip. "Don't know what you're talking about. I didn't touch nothin'."

"Liar. You know exactly what I'm talking about. I had an important item downstairs. You're not supposed to go down there." Why did he have to be back here dealing with her? He hated that he had messed up. *Dammit.*

"That basement isn't yours! You've been gone for years. You can't just show up and think you're welcome here." Her voice shrill as it rose several octaves, she stood up and stared at him with bulging eyes.

"That basement is mine as long as I say so. You bitch! What the fuck did you do?" He had almost made it home when he realized he had forgotten his prize. *Stupid.* He had to turn back. *Stupid, stupid!* The only thing that would stop his eye from twitching was to come back for Reddy's eyes.

"Nothin'. I told you. I didn't touch nothin'!" She stared at him, her face turning red. "What the hell are you doing here anyways? I heard you, the other night. I *know* you were down there doin' somethin'."

"Then were did my *stuff* go?" He towered over her, his long, tangled hair slipped over his shoulders, sticking to his sweat drenched face.

"I don't know," she spat back at him. "And even if I did, why the hell should I tell you? You're the one who left. You weren't here. Seth needed you. And you weren't here!"

"Seth? Needed *me*? What the hell are you talking about? Seth's *your* kid. Not mine."

"They took him away," she screamed. Her fat, pale knees shook. Her fingers dug into the worn floral material covering her frumpy frame. "*You!* You made him what he is."

He raised his arm, his fingers pumping into a fist. "Don't you talk to me that way, you worthless whore. *You* turned him into whatever piece of shit he is."

"There were people here." She raised her hands, shielding her face. "I couldn't stop them." She stole a glance out the window. Where was the police cruiser? She could have sworn it was there not a half hour ago.

He lowered his fist. "What people?"

"Police. A detective. And some FBI woman."

"What?"

"Yeah. Yeah, they came here, I couldn't stop them. They had a *warrant.* They went downstairs. But I didn't see them take anything. I swear."

In a flash, his fist flung high and punched her hard in the cheek. She toppled over.

"Why the *fuck* would you let anyone in here?"

Kneeling on all fours, she looked up at him, her teeth clenched. "I told you, there was nothin' I could do. It was the *police.*" She spit bloody saliva onto the floor.

Pacing back and forth, stringing his hair through his hands, Jud snickered. "Of course, nothing you could do. You probably *wanted* to help them. You want them to find me, don't you?" He halted. He stared at her. Her disgusting, fat body crumpled on the ground. Her torn nightgown, stains all down the side, barely covered her gross flesh. *Useless. Disgusting. What the fuck did I ever want with her?*

He leaned in close to her face. "Did you say anything to them? About me?" Spit flew from his mouth, landing on her cheek.

She sat down onto her ample ass. "No."

"Are you sure?"

"I didn't say a word. Told them I hadn't seen you since you left."

Searching her eyes for any doubt, he walked into the kitchen. Rummaging through a cabinet, he found a glass. He turned on the rusty faucet and watched the orange-brownish water pouring out. "What's wrong with your water?" he yelled into the other room. He crouched down, opened the cabinet underneath the sink, and peered inside. Droplets of water dripped from rust coated pipes. *Stupid Doris. Pipes need cleaning. She's got rust tainted water.*

"I don't know. There're some bottles, in the fridge."

He turned the faucet off and walked over to the fridge. Opening the door, peering into the waft of cold air. *What the hell? There's nothing in here. She's just a pig.*

He backed out of the fridge and closed the door. A loud thud rang through his ears as something hit the back of his head. Pain seared through him. The world around him turned black.

Chapter Thirty-five

Egyptian Store

The driver's side door creaked as Mahoney pushed it open. He stood tall and settled his derby onto his head. A rattling noise erupted from the passenger's side. *Damn handle.* He swiftly made his way around the car. Grabbing the handle, he gave it one hard pull. The door creaked open. Fire hair appeared. A platinum boot clicked the pavement.

"Mahoney. Really. You should junk this thing."

He cringed. "Some things are worth keeping."

"Yeah. Till you get stranded on the highway. Or in the woods at one of your crime scenes."

He pondered the comment. It would put a crinkle in an investigation if he did get stranded. And his boys would never let him forget it. He looked at the bright-orange paint. *Nah. She's got a few miles left in her.*

Inspecting the row of shops comprising the run-down mini-mall, his eye caught the sign he was looking for. Rusting golden letters spelled out *Caesar's P lace.* The one place that sold canopic jars in the city—according to Dara's searches. After writing up the warrant, rushing it through approval, scouring Doris' house, grilling her, and getting a patrol car set up outside, they'd barely made it here before closing time. He'd left the lone officer tucked in an alley way between houses, watching Doris, hopefully undetected. Might as well squeeze in one more lead while the eyeballs in a jar and flesh on a hook were being processed.

Pulling his notebook from his coat pocket, he flipped it open. "Must be it. Looks like the *Palace* has become a simple *Place.*"

They walked up to the black door. He reached out and turned the golden knob. He pushed the door. It stuck. He pushed again. There was a thud as it dislodged. It creaked open.

"Why do my investigations have to include such strange places? You should have seen that apothecary Blackwood and I visited on the last case. Something tells me this will be reminiscent."

"You've just dug up two boys with doll eyes, and *this* you're calling strange?" She smirked at him.

Mahoney walked through the door and scanned the cluttered space. Ornately woven rugs of golden and silver thread were plastered against the walls, like makeshift wallpaper. Solid-looking golden statues were perched on top of high pedestals, creating shrines to Egyptian gods. Welcoming them, two marble black cats sat poised, tails wrapped around their hinds, eyes glittering with emeralds, narrowed at them, inspecting them. As if they were intruders.

Something cold walked down Mahoney's spine. *C'mon, Bug,* he scolded himself. Yet, deep down, he believed there was a reason for the cold. The room was almost circular, and appeared to have several tunnel-like offshoots.

"Odd layout." Quesnel walked ahead.

He followed her into the centre of the circle. To their left, a counter with a golden top sat unattended. An eerie music drifted through the space. It sounded like it was coming from one of the tunnel-like openings across the room. A bell chimed. Mahoney jumped. Another bell followed. It was part of the song.

Quesnel giggled. "On edge?"

He glared at her. Walking along the circle, he inspected each elaborate display. Nothing looked familiar. He moved to the next wallpaper rug and looked at the long table perched in front of the wall. An ice wave cut his gut. A series of intricately carved jars lined up, forming a perfect row. He pulled a photo from his pocket and held it up beside the jars. Four clay jars with intricate heads carved into the lids stood side by side. Just like the ones that held Caleb's stomach, intestines, lungs and liver.

A tinkling noise pierced his line of analysis. A man walked through the opening where the music was coming from. Little bells hung from his long, purple robe, chiming in rhythm to his long strides.

"Welcome to Caesar's Palace. May I be of assistance?" His voice was low and thick.

Mahoney darted a glance at Quesnel. "We are looking for canopic jars. Like these ones." He pointed to the table beside him.

"Oh? What would be your intention for them?" The man narrowed his eyes at Mahoney.

My intention? What is this? "I'm Detective Mahoney. This is my colleague, Agent Quesnel. We're investigating a murder."

"Murder?"

"Yes. A murder. Jars, just like these, were found with the body."

The man's face went white. "Excuse me. I must sit down. Please." He motioned toward the counter. He walked over and sat behind it. Closing his eyes, he took several deep breaths.

Mahoney glanced at Quesnel. She shrugged her shoulders. They stood and waited.

The man opened his eyes. "I do apologize. These jars, they are a special part of a ritual. To hear that they may have been used as part of, well, such a terrible act, that would create a shift in the afterlife of the souls involved. It's quite disturbing." He shook his head, rubbing the back of his neck.

Did this guy have something to do with Caleb and his organs? Mahoney placed the photo of Caleb's jars onto the countertop. "These jars, the ones we found, they look just like those on that table over there."

The man stood and walked to the countertop. He looked at the photo. "These do look like the ones I sell, yes."

"What does the blue writing on the lids mean?" Mahoney asked.

"Each jar is inscribed to indicate the dedication, according to the organ it holds. This one..."—the man pointed at the photo—"the inscription is a dedication to the goddess Isis who protects the liver."

"The jars on your table, they're lined up. Does the order mean anything?"

"Yes. They are ordered according to the manner in which the internal physical organs of the lost soul are removed. The ritual for preparing the body requires the order to be followed. This is so the soul can prosper in the afterlife. The order must be followed precisely." The man folded his hands and rested them on the countertop.

Mahoney took the picture and looked at it.

Agent Quesnel asked, "The heart, is it usually removed as part of this process?"

The man shook his head. "Oh no. The heart is sacred. It must be left within the body. If it is removed, the soul cannot enter the afterlife. The soul will be left between worlds to suffer for all eternity." His eyes bulged. "That would be a terrible plight. The lost soul, and their loved ones, would suffer."

"Do you maintain sales records?" Mahoney asked.

"I try to. It's a paper system. But I have to keep track. It can be difficult to estimate how many of these specialty items will be purchased."

"Would you have sales records for ten years ago?"

The slight colour that had returned to the man's face faded in a flash. "I might. I'll have to check."

Mahoney towered over the counter. "We'll wait."

"Of course. One moment." The man walked around the counter, passing them on his way to the tunnel opening. The *tink-tink* of bells rung from his robe.

"We're heavy on behaviour. Light on physical evidence." Mahoney rubbed his chin.

"He might be able to give us a name. This killer, he knew about Egyptian mummification processes, both the physical process and the ritualistic side to it. He deliberately left out the heart. If he was only aiming to preserve the body for whatever acts he was planning postmortem, then why go to the trouble to leave the heart? Any internal organs left pose a risk to the preservation of the physical remains. Someone this organized, this careful, would remove any risk that could ruin his plan."

Mahoney wrinkled his brow. "True. He needed to follow this Egyptian ritual to a tee. I guess."

"It's part of his fantasy. He didn't see Caleb as just an object—even after he was dead. Maybe he was trying to help him."

Tinkle-tinkle. The purple-robed man returned, carrying a box. He plunked it onto the countertop and lifted the lid.

"I do apologize. I have records, but these older ones are not well maintained." He flipped through the folders stuffed tightly into the box, pulling out the one labelled *Sales Records 1977-1978*. He set the folder on the counter and turned it to Mahoney. "I opened my shop in 1977, so, this is as far back as the records would go."

"1977?"

"Yes."

"When in 1977?"

"February." The man responded without hesitation.

Mahoney nodded. "We need to look for a Sid, Sydney, Mick...and any purchases of multiple sets of jars." Mahoney grabbed the folders and handed half of them to Quesnel.

"Multiple sets? Oh my." The man sat back down.

"What?" Mahoney asked.

"I thought I was overreacting. Now I have such a feeling." The man shook his head, staring vacantly across the room.

Mahoney narrowed his eyes. "What are you talking about?"

"I remember this customer. He was the only customer I ever had that purchased more than one set. I had just taken over this shop. It was the day after my grand opening. He bought five sets of jars. I had a bad feeling about him. But, he said he ran a funeral home. There was no logical reason to deny him the sale. I decided I was overreacting."

"When was your opening?" Mahoney asked.

"February fourteenth. I remember because apparently there is a celebration for this Valentine's Day here, which I was unaware of." The man replied.

"What was here before you took over?"

"I think it was an old bookstore."

Mahoney flipped open the folder, broke the stack of papers into two, and handed half the pile to Quesnel. "Look for Sid or Sydney. Or a purchase of five jars."

"Let me help." The man reached out.

Mahoney handed him a portion of the papers.

Quesnel plunked her pile onto the counter and sifted through them.

Mahoney focused on his stack. Glaring at the dates as he flipped the corners of the papers, willing the date to settle where he wanted it. "These aren't in order."

"No, I'm afraid not."

They shuffled in silence. Mahoney willed a record for Sid to appear. He halted, staring at the paper in his hand. "This could be something." He slid a sheet of paper over to Quesnel. "1977. Five sets of jars."

Quesnel scanned the page. "Douglas Morrison."

"It's no Sid. But, look, he bought five sets of jars," Mahoney said.

Quesnel looked down the page. "It says he paid with a credit card. Maybe Dara can dig something up on this guy."

"I hope so." Mahoney looked back at the stack.

The cold returned, walking insect legs up Mahoney's back. *Five sets of canopic jars.* Five. Five. Did this purchase have anything to do with Sid? Were there four more little bodies mummified in the ground somewhere?

He looked at the man. "Do you remember anything about him?"

The man rubbed his forehead and squinted his eyes hard. His eyes sprung open. "He told me he worked at his family-owned funeral home, and they'd had a request for these jars. He had proper identification, valid credit card. I had no reason to doubt him. Just a feeling in my gut. My family is always telling me I am too emotional. So I sold him the jars."

The cold insect legs walked up Mahoney's neck. "What did he look like?"

"He dressed in work clothes. Jeans. Plaid shirt. And he had long, reddish, blondish hair." The man swallowed. "I know it was a long time ago, but, this man, he had a cold aura about him. And he had a tattoo on his arm."

Mahoney jolted. "A tattoo?"

"Yes. A tree. With fruit hanging from the branches."

"Quesnel."

She stopped shuffling papers. She flipped her fire hair over her shoulder as she turned to look at him.

"Five sets of jars. Tree tattoo. We need to look into this, now." He looked at the man. "We'll need access to your files. We need a more thorough search in case there's another suspicious purchase in here. I'll send some detectives by."

"This is all legal?" Alarm rung around the man's eyes.

"Of course. I'll have them bring all the paperwork. Based on what we have seen here, we have ample grounds to require a full search."

Quesnel interjected, "You mentioned that if these jars were used for someone who had been murdered, there would be dire consequences?"

His eyes widened again. "Oh, yes, miss. Definitely."

"What exactly would happen?" she asked calmly.

"If a soul, which has left a body that has been taken from this earth by another human being, is encapsulated within canopic jars, then that soul can never enter the realm of the afterlife. It is a curse that befalls the lost soul, as the soul has not been lost by natural causes, but by the hand of a neighbour in the physical realm."

An image of young Caleb, wandering on the side of a long, unending road, flashed into Mahoney's mind. Blond curls stuck to the sweat pouring down his hot face. The sparkle in his blue eyes dimmed, fading away, turning to a look of hopelessness. The cold insect legs made their way over Mahoney's flesh and walked down his insides, creeping along, one prickly step at a time.

Chapter Thirty-six

Near Capture

His head pounded. *Thump. Thump. Thump.* With every throb of his temples, pain seared down the back of his head, stretching into his neck. Jud opened one eye. Then the other. *Where the fuck am I?*

He pushed one hand against the cracked linoleum and raised himself to seated. He leaned back against the wooden cabinets. Hooking loose strands of wet hair behind one ear, then the other, he looked around the small kitchen. *Right. Doris. My jar. Where the hell did she go?*

"Doris! Where are you?" Claws scratched down his throat. His eye twitched.

Not a shuffle. Not a sound. *No thumping. Is she hiding?* He leaned over and started to raise himself to standing. The chipped white stove, rusted-orange fridge and snot-green counter whirled around him into a streak of blended colour. He fell onto his knees, bracing himself with his hands. Stroking the back of his head, something wet and gooey slid across his fingers. He moved his hand in front of his face and stared at thick blood.

What the hell? He racked his brain for a clear picture of the last thing he could remember. *Doris.* On that stupid oversized chair. In her filthy nightgown. He had yelled at her. He had walked into the kitchen, looking for a glass of water. The fridge. He had opened the fridge.

"Bitch hit me. Hard. With something."

The spinning slowed down. He crouched onto the steel toes of his boots. He scanned the kitchen. A heavy frying pan lay on the floor next to the fridge. *Dammit.*

He raised his torso, uncurling his back, one vertebrae at a time, then straightened his legs at a snail's pace.

"Doris! Where are you?"

He stood in the silence of the apparently empty house. He walked over to the fridge and bent to pick up the pan. Shuffling his feet, he moved over to the sink and turned on the tap. Squinting at the brownish wash sponge covered in a slimy green goo, he cringed.

What a pig. He ran the pan under the tap, giving it a once over with hot, brown water. Thick, red streaks formed in the rusting sink. Scanning the counter, he opened the cupboard underneath the sink and peered inside. *No soap. Dammit.*

He looked at the cracked clock on the wall. *Dammit. Dammit.* His *Bug* had found his message by now. Why else would they have been here? He had to get of here. Now.

Abandoning the pan, he turned the water off and trudged to the back door. *My glass jar was gone. She whacked me, hard. Lucky no one came. Gotta get outta here. Fast.* His eye twitched. He ignored it. No time for details. He hated such a panicked exit without a careful scouring of the place. But with a Bug crawling close by, he wasn't going to hang around.

Chapter Thirty-seven

Walk Down Memory Lane

Seth stared at the table, head lowered, dark hair falling over his face.

Mahoney walked up to the table, slid a chair out, and sat down across from Seth. "Seth I'd like to talk to you for a few minutes."

He settled in against the back of the chair and waited. The black locks of hair hung around Seth's face. *C'mon, Seth, let's play our game. I get you stuff. You tell me things. Things I don't want to hear. But things I need to know.* "How about a cold drink? Maybe a smoke?" *C'mon, you sick, broken psycho.*

Seth raised his head. Dark locks slid away, exposing his pale face. "A smoke."

Mahoney waved at the uniformed guard standing at the locked gate.

"Detective?"

"Can we please get a cold drink—a Tab, and a couple cigarettes for the patient here."

The guard nodded.

Seth grinned. "Why are you here again?"

"Well, it seems you and I have something in common. We both have the same enemy."

A cloud darkened Seth's eyes.

"Do you remember what we talked about the last time I visited you?"

"Yes." Seth glared. "The cave."

"And?"

"And...Sid."

"Yes. Trust me, I know it isn't easy to talk about him. But, if you can do it, you'll get that smoke you want, and a cold refreshment."

Seth's face relaxed a little.

"And you might be able to help me get Sid. Catch him. Make him pay for what he did to you."

Seth sat up, leaned back against his chair, and plunked his folded hands onto the table with a clink of metal cuffs. He narrowed his eyes. "For real?"

Mahoney leaned in toward Seth. "Oh, I assure you, I am completely serious. Like I said last time, I know you didn't have anything to do with what happened to the kid in the cave. You were just a child. You were a victim. If you help me, I'll catch him. I'll put him away. He'll get what he deserves." He sat back against his chair.

Seth stared at him. Beads of sweat sprouting across his forehead, his shoulders tightened around his neck. "Make him *pay*." He spat out the last word.

"Detective." The guard walked over to the table and set down a can of pop, three cigarettes, an ashtray, and a lighter.

"Thank you." Mahoney nodded. He pulled open the silver tab on the can. The pop hissed. He slid it over to Seth.

Seth picked up the can between his palms, curling his fingers around it. He took a long swig and swallowed hard. He set the can down.

Mahoney picked up a cigarette and passed it to Seth. Seth put it between his lips. Mahoney lifted the lighter and Seth leaned in toward him. Mahoney flicked the wheel. Sparks flew, a flame lit, and Seth guided the cigarette toward it.

Taking a long, slow drag, Seth settled back against the chair. He stretched his legs out under the table, and his shoulders relaxed. He looked at Mahoney. "All right, Detective. What do you want to know?"

"To find Sid, I need to know who he is. What's his full name?"

Seth closed his eyes and sucked on the cigarette. He exhaled. His eyes popped open. "He told my mom his name was Sydney Smith. I think it was a made-up name. I snooped around the basement one day while he was out. I found some driver's licences. With different names on them. They all had his picture."

"Do you remember any of the names?"

Seth closed his eyes again. "One of them did say Sydney Smith. I think it was fake."

"What about the others?" Mahoney leaned over the table.

Seth closed his eyes and rubbed his temples with his fingers. Smoke swirled from the cigarette around his head in a wispy cloud. He opened his eyes. "Dammit. I wish I could remember. There were at least two others. One said

Sid. But I can't remember the last name. I think it started with a P. The other one...Mick something."

"You're sure you can't remember?"

"I don't know. I was nervous, thought I heard someone upstairs, so I got out of there, fast. He would have *killed* me if he caught me snooping." Seth loomed over the table. His stare pierced Mahoney.

"No problem. This is good." *Dammit. Who is this Sid?* "What did Sid look like?"

"Long hair. Reddish blond. Muscular. He worked in the garden in the back, a lot. He was tough."

"The garden?"

"Yeah. He was real obsessive about it. Loved his fruit trees. He was always frustrated that it was so damn cold up here so much of the year. Said it was impossible to grow a proper tree garden. It was weird. For such a tough guy, he loved his freakin' trees and flowers." Seth shook his head and frowned. He took another drag then flicked the cigarette. The butt flared red. Ashes trickled into the pile of grey dust in the cheap plastic tray.

"Do you remember anything else about him? Anything distinctive about his looks? Anything else unusual?"

Seth's lips stretched into a thin line. "Average height. Muscular build. Always wore work clothes, jeans, plaid shirts, and work boots. That's it. Nothing weird, I don't think."

"You're sure? Think hard." Mahoney's eyes darted toward the two remaining cigarettes.

"Fine." Seth closed his eyes. The sweat beads multiplied on his forehead. He frowned. His leg twitched. He snapped his eyes open. "He had a small tattoo, on the inside of his wrist." He gulped.

"What was it?"

"A tree. With little round fruit hanging from it."

"Which wrist?"

Seth's shoulders shivered. "His right wrist. Inside. I stared at that fucking tree a lot." His shoulders shook hard.

"Seth." Mahoney leaned in across the table. "Stay with me." He found Seth's eyes with his own and slid the cold can toward him. "Take a break. Have a drink." *Damned if I'm gonna lose this sick psycho now. I need info.*

Seth's eyes watered as he looked back at Mahoney. He took the pop and gulped it down.

Satisfied that he hadn't lost Seth to another catatonic episode, Mahoney sat back in his chair. "Do you remember when Sid left?"

"Yeah. The day after I followed him into the cave. It was my birthday." Seth's hands shook, metal cuffs clinking against the table.

"All right. How about another smoke?" Mahoney rolled a cig over to Seth. Seth picked it up. Mahoney lit it for him. He watched Seth take several long puffs. *Ease up, Bug. Keep him here.*

"How old were you, that day, on your birthday?"

"Twelve. I remember cause my mom made a big deal about it being my last year before I became a teenager and didn't need her anymore. She baked a cake. Only cake she ever made for me. Even had icing. But then...well, when Sid didn't come home for dinner, and she found his half of the bedroom empty, all his clothes gone, she threw the cake across the kitchen. It smashed into the wall." A tear burst from the corner of Seth's eye and slid down his cheek.

"I'm sorry, Seth." *For fuck's sake. What am I? A therapist? Easy, Bug. Easy.* He forced a smile. *Twelve. Fits the timeline.*

"Yeah. I'm sure you're real sorry." Seth spat the words out. A glower washed over his face. "I'm done talking about Sid."

"I *am* sorry." Mahoney opened his briefcase and pulled out the teddy bear with the purple cross eye. He placed it on the table.

Seth went rigid. "Where d'you get that?" His eyes blazed.

"We found it. In the basement, at your house. Your mom's house."

Seth clenched his teeth. His hands shook, rattling cuffs against metal.

"Seth, we just found this. It wasn't there before. Do you know how it got there?"

"He stole it."

"You mean Sid?"

Seth licked his lips. "Yeah. I'm sure it was him. It went missing the same day he left. That psycho took everything I had. Don't know why he wanted my bear." He looked down at his lap. "Wasn't the only thing he stole."

"Look, you've given me some good information here."

"Yeah, fine, whatever. I'm done." He flicked the cigarette. The tip glowed orange as grey ashes fluttered into the tray. He looked straight into Mahoney's eyes. Something washed over Seth's face. In a flash, the young, hurt boy transformed. The look in his eyes pierced into Mahoney. Seth's face grew a shade paler and took on a greyish hue. Something glinted behind his eyes. Something cold. Something dark.

"Are you sure there's nothing else you can tell me? About Sid?" *C'mon sicko. Don't leave me.*

"Sure. Sid. You know he had many friends." He paused. "*Special friends.*" The words drew slowly out of Seth's mouth as he enunciated each syllable. "He told me once I was his *most special* friend. But he was a liar. Dammed liar." Anger pulsed from Seth's voice. His face flushed. Sweat trickled from his forehead, down his cheeks. "You know, he had dozens of special friends. How special could I have been?" His piercing stare searched inside Mahoney, demanding an answer.

"Dozens?" Mahoney swallowed. *Is he full of shit?* He forced a blank stare onto his face.

"Oh yeah. At least he taught me something. You're nothing if you don't have *dozens* of dolls to play with. You don't know nothing 'bout keeping toys until you have *at least* twelve."

Mahoney's shoulders tensed. His gut clenched. "Wow. You had a dozen dolls, did you?"

"*Have.* Over a dozen. The ones that weren't stolen. They're safe. I'll get back to them. I will."

He's full of shit. "That's amazing." *His vocation. Praise. He needs praise.* Mahoney swallowed against the bile rising in his throat. "That's an impressive collection. Did you give them nice places to rest, until you return?" *Sick game.*

"Of course. There's this one, oh, the beautiful bed I built for it. It's spectacular." A fiendish smile stretched across Seth's face. "I laid it in a place fit for a queen."

"A queen?"

"Yes." Seth's eyes sparkled. "A place where special souls can be scattered."

Scattered? Does he mean ashes? Mahoney glued his eyes to Seth as he pictured small scattering grounds behind the cemetery he'd been to a long time ago.

"I gave it a home. The most beautiful fir you've ever seen."

A picture of a massive fir tree shot into Mahoney's mind. "That's impressive. Can you tell me about any of your other dolls? The nice places you gave them to rest until you can play with them again?"

Seth took a long drag and leaned back against the chair. "Now why would I tell you? You'll just go stealing them again, won't you?" He smirked. "I'm done talking. Thanks for the smokes." He pushed the remnants of the cigarette into the pile of grey ashes in the plastic tray and summoned the attendant.

Chapter Thirty-eight

The Ghost Gets Away

Mahoney plunked down into the driver's seat and closed the door with a creak. He twisted the key in the ignition and turned the volume down on the tape deck, simmering the sounds of the rock god he'd been getting reacquainted with.

His phone buzzed. He snapped it open. "Mahoney."

"It's Sutton. We have a problem. I swung by, to check on the patrol car watching Doris. It was gone."

"What?" Mahoney's temples throbbed.

"Yeah. I settled into the alley, then called in right away. They don't know where he went."

What the holy hell. The veins in Mahoney's neck pulsed. "How long you been there?"

"Ten minutes tops. Got here. Called in. Called you."

Mahoney gritted his teeth. "OK. Stay there. Watch the house. I'll find out what happened."

"You got it, boss. I won't move till I hear from you."

Mahoney snapped the phone shut and threw it onto the passenger's seat. His shoulders clenched. He'd specifically left a single car, strategically placed, to prevent spooking Sid. If they hadn't already. *Dammit.* If they hadn't scared him off when they were searching the basement, he could have taken the patrol-car-free window to slip back into Doris'. If he went back. Mahoney clenched his hand into a fist and pounded the steering wheel.

Slippery Sid was sliding right through his fingers. He reached over and cranked the volume on the tape deck, revved the engine and sped off.

Chapter Thirty-nine

Lost Doll

Mahoney rapped firmly on the office door. He stared at the golden letters: *Sergeant Jackson.* He hated asking permission. Charging forth was more his forte. But he knew this would strain resources, and he couldn't risk slowing down the current investigation. His sergeant would give him some extra manpower on the side. He'd find the boy Seth left in Queen's Park. A place fit for a Queen, with a place to scatter souls. It had to be.

"Come in," came Sergeant Jackson's rough voice, muffled through the door.

Mahoney swung it open and strode up to the desk. "Sarge."

"Detective. Something new in your case?"

"Yeah. I need a search, at Queen's Park. Could be another victim of Seth buried there."

"No."

"Why not?"

"You brought in the FBI, behind my back. You gave Sergeant Red-Coat sifting equipment and told me about it after the fact. I can't even get you more manpower on your *current* case."

"But there's a dead college kid in Queen's Park."

Sergeant Jackson leaned over the desk. "Mahoney. Focus on *this* case."

"Sarge. It's Seth. I've pulled more information from him, for *this* case. He divulged more about his own trail of bodies. He's cracking. I know exactly where to look. It'd be a clean search. In and out."

The sergeant sighed. He sat up, pressed his palms against his heavy wood desk, and looked Mahoney squarely in the eye. "No. If you can't spare any of the extra resources you've already indulged in, then this'll have to wait until you can."

His neck burning, Mahoney loosened his collar. "Think of the family. They need to know. What if it was your kid?"

"I might not want to know. Sometimes parents move on, you know. They create their own explanation—they don't want the truth. They have to let it go."

A rage of regurgitated food rose up his throat. He swallowed hard against it and pulled at his collar. "You really believe that? If it was *your* kid, you could let it go? Without ever *knowing* what happened to him? Why he simply vanished into thin air." The veins in his neck throbbed. He stared hard at his sergeant.

"Relax. Seth isn't going anywhere. Finding another body now won't help anything." He motioned for Mahoney to sit.

"I don't need to sit." Mahoney paced along the desk.

"Listen. The priority is to find the perp who killed these two boys. I need you to stay focused. Find him. Before he hurts another kid. Seth can't hurt anyone right now. This perp can."

Mahoney spun on his heel and faced the sergeant. His heartbeat thumped in the sides of his temples. He exhaled sharply. "I'm trying to find him. I had a patrol car on Doris' house. He disappeared."

"Ease up. I just got a call. The officer had a family emergency. He had to leave."

Mahoney glowered. "He should have waited for a replacement."

Jackson slid his glasses further up the bridge of his nose. "His three-year-old daughter was rushed to the hospital. His wife called him. He panicked. Took off. When he got to the hospital, he called it in. They were sending another car. Seems you got Sutton over there before the car arrived."

Ripples of tension clenched at Mahoney's shoulders. He took a deep breath. "I see."

"You get this guy. Then we'll talk more about Seth, and your search." The sergeant waved his hand in the air. "In the meantime, take it down a notch. You're looking a little ragged. Don't bust out on me before the end of this case."

Mahoney took a deep breath and rolled his shoulders a couple times. "Fine." He turned toward the door.

"Mahoney."

He cranked his neck. "Yeah?"

"You'll get him. Just listen to that gut of yours."

Chapter Forty

Tight War Room

Mahoney hung at the back of the small room by the coffee pot, watching Dara set up her typewriter. The door swung open. Agent Quesnel entered the room. He made eye contact with her. She gave him a nod. Sutton sat at the long centre table, wolfing down a burger out of a grease-spotted paper bag. Mahoney longed for the day to end. *Get moving, old man.*

He walked to the front of the room, itching to harness his team. *No more red-coat weight.*

"OK, everyone, let's get a move on." He scanned the room. Agent Quesnel crossed her arms and leaned back against the wall, facing him. The room was quiet.

"I just checked in with Officer Williams. Hayes has been out in K-Country with him all day. Looks like they're spending the night out there. They dug deep. Literally. They worked the cave over again, underground. They found another concrete box. In the opposite corner of the cave."

Sutton whistled. "Doozie. Two concrete boxes, both buried in the same cave."

"Yeah. Chances are, it's the work of the same killer. We won't have anything conclusive until the contents are examined. Blackwood's headed out there. The box won't be opened until she arrives. Can't risk air exposure."

"For this killer, two is just an appetizer." Agent Quesnel leaned against the back wall, her arms crossed.

"You think there's more, in the cave?" Sutton swallowed a bite of meat.

"It's possible," Agent Quesnel said. "The boxes were buried deep. The scenes are intricate. Going to all that trouble to hide these bodies, and finding such a remote spot, well, the killer could have used the secluded area multiple times."

Sutton nodded, wiping his fingers on a thin paper napkin.

"Sutton, the doll eyes? Any progress?" Mahoney asked.

Sutton crumpled the paper bag. "I went to every doll and hobby supply shop on the list from Dara. Got a list of all recent purchases of black, glass eyes, over the last two weeks. More than you would think. Most are paid in cash. None of the credit card receipts raise any flags. None of the sales people remembered anything noteworthy. And no one I talked to worked at any of these stores ten years ago. All fresh staff."

Mahoney walked over to the cream-coloured wall and stared at the bright-blue eyes of Caleb's photo looking back at him. Shaking his head, he turned to his team. "Did you find anything on the embalming chemicals?"

Sutton nodded. "I was able to hit about half the places on the list from Dara. They keep close tabs on every employee, given the nature of their work. I secured a record of all personnel licensed to purchase embalming supplies between 1975 and 1980. It's a start. They'll have to be analyzed."

"OK. We'll figure that out. Agent Quesnel accompanied me to the Egyptian store to locate our canopic jars. We accessed sales records. Initial scan gave us a strong lead. There was a purchase, the year we were looking for. Guy by the name of Douglas Morrison. He bought five sets on a credit card. Shop owner's description fits."

Wrinkles crossed over Sutton's forehead. "What? *Five?* But we only have one set of jars, from the cave."

"Yeah. Well, Williams might be finding us another set shortly."

"But that would leave three more," Sutton said.

Agent Quesnel said, "I know this is gory. But we need to prepare ourselves. The kind of killer who went to the amount of effort with the first mummy found in the cave, well, let's just say he probably had practice before killing that boy. And he didn't stop there. He needed to perfect his script. His hunger for the perfect fantasy grew."

Mahoney continued, "Dara, we'll need a search on this name as soon as we convene."

Dara nodded, her fingers typing away.

Mahoney's gut tingled. He cleared his throat. "I paid a visit to Seth. He said he found several driver's licences, all with this Sid guy's picture on them," Mahoney said. "The only full name he gave me is Sydney Smith. He couldn't remember the rest of them. One was Sid P, and one was Mick. That's it. Doris said the same thing. Dara, I'll need name searches. Sutton, we need a thorough search of the sales records at the Egyptian joint. Look for other purchases for multiple sets of jars. And look for any other records in any of these names—partial or full. We have to figure out who this guy is. I've already set the paperwork in motion, and lined it up with the shop owner. You'll need to spend the day there tomorrow. I'll try to get you more manpower, but I can't promise."

"No problem. I can handle it." Sutton nodded.

Mahoney asked, "Dara? How are the computer searches coming?"

"I wasn't getting anywhere with the messages and the symbol. I left that for now and focused on the cross-Canada search you gave me." Her eyes darted around the room.

"For other bodies, similar to our victims," Mahoney filled in for her.

"Yes. I found three. In BC. All buried in wooden boxes, deep, in the forest. Appears the cases were never linked. They were in different jurisdictions, so there wasn't any reason to connect them. I've requested the files. We should have them overnight. The information I have on my computer is spotty."

Sutton sucked the remaining life out of his Big Gulp, shaking his head. Agent Quesnel leaned back against the wall and closed her eyes.

"Team. As tragic as this is, it's good we found them. We'll be the ones to make the link. Dara, let's get the files together for our meeting first thing tomorrow. Anything else?"

No one spoke.

"All right. Sutton, you get to spend the day in a weird Egyptian store. Shop owner agreed to let you in early. Those files are a top-priority item."

Sutton nodded.

"Quesnel, let's cook up a plan to dig into those files on the embalmment licensing."

"Dara, I'll be by your desk pronto. Let's get these crime scenes mapped out."

Chapter Forty-one

Dessert Will Have to Wait

Speeding down the main road into the dark belly of the downtown core, Mahoney leaned back into the seat. He'd been in this city—his city—his whole life. He loved everything about it. Even the dark side that came out of the trenches when the sun went down. He cranked the volume on the tape deck. The wails of a rock god from long ago seeped through car. Words of the end being his only friend doused the millions of thoughts racing through his head. He needed a good drive to help clear his cluttered thoughts.

He stole a glance at the leather book snuggled into the passenger seat. It would take him all night to read Seth's journal. His mind would be full to the brim of dark memories and torture. For the few minutes he had behind the wheel of his trusted Pony he could get lost in the sounds of rock and blues. His shoulders sank into the back of the seat. The swirling in his mind slowed. He breathed deeply.

A grumbling quivered through his stomach. Did I have lunch? He searched his mind, but nothing resembling a lunch could be found. He thought of his fridge. It was pretty bare. Bottle of ketchup. Half a jar of pickles. Some questionable cheese with fuzzy white circles starting to appear. *Guess I better make a pitstop. Where can I get a quick, no-hassle bite?* The pulsing blue neon sign flashed into his mind. Cotton-candy lips followed. Bingo. Dinner and distraction, to go.

Rerouting slightly, he pressed the gas pedal hard and sped through the dark. Easing up as he pulled onto a dimly lit side road, pulsating blue neon caught his eye. He swung into the parking lot and rolled into a stall.

Sliding the keys out of the ignition, he slipped out of the driver's side. His hiking boots gripped the pavement as he walked around to the back of the car. Popping the trunk, it creaked as he lifted it. He grabbed a pair of shiny black shoes, and dropped them to the ground. He bent over, untied each hiking boot, and switched them for the shiny black. Closing the trunk with a loud *clunk,* he locked the car and walked toward the black door.

A buzz of voices and the strumming of an acoustic guitar welcomed him. The place was about half full. People were scattered around the room, chattering, clinking beer glasses, and swaying to the crooning of a long-haired hippy up on stage, strumming away. Mahoney made his way across the room to the bar and hoisted himself up on a high stool.

Blonde curls swayed across her shoulders as she turned his way. He danced his eyes over the caramel-coloured dot, lingering over the creamy skin of her left breast.

"Mr. Detective. So nice to see you." She flashed him her candy-floss smile. A puff of strawberry floated around him. "Ginger ale?"

"Please. And a pepperoni pizza. To go."

She fake pouted. "Oh, you can't stay and dine with me tonight?"

"I'm deep into a case."

"Well then, I'll get that pizza going for you, right away." She slid a tall, icy glass his way.

"Thanks." He took a long sip. The ginger bubbles soothed his throat. He watched her blonde curls bouncing against her back, tight black pleather following the contours of her curves down to her ample ass. She leaned into the makeshift window between the back of the room and the kitchen. As she turned back toward the bar, he shifted his gaze to the shiny countertop.

"Your order's in. Too bad you can't hang around. I get off in an hour." She leaned over the bar toward him. The small, brown circle at the top of her breast lingered in front of him. He wondered if it was a birthmark.

He snapped his gaze to her eyes. "Yeah. Maybe next time."

"I missed you at The Roxy last Thursday."

"Case got a hold of me." He remembered sitting in this exact spot, realizing it was Thursday.

"Must be an important case."

"Well. It's always murder."

"Right." She stood up. "You must see a lot. I could take your mind off that, sometime...if you ever get a day off." She twirled a blonde curl around her pink fingernail.

I'm sure you could.

"Would still love to hang with you at The Roxy sometime. I'm there every Thursday."

Bet every part of you tastes like strawberry. He shifted in his seat. He'd give anything to trade dead boys for a night of dipping into her. He shook off the tingling, and focused his mind. *Pizza. Journal. That's all you get tonight.*

"Not tonight," he answered gruffly.

"Awww. All right." She pouted again.

"Sasha. Order's up," the cook yelled from the back of the room.

"Be right back."

Sipping his cold pop, his shoulders slumped. He thought about the journal. A cold crept up the back of his neck. *No treats for you, Bug. You got psycho Sid to catch.* His mind whirled again. How could there be no trace of this guy? Multiple matching descriptions. The same tattoo. Dara's initial searches—on both Sydney and Douglas—had turned up nothing. Poof. He was gone. Vanished into thin air. Mahoney's mind wrenched.

Sweet strawberry brought him back to the bar. She slid a white box toward him. "Your dinner. Too bad you gotta eat that alone."

"Yeah." He slipped a couple of bills across the counter, jumped down from the chair and turned away. He had all the temptation he would get tonight. *No strawberry candy for you.*

"Hey. Mr. Detective."

He spun on his heel.

"Yeah?"

"Your change." She held her hand out over the bar, her breasts reaching for him.

"Keep it." He turned and walked toward the door, fast, before he could change his mind.

Chapter Forty-two

Psycho Journal

The clank pierced the quiet apartment as Mahoney dropped his keys onto the small table in the tight entrance way. Placing his derby next to the keys, he slid off his shiny black shoes. The cavern worn into the couch welcomed him as he plunked down. He set the pizza on the glass coffee table and nestled his briefcase on the couch next to him. He dug into his briefcase and pulled out the leather book. The weight of the book pushed into his legs as he set it down and stared at it. It took a thorough search of several boxes of evidence from the last case to find it. It had been processed and stored. Now it was in his hands for the sole purpose of deciphering the entries. He hoped his memory of the horror inside had been amplified in his mind by lack of sleep. He opened the cover.

Journal

of

Seth

Henderson

Turning the page, his eyes found the first entry.

April 3, 1975

I wish he would just kill me.

Hell. This wasn't exactly the book he would choose to reread. He needed to go through it again, looking for a killer called Sid. How could someone be everywhere and nowhere at the same time?

April 4, 1987

Dear Doris,

I'm not your fool...

The entry that matched the description fitting the first corpse Seth left in his wake. Or at least the first one Mahoney's team had found. Flashes of ghastly ligatures circling a pale neck and a shimmering black cloak jarred Mahoney's mind. He flipped through a few more pages.

April 11, 1987

Dear Doris,

I want to watch you bleed...

He remembered this entry. It was a soul-exposing capture of Seth's inner torture that drove him to kill a young man, paint his face white as a ghost, force his dead legs into tight black pleather, dye his hair orange and tease it wild, then leave him perched at the back of a dark, wet cave.

Not it. He kept flipping pages.

April 18, 1987

I am a carcass. I have no soul.

Another deep dive into Seth's inner thoughts. A look at the lack of soul he felt he had as a result of the abuse by his mother, driving him to hang an innocent young man by his wrists from a rock roof in a forest. Forcing his hand to pump the young man full of toxins until he couldn't breathe. Mahoney could still hear the last gasps of breath the young man took as he lay in Blackwood's arms.

Mahoney set the book down on the table, and pressed circles into his temples with his forefingers. He opened the pizza box and lifted out a slice. The gooey cheese stretched as he pulled the piece from the pie. The greasy meaty smell called to him. He took a bite and leaned back against the couch. He devoured the slice. He needed a drink to wash it down. Walking over to the small bar against the wall, he twisted open a bottle of Maker's Mark and splashed a small dose into a crystal glass. *One won't hurt.*

Drink in hand, he walked back over to the couch. Crystal clinked against glass as he set the drink down. He plunked back into the well-worn couch and wolfed down a second slice of pizza. The grumbling in his stomach had eased. He closed the pizza box and shoved it to the edge of the table. After a thorough wipe down of his hands with a paper towel, he picked up the book and continued flipping through entries. Mahoney relived the world through the eyes a young, tortured boy, absorbing the details of the emotional turmoil that brought the killer within the boy to surface, sending him down a spiral until he took one life after another.

Night descended upon the small apartment. A streetlight pierced a window, casting an eerie glow over the otherwise dark room. He stood up, stretching his numb legs, and walked across the room. He snapped on the only lamp. A warm glow softened the vibe.

He shuffled back to the couch, back to the book, and continued his dreary task. He flipped to another entry. The word *Dad* caught his eye. He scanned the page.

April 25, 1987

Dearest Fucking Fake Dad,

Bingo. Must be it. Sid. Mom's boyfriend. Fake Dad. Yup. He stood, walked over and poured himself another drink. He settled himself back into the cavern of the worn couch and continued reading.

Was my whole life simply wasted time?

Was my only purpose to be your toy?

How can you live with yourself, knowing what you have left behind?

You didn't see me as a young boy. You only saw me as your doll. Your doll to play your games with. Your sick, twisted games.

You stole every shred of that little boy's innocence. There is nothing of him left but a carcass.

A carcass searching for a soul.

How can you live with yourself?

Do you have delusions? Or am I the only one left haunted by the visions you drove into my mind?

You said I was special. You said I was marked, that I would never be corrupted, rotten to the core. That you would protect me from her. From her poison. That you wouldn't let her rot my soul. You branded me with a symbol of innocence.

Mahoney jolted. A tingling crept through him. Like an imaginary caterpillar walking down his insides, little insect legs creeping along, dragging a chill through him.

He stared at a crudely drawn symbol. The swirls pulled him in, whirling around into a vortex. The fence at the park flashed into his mind. Caleb's face looked at him from the cream-coloured crime scene wall. The carving on the tree materialized. The symbol in Seth's journal matched what was carved on that fence and on the tree in the park. He was sure of it.

He dropped the book onto the table and dug into his briefcase in a hasty search. Pulling out a stack of photos, he spilled them onto the table. There it was. The picture of the fence, in the park Caleb disappeared from. He placed it next to the open journal.

It matched.

A cold feeling washed over him. His eyes explored the strong, winding circles. *What the hell is this?*

He read the journal entry again, slowing down over the important words.

You branded me with a symbol of innocence.

Innocence?

He reviewed the words again.

Protect me from her.

From her poison.

You wouldn't let her rot my soul.

You branded me with a symbol of innocence.

Innocence. He couldn't get past the word. Was Seth saying this sicko Sid had branded him in order to protect him? Was Sid leaving a symbol of innocence on the very children that he killed?

Mahoney's mind buzzed. Sipping back a long swig of bourbon, he let the sweetness linger at the back of his tongue, the burn crawl down his throat, and the numbness trickle down his arms.

Sid. A handful of people described this long-haired man in work boots with a tree tattoo on his arm. Yet there was no record of him. Sydney Smith. Sid was a ghost. Everywhere but nowhere. Was this symbol the first step to finding Sid? Mahoney sighed. His gut told him the only way to catch the killer was to unravel another sick fantasy. He stared at the symbol of innocence and pondered his next step.

BOOK OF
THE DEAD

Chapter Forty-three

Loose Links

Jud took a sip of coffee and smiled at the shit-brown mug. The simple things in life gave him unexpected joy lately. He picked up the Calgary Chronicle and scanned the front page.

"Two Mummies with Loose Ties"

"Local Homicide detectives left floundering as they try to piece together the bodies of two young boys. The 'Cave-Mummy,' found in the back of a cave near Wash-A-Way Point on Saturday, May 9, and the body of a young boy found Thursday, May 28, deemed the 'Fresh-Mummy,' are two of the highest profile murder scenes that Calgary has ever seen. Some aspects of the scenes and the bodies have striking resemblances to one another. Both bodies were wrapped in white cloths. The eyes were missing from both victims. Aspects of the scenes, however, are vastly different, leaving Detective Mahoney and his local Homicide team to wonder if this is indeed the work of one killer. The Cave-Mummy was found in a concrete structure and was well preserved using sophisticated processes, including embalming. The Fresh-Mummy was found in a freshly dug plot, and no indication of preservation has yet been found. The single most disturbing part about both scenes was the black doll eyes left in the eye sockets."

Jud took a long sip of coffee. He placed the mug on the faded cherry wood and laughed. *Yeah. Things are good. Watching a Bug squirm even makes you look good, stupid shit-brown mug. Squirm, Bug, squirm.*

He picked up a piece of toast and spread a thick layer of Crab Apple jam onto it. Taking a large bite, he savoured the mix of tart and sweet dancing on his tongue. He loved his Crab Apple tree. It had been one of the first he had planted in his garden. And Timmy had settled in real nice with the Crab Apple tree. They were a good pair.

He picked up the paper and continued reading.

"Sergeant Jackson gave his strong assurance that everything would be done to solve this case before any more children were harmed."

A full, cynical laugh rumbled up Jud's throat, escaping from his mouth. He slapped his hand against the cherry wood.

"Before any more children are harmed. They won't be. I've been looking out for them for a long time. When you were a rookie detective, Bug, I was starting my own career. You squirming little critter."

He emptied the last splash of coffee into his mouth, stacked up the dishes and stood. *Enough comic strips for today. It's time to go to work.*

Chapter Forty-Four

Search for Sid

Mahoney sipped cold coffee from cheap Styrofoam. He leaned in over Dara, watching her fingers tapping ferociously over little black keys. *Tap-tap, tap-tap, tap-tap.*

"Bug..."—she continued typing—"we got something on your Sydney Smith. I was able to go back further, into expired records. Look." She shifted away from the screen.

SYDNEY SMITH

The letters flashed back at him, bright green, and daunting. He had to be their guy. He had to exist.

All descriptions—from Joseph, the Egyptian store owner, Seth, and even Doris—indicated this reddish blond long-haired, heavy-booted, muscular mystery man. To tie a knot in the whole thing, there was the tattoo of a tree. They all saw it. Seth more than the others. On the inside of his wrist. His right wrist. This had to be their guy. Mahoney could taste the satisfaction of stopping this sicko dead in his tracks. *No more dead kids.* His gut tingled. *C'mon, c'mon.* He willed the strings of bright-green letters to halt. He wanted an answer. And he wanted it now.

No paper trail. No record of who this man was. The only name they had—Sydney Smith—came from the mouths of two crazies. Doris and Seth. Mahoney clung to the possibility that Sydney Smith would materialize in neon letters on Dara's computer screen.

A soft slurping sound crept through his ears. Dara sipped from a floral teacup. *Clink.* She set the teacup into a matching saucer.

Bright green halted, still letters glared back at him from the black screen.

OPERATOR'S LICENCE

No. 134711-666

SMITH, Sydney

Expires: 10 NOV 1978

99 Rosemont Street NW

Calgary AB T2T 3A3

DOB 13 APR 1947

Dara pressed thick black glasses against her face. "Got one match on the name. A driver's licence. It's expired. That's it. Nothing else. No other pieces of identification. No permanent residence listed. No accounts in his name, utilities, phone, nothing. This is strange."

Dammit. "The address matches Doris'."

"Yes. But the house was solely in her name. All the bills associated with the residence are also in her name. This Sydney, the only thing we've got here is this expired driver's licence."

"Other than that, it's like he didn't exist."

"But he does. Look at this." Dara tapped the keys.

A picture of a man materialized on the black screen. A photo, taken when the license was issued. The chiselled face revealed rough features and tanned skin. Long, sandy blond hair fell over broad shoulders.

"It's only a head shot. But it fits our description." Mahoney said.

Dara nodded. "I also found something on the name you got on the purchase of the canopic jars—Douglas Morrison." Her fingers flew over the keyboard again. "The credit card was cancelled two days after the purchase. Douglas Morrison owned Morrison Funeral Home."

"Really? Lines up with the story the store owner told us. He sold the guy multiple sets because the guy indicated his family ran a funeral home. Where is Douglas now?"

"He died. In 1979. That's why my initial searches came up empty."

"What? So, Douglas purchases five sets of jars. He runs a funeral home, maybe the purchase is justified. Why cancel the credit card two days later? And how did a set of those jars get in the coffin in the cave? Was this Douglas involved? Or, does Sid exist, and he knew Douglas?" Mahoney paused and took a deep breath.

"Morrison Funeral home is now run by Don, Douglas' son. Look at this."

Mahoney stared at the screen. A photo of Douglas Morrison stared back at him, bearing no resemblance to Sydney Smith's head shot.

"OK. I'll have a chat with Don then." Mahoney flipped to a fresh page in his notebook and jotted down the address for Morrison Funeral Home. "In the meantime, we need to find more on this Sydney Smith. Can you widen the search? Cross-Canada? And try credit cards."

"Will do."

"Let's toy with the name. We've got this Sid P. And we've got this Mick. Maybe Mick Smith? Mick P?" Mahoney shook his head. "I don't know. Whatever you can think of."

Dara placed a hand on his arm. "I'll work on it, Bug."

Mahoney rubbed the bristle on his chin. His eyes narrowed. *Sid, Sydney, Mick, whatever the fuck his name was, this guy has to exist.*

"Anything else, Bug?"

"No. Focus on this. This guy exists, physically. He's been seen. We need to find him in your cyber world." He grabbed his derby. "Thanks, Dara." He walked away.

Chapter Forty-five
Bubblegum Plum

His shirt drenched in sweat, Jud plunged the shovel deep into the earth. Bending his knees, he hoisted the shovel, heavy with soil, over his shoulder. Fresh dirt flew through the air, landing on a tall pile behind him. He paused, wiping the sweat trickling down his brow with the bottom of his t-shirt. Taking a few breaths, his heart steadied.

Looking over to the fresh tree waiting to be planted, he nodded his approval. This one was a rare find. He'd had plum trees before, but not like this one. His eyes scanned the smooth, vase-like shape of the trunk. Good 'ole Kent had even found one that was partially mature. He wouldn't have to wait years for it to bear its luscious fruit. Closing his eyes, he imagined the fragrance of sweet bubblegum wafting from round, ripe, red plums.

Snapping his eyes open, he plunged himself back into his work.

"Bubblegum Plum. Special tree. Might take a while to find you a match. I'm sure going to enjoy the hunt."

A few more digs of the shovel and Jud stepped back to examine his work. He had dug the hole at the apex of his circular garden. The new plum tree would sit at the head of his sanctuary. Putting the shovel down, he walked over to the tree, wrapping his arms around its base. The muscles in his arms bulged as he lifted it up, moved it over to the fresh hole, and lowered the vase-like trunk into the dark soil. Grabbing the shovel, he worked at the pile of dirt, moving it back to where it came from, securing the tree.

When he finally finished, he walked over to the centre of the circular garden. He had built four benches, one facing each side of the garden. He plunked himself down onto the one facing his new tree. Rubbing his right shoulder with his left hand, he sunk against the back of the bench. Mopping up the moisture drizzling down his face with his shirt, he admired his work.

"Now, don't you look lovely up there at the head of the table? I knew you were a special tree the minute I saw you. You're gonna fit in real well around here."

Picking up a leather-bound book, he unravelled the sinewy tie holding it closed. He scanned each page as he flipped through them.

The Crab Apple. You were the first tree in this garden, my final sanctuary. You've stood through the test of time. How long has it been now?

Scanning the page, he found the date scribed in the top corner.

April 10, 1979. When I met little Timmy.

Looking up from his book, he turned his head, finding the Crab Apple tree. The trunk was thick, the branches were ample and sturdy, stretching far out on all sides of the tree. Little flowers smothered the branches, weaving a white blanket.

Little Timmy. We should have a playdate soon.

He skimmed the pages detailing the orange, lemon and lime trees he'd planted when he first built this garden. He'd started out simple. Flipping through the book, he glanced at the entry describing the Babcock Peach. Now there was a juicy delight. He flipped to the page about The Flavour King Pluot. What a special treat. Known as the love child of the apricot and the plum. They required a climate with certain chill hours. Why he hadn't migrated here sooner, he didn't know. He loved the heat of the day and cool of the night. Just like his trees.

Finding a fresh page, he slid a pen out from a small, circular holder attached to the spine of the book. He scribed a new entry on the clean page.

May 31, 1987

Bubblegum Plum. Planted at the head of my sanctuary. A placeholder for a real special friend.

Closing the book, he sat back against the bench, staring at the plum tree.

No need to rush this one. Patience will bear the sweetest of fruits. "Who will we find to rest under your beautiful branches? Hmmm?"

He shuffled through his mind, looking for the right hunting grounds. A short drive took him into the nearest town. There were several schools within reach, and playgrounds along with them. But he didn't want any friend. He wanted a real special friend. Someone who was a match for this new tree. This special tree. Red fruit that smelled of bubblegum. He would need someone one hundred percent unblemished. Clean and pure. Not an inkling of rot. A tingling shot through his insides. This one might take a while. And he would definitely need a lot of patience.

Yeah, patience. It'll pay off. The pleasure will be worth it.

He licked his salty lips and swallowed hard. A tidbit of saliva caught in his parched throat. A cold glass of lemonade flashed through his mind. He closed the leather book, carefully tying the cords. Placing the book down on the bench, he stood up, gathered his tools, and walked toward the shed.

A moment later, book in hand, he strode to the back of the circular garden. He ducked under a branch thick with lush green leaves protruding from a massive Cypress tree. Opening a small door, he hunched over, bending his head under the doorframe. The cold air hit him like a refreshing shower. He squinted into the darkness until he could make out the narrow tunnel. Weaving his way through the darkness, book in hand, his mind wandered, thinking of the delight the plum tree would bring him.

Chapter Forty-six

Cave and Parks

Wafts of strong, cheap coffee violated Mahoney's nose. He slid the small glass pot back into its holder. He winked at Dara and raised the chipped mug toward her in a fake toast. "Here's to cheap Homicide coffee and chipped mugs."

"Oh, Bug. I know you like your fancy dark roast. No budget for that around here."

"Perks of the job, Dara, perks of the job." He took a long swig and grimaced. At least it was strong. He needed a jolt if he was going to deal with Williams and his red-coated sidekicks.

The door swung open. Agent Quesnel slid into the room. "Mahoney. Late night? You look like you've been through the ringer."

He pictured the dark circles around his eyes staring back at him in the bathroom mirror. "Yeah. I had a date with Seth's journal last night."

"Sounds thrilling."

"Oh, yeah. Torture and rape. Just my type of book."

"Find anything?"

"A symbol. Strangely similar to the one on the fence, on the wrappings, and carved into the tree at the second scene. It was hand drawn in pencil, in an entry about this Sid and what he did to Seth."

"Any indication of timeline?"

"The entry with the symbol was dated 1987—so it was written earlier this year. Seems like the torture started in '75 and ended somewhere around '77."

"So this further confirms Sid did the same things to Seth he is doing to these boys. Minus the murder and preservation. But we don't have a source on these symbols." Quesnel's eyes narrowed.

"I met with Dara this morning. Still no leads on any source for these messages. I don't know...maybe this mysterious Sid doesn't exist. Did Doris and Seth concoct an imaginary monster to cover up a series of murders? Could Seth have been involved ten years ago? What about the most recent body—is Doris the killer? I don't know what to believe."

"All those theories are possible. Regardless, these messages are important. Ever seen the movie Taxi Driver?"

Mahoney shook his head.

"It was based on a best-selling novel. I met a serial killer who knew every word in that book. It was like his bible. The premise of the story was this guy—a taxi driver—cleaning up the filth in New York City. By killing people. It could be that our guy has his own bible. It's worth looking into."

The door swung open again. Sergeant Williams entered, Constable Rudson in tow. Sutton scrambled in behind them.

"Sergeant. Constable." Mahoney forced a smile. He topped up the chipped mug and tipped it toward Dara. "Time for the show." He strode to the front of the room. "Let's get moving. Sergeant Williams, thank you for joining us. Word is you had a long night."

Shadows crept under Williams' eyes, his face pale. "We did. Detective Hayes and Officer Roberts are still at the scene. Crime techs are still there too. Your medical examiner, Blackwood, she departed with the body." He swallowed, his cheeks flushed. "I guess you were right, Agent Quesnel. And your Detective Hayes, his instincts to keep digging were on track."

Agent Quesnel nodded.

Mahoney pondered the sheepish look washing over Williams' face. Swallowing down the temptation to throw in a jackass remark, Mahoney chose a polite tone. "All that matters is you found what was there. Can you fill us in?"

Williams cleared his throat. "It's almost identical to the first body. Concrete, coffin-like box. It was buried several feet under the sand, in the opposite corner of the cave. The body was in white wrappings. The medical examiner didn't want to risk exposure—said she would unwrap the body back at the morgue."

"Was there anything new? Anything different?" Quesnel probed.

"Everything was...the same. Except..." Williams waved a hand at Rudson.

Rudson walked up to the centre table, placed a briefcase down, snapped open the clasps, and raised the lid. He pulled out a large, clear-plastic bag. Rudson snapped on a pair of gloves, removed the item from within the bag, and held it up.

Between both hands, Rudson lifted a cardboard square displaying a half-sketched, half-painted face. Dramatic lips were poised as if ready to speak. High cheekbones accentuated the dramatic flare of the face. Eyes pierced every soul in the room, seeking answers. A tiger mane waved around, floating over the cover, dancing on shoulders. White scratches had torn away the colouring across the top.

Rudson said, "It appears to be an LP case. It's empty. And the title's been scratched out."

Mahoney rubbed the bristle on his chin. "It's The Doors." His mind shot to his old collection of LPs collecting dust in the bottom of his closet.

"It was placed on top of the body," Rudson said.

"Everything about the scene matched the other plot. Everything. Except this," Williams added.

Mahoney nodded.

Rudson slid the LP case back into the plastic bag and secured it shut. He set it on the table and stepped back into the red-coated corner.

"Look, Detective, I realize our approaches are different," Williams said. "But now, two bodies on the same scene. On my team's turf. I've allocated more men to the scene, at least for the next week." The wiry moustache stretched in a thin line across Williams' pursed lips.

Play nice, Bug. He's co-operating, just like you wanted. "You can keep Hayes. What else can I do?"

"Well, I propose that my team will take care of the scene. We'll do a thorough job. Document everything. I also propose that your team keep the investigation. You obviously have the knowledge for this." He scanned Mahoney's team.

Ha. Flattery. Mahoney nodded. "You've got yourself a deal, Sergeant."

"We should head back. I'll be sure to let you know if anything else arises."

"Thank you, Sergeant." Mahoney watched the two red-coats depart. Then he eyeballed his team. "Why would he leave an album cover on the body?" He walked over and stared down at the face sketched across the cardboard.

"The guy on the cover looks dramatic. His eyes...it's like they're piercing right into me," Sutton said.

Dara added, "Yeah. He looks like a deep thinker."

"Jim Morrison. He was a poet. All the tracks on this album are spoken word over musical backgrounds." Mahoney looked at Dara, then Sutton.

Sutton asked, "Not your typical blues?"

"No. I'll dig it up and have a listen. Maybe the lyrics will tell us something. I'll ask Seth too. I have to pay him a visit anyways, see what he can tell me about the symbol in his journal. Maybe he knows why Sid would leave an LP on a mummy." He took a sip of cooling coffee. "I'll catch up with Blackwood. Dara, keep searching for our ghost Sid. And for the messages and the symbol." He shook his head. "This Sid is everywhere, yet nowhere."

"The physical evidence is lacking. Unravelling his fantasy might reveal things about his behaviour that could lead us to him," Quesnel said.

Mahoney nodded. "Sutton, what's your update?"

Sutton flipped open his notebook. "I spent several hours in that Egyptian shop this morning. Weird place. I've gone through the records from '75 to '80. Most of the purchases were made in cash, no names. Nothing with Sid, Sydney, Mick. Dead end so far. No purchases of multiple sets."

Mahoney nodded. A chill crept down his neck.

"Quesnel, what about those licences?"

"I've gone through a good chunk of the print-outs Sutton brought in. Nothing yet. It'll take some time to go through those."

Mahoney rubbed the bristle on his chin. "I'm not sure that'll get us anywhere."

"He may have stayed under the radar. He could have persuaded someone to give him those supplies, without a licence," Quesnel said.

"Yeah. But it's worth a shot. So far we have all these versions of Sid and Sydney. But no person. He's everywhere, and he's nowhere," Mahoney said.

Dara frowned. "I'll keep digging."

Mahoney nodded. "Let's review the new bodies that Dara found." He walked over to the crime scene wall, plastered with two mummies. With the new one in the cave, and the ones in BC, it would soon be six.

Sutton asked, "You found three in BC?"

"Yes. Young boys. Buried in wooden boxes. Wrapped," Dara said.

"What are the timelines on those boys in BC?" Mahoney asked.

"They were discovered in..." Dara peered down her nose at her notepad though her thick glasses. "One in 1983, one in '85, and one in '86. I don't have anything about COD or time of death yet. I talked to all three jurisdictions, they all agreed to consolidate everything they have and fax it over right away. I was hoping to have all the files for this meeting." Her frown deepened.

"We can follow up with them when we're done here." *Eyes were a dead end. Symbol is a mystery. All the weird clues are leading nowhere.* "Assume our Sid exists. He leaves Caleb in the cave. Seth sees the whole thing. Sid gives Seth the beating of his life, takes off. Sid hates the cold. He wants to garden. Only place in Canada to go would be out west. He heads there. Continues to hunt. Keeps working his sick ritual. Leaves a trail of boys behind, but well hidden and scattered. Takes a while before they are found. And no connection is made. Cross-jurisdiction didn't appear required, with only one body in each zone."

Quesnel interjected, "Maybe he headed south."

"South? You might be onto something here," Mahoney said. "Seth said his Sid loved to garden. Fruit trees. And this Sid was always complaining about how cold it was here and how hard it was to grow a proper garden. Let's broaden your search on those names. Not just Canada-wide. Go south, Dara, go south. Warm places. Where people garden."

Crossing her arms and leaning against the back wall, Quesnel flashed a smile.

"Sutton, camp out here and look into the rest of those embalming chemical purchases. If you don't find anything, go to the rest of the places—except the Morrison Funeral Home. I'll take that one. Dara, Quesnel, put your heads together and take another look at that symbol. Find me a Sid."

All heads nodded.

"I'm going to try and get some solid answers out of a crazy man." Mahoney grabbed his derby and bolted through the door.

Chapter Forty-seven

Morrison Funeral Home

Gravel flew through the air as Mahoney spun a hard left into the parking lot of the Morrison Funeral Home. He hit the brakes, killed the engine, and looked up at the black, daunting building.

He'd expected something more welcoming for a place that helped families deal with loss. While waiting on the results from the crime lab regarding the flesh on the hook in Doris' basement, and while his team tried to find him a Sid, he wanted to find out about this Douglas Morrison who had purchased five sets of canopic jars, then cancelled his credit card two days later.

He slammed the creaky car door shut and strode up a concrete staircase. A large, burgundy door with an ornate, golden knocker loomed over him. He tried the handle. It wasn't locked.

A wave of dust and chill swept across his face as he entered the funeral home. He squinted down a long, dim hallway. "Hello? Anyone here?"

A slight man in a pristine, dark-blue suit appeared through a doorway. "Hello. How many I help you?"

"I'm looking for Don Morrison."

"I'm Don." Don walked briskly down the hallway, his black shoes clicking against the polished floor. The wide, high-ceilinged hallway ate his waif of a frame, like a giant throat swallowing a morsel. Don approached, extending a thin arm.

Mahoney shook Don's hand. "I'm Detective Mahoney. I was hoping to ask you some questions about your father."

"My father? You know he died, nine years ago?" Worry etched Don's face.

"Yes. A purchase was made, for canopic jars, with his credit card. Ten years ago. A set of these jars is connected to a case I'm working on."

"Canopic jars?" Don looked confused.

"Jars used in the Egyptian mummification process, to store internal organs."

Don's eyes widened. "Oh. I see. Why don't you come in and sit." Don led Mahoney down the long hallway, hooking a right back through the door he had materialized from.

Don motioned to a chair, then settled himself behind a thick, cherry-wood desk.

Mahoney sat down. A thin cushion provided less-than-adequate padding against the metal seat of the chair. *Aren't they supposed to make you comfortable in these places?*

"What was this about a purchase of…what did you call them? Canopic jars?" Don swept a lock of blond hair away from the corner of his grey eye.

Mahoney pulled a photo from his tweed coat pocket and slid it across the smooth wood of the desk. "This set of jars here, they were purchased at Caesar's Palace, a local shop. The purchase was made with your father's credit card, on February 15, 1977. Would you know anything about this purchase?"

Don rubbed the back of his neck as he stared at the photo. "No. I don't. '77?"

"Yes."

"That was the year after my dad started to deteriorate. His decline started right after my twenty-first birthday. I spent most of the following year shadowing him. He was intent on my taking over. I think I would have remembered seeing jars like these. They're quite distinctive."

"Yeah. Well, this set, in the photo, was purchased with your dad's credit card. Two days later, the card was cancelled."

"Cancelled?" Don's eyebrows slanted toward his grey eyes. "Right. I remember that. He was teaching me the business. We had to make some purchases, and he couldn't find his card. We assumed he'd lost it. By then he was having trouble keeping track of things. He'd stopped driving. We, my mother and I, made sure that one of us was always with him." Don frowned, shaking his head.

How could Douglas murder a kid, or even purchase these jars, if he was on 24/7 chaperone? The stolen card story sounded legit.

"One of you was always with him?"

"Yes."

Mahoney rubbed the bristle on his chin. "And you don't recognize these jars?"

"No."

"How long did you say you were shadowing your dad?"

"Since right after my twenty-first birthday. I started helping him when I was sixteen, but not with the business side of things. I helped him with cleaning and body preparation."

Strange. Did Don take his dad's card for a spin? Am I looking at my Sid? Mahoney stared at Don's smooth skinned face and light blond hair, nothing like the rough skinned, reddish blond, long haired Sydney. He pulled a print-out from his pocket, unfolded it, and turned it to face Don.

"Do you recognize this man?"

Don stared at the print-out of Sydney Smith's driver's licence headshot. His thin, blond eyebrows caved in around his grey eyes. "Hmmm. Not exactly. But..." Don's thin lips contorted.

"What is it?" Mahoney leaned toward the desk.

"It's odd. I've never seen this man, but...that hair...he reminds me of this kid I used to play with. It's a long story, really." Don looked up from the photo.

"I've got time." Mahoney leaned back against chair, the thin metal pressing hard against his back.

Don swallowed. "My dad opened the funeral home in 1960. I was only five at the time. But I have faint memories about moving into the house next to the big, black, scary building." He chuckled. "Anyways, when my dad opened this place, we moved into the house out back. There's a separate guest house. A couple years after we moved in, my dad rented it out to a woman. She had a son. I think he was about fourteen or fifteen. I was only about seven then, but sometimes he let me play with him. There wasn't much to do out here." Don paused.

"And?"

"And, they lived here for a while. A year or two, I guess. Then this horrible thing happened. It was late one night, I was in bed. There was a huge commotion. Police sirens and all. I went downstairs and looked outside, tried to see what was going on. My mom came in, frantic, in her night gown, waving her hands, and told me to get in my room and stay there. I think someone died. I never saw the woman or the kid again. I never looked into it when I got old enough. Taking over this place—well, I just didn't want to know." Don's thin lips turned down.

"Quite a commotion. Do you remember their names—the woman and the kid?"

"The woman…I want to say Eve, or Eva? I'm not sure. The kid, he called himself Mick. He was kind of…strange. I used to find him in my father's office, reading old books. On Thanatology."

Mahoney looked up from his notebook. "The science of the dead?"

"Yeah. My dad had them around to study up on body preservation. Not sure why a teenaged kid would want to read them."

"Recall their last name?"

Don shook his head. "No. Not sure I even knew what it was. I don't know any Sydney Smith, but, like I said, for some reason that photo you have reminds me of the kid.

Mahoney snapped his notebook shut and rubbed the bristle on his chin.

"Say, if your dad had purchased those jars, where would he keep them?"

"I guess in the storage where we prepare the bodies. But like I said, I've never seen anything like them."

"Do you use embalming fluids, to prepare the bodies?"

"Yes, we do. Standard practice."

"You mind if we take a look through your body preparation area?"

"No. Not at all." Don rose from his chair, his face calm, and free of perspiration. He turned and led Mahoney out of the black door.

Chapter Forty-eight

Hidden Symbol Memory

Seth slid his legs onto the couch. Bending his knees, he pulled his legs to his chest and wrapped his arms around them. He looked at Doctor Morin.

"It's OK, Seth. I'll be here the whole time." Doctor Morin reached out and placed her hand on Seth's shoulder. Curly brown locks slipped over her shoulders.

Seth nodded. Long, dark stands of hair slipped away from his face as he laid his head back against the arm of the leather couch.

"Detective, please, have a seat." She motioned to a chair at the foot of the couch. She took her position in a chair near Seth's head.

Mahoney removed his derby, sat down into the plush chair, and watched as the doctor proceeded.

Doctor Morin looked at Seth. "I want you to close your eyes, take a deep breath and try to relax."

Seth closed his eyes, inhaled loudly, then exhaled a long, slow breath. His arms sunk into the couch beneath him.

Doctor Morin continued her gentle guidance, "Good. Now, just listen to my voice. If you feel uncomfortable at any time, just take another deep breath. Try to keep your eyes closed until I tell you to open them. Are you OK?"

Seth nodded and whispered, "Yes."

"Seth, I am going to count to ten. When I reach ten, you will be in a deep state of relaxation. You will remain there until you hear me tell you to count to ten again."

Doctor Morin counted slowly, starting with the number one. When she reached the number ten, Seth's arms and legs lay limp against the couch. His eyes slid back and forth underneath his eyelids, as if he had reached a deep state of sleep.

Doctor Morin looked at Mahoney. "He isn't asleep, nor is he unconscious. He is in a deep state of relaxation. He will be aware of the sounds around him, and able to respond to the questions I ask him. The state he is in will allow us to access areas of his mind that he has the ability to shut out when he is awake and active. He may be able to recall memories that are actively suppressed when he is in a normal state of interaction."

Mahoney nodded.

She leaned in toward Seth. "Seth, this is Doctor Morin. You are resting comfortably in my office, the same one we meet in everyday. Nod if you understand."

Seth nodded.

"I am going to ask you a series of questions. Respond with yes or no. You can also talk freely as you wish. Do you remember the house you lived in with your mother, Doris?"

"Yes. Old house. Beat up."

"Did you live there for a long time with your mother?"

"Yes. Since I was four."

"Did anyone else live with you?"

"No. Not at first. Later."

"Who lived with you later?"

"Sid."

"Do you remember how old you were when Sid moved in?"

"Yes. Eight."

"Do you remember when Sid left?"

"Yes. Mom was mad. Mom hated him."

"How old were you when he left?"

"Twelve. My birthday. Never came back."

"Where did Sid spend his time?"

"At home. In the back, growing his garden. In the basement."

"What did Sid do in the basement?"

Seth's head shook back and forth. He remained silent.

"OK, Seth, never mind the basement. Let's just talk about Sid. How did you feel about Sid?"

Seth's teeth clenched. "Hated him. He was mean to me."

"What did he do to you?"

Sweat sprouted on Seth's forehead. His teeth clenched harder. He licked his lips. "Made me stay downstairs." Seth's Adam's apple bobbed as he swallowed.

"Seth, what was downstairs?"

Seth's nostrils flickered. His eyes darted back and forth under his eyelids. "The dungeon."

"Did he make you stay down there, when you didn't want to?"

"Yes. Mom didn't care."

"Did Sid take anyone else down there?"

"Uh-huh. Other boys. Younger boys. Said I was too old. I was overripe. I was rotten." Seth's lip quivered.

"Do you remember writing in your journal, about Sid?"

"Yes."

"Do you remember drawing a symbol when you wrote about Sid?"

"Yes."

"Do you remember what the symbol means?"

"Yes. Sid told me it was my symbol. He told me it would protect me, keep me innocent. Even after I died." His eyes rushed back and forth under his eyelids. In his hypnotic state, he sat up on the couch, curled his back over his legs, and grabbed the back of his shirt with his trembling hand. He lifted his shirt. A circular, malformed blotch of red-pink skin protruded from the center of his back. It looked like a healed burn, as if the folds of skin had attempted to reform and failed. Seth released his hold on his shirt and settled back against the couch.

"He cut it into my back. Told me he was protecting my innocence. I hated it. I burned it out." Sweat drizzled down the sides of Seth's face. His eyes darted in wild patterns under his eyelids.

"OK, Seth, stay with me for just a little longer. When you were down there, in the dungeon, with Sid, what did he do to you?"

Tears escaped from the corners of Seth's closed eyes. He squeezed his eyelids hard, his eyebrows closing in. His hands trembled. "Tied me up. Couldn't move, my hands, my feet. He tied a scarf around my neck, tight." His hand rose up to his neck, and his fingers clawed at his skin. "He made me lay on my stomach. It hurt. It hurt! No. Nooo..." Seth's hands flew to his head. His hands clawed around his scalp. He pulled strands of hair away from his head. His shoulders trembled as he wailed.

"It's OK. It's Doctor Morin. I am here. Listen to me." She counted to ten. Seth's hands flopped back onto the couch. The trembling eased, his hands and shoulders shaking. His wailing halted. "Take a deep breath, then open your eyes."

Seth's chest rose as he inhaled deeply. A swoosh of air wafted from his mouth. His eyelids opened slowly and he looked around the room.

"You are in my office. You are safe. You are here with me, and Detective Mahoney."

Seth's eyes focused as he came to. He looked at Doctor Morin. Then he turned his eyes to Mahoney. His face changed. Something washed over it. The fear in his eyes turned to fire. The hesitation in his face vanished. His lips sneered into a grin. "Detective. Did you get what you wanted?"

Mahoney looked at Doctor Morin. She motioned him forward. "Go ahead. You can ask Seth questions if you'd like."

"You gave me something to work with, yes. It's a start."

Seth stared, his eyes glued to Mahoney.

"Seth, you do realize I'm trying to help you too. If we find Sid, we can stop him," Mahoney said.

A sadistic laugh came from Seth.

Mahoney leaned over, pulled a plastic bag from his briefcase, and held it up. "Do you know anything about this?"

Seth stared at the plastic-coated album cover. The man on the front stared back. His fire hair almost came to life. Seth's mouth pressed into a thin line.

"We found another body, in the cave. Where we found your pendant. This was left. Did this belong to Sid?"

"Sid's true god. The only one he looked up to." Seth spat out the words. Anger pulsed in his eyes.

"It belonged to Sid?"

"Yes."

"Why would he leave it, in the cave?"

"A symbol of what he wanted to build."

What? "What does that mean?"

Seth stared back in silence.

Mahoney waited. "Seth. What did this album mean to Sid?"

More silence. After several moments, Mahoney stood and loomed over Seth.

"What did Sid want to build?" Mahoney glared down at Seth.

Seth glared back up at him, narrowing his eyes. "I'm done talking."

Mahoney grabbed Seth's arm. "Help me find Sid. I told you, we can stop him."

"Why do I care?" Seth spat the words back at Mahoney.

"Because, you can help me. I can stop him from hurting other kids." Heat simmered across Mahoney's face. His grip tightened on Seth's arm.

Doctor Morin stood, touching Mahoney's arm. "Detective. Please. Sit."

Mahoney let go of Seth and backed away. *We were so close.*

Seth glared, tight lipped, sitting silently.

Doctor Morin looked at Seth. "What did you mean, it was a symbol of what Sid wanted to build?"

Seth shook his head. "I don't know." He looked down.

Doctor Morin waited a moment, then continued, "You don't know, or you don't want to tell us?"

Seth's arms shook. He keeled over onto the couch in convulsions.

Doctor Morin sprung into action. She flung a drawer in her desk open, pulled out a syringe, ripped the cap off and stuck it into Seth's arm. Seth went limp against the couch.

She stood and looked at Mahoney. "I'm sorry, Detective. We'll have to end the session."

"Why? What's wrong with him?"

"It could be a response to his memories of Sid. Sometimes he becomes catatonic, sometimes he goes into convulsions."

"He could be faking the whole thing."

She met his gaze, dead on. "It's a possibility. But I'm not willing to risk his health."

Mahoney sighed. "Understood. But I'll need to finish this conversation with him."

"Of course. I think he's torn. He wants to help us, but his memories are vivid. He could be scared. He simply could be unsure about helping the man who locked him up." A slight smile touched her lips. "Be patient. We might get more out of him."

Heat built in his belly. Why did he have to play these games? He wanted information. He wanted to find Sid. "All right. Let me know when he can talk again."

"I will."

He turned and headed for the door, pulling his notebook from his pocket. He scribbled down the cryptic clues Seth had spouted. *Sid's god. The one he looked up to. Symbol of what he wanted to build.* He opened the door and walked through, wondering how long he'd have to play these games.

His phone buzzed. He grabbed it from the holster on his belt and snapped it open. "Mahoney."

"It's Quesnel. Meet me at the central library, downtown. Dara found the source of the messages. The Book of the Dead."

"Got it." Mahoney snapped his phone shut and stepped up his pace. Maybe this book would get him some solid answers on at least one of the two sadistic psychos in his life.

Chapter Forty-nine

Book of the Dead

Mahoney looked up at the large door looming in front of him.

"Geez. This looks more like a castle than a library."

Agent Quesnel snorted a laugh. "You've never been here? Dara said it's the oldest library in Calgary. The building is historic. Let's go." She reached a hand out and latched on to the ornate, golden handle.

The door creaked. He followed her in. The bright sunshine vanished. His vision blurred into a collage of rainbow splotches. He blinked hard, trying to make out the shadows weaving across the dark room. A musty odour suffocated him.

The click-clack of heels faded away from him. "Quesnel. Wait. How can you see anything in here?"

The click-clack halted. "Over here."

He followed the echo of her voice. *Geez, where the hell are we?*

The blurry spots fading, the shadows formed concrete shapes. The vast space stretched out in all directions. Long, rectangular tables lined the centre of the room. A handful of people scattered along the tables, their noses deep in the open pages of the books they had selected. One side of the room housed massive bookshelves almost touching the ceiling. The other side held a desk spanning wall to wall, separating them from a series of filing cabinets.

Summoned by clicking boots, Mahoney trailed Agent Quesnel over to the desk. He cranked his neck, scanning all directions behind the desk.

"There's nobody here," he blurted.

"There's a bell." She pointed a finger and snapped the top of a round, golden bell. A sharp *bing* rang through the air. The golden tip bounced back from the centre of the bell.

"This place is archaic." Mahoney noted.

"I spent a lot of late nights in places like this when I was doing my research."

Shuffling jolted his attention behind the desk. A woman approached them. "Could you please keep it down."

"Uh, yes, ma'am." Mahoney smirked.

"How can I help you?"

Agent Quesnel rolled her eyes. "We're looking for a copy of a specific old book. The title is The Book of the Dead. Its contents are part of the ritual for the Egyptian mummification process."

"Oh my. Well, let me have a look." The woman shuffled away toward a row of filing cabinets.

A screech pierced the silence. A chill trickled through Mahoney. His mind sprang back in time to the blackboard at the front or Mrs. Matteson's grade five class. He could see his goofball classmates scratching their nails down the day's lesson.

"Get a load of this." Agent Quesnel pointed to the librarian peering into a long, rectangular drawer leaning precariously out of one of the filing cabinets. "I think these cabinets could use a good oiling. I guess they don't have any plans for a computer inventory system."

"This could take a while."

"Yeah. Reminds me of those boxes of files at the medical institute when we were looking for Seth's straitjacket."

He whistled. "That was a long night."

The librarian looked up from the file cabinet, placed her pointer finger over her lips and glared at them. "Sssh."

"Oooh. You're going to get me in trouble, Detective."

"I'm sure you get yourself into plenty of trouble on your own."

She shrugged.

The librarian shuffled back over to them, an index card in her hand.

"Here you go. Section 23 C. The shelf on the very left, about half way down. There's a ladder hooked at the end if you need it."

Mahoney took the yellow card, then followed Agent Quesnel over to the bookshelf.

"Let me see that." She snatched the card from him. "OK. That'll be...right about here." She looked up at the shelf towering over her. "Yeah, we're gonna need that ladder."

He walked to the end of the shelf. *This is going to take a while. Better be the right book. Freakin' messages.*

He slid the ladder along the top of the shelf, resting it beside Agent Quesnel. He latched a hand around a rung. Before he could lift a leg, her boots had clicked their way halfway up the ladder.

"I got it."

"Be careful."

A *schwooop* broke through the thick quiet as she pulled a large book from its snug spot in a line of tightly packed books. Her black boots pattered down the rungs.

"Let's go over to that table in the corner. Maybe you won't get me in trouble over there."

He followed her to a smaller, round table and sat down across from her.

The book thudded against the cherry wood. *The Book of the Dead* dripped down the black cover in ornate, golden lettering.

"What the hell is this?" Mahoney asked.

She opened the black cover and scanned the page. She turned the book and slid it to the centre of the table. "Book of the Dead. English translation based on the version by E.A. Wallis Budge—240 BCE."

"BCE?"

"Yeah. Before the common era. Same as before Christ. But, less religious." She glanced his way.

Mahoney rolled his eyes.

"Looks like this one was printed in 1972. Dara said the first version of the chapters and spells were written down in 1600 BC—on papyrus. No two copies were the same—until print came along. Look at this. It's an introduction. It says here this book contains a set of negative confessions, otherwise known as declarations of innocence. Each one is an assertion of blamelessness. Together, they are a collection of spells that enable the dead to navigate the afterlife." She looked up and shook her head. "Nah. Not creepy at all."

"Let's check if our messages are in the book." He pulled a folder from his brown briefcase and set it on the table. Opening the front, he pulled out several pages. "I have committed no murder. Written on Caleb's cloth."

She flipped the pages. "Look at this. Negative confessions." She ran her finger down the yellowing paper. "It's here. Number four." She flipped more pages. "'Hail, Devourer of the Shade, who comest forth from Qernet, I have committed no murder, I have done no harm.' There's a series of symbols here at the bottom of the page. Look at this one." She pointed to a swirling vortex printed on the page.

"Matches the one we've been hunting." Mahoney shivered. "What about the message left on Benjamin's cloths." He flipped open his notebook. "'Neither have I sinned against the God of my own town.'"

More pages fluttered. She ran her red-polished finger down the text. "Here. Number forty-one."

Cold crept down Mahoney's throat. "Forty-one?"

"Yeah."

She looked back at the book. "'Hail, thou who bringest thy arm, who comest forth from the city of Ma'ati, I have not filched the food of the infant, neither have I sinned against the God of my native town'. More symbols, including our vortex."

Mahoney rubbed his temples with his fingers. "What do these messages mean? Why is he leaving them on these kids?"

"Wait." She turned back to the front of the book. "Negative confessions. Didn't the team think these messages sounded biblical, but more like a declaration that commandments had not been broken?"

Mahoney narrowed his eyes. "Yeah. You said negative confessions?"

"That's right. He's extracting a portion of each message, to leave on the wrappings. Maybe he's choosing what serves him."

"The symbol—innocence. Maybe he's declaring the innocence of the child, not of himself. I mean, he did commit murder, yet he leaves the message I have committed no murder. The symbol Seth drew in his book—he wrote about it being a mark of innocence."

"I like where you're going. He saw these children as innocent. He wanted to maintain their purity."

"How many of these declarations are in there?"

She scanned the page. "Forty-two."

"Geez. You don't think he's killed forty-two kids, do you?" He tried to swallow, but his mouth was dry as a desert.

She looked at him, pursing her lips. "It's possible."

"What's message forty-two?"

She flipped the pages toward the end of the book. "'I have not slaughtered with intent the cattle of God'. The number, the sequencing, it's organized. Meticulous. It fits with his need to control. And aids him with his inventory."

"His portfolio?"

"Yeah. Same idea. He needs to keep careful track of every one."

"Do you think this declaration of innocence has anything to do with his need to remove the eyes?"

"Good point. He removes their sight. He doesn't want them to see. What if he was trying to protect them from seeing something? Maybe he saw something. Something that changed him forever. If he saw them as innocent, it would make sense that he would want to protect them from corruption. Layer this on top, he's trying to protect them even after they're dead."

"But forty-two."

"It's a lot. I've been exposed to cases where the number was reaching toward a hundred."

"Please don't give me any examples."

She smirked. "I'll resist."

He ran his fingers through his hair, pulling at the strands. "So, where does this lead us?"

"What about the new bodies?"

"The ones from BC?"

"Yeah."

"Dara got those files in. Didn't seem to be anything about messages. I don't think the cloths were examined closely."

"Hmmm. Let's go back to the eyes. Doris is in her forties. If there is a Sid...is he the same age? What did that driver's license say?"

"He was born in 1947. He's forty."

"How do we find seriously damaged kids from thirty years ago?"

"That's a hefty search. We could talk to Dara. We wouldn't be giving her much, though." He paused. "When you called, I was leaving the Morrison

Funeral Home. Don, the son who runs it now, he said his dad—Douglas—started deteriorating, just over ten years ago. When the jars were purchased, Douglas thought he'd lost his card. He cancelled it. Some embalming fluids also went missing around the same time. They blamed it on poor Douglas' failing mind." Mahoney rubbed the bristle on his chin. "Don said something really dramatic happened about twenty-five years ago, involving the woman renting the guest suite. Police were called. Her son was there too, but he vanished."

"Hey. Aren't you chummy with that young journalist, at the paper? If something crazy happened here, maybe it was in the paper. We might be reaching, but..."

"It's too weird to ignore."

"Yeah." She looked at him.

"I'll give him a call. I need get the status on those subscriptions. Warrant should be in this afternoon." He shook his head. "I feel like we're looking for a ghost."

"I know. It's what these guys are good at. Vanishing. For a long time. But they always get caught."

"I hope you're right." A cold slithered over his gut. He imagined long-haired, tree-tattooed Sid slipping through his fingers.

Chapter Fifty

Plethora of Profiling

Mahoney walked into the small, bright room. It was quiet. The temperature was cooler than usual. A mist of citrus and pine floated toward him. The only one in the room was Dara, up at the front, attempting to tack a massive print-out to the wall. The top ends rolled down on her as she stretched her short arms out in a wide Y.

Mahoney set his cup on the long centre table. "Let me help you with that." He walked up to the front wall and pressed his hands into the top corners of the thick paper.

"Thank you, Bug." Dara pressed a bright-orange tack into the top right corner. She shuffled over to the left side and pierced the peeling wall with a blue tack.

Mahoney stepped back and scanned the poster. An enlarged map of Canada and the United States spread out over the wall. Bright orange and red colour coded chunks dotted the map. "What are the colours for?" He walked over to retrieve his Styrofoam cup.

"The orange indicates the locations of the scenes from before—the ones in BC. Red indicates the new ones—here and in Saskatchewan."

"You've got a strategy?"

"Agent Quesnel does." She walked to the centre table, grabbed a photo, then walked back to the map. She held the enlarged driver's licence photo of Sydney Smith against the wall and poked a bright red tack through the centre of his forehead. "We have some proof that Sid might exist. We also have a series of crime scenes with extremely similar bodies."

Mahoney walked up to the map. He nodded and smiled.

"You suspected that Sid could have moved somewhere warm, chasing his passion for gardening. Animals move south for the winter. This Sid, he may have his own migratory pattern."

He homed in on the orange blots. "OK. Let's assume Sid killed the kid in the cave. The crime scenes in BC insinuate that he moved west after he left Caleb in the cave."

"Precisely."

"But what about the kid from Saskatchewan? The location seems random."

"I know." She stared at the red spot on the map, fiddling with the string of sparkly beads hanging from her neck.

A cold trickled down his sweaty neck. *What are we missing here?* He sipped coffee from the spongy cup. He stared at the map. *Where are you, psycho Sid? And what have you left in your wake? Dammit.*

Chatter seeped through the door. It swung open and Sutton and Quesnel shuffled into the room.

Agent Quesnel clicked her way up to the map on the front wall. "Looks good, Dara."

"Thanks." Dara made her way to her usual back corner.

Sutton walked up to the map. "What are we looking for?"

"Sid's migratory pattern," Quesnel responded.

"OK. We've got some indication that this Sid exists." Mahoney pointed at the photo of Sydney tacked to the wall. "And we've got bodies following a timeline from here and through BC. But what about our fresh crime scene? The kid from Saskatchewan. It seems random." Mahoney shook off the lingering chill creeping up his insides. "And even if our Sid did go south...we're speculating here. And we can't search everything south of here. We need to narrow this down somehow."

What now, Bug? He scanned the room. They all stared at the colour-coded map. His back broke out in a full, cold sweat. He shifted on his feet, trying to unstick his shirt from his body. *Psycho Sid. Where the hell are you?* Pictures of young boys floated through his mind. Young, dead boys, ghastly white faces, black doll eyes staring him down. He shuddered, grabbed the Styrofoam and took a big gulp, swallowing cold, black liquid against rising bile.

"Let's narrow it down," Quesnel said. "We're focused on 'what.' Let's focus on 'why' for a bit. I've worked on some complex cases. The clues seemed bizarre and disconnected at times. Looking beyond what we assumed to be obvious impulses, and digging into the motivation behind them resulted in an answer. Adding the *why* led to the *who*." Quesnel crossed her arms and leaned against the wall.

Mahoney walked over to the investigative triangle he had drawn on the whiteboard only days earlier. "OK. How do we proceed?" He picked up a blue marker and flipped off the cap.

"My team has developed a taxonomy. A set of categories to flesh out the behaviour side of an investigation. We've found that serial killers are either organized or disorganized. This Sid, or Sydney, or whoever is killing these kids, he's organized," Quesnel said. "We've already seen the extent he goes to when he prepares the bodies. Especially the cave boys. His methodology is detailed and planned. Before, during and after the murder. Killers of this calibre tend to have a substantial amount of practice. It's likely that our Sid has practised and evolved. Probably both his script, premortem and postmortem, and his setup." Quesnel walked up to the photo of Sydney. "Whoever our killer is, I doubt the trail of bodies ends in BC. We need to examine why he killed these boys, and determine where he went." Quesnel looked at Mahoney. "Let's go through your usual review of the evidence, and we'll put a behavioural filter on it."

"I joined Seth and his doctor for a deep dive into his mind," Mahoney said. "Turns out that symbol—on Caleb and in Seth's journal—it's a sign of innocence. In his deep doctor-induced trance, Seth revealed the version Sid had carved into his back. Anyways, it added a final layer on Dara's search. The messages came from The Book of the Dead."

Sutton raised an eyebrow. "The Book of the Dead?"

"Yeah. Part of the ritualistic process associated with Egyptian mummification. Dara found us a copy at the central library. Quesnel helped me dig into it. Seems like Sid declared the innocence of the kids he killed. Maintaining their purity. Quesnel, what was it you said about him losing his own innocence?"

"I think he's mourning the loss of his own innocence," Quesnel said. "He's projecting that loss onto these kids. He thinks he's saving them by declaring their innocence and killing them before they can lose it. I think it goes further. The eyes are a critical part of his ritual. Even when he was in a hurry with Benjamin, he still took the eyes. I think he saw something as a child that took away his innocence. He's got this convoluted view that he can save these kids from losing their own innocence."

Sutton stared with wide eyes. "Wow. That is messed up."

"Convoluted. Yes." Quesnel crossed her arms and leaned against the wall. "Tell them about the funeral home."

Mahoney nodded. "A Douglas Morrison purchased five sets of canopic jars, with a credit card. He used to run Morrison Funeral Home. When he passed, in '79, his son, Don, took over. Don is very co-operative. Turns out Douglas thought he lost his credit card, right around the time the five sets of jars were purchased. He cancelled it. Don and I walked through his records from the months leading up to and following the credit card cancellation. The jars showed up. Embalming fluids also disappeared around the same time. Don and his mother blamed it on Douglas' failing memory. Don and I took a walk through his storage facility. Nothing seems off. Jars weren't there."

Sutton asked, "You don't think Don could have been involved?"

"No. Nothing about his response was suspicious. But I asked him his whereabouts on all the key dates. He was quite busy taking over the family business during '77. Had a detailed account of all the services he was running and logging in and out of the morgue."

"We need to verify it." Sutton raised an eyebrow.

"Of course. I'll give you the print-out from Don, you can double check."

Sutton nodded.

Quesnel said, "Tell them about the weird incident."

"It's nothing yet, but I'm looking into it. Apparently, Douglas rented out the guest suite beside the house at the funeral home. A woman and her kid. Something crazy happened, police were called. Don was young, doesn't know the details. But the driver's photo of Sydney triggered Don's memory of the story. Apparently, adult Sydney reminded Don of the woman's kid."

"If this incident is related, it could help us unravel any Douglas, Don, Sid connection." Quesnel clucked her tongue.

Sutton nodded.

Mahoney said, "This tells us *why* he is doing this. But not who he is. We need to layer this on somehow. I'm gonna stop by the paper, talk to that young journalist again. I wonder if there's any way to dig up old news headlines. Whatever happened, it would have to be something traumatic to shatter a young kid like that."

"Maybe. These guys can be wired differently. Something that wouldn't destroy the typical person could have altered his path forever. It's worth a shot," Quesnel said.

"Yeah." Sweat stuck to Mahoney's neck, gluing his shirt to his skin.

"Back up to Seth. Did you ask him about the album cover?" Sutton asked.

"Yeah." Mahoney shook his head. "He indirectly confirmed it belonged to Sid. He said…"—he flipped through his notebook—"he said 'Sid's true god. The only one he looked up to,' and that it was a symbol of what Sid wanted to build. I have no clue what that freakin' means. He went into convulsions. The doctor ended the session. I think I've got an old copy of the album. I'll dig it up and have a listen."

Sutton nodded.

"Wherever this guy went, I bet he left a trail of mummies in his wake. Dara, you think you can help me with some searches?" Quesnel asked.

Dara smiled. "Of course."

"Two bodies here. Three in BC. Then this one from Saskatchewan." Quesnel narrowed her eyes at the map. "Mahoney, Sutton, help us fuel our hunt for a migratory murderer. What have we learned about this killer—the behaviour stuff?"

"Sid likes to garden." Mahoney rubbed the bristles on his chin. "He had a garden in Doris' backyard. He has a fruit tree tattooed on his arm. Seth said Sid focused on how much he hated the cold. If you hated winter, where would you go?"

Quesnel pitched in, "Year-long summer."

"California," Sutton said.

"California, yes," Quesnel said. "There's a good handful of states that would provide a sunny hideout yearlong."

"Good. We need all year-long summer stakeouts." Mahoney stood and scanned the map. His gut tingled. He plunged his hand into his pants pocket and grazed the smooth, pink stone. *Focus, Bug.* "What do you do when you're smart and you need knowledge to maintain an elaborate garden and preserve bodies?"

"School. More courses," Sutton said.

"A good library," Quesnel added.

Mahoney flipped open a marker and jotted on the whiteboard. "Good. So, he needs space for a garden. Fruit trees. He needs a school—something post-secondary with his specialized topics—or a good library. Or both. And, if his basement at Doris' is any indication, he'd also need a place for a hideaway. For his less-than-acceptable habits. I wonder if he has a plot of land somewhere. But, not too far from a city, or a decent town. Somewhere he can take classes or check out books from the library." He paused and looked at the bright-blue notes on the shiny whiteboard. "What else?"

"He needs to hunt," Quesnel said. "Supports your argument for him being close to a town. He needs access to kids. Schools. Playgrounds."

"Geez." Sutton took a loud sip of his Big Gulp.

Mahoney scribbled wildly, bright-blue letters on shiny white. He turned back to the colour-coded map. "We could filter this. Take out places with winter. Then zoom in on the remaining areas. Look for towns with post-secondary schools, big libraries, and lots of playgrounds." He nodded at his own conclusion. "It's a start. Dara's computer skills will help us here."

Quesnel said, "Start with small cities, or towns on the verge of becoming a city. Bigger cities would require a lot of travel time, in and out. Look for towns that have ample acreage space on the outskirts. I'll bet he's somewhere with enough population to warrant the services he needs, but a place that tends to stay under the radar. And where living on the outskirts, off the grid, is common. He'd blend in better."

"And supplies. He needs supplies," Sutton said. "To preserve the bodies."

Quesnel said, "Of course. His fantasy involves this mummification process. He's not going to deviate from that. Not when he has a dedicated space to live it out to the fullest. He'll need the embalming fluids, canopic jars, wraps, and other odds and ends."

Mahoney said, "That'll be a big filter on potential locations."

Quesnel said, "It's a start. We'll keep working, add more to the filtering. Dara, I'll stick around, work with you on this. I'll reach out to my colleagues. If this killer did migrate to warmer pastures, he might have left us a trail of bodies."

Sutton asked, "Why wouldn't we have heard about this before, if there are a bunch of bodies?"

"They could be spread out. Serial killers can be smart. I've seen a few cases where the remains were scattered in multiple jurisdictions. Dara, didn't you say the three scenes in BC were in different jurisdictions?"

Dara nodded.

"It takes longer to connect the dots, if any link is made at all." Quesnel paused, narrowing her eyes at the map. "Also, the bodies could be in remote places. There's a lot of open space, parks, mountains, forests providing the perfect place to hide bodies."

"OK." Mahoney snapped the cap on the marker. "Sutton—licences. Let's make sure there aren't any other suspicious missing supplies. I'll get to the paper, then the album. Dara, Quesnel—you hunt for bodies and places without winter. Let's try and dig up more evidence."

Mahoney scanned the room. A cold chill crawled spiny fingers up his insides. They were grasping. He could feel Sid slipping through his fingers. He wanted to find him. He watched his team file out of the room, then turned and looked back at the crime scene wall. The bodies were stacking up. Cold fear trickled through him. *What if we never find Sid? How many kids would there be?* He gritted his teeth and looked into Caleb's eyes. No. He couldn't let that happen. Heat flushed away the chill. His gut vibrated. No. He wouldn't let Sid slither away.

Chapter Fifty-one

Newspaper

Mahoney burst through the door and stomped into the dimly lit office of the Calgary Chronicle. The only light on was the one he'd hoped for. He trudged over to the desk of the young journalist, hoping the kid had come through for him.

The young man looked up from his computer, his small desk lamp glowing over his face. He stood, adjusting his belt. "Detective. You're back." The kid glanced around the room, swallowing as he nervously perused the office space.

"I'm back. I got the warrant. Tell me I can leave here with a list of subscriptions."

The young man smiled. His shoulders dropped. "Yes. I dug up the list for you, last night, and whenever I could between work today."

"Let's see it."

The kid smiled awkwardly. "The warrant first, please."

Mahoney smirked. "Sure, kid." He slipped his hand into the pocket inside his tweed coat and pulled out a stack of papers. He sifted through them and produced the warrant, handing it to the kid.

The journalist unfolded it and scanned the paper slowly from top to bottom.

"You know what you're looking for?" Mahoney asked.

The journalist ignored him, continuing to eyeball the paper. When he reached the bottom, he looked up. "Yeah. I do. I've seen warrants before."

Mahoney chuckled to himself. "All right then. How about that list?'

"Of course." The journalist sat back down onto the chair and leaned toward his computer. He tapped quickly over the keys of the keyboard, causing a series of bright-green letters to flash in full sentences down the black screen.

The kid reminded him of Dara.

The young journalist looked up from his computer search and met Mahoney's gaze. "Here." He pointed to the screen.

A long list of names filed down the page in neon lime.

"This is just the first page. We have tens of thousands of subscribers within the city. And a surprising number outside of the city. Even more surprising is how many there are out of country."

"I need a printed copy."

"Do you want it filtered? I mean, I could organize it for you, by city, province, state, that sort of thing. Or by name."

"Let's start with name. Sid or Sydney. Maybe Smith, but I'm not sure."

"Sure thing." The journalist typed away. The list vanished, then reappeared, much smaller. "There's only about a dozen by that name. Sid or Sydney. They're all local. None have the last name Smith."

"OK, print that. Then we'll look by location."

"You got it." The journalist clicked at the keys. A zipping noise a few desks over erupted through the quiet space.

"How else should we filter?"

Mahoney scratched at his chin.

Bang. A door closed. A stout man stomped into the room. "What the hell is this?"

Mahoney looked at the intruder. It was Editor-in-Chief Hammington. Their meeting hadn't gone so smoothly the other day.

"Mr. Hammington, I'm Detective Mahoney."

"I know who the hell you are. What are you doing here?'

"Delivering the warrant, for the subscriptions."

"Let me see."

The journalist stood and handed the crumpled warrant to Mr. Hammington.

The editor-in-chief snatched it, causing it to tear along the side. "Let's see here." He scanned down the page. Warrant in hand, he stomped toward his office at the head of the space, facing the large window. "Fine then, Detective. We'll be in touch."

The journalist waved his hands. "But Mr. Hammington, I have the list here, I was just going through it with the detective."

Mr. Hammington spun his stout body on one heel and glared at them. "I'll have the warrant reviewed by my legal team. It is my duty to do due diligence with respect to the privacy of the subscribers to my paper. *If* this is all in order, then you'll get your list," he spat the words out, his face turning red. "So, *Detective,* I will be in touch." He looked at the journalist. "And you, I suggest you pipe down. What are you doing here so late anyways?"

"Finishing up the morning run."

"Fine. Then finish up." He turned, walked into his office and slammed the door.

The kid looked up from his desk, worry wrinkling his young face.

"Dammit. OK, kid, you heard your boss. You've still got my card?"

"Yeah."

"If you feel like sharing after he's left, give me call."

The kid smiled. "Sure thing."

Mahoney stomped back to the elevator. *Dammit. This Hammington is really getting on my nerves.* He took a deep breath. *But the kid, yeah, he'll call me later.*

Chapter Fifty-two
Playdate with Timmy

It was time to get Timmy. Jud walked over to Timmy's concrete bed where he'd already placed the lifting machine. He slid the sharp end of a metal hook into the ring on one end of the concrete lid. Walking to the other end of the rectangular box, he repeated the process. Two metal hooks, two rings, both ready to go. He stepped away from the box. Grasping the handle of the lever, he began pulling it, focusing intensely on the lid, eyes darting back and forth between the two hooks. The last thing he wanted was any damage to Timmy's carefully carpentered box. It had taken him several months to finish this one. Timmy was special. He deserved an intricately designed home.

Pulling the lever slowly, eyes continuing to watch as the hooks inched their way upwards, pulling the lid away from the box, he held his breath. This was always the riskiest part of the process.

The lid lifted away, the contents of the box revealing themselves. At the first sight of white cloth, an electric buzz surged through him. Moving his gloved hand to the square-shaped control panel next to the crank, Jud pushed down on a circular button with his pointer finger. The machine whirred. The hooks jolted the slab, then moved it smoothly away from the box. Releasing his finger, he pushed the next button in the assembly line. The lid lowered, gently landing on the hard-packed dirt floor. Powering down the machine, Jud slithered toward the box. He stared down at the small, motionless figure, wrapped in lengths of what had once been clean, white cloth. The wrappings were now tinged with yellow.

Rubbing his gloved hands together, Jud licked his lips, looking down at his boy-mummy.

Timmy. My special friend.

His doll. A prized item in his growing collection. "Hello, Timmy. How are you, my special friend?"

Eerie whispers echoed through the room. *"Jud. I'm well. Thank you for coming to play with me."*

"Of course, Timmy. My special friend." He rubbed his gloved hands together.

Jud scanned Timmy, slowly, from head to toe. All three feet, four inches of him. "I see your wrappings are well intact. That's good. Looks like we did a good job when we tucked you away in bed, now, didn't we? Yes, well. That's good."

Jud gingerly picked up the end of a wrapping resting on Timmy's forehead, between his thumb and forefinger. He ever so gently pulled at the wrapping. It gave, following the lead of Jud's fingers. Jud pulled, wrapping the cloth into a ball as he made his way around Timmy's head. Pausing to gently lift Timmy's head with one hand, pulling the wrapping with the other, he weaved the cloth away, making several rounds until little Timmy began to appear.

"Oh, there you are."

A whisper echoed again. *"Here I am."*

Blood rushed down Jud's body, pumping through his veins. His arms tingling, beads of sweat forming on his face, he exhaled loudly. "Oh, Timmy. The mere site of you brings me to life. It's so hard to find a good friend. Someone who won't hurt me."

Swallowing hard, he calmed himself and focused on his work.

"We must be patient now. Not till we're both ready."

Jud turned all his attention to the slow process of unwrapping his special friend. As the yellowing strips of cloth were removed, Timmy's doll eyes revealed themselves. Jud stared into the black nothing eyes, polished and cleaned the last time they had played together. They were special gems that Jud had placed in little Timmy's eye sockets when they first met. Obsidian windows for Timmy to see through, shielding him from the evils of the earth so he would remain pure and innocent. Preventing him from seeing the gruesome acts of the world that could decay his innocent soul.

"You'll never be a rotten piece of fruit like I am. No. You are preserved. Your innocence is intact."

Jud removed one of his gloves. He caressed Timmy's cheek with his fingers. "Oh Timmy, how I've missed you." Heat flushed through Jud. His arms swelled with warmth. The room whirled around him. "Now, just wait. Not yet."

Another whisper echoed off the dirt walls. "Not yet."

Jud snipped away the cloth, releasing the substantial ball that had formed. Pulling at the end still attached to Timmy, he continued the unwrapping process, exposing Timmy's chest, shoulders, arms and torso. Jud's shoulders relaxed as he peered at Timmy's skin.

"Looks like you're still in good shape. We still have time together. That's good." Jud's eyes snaked their way down Timmy's body, fixating on his waxy skin. Jud removed his other glove.

Grabbing a bottle, he squeezed a dollop of oil into his palm. Rubbing his hands together, he worked the oil into circles. He reached out his arms, finding Timmy's soft skin with his hands. Jud's body shivered.

"You always loved me." Closing his eyes, he massaged Timmy, rubbing the oil over his chest, down his body, toward his abdomen. His eyes snapped open. "Oh, Timmy. Your innocence overcomes me. I can only wish I were as pure as you."

Caressing Timmy with his bare hands, the room spun around him. The blood rushed from his head, down his body. His chest slick with sweat, he licked his lips.

"You have everything I have lost. You are my salvation."

Swallowing hard, he gasped for air. He shuddered. His entire body relaxed. The room slowed around him as his eyes opened. *Timmy. So innocent.* Timmy's ether floated through the air over to him. He let the innocent molecules of Timmy's being wash over him, transforming his own rotten ions into pure particles.

Why did she steal my innocence? I was just a boy. No. No bad thoughts right now. Just Timmy. Just his pure, delicious core, seeping into mine, making me whole again.

"Thank you. For making me whole again. I have taken from you. Now I must give back."

A young voice whispered through the cave, *"You're welcome, Jud."*

"I will tuck you in for the night. I will come back tomorrow. We shall play together again."

"Good night, Jud."

Chapter Fifty-three

The Roxy

Mahoney walked up to the main entrance. Pausing at the end of the red-carpeted walkway, he looked toward the door. A thick man with a buzzcut stood at the doorway, arms bulging, eyes darting along the sidewalk. *What the hell have I gotten myself into.* Looking down at his freshly polished, black dress shoes, he thought about turning around. Candy lips dripped across his mind. The smell of sweet strawberry wove through his nose. *Dammit.* He proceeded toward the doorman.

"Good evening, sir." A thick arm extended, opening a large, red door with a golden handle.

"Good evening." Mahoney slipped through the red door. The dimly lit room glowed orange-red. Small tables were sprinkled around the front entrance. Well-dressed people stood at the round tables, sipping fancy cocktails. A constant hum buzzed through the room as people chattered over the acoustic guitar music floating from an undisclosed location.

"Can I help you, sir?" a woman in a sparkly, flapper-style dress asked.

"Oh, yes. I'm meeting someone here."

"Very good, sir. Do you know if the rest of your party has already arrived?"

"I'm not sure." His eyes darted around the room, searching tables and booths along the walls. Red-velvet lamps lit his way. His eye caught a flash of blonde curls and candy lips. "Oh, I believe that's her over there."

"Very well. Enjoy your evening, sir."

"Thank you." Removing his tweed herringbone overcoat, he hung it over his arm. Adjusting his corduroy jacket, he rolled his shoulders back. *OK, Bug, not exactly what you were expecting. It's fine.*

Walking across the room, he scanned the eclectic crowd. Not exactly business attire, but there was a certain class to the way these people dressed. No pint glasses.

Martinis, champagne and concoctions served in crystal glassware settled on the tables he passed by. The conversations appeared civilized. The room was buzzing, but it wasn't loud. An intimate vibe clung to the air.

Approaching a booth along the back wall, he slid right up without hesitation.

She spotted him before he arrived. "Mr. Detective." Slipping from the booth, she walked right up to him and gave him a quick hug.

Her ample breasts pushed against his chest. His back tensed. "Hello, Sasha."

Shooting him the usual wide smile, her white teeth gleamed against candy-pink lipstick. She looked entirely different than the image she portrayed at *LiveWire*. A simple black dress clung to her curves, long sleeves weaving down her arms, a high neck winding around her throat. Her hair was intricately woven around her head, a plethora of red barrettes sparkling against her blonde hair. Had he misread her? He was sure she was a sweet treat, a simple distraction, young and fun, not wanting anything serious.

"You look lovely."

Blushing, she looked down at her dress. "Yeah, well, I realize this is a tad different than my getup at the bar." Looking him in the eye, she smiled again. "Thank you. Detective, please join me." She waved an arm over to the booth.

Mahoney slid into the booth as encouraged. Sasha slid in next to him, her hip close to his. An intoxicating blend of strawberries and vodka drifted from her. *Geez, Bug. Some profiler you are. You had her pegged as a rocker chick.*

A waitress slid up to the table. "Drinks, anyone?"

Sasha replied, "I'll have a French martini, please." Turning to him, she inquired, "Ginger ale for you?" Her eyebrow raised playfully.

"I'll have an old fashioned, please. Maker's Mark."

"Very good." The waitress departed.

Sasha turned to Mahoney and smiled. "Look, I know this is a little different from the dive joint, I hope it's OK for you."

"Yeah. It's swell."

"Working at *LiveWire* is a rush. I work hard, management treats me well, I'm guaranteed my hours, and I don't get harassed. The crowd may be weird, but they're there for the music. Not like other places where the guys are creepy. And the tips are good. But, this place, well, look at it. I feel like I'm in Paris or something. You know, somewhere that I'll never go but that I dream of, and I can pretend for a night I'm there."

"Sounds nice."

The waitress placed their drinks on the table.

"Thank you." Mahoney eyeballed his drink. Crystal glass. Single, square cube. Promising. Taking a swig, he closed his eyes and savoured the sweet mix of bourbon, simple sugars and dark cherry.

"Good drink?"

"I'm impressed."

"You look like a guy who knows his bourbon."

"Yeah, I guess I do."

"But you stick to ginger ale?"

"When I'm on an active case, I gotta keep my head clear." A white face with black, glassy eyes intruded his thoughts. *What about the case you're on now, Bug? Did you forget about that?*

"Hmmm. So bourbon's your treat?"

Looking at her glossy, pink lips, he met her eyes with his own. "You could say that. Among other things."

Giggling, she touched his arm. The warmth of her fingers seeped through the thick corduroy. His stomach seized. He took a big swig of bourbon. Her candy lips dipped into the translucent pink drink, shining fluorescent through the martini glass. A bright-red cherry rolled down the inside of the glass, landing against her mouth. She slipped the cherry onto her tongue, sliding it between her lips. Placing the glass down on the table, she rolled the cherry around in her mouth.

Moving along the booth, closer to him, her hip rubbed against his. His leg tingled with bursts of electric energy.

She played with the cherry stem between her lips. Pulling the stem from her mouth, she chewed the fruit. Her lips dipped into the martini for another sip. "You know, Mr. Detective, since this is your night off, we could have a little fun."

Geez, Bug. What are you up to? "What do you have in mind?"

"Let's start by getting this coat out of the way." She pulled at his corduroy sleeve, slipped the jacket around his back, and slid it off his other arm. Tilting her head to his almost empty glass, she shoved the jacket aside. "And maybe another round. See where it leads us."

She's so playful. But dressed all fancy. Is she serious? Or is she just a treat? "Sounds nice." He sunk back into the high cushion of the booth surrounding the round table. *She's young, free, won't expect anything you can't give.* Scanning the classy joint again, his gut told him otherwise.

"Another round?" the waitress sweetly inquired.

He looked at Sasha, her porcelain skin, her hot-pink lips, her wide smile. "Why not?"

"Well, that's a great start." Sasha cuddled closer to him.

Ignoring the droplets of sweat bursting over his neck and down his back, he smiled back at her. Little hands of instinct clawed at his gut. He ignored them and focused on her pink lips and forced himself to speak. "Like you said, just another round. We can let the evening guide us where it wants."

Mahoney cozied up to Sasha. Her lips summoned him like sweet cotton candy beckoning a kid at a fair. Plumes of strawberry floated from her, filling his nose and clouding his mind. Touching cold crystal with his lips, the sweet bourbon lingered on his tongue then burned his throat. Numbness wove through his arms and legs. The glowing red of the velvet lampshades dotting the room pulsed. Images swirled through his mind. Shiny black tassels flapped. White ghost faces moved their bloody lips.

There are six boys dead, Bug. And how many are out there? Would he ever find out? Black, glassy eyes stared at him, their haunting gaze piercing into him. How many mummy children will there be? *Are you smart enough, Bug, to catch this killer?*

He lifted the heavy crystal again and tossed back the rest of the amber liquid. The large rectangular ice cube clanked against the glass as he set it down. Sasha was talking. Her voice trickled into his reverie. The waitress set down their second round. He immediately lifted the glass to his lips. He focused on Sasha, nodding in response to her smooth voice.

He thought of his wife. Well, he couldn't call her that anymore. He hated the term *ex.* It was so final. The scent of lavender hit him. A blue scarf floated through his mind. Strawberry curls followed. It's all he had left of her. He'd lost her long before she walked through the front door of the cozy cottage in the woods that he had plowed all his savings into. She'd walked through and never came back. He'd chosen a dead body over her one too many times. No. More than that. Dozens of times too many. He couldn't stop himself. He froze every time, even as he watched those blue scarves slip through that cottage door.

Well, you got what ya wanted, didn't you, Bug? Now it's just you and your corpses.

Cotton-candy lips moving toward him pulled him back to the glowing red room. Sticky sweet pressed against his cheek. He breathed her in. He wanted to taste this fresh strawberry. Every part of it. He nodded and smiled, letting his eyes wander over her tight dress. *She's just a treat. A distraction. She won't expect anything more from you.* He stared at the oval opening in her high-collared dress, resting his eyes on the caramel-coloured circle on the inside of her milky left breast.

She giggled, running her finger down the side of his cheek. "It's a birthmark."

He met her gaze.

"There you are. You were far away."

"Yeah. Sorry. I'm all yours." He downed another swig of bourbon, welcoming the haziness descending over his mind.

"Good. We'll finish the next round. Then head back to my place." Her warm candy breath tickled his cheek. Her hand slid down his chest, onto his thigh, then she trickled her fingers over the inside of his leg.

Tingling electricity vibrated through his gut and up his arms. *It's fine. She's young. Free. She's just using you, old man.* Her candy lips found his. She slid her sweet tongue into his mouth and ran it along his lip. Hot blood pumped through his veins.

Clinking of glass against the table jolted him. Sasha slid away. The waitress vanished without a word. Sasha pushed his drink toward him. Freshly burned citrus mixed with sugar and cherry beckoned him. Sweet bourbon stung his throat. The red glow of the room engulfed him. He let go. Of every ghost face. The smell of lavender. And the clues hounding his brain.

All he could think of was the sweet taste of strawberry.

Chapter Fifty-Four

Blow Up My Insides

Mahoney shoved the front door of his apartment open and tossed his keys toward the wobbly, wooden table. They clanked as they hit the side of a glass dish. A sharp, red chip flew through the air. He yanked his shoes off and trudged to his bedroom.

He thought about Sasha. He'd snuck out of her place, quietly. But not without a last glance. The black lace hugging her hips, her ample, milky ass cheeks concealing her g-string. Her head tilted, luxurious blonde waves of hair spilling over her pink, satin sheets. The cloud of strawberry emanating from her every pore. A blue scarf floated through his mind, concealing his image of Sasha. *Bug. You'll never replace her.* He wasn't trying to. He'd never open up to another woman the way he'd given himself to his wife. *You're sick. Using a young rocker chick for kicks.*

He stripped down to his underwear and shuffled over to the bathroom. He looked at himself in the mirror. *You're nothing but a fuckin' shell, old man.* The room spun. He closed his eyes and leaned over the sink.

A beach shimmered through his thoughts. Stella. His daughter. She stood at the water's edge, pleading with her eyes for him to join her. He took a step over the warm sand. A carcass flung itself in his path. White strips of cloth unravelled as the skeleton crawled over the sand. A young boy's fear-stricken face looked at him. The boy's body ripped apart into scraps, his flesh tearing, blood drenching the white cloths. The boy's fingers dug into the wet sand, grasping desperately, pulling his hands, his arms, his body, away from the horrific torture tearing him to pieces. The boy's mouth stretched wide open and screams escaped, vibrating over the sound of the crashing waves, calling for help. Mahoney scanned the beach frantically. He was the only one there. He was the only one who could help this boy.

He snapped his eyes open and stared into the mirror. *You chose dead boys over your daughter. You put the corpses on hold for bourbon and sex. So, what? Babes and bourbon are more important than Stella?* Why had he let himself drown the images of dead boys with mere pleasures. He should be finding Sid. He should be putting an end to this case. He should be on a plane to see Stella. His stomach swirled. He imagined pulling the ring out of a grenade, sliding it down his throat and blowing up his insides.

The booze washed over him, spinning his head. He'd lost count after the fourth bourbon. He leaned over the sink, turned on the faucet and splashed water over his face. Nausea pulsed in his stomach. A sweaty heat broke out over his face, neck and chest. He wobbled over to the toilet and fell to his knees.

Plunging his face toward the cold porcelain, he willed the torrent of booze, strawberry perfume, and candy-floss kisses to exit his body in one foul swoop. Bile rose up his throat. A wave of hot, sour vomit followed. He heaved and heaved, expelling all the poison. Every last drop. He crumpled to the floor in a heap, resting his hot cheek against the cold tile.

He closed his eyes and mumbled meekly, "You thought you could drown out all those little mummies and doll eyes, huh?" A demented laugh gurgled in his throat. "You think bourbon and babes can take away the sting of your failures, huh, *Bug?*"

He rolled over onto his knees and stood slowly. Walking back to the sink, he leaned against the porcelain and turned the tap on. Scooping several handfuls of cold water into his mouth, he swished it back and forth. Chunks of half-digested food scraped against his cheeks.

He spat and turned his eyes up to the mirror. He stared at himself. Dark, bloated skin bulged under his eyes. Wrinkles snaked over his forehead and around his mouth. He ran his fingers through his hair. "Ha. Scour the facts. Analyze the behaviour. You can't catch this sly Sid. He's too smart for you." He shook his head. "Then you've failed the dead kids and your daughter."

He turned and walked over to his bed. Letting go of every pair of doll eyes, every message clinging to a cloth, every little body wrapped for eternity, he let himself fall onto the bed with a hard thump. The soft mattress caved in the middle as he sunk into the crumpled sheets.

MUMMY
HUNT

Chapter Fifty-Five

Bourbon-Coated Severed Garden

Mahoney opened one eye halfway. The room was dark and quiet. A steady thumping worked its way through his head, reaching around to the base of his neck. Candy-floss lips popped into his mind. Blonde hair flowed over a black dress. *Sasha. I had drinks with Sasha.*

His mind lunged forward through the events of the evening. The bar dotted with red velour lamps. Sasha sipping on pink cocktails with cherries. And the bourbon. *Oh god.* The bourbon. How many did he have?

Flashes of black lace slipped through his mind, followed by pink cushions and satin sheets. He'd gone to Sasha's place. Right.

His mind lunged further forward, back to his apartment. He saw himself facing his ragged reflection in his bathroom mirror. His mind spun. He relived the moments, the bathroom swirling around him, his knees buckling, hitting the cold tiles, and his head plunging into the white porcelain.

Get yourself together, old man.

The cracked radio clock blinked red numbers at him. 4:17 a.m. He lay back down against the pillow. The ceiling was still. His head throbbed. His body ached. Sleep wouldn't be coming back.

Sliding his feet onto the rug, he wrapped his bathrobe around him and shuffled into the kitchen. The light buzzed as he flicked the switch. The tiny space pulsed an eerie glow. The rest of the city was still sleeping. He shuffled over to the cupboard and proceeded to make a cup of dark roast. As it percolated, he poured an ample glass of cold water and chugged the whole thing in one shot. The cold rushed through him, flushing out the remnants of the night.

The aroma of dark roast wafting through the room, he left the coffee to perk and walked over to a small, spare room. It had become a place to store things. The closet door creaked as he opened it. He looked down at the brown-stained rug, housing a collection of items under a thick coat of dust. He eyeballed the selection, finding what he was looking for.

He walked over to a box labelled LPs and pulled the filthy lid off the box, dropping it onto the rug. He shuffled through them, looking for the fire-haired man with piercing eyes. The man came into view. He slid the LP from the box and stared into the man's eyes. He hadn't listened to this one in a long time. The same album that Sid left buried with a boy wrapped like a mummy. How was it that psycho Sid had the same musical taste as he did? Or was it the other way around? Did he have the same taste as Sid? He shuddered at the thought.

He rummaged around in the back of the closet until he found the box marked "Electronics." Well, they weren't exactly *electronics* by today's standards, but they had been...ten years ago. He lifted the box, placed it on the rug, wiped the coat of dust off with his hand, laid the LP on top, then carried the box and LP out to the living space.

The small room now filled with spice and smoke aromas, he breathed it in. Forcing the delicious smell to settle against his raging stomach, he placed the box in the middle of the room then walked to the kitchen to pour a cup of coffee. Passing up the brilliant blue with yellow words of lies, he chose a plain, black mug. The coffee reached for his nose as he poured. He took a long, slow slip, then turned to face his task.

The box still held all of the contents required. Within minutes, he'd set up the record player and had the black disc set atop. The needled handle rested on his finger. Flipping the on switch, he held his breath. The table turned. He dropped the needle.

A dark, bluesy riff immediately wiped through the room. The deep voice of a dark poet rode along the air waves, reaching long fingers of sound toward his ears. He sat down into the cavern worn into his couch, lifted the coffee cup, and leaned back against the tattered cushion. Closing his eyes, he willed his mind to absorb the words, seeking the answer to who Sid was, what he wanted, and where he was.

The voice spoke to him, creating fuzzy images in his whirling mind. A baby appeared, wrapped in red sparkling rubies. A garden sprouted, plants being plowed by dark figures. He sipped his coffee and listened to the words. The song ended. There was nothing new in these words. The words that made sense didn't tell him anything. It was obvious Sid had a garden. Somewhere. The rest of the lyrics were broken fragments of meaning.

He swallowed back the rest of the coffee in his mug, then walked over to the record player. He lifted the needle and set it down at the beginning of the song. Shuffling back over to the couch, he plunked down again, willing the words to lead him to Sid.

Chapter Fifty-six
Scrapbook of Mummies

Mahoney flicked the switch. The fluorescent tubes buzzed to life, electrifying his eyes. The empty room engulfed him in a cloud of silence. Tossing his tweed coat, derby and tattered brown briefcase onto the long table running down the centre of the room, he walked over to the cream-coloured crime scene wall.

A massive collage of crime scenes plastered the chipping paint. Like a memory book of bad dreams, each page transformed a young glowing child into a lifeless, dehydrated skeleton. Scanning the collage of gruesome scenes, Mahoney's eyes stung, a freeze of fear immobilizing his limbs. Pressure built in his brain as his scalp tightened. His shoulders tingled.

Six small faces stared back at him. His team had migrated south, across the border, looking for more child mummies. They'd been right.

The investigation had already uncovered six small bodies—two in the cave, the fresh one in the park, and three in BC. The wall recreated six additional crime scenes. *Six.* His gut told him they weren't done digging. *A dozen bodies.* He swallowed hard, stabilizing the remnants of his late night churning in his stomach. Glancing at the white-faced clock glaring at him from the front of the room, he turned back to the crime scenes. Focusing on the photos, he scoured the gruesome remains of each young child for the slightest clue.

Frick. This guy is sick. Real sick. He won't quit. Someone has to stop him. He tugged at his collar, peeling it from the coat of sweat drizzling down his neck. He stepped closer to the wall, peering at the pictures of the first scene.

Max Simmons. 12 years old. Chocolate-brown hair. Last seen April 5, 1977. Found on April 12, 1983. Staring into Max's dark pupils, a shiver ran down Mahoney's arms. Shaking it off, he moved his gaze to the next photo. A small figure lay, wrapped in white cloths stained with dark brown-and-green streaks, in a plot dug into the soil. The plot was located deep in the forest of Olympic

National park, surrounded by bright-green ferns. It lay at the base of a spongey moss-covered tree trunk.

Mahoney's gaze landed on the unwrapped remains of Max's body. His gut tingled. He stared at a skeletal framework covered in paper-thin brown patches of skin. Glassy, black spheres stared back from Max's eye sockets. Mahoney's gaze was glued to the non-eyes. He forced them away, looking at the page of facts plastered beside the photos of Max's crime scene.

Sliding his feet along the rough, torn carpet, he moved to the next collage. He took a long sip of lukewarm coffee, then stared at a photo of the next child in line.

Lucas Johnson. 12 years old. Red hair and a spattering of freckles. Last seen May 13, 1977. Found June 6, 1982. Snapping his gaze to the next photo, he stared at Lucas, nothing more than a small mummy, lying in an earth plot. The plot had been dug directly beneath a massive fir tree. Moving his eyes along the line of photos, the view from the bottom of the plot opened up onto a vast lake. The white-and-blue peak of Mount Hood reflected off the clear water. A calming energy seeped through him. Forcing his eyes to move along the series of photos, an ice wave cut through his gut. He stared at young Lucas, naked, lying on a steel slab. More thin sheets of skin clung to bones. Another pair of non-eyes stared back at him.

He swallowed. Small droplets of moisture scraped down his throat. Shuffling along the rough carpet, his toe caught on a rip. He stepped over it and faced the next boy.

Oliver Miller. Twelve years old. Sun-bleached hair and bright-blue eyes. Buried in the soil at the top of Crater Lake, under a fir tree overlooking the crater, once active with hot lava, now housing a lake of the clearest water on earth. He went missing June 23, 1977. He was found August 12, 1984.

Mahoney shot his gaze to the next body.

Liam Winston. Ten years old. Dark hair and eyes. Pale complexion. Buried six feet into the soft soil at the top of a climb covered in a thick forest of firs in Six Rivers National Forest. He went missing August 11, 1977. Found on July 7, 1986, he was at the end of an offshoot from the main path. Less travelled. Untouched for some time.

Mahoney shuffled along the tattered carpet, forcing his gaze onto the next set of photos.

Jordan Thompson. Ten years old. Sandy-blond hair, creamy complexion. Last seen October 6, 1977. Found July 5, 1985. The photos revealed a fifth mummy, buried deep in the earth at Yosemite Falls. Mahoney stared at a massive waterfall plunging over a cliff into a spray of white.

He moved his eyes to the next photo, a skeletal frame covered in brown, paper-thin skin, staring back at him with black void eyes.

A chill crept up Mahoney's back. He swallowed a gulp of cold coffee and shook off the eerie cold creeping through him. His breakfast swam in a violent revolt.

Darting his eyes to the last collage on the wall, he stared at six-year-old Henry Jones, strawberry-blond curls framing his face. *Six years old.* He took a big sip of cold coffee, trying to wash away the pins pricking up his insides. *Geez. Six years.* Shaking his head, he willed his mind to stay clear. Of the half-dozen small mummies plastered to the crime scene wall, this was the only one of which the cloths had been examined under a high magnification, revealing the message, *"I have not burned with rage."* Negative confession number twenty-five in The Book of the Dead. *Twenty-five.* Did that mean there had been twenty-four bodies before Henry?

He forced himself to focus on the photos of the scene where young Henry was found. Staring at the smallest mummy in the line up, his eyes explored the surroundings. *This is different.* The plot was dug into brown sandy earth, out in the open of a vast, barren wilderness. The landscape was dotted with scraggly bushes, red rocks, and dry, brownish grass. The body had been laid to rest in a barren park, on the fringe of being desert. Hovering over the abandoned boy, a two-pronged tree sprung. The kind of tree that looked like it didn't belong anywhere. One of the prongs broke off into its own forked branch. Tufts of green spikes shot from the tops of each branch, like prickly pom poms.

Strange. All these scenes involved forests. Big trees. Lush green. And then this one. The youngest boy. The most barren scene.

Mahoney rubbed his bristly chin, stepping closer to the desert scene. Squinting, he peered at the strange tree. He stood back from the wall and rescanned the series of images. Forests dissolved into open, barren desert. *Is this his migratory pattern?*

Stepping to the end of the scrapbook, he narrowed his eyes and looked hard at the strange tree perched in the desert scene. He moved his gaze over the series of pictures, the display forcing him to relive the fate of six-year-old Henry

Jones. A photo snatched his attention. He halted, staring at a collection of items displayed over the dry, brown dirt. Leaning close to the photo, his suspicions were confirmed. A small jar, reminiscent of the bizarre pottery creations he'd been hunting down, sat in the middle of the crime scene in the desert park. Scanning the six crime scenes again, he found similar photos of jars at each of the three scenes in California. He pulled the three photos from the wall and set them on the table running down the centre of the room.

Mahoney took a deep breath, closing his eyes, then stepped back up to the half dozen crime scenes. He reread the message magnified in the photo of the cloths wrapped around Henry. *I have not burned with rage.* It was hard to believe that a killer who could do this to young boys didn't have rage burning within. Rescanning the collages, he found pictures of the cloths wrapped around the other five boys. He wondered if they too had messages left behind with them.

Jumping over to the centre table, he fished his cell phone from his briefcase. Pushing the buttons in a hurry, he held the phone up to his ear.

"Blackwood. It's Mahoney. We've found a series of crime scenes, from a while back. I need someone with access to powerful magnification."

"You called the right girl."

"I'm gonna send you a series of photos. Can you zoom in, identify anything that looks like a canopic jar?"

"You got it."

"And the photos with white mummy wrappings, can you get them processed to see if there's anything on them."

"Of course."

"Thanks."

Snapping his phone shut, he placed it on the table.

Walking back over to the cream-coloured wall, he stared at the line of crime scenes.

He spoke to the photos of the dead boys. "So, what? His victims are getting younger? Or was little Henry just a one off? And why these states? Is it the parks? The wilderness? Why did you move south?"

Moving over to the table, he pulled out a chair and sat down, facing the crime scenes. Playing with his Styrofoam cup, he clenched his jaw. His eyes wandered down the list of states he'd scribbled in his notepad. Washington. Oregon. California. He spent time in California.

"How far south did you go?"

He stood, walked up to the wall, and pulled down the fading pictures taken years ago, depicting evidence collected at each crime scene. The scenes may not have been thoroughly scoured back then, but the photos remained. *Follow the trees. Find the jars. Find the messages. Find Sid.* He was grasping, trying to find a ghost at the end of a migratory path.

Chapter Fifty-seven

Losing Timmy

Jud's feet were heavy with the weight of his work boots and each stair creaked as he made his way into the dark tunnel.

Overhead, blossoms of pink and white littered the freshly cut green grass. Trees stood tall, their branches heaving under the weight of a plethora of ripe fruit. The sun shone, glaring over the pastel-blue sky.

Down here, underneath the garden, a circular cave served as his sanctuary for his special friends. In the depths of the underground, he had placed each friend directly below one of the fruit trees blossoming above in the garden, according to his meticulous design. He'd used the remains of the Evelyn Mine to create tunnels, spreading like fingers through the underground, to the dark sanctuary. The glimmer left from the remnants of the gold, silver and copper raped from the internals of the old mines created a delightful glow in the dark passageways.

Jud stepped through the black door into the cave and pulled his wool sweater tighter around his chest. He didn't mind the cold. It was imperative for the preservation of his special friends. His prized possessions. The dark could easily be taken care of. He snapped a light switch on. The room buzzed with the echoes of fluorescent tubes, strategically placed to provide even lighting throughout the cave.

He walked over to Timmy. *Timmy. I'm here. One more visit, then I must put you away. For now.*

Working the machine, he soon had the lid removed from the tomb. Walking up to the body, he drummed his fingertips together in anticipation.

"It's time to come out and play." Jud walked up to Timmy's bed and peered down inside.

Jud froze. His scalp seized. His heart skipped a beat.

"Timmy!" Jud's hands slapped against the sides of his face. "What has happened to you?"

Jud scanned the body from head to toe. What had been soft, waxen flesh had turned to thin, brown scraps of skin barely clinging to the bones.

"What has happened? I only left you for a day. We've done this before. Why? What?" Jud vigorously ran his fingers through his hair, grasping at the roots. Stepping back, away from Timmy, Jud implored his mind for answers. *I don't understand. He wasn't re-wrapped, but he was in his box. His air-tight box. And down here, in the cold, dry cavern. Away from exposure. Did air get in?* Jud scanned the box frantically, his eyes searching every inch, seeking to find some fault. *A hole? A crack?* His fingers running over the concrete, he searched for the cause of Timmy's demise, to no avail.

Stepping away from the bed, sweat trickled down his back. *What have I done? Did I miss a step? Is something faulty? What mistake have I made? Didn't I stick to the script?*

Jud searched the corners of his mind, attempting to replay his actions over the last twenty-four hours. His mind walked through the previous day, reviewing each movement, each thought.

He remembered his time with Timmy. He'd tucked him in, and replaced the lid on his bed. *Yes, the lid. It was on. I even checked the entire perimeter to ensure it was air tight.* He saw himself walking over to the thermostat, rechecking the temperature in the room. *It was perfect.* The needle pointed at thirty-two degrees Fahrenheit.

Then his mind showed him turning off the fluorescent lights, scanning the room to ensure it was dark. *Then I went up the stairs, down the tunnel, into the garden and back to the house.* He could taste the sweet rye he had poured over ice, feel the burn in the back of his throat as he tossed it back. *That was it. Nothing. No intrusions until now.*

He couldn't understand it. There was no answer to his predicament. But it was real. This was really happening.

Sauntering back over to Timmy, a dark fear crept through him, wrenching each of his internal organs in turn, crawling up his throat. Clenching his teeth, he looked into Timmy's bed. Timmy's brown, flaky skin caked around white, decaying bones. Timmy's obsidian eyes slipped away from his eye sockets without their bed of waxy white skin to hold them in place.

No. Timmy. I don't want you to see. Your soul will be destroyed.

He paced back and forth along Timmy's tomb, running his fingers through his hair. Thoughts darted through his mind. *No more Timmy. I need his innocence.*

Jud's eye twitched. His boot thumped against the dirt floor, halting his body. He looked down at the small body. Taking a deep breath, he prepared himself to face his glaring reality.

"Timmy."

He waited. His ears perked, searching for a whisper. Nothing.

"Timmy."

He waited again. No echoes. No whispers. Nothing.

He walked up to the body. Caressing the brown, flaky cheek, Jud stared at the non-eyes, slanting sideways, teetering on the corners of Timmy's eye sockets. *Why? Did I rot him?*

"I'm sorry. I don't know what went wrong. I have failed you." He gulped a few drops of saliva down the back of his dry throat. A deep sigh seeped from his nostrils. "Goodbye, Timmy. Goodbye."

His heavy boots thudding against the packed dirt, Jud walked across his sanctuary up to the head of the circle. Sliding his finger along the carefully arranged row of LPs, he selected the one appropriate for the occasion. He needed a dose of a true king to soothe his pain. He pulled the album from the shelf and slid the shiny black disc from the cardboard cover. Setting the record onto the player with care, he lifted the arm and placed the needle as close as possible to the beginning.

A special release, each track was spoken word, by the poet himself, over background music by the band. An eerie riff floated through the dark space. A deep voice half-spoke, half-sung over the instruments. Words drifted around Jud, telling him of roses, gardens and plowed plants. Jud was transported back to a time when he severed his first attempt at the dream garden in his mind. A time when he broke his ties with a cold land and migrated to the place where his trees could flourish.

Jud turned and walked over to the far side of his sanctuary. He slipped through an opening in the dark wall and returned with an orange tarp. He spread the tarp out on the dirt floor. Picking up the small, decaying body, he laid it down gently on top of the orange plastic. The deep voice seethed from the spinning black disc, talking of a severed garden and angels finding their way from death.

Staring at the non-eyes, he pulled one side of the tarp over the small body, then the other. It was Timmy's time to be an angel. A zipping sound pierced the quiet cave as Jud pulled a length of silver duct tape from a roll. He snapped the length free, pulled each end with one hand, then leaned over and secured the opening of the tarp with the sticky tape.

He hoisted the orange-tarp-wrapped body over his shoulder and walked toward the black door. Weaving through the dark, cold tunnel, his thoughts wandered. *What have I done? Why did Timmy have to go? It's all my fault. My rot destroyed him.* Red lips flashed through his mind. *She took my innocence.* The woman who was supposed to be his protector had sucked his innocence away just like she had sucked the life out of all those cocks. *Evelyne.* How many times had he hid in the closet, trembling, watching the one who had given him life drain it right out of him? *Whore. Not a mother.* She had caused him to rot from his core. Now he had spread his rot to poor little Timmy.

His mind spun faster and faster, thoughts racing, clouding his thoughts with a heavy, dark gloom. Working his way through the deserted tunnels of Evelyn Mine, a sense of satisfaction washed through him. Plowing through the deserted core of a mine named after the woman who had ruined his life gave him a sense of satisfaction. As if he was invading her insides in return for the rot she'd infused within his core. At the end of the last tunnel, he ascended a short staircase, and opened another black door. The sunlight stung his eyes. He blinked rapidly, coloured blotches concealing his vision. He stood for a couple of moments, the heat of the sun burning his skin. Once his eyes adjusted, he walked over to the Crab Apple tree. He set tarp-wrapped Timmy down, underneath the fragrant, white blossoms running across the long branches. Kneeling, sitting on the heels of his boots, he stared at the boy.

"Timmy. I'm sorry. It is your time to leave me now. You have given me so much. I will put you underneath your tree. You will be able to smell the fresh blossoms of your Crab Apple tree every year. Oh, Timmy. My special friend."

Jud stood up and walked over to the shed to retrieve the tools he would need to put his special friend into his forever bed under the Crab Apple tree. Now that Timmy didn't speak to him anymore, he needed to put him in the garden, where he'd become one with the earth. Free a bed in the underground sanctuary for another special friend. Although, it was too soon to think about that now.

Chapter Fifty-eight

High-Powered Serial Numbers

The morgue door heavy against his arms, Mahoney pushed it open. A rush of cold air hit him. The room was dim. Blackwood stood in her usual corner, hovering over a microscope.

He walked briskly across the room, his eyes adjusting to the lack of light. A few still bodies lay, covered in thin sheets. No one else was in the room. Just him, Blackwood, and a bunch of corpses.

"Blackwood," he warned her of his impending approach.

She looked up, her almond-shaped eyes peering from behind thick, plastic goggles. "Mahoney. You've got to see this." She waved him over as she lowered her head, peering into the lens again.

"I found a jar in three of the photos." She looked up, lowering her plastic goggles, exposing her eyes. Lavender wafted over to him as he approached.

His heart thumped. It was getting harder to ignore the effect she had on him. "Three?" He'd just walked away from a mind-numbing night of sex to escape from the sea of corpse faces drowning him. Opening up his heart was out of the question.

"Yeah. The three scenes in California. Each photo captures a collection of items from the crime scenes. I had to isolate each jar, zoom in, then focus the magnification." She shook her head, the silver streak in her black hair shining under the single light brightening her corner of the room. "Take a look. This is the one from the Joshua Tree scene."

He removed his derby and lowered his face toward the microscope. Closing one eye, he peered with the other eye into the lens. A small jar came into focus. He wondered if it had contained one of Henry's organs.

He stood up. "Why would the killer leave jars at three of the scenes?"

"That, I don't know." She handed him a stack of photos. "These are magnified versions of each of the three jars I found. It appears the serial numbers were intact when the photos were taken."

"Maybe we can find out if these are the jars missing from our set of five." He rubbed the bristle on his chin. How many days since he'd shaved? "Why the scenes in California? Why not the other ones too?"

"I've been on more than one case where the killer practised his script. His later kills include steps and details that weren't present in his earlier ones."

"Really?"

"Yeah. It's strange. It's like they're perfecting their process. Adding in details until it's perfect. Once they settle on a location, they execute their most detailed kills." Blackwood said.

He shook his head. "Wow. Maybe California was the final stop for our killer."

"There's more. The photos with the wrappings, I've sent them off to go through a high-powered magnification process. Upon initial examination, it looked like there may be messages written on them. I put a rush on it."

"Thanks, Blackwood. This is great." He waved the stack of photos.

"Don't thank me yet. Let's see if anything comes back."

He waved the stack of photos depicting magnified canopic jars. "Keep me posted."

"You know I will."

Her lavender scent followed him out of the morgue and into his car.

Chapter Fifty-nine

Drive-Thru War Room

The sun had made a full appearance since he'd entered the morgue. It hung low in the sky, a bright-yellow bulb waking up the city. Creaking sounds echoed as Mahoney opened the driver's side door. He slid in, placed his derby on the passenger's side, and started the engine. Rumbling soothed his nerves.

How long had he been in there? His watch told him it was past the start time of the morning meeting in the stuffy war room.

Flipping his phone open, he punched numbers in, then held it to his ear.

Sutton's voice chirped through the phone, "Detective Sutton."

"Sutton. It's Mahoney."

"Boss. Where are you?"

"You all assembled at HQ?"

"Yeah. We're waiting for you."

He pictured Dara perched in her corner, Sutton wolfing down a greasy breakfast, and Quesnel looking cool, her arms crossed. "Don't wait. I examined the crime scene photos."

"The new ones? All six of them?"

"Yeah. There were canopic jars, in three of the scenes. Blackwood directed a powerful lens on the situation. We found serial numbers."

"Really? Think they could be our missing jars?"

"Yeah. I've got magnified versions of all of them. I'll call the Egyptian store, give him the numbers. Can you get over there and see if he has any record of serial numbers? We need to confirm if they match that purchase made on Douglas Morrison's missing credit card."

"You got it, boss."

Mahoney ended the call with a click. He punched in a new set of numbers.

"Mahoney, is that you?" Agent Quesnel's cool voice seeped through the phone.

"Yeah. How'd you know?"

"I'm standing next to Sutton. Or I was. He dashed off."

"You looking at the photos?"

"Yeah." She whistled. "My colleagues helped me dig up another half a dozen. There's probably more."

"If you look close, you'll see a canopic jar in one of the evidence photos from each of the California scenes."

Silence. He waited.

Her voice returned. "Oh yeah. That's what you're off chasing?"

"Yeah. Blackwood magnified them for me. Got me a set of serial numbers."

"Only in California?"

"Yeah." Mahoney took a swig of cold coffee from the Styrofoam cup perched in the centre cup holder.

"Hmmm." Quesnel's thin-lipped thinking face flashed through his thoughts. "He saved those jars. He was practicing. Looking for the perfect spot to execute the best version of his fantasy."

Mahoney cringed at the cold coffee slipping down his throat. "That's what Blackwood said."

"She's smart. I was on the hunt for more mummies. I'll narrow the search to California. Three kills there. Maybe he was settling."

"There's more. There may be messages on the cloths from the scenes down south."

"Really? That would be helpful."

"I'll get back to HQ as soon as I can."

"See you soon."

He flipped the phone shut, cranked up the tape deck and backed his car out of the lot. He'd been on the road for two minutes flat when his phone buzzed.

"Mahoney."

"Detective. It's Jake."

"Jake?"

"From the newspaper."

Mahoney chuckled. "Oh yeah. Sorry, kid, I've had one helluva morning here." He forced down another gulp of stale coffee.

"No problem. Listen, my boss, he's playing hardball. He told me to get the subscription list to you, but not to spend any time filtering. Just print the whole shebang."

"He's obstructing my investigation." Mahoney gritted his teeth.

"But I can un-obstruct it."

"Oh yeah?" His shoulders relaxed.

"Yeah. This is between you and me. That list, of the twelve Sids. They're all local, and they're all recent. I don't know what that means. None of them have the last name Smith. Five of them are Sid. Four of them are Sydney—with a Y. And three of them are Sidney—with an I."

"You got addresses?"

"Yeah."

"Are any of them 99 Rosemont?"

"No."

"OK. Can you fax that list to my office?"

"Yeah."

"The number's on the card I left on your desk."

"Got it. What other filters were you gonna have me do? I mean, before my boss stormed in?"

"Head south of the border."

"OK. Hang on." Clicking sounds erupted through the phone. "Wow. There're hundreds here. I'm shocked."

"Snowbirds."

"Snowbirds?"

Mahoney smirked. *Little grasshopper.* "Yeah. The old folk. They migrate south for the winter. To stay warm."

"Like birds."

"Yeah." Mahoney chuckled.

"OK, well, there's a lot of them. I'll sift through. What am I looking for?"

"Start with Sid, Sydney, and any derivation you can think of. And look for year-round summer."

"OK."

"Oh—focus on California." The barren scene with the strange tree flashed through his mind. "And the desert areas."

"On it. I'll call you when I have something."

"Sounds good. Thanks."

"No problem."

"Hey kid, how far back do your archives go?"

"A long way. Why?"

"I'm looking for a headline. Something happened at Morrison Funeral Home. Early sixties. The family that ran the place leased out a room to a woman and her son. Something happened. Police showed up. They may have taken her away. The kid disappeared."

"I'll dig."

"Hey, Jake?"

"Yeah?"

"You ever thought of a job in Homicide?"

"Uh…no."

"You happy where you are?"

"Uh…no. Not exactly."

"OK. Get on that list."

"Done."

Mahoney snapped his phone shut and dropped it on the passenger side. He cranked the music up again and sped through town.

Chapter Sixty

Vanilla Bean

Jud cruised down the street in his rusty green Chevy, slowing to a playground-appropriate roll. He pulled up alongside the curb and parked under the cool shade of a large orange tree. He turned the key toward him, killing the ignition while allowing the music to continue wafting from the cassette player.

He listened to the story of air, water, and trees floating from the black speakers. Ruffling through the pile of cases on the passenger seat, he found the one he'd stolen from Seth's collection. He opened the case and slid out the insert. Flipping through it, he looked at the photos of the tight-panted, long-haired men. The album was much newer than what Jud usually listened to, made in a time that mixed men, hairspray, eyeliner and pleather. The leader of the pack looked back at him, long, scraggly hair falling around his shoulders, his chin unshaven. He looked dishevelled, yet his eyes said he knew exactly where he was going. Jud slid the cassette out of the case, pushed eject on the tape deck, and replaced his Lizard King with Seth's crazy rockers.

He'd parked the Chevy directly across the street and halfway down the block from a school, allowing him a prime view of the hunting ground while remaining inconspicuous. He hadn't been to this spot before. He never found friends in the same place twice. And this time he drove further. He needed to find the perfect pair—mother and son—to execute the final part of his plan.

Jud reached over to the passenger's side, and picked up his binoculars. Peering through the circular lenses, he adjusted the wheel until the children running through the playground came into clear focus. *C'mon. Give me something good here.* He'd had several hunting days now. It was time to find what he was looking for.

The raw voice seeping from the small black speakers sung to him of a garden full of teasing flowers, where everybody had gone. Jud tapped his foot to the beat, soothed by the lyrics. It was time for him to move forward with his garden. Moving his head slowly from side to side, he inspected the erratically moving flock. Vanilla, chocolate, strawberry, freshly washed, shiny locks bounced through the air. Little legs ran, skipped and trotted. Jud scanned and rescanned, carefully inspecting each little friend. Running his eyes down a particularly fresh-looking blond boy with bright-blue eyes, he surged with hope. *Well, look at this. Are you my next special friend?*

The guitar riff seething through the cab of the truck grew wild. The voice slithering through his ears became gruff, telling him he had not lost his mind, that he was just in a garden. A flash of shiny strawberry pulled his gaze away from the blond locks. Moving his spying glasses slowly down the little body, he looked at the red strands of clean hair, the freckles dotting the fair skin, and the pink lips. A large, brown blemish on the white cheek loomed in front of the lens. Jud jolted. *Oh, that won't do.* Moving the binoculars back over the crowd, he searched for the blond locks again. *Oh, there you are.*

Inch by inch, he executed a meticulous scan of the small figure. Creamy, white skin. *Just like Timmy. But creamier.* Shiny, blond locks. *Just like Timmy. But with a brown tinge. Like a vanilla bean. I bet he smells like fresh baking.* Bright-blue eyes, sparkling with youth and innocence. *So sparkly. So bright.* Cherry lips. *Like I've never seen before.*

A bolt of electric excitement jolted through him, from his buzzing brain down to his steel-covered toes. He lowered his binoculars and rolled his shoulders. *OK, Jud. Don't rush. Scan again. Then again. Make sure.* He couldn't believe this could be the one. The one who might be a match for the most special tree he had ever planted. His most special friend. And this time he had a new plan. A better plan. A more evolved plan.

It was time to live out the final piece of his script—the act he had been saving until he found the most special little friend he'd ever had. The voice from the speakers smoothed out, telling Jud to look inside for his own garden. He grabbed his notepad from the passenger's seat and flipped it open. As he reread each carefully scribed instruction, he rechecked the clock on the dashboard.

1. Lunch Bell Start 12:00

2. Lunch Bell End 12:45

3. Parent Arrival in Loading Zone 2:45

4. School Day End (Bell) 3:00

He needed to be positioned in the loading zone at the back of the school no later than 2:40. The parents started pulling their minivans up around 2:45, at least the keen ones did. He wanted to make sure he had a prime position to examine the mother of the vanilla boy. The mother who would play an important role in the last step in his final script. Then he would find a nice cool, quiet spot to hide until loading time approached.

He reached over to the tape deck and turned the volume knob to the right. A deep voice resonated through the small cab. The words washed over Jud, seeping into his soul. It was his time. He knew it. He picked up the binoculars, and settled them into the perfect view of the creamy skin and the vanilla-bean locks.

Chapter Sixty-one
Trail of Bodies

A series of collages plastered the cream-coloured crime scene wall. Each set of photos depicted the gruesome acts done to a young being. The images of lush forest backgrounds collided with those of the dead, skeletal boys. It was a bizarre juxtaposition that caused a chill to creep down Mahoney's spine.

He walked up to the death collages. He turned to face his team. "Hayes, good to have you back."

"Thanks, boss. It's good to be back. Sergeant Williams and his team are closing what remains of the search in the cave. Didn't seem like there was anything else to find."

Mahoney cleared his throat. "OK. Looks like we got a trail of bodies." He pointed to the map plastered to the front wall. "Three in BC." He indicated the orange dots on the map. "Six more scattered in different states." He ran his finger along the blue spots.

Hayes said, "They're scattered. No two are in the same jurisdiction."

Mahoney looked down the length of the map. "Yeah."

Quesnel uncrossed her arms, then walked up to the colour-coded map. "I've seen this before. Each body in a different jurisdiction. No reason to link them. Until there's enough to notice."

Mahoney looked at the trail of dots running across and down the map. "West through BC. Then south. Washington. Oregon. California."

"Three in California," Sutton said.

Hayes walked up to the colour-coded map. "Yeah, maybe he liked it there. Do you think there are more?"

Sutton swallowed a sip of his Big Gulp. "Yeah. Look at the messages. They're in order, but many are missing. There are forty-two negative confessions, according to this Book of the Dead?"

Mahoney nodded. "Yeah. But he left…" He flipped through his notebook. "Message eleven, twelve, thirteen, sixteen, eighteen, twenty-five." He looked up from the page. "Those are the order of messages for each scene found south of the border. Messages weren't found on the victims in BC."

Quesnel said, "It doesn't mean there weren't messages. Between the quality of the photos of the wrappings on the victims in the states, and Blackwood's magnification power, the messages were revealed. There may have been messages on the wraps on the victims from BC. The photos don't provide the required insight."

Sutton asked, "So there could be more bodies?"

Quesnel said, "Not that I could find. I conferred with all my contacts. It's possible. But a crime scene like this would likely be on the radar of the BAU." She clicked her tongue. "Unless they haven't been found yet."

Hayes asked, "What were the messages?"

Mahoney popped open his notebook. "First body we found, in the cave, the message was 'I have done no murder.' No messages were found on the bodies recovered in BC. Messages on the wraps covering the boys found south of the border, in order. Washington, 'I have not committed fornication.'" Mahoney cleared his throat. "Mount Hood, 'I have not caused shedding of tears.' Crater Lake, 'I have not dealt deceitfully.' Six Rivers National Forest, 'I have not laid waste to the plowed land.' Yosemite Falls, 'I have not set my lips in motion against anyone.' Joshua Tree, on Henry, 'I have not burned with rage.'"

Hayes said, "Wow. Really weird."

"Yeah," Sutton agreed.

"They all match the copy of The Book of the Dead that Quesnel and I read through. It was the only copy the library here had. I wonder if our killer read the same copy."

Quesnel added, "There are many versions. These negative confessions—they differ from copy to copy."

Hayes asked, "What does it all mean?"

Quesnel replied, "It seems the killer may have been declaring the innocence of these boys. Running through the set of confessions. To decipher any deeper connection to the words may require a deep dive into the killer's mind."

Sutton asked, "What about the second body at the cave?"

Mahoney flipped a page in his notebook. "Number ten. 'I have not caused pain.'"

Sutton walked up to the whiteboard, flipped a marker open. "So, numbers four and ten in the cave." The marker squeaked as he wrote the numbers on the whiteboard. "Nothing in BC. Then eleven, twelve, thirteen, sixteen, eighteen, twenty-five—through the states." He looked up. "Then what number was at the latest scene—here in the park?"

Mahoney looked at his notebook. "Forty-one. 'Neither have I sinned against the god of my own town.'"

Sutton wrote the number on the board. "Own town."

Mahoney's gut tingled. "It's like the killer is declaring this to be his town."

Quesnel said, "That wouldn't align with the use of the messages to declare the innocence of each boy. But, the newest scene, left here, it was out of line with all the others. It was more like a direct message."

Mahoney scanned the crime scenes left in Oregon. The mountain reflecting off the clear water glared at him. "The first scenes, they've got big mountain and forest backdrops. Then the scenes get more barren."

Hayes said, "Yeah. That last one looks like the desert."

Quesnel said, "He might have settled in California. There are three kills there."

Mahoney said, "That last scene irks me. It's so barren. Maybe he went to the desert."

Dara looked up from her typing. "Desert-like conditions are ideal for growing fruit trees."

Sutton asked, "Really? Doesn't it get cold at night?"

Dara continued, "Apparently, the temperature range is perfect. The heat of the day and the cool of the night."

Mahoney shook his head. "Are we reaching?"

Quesnel said, "Maybe. Maybe not." She pointed to the colour-coded map. "Is it really a coincidence that the order of the scenes trails south toward warmer, fruit-tree-growing pastures?"

Mahoney nodded. He looked back at the map. "In California, he left three scenes, each with canopic jars. Sutton, did you get a confirmation on those serial numbers?"

Sutton nodded. "Yeah. The numbers weren't on the sales receipt. Shop owner and I had to dig through another box of files, but we found the inventory record for the purchase of the five sets of jars. Serial numbers on three of the sets matched the ones you got from Blackwood."

Blackwood. She came through, again.

"And, get this," Sutton said. "I called the crime lab, got the serial numbers on the two sets of jars found in the cave. They also matched the purchase made by Douglas Morrison—or his credit card, at least."

Mahoney's shoulders relaxed. His gut settled. "Great work. We're not reaching. Five sets purchased. Two left at the cave scene. Three scattered through California. Whoever used Douglas' card left us a trail."

Hayes said, "He kept those jars all that time. Took them to California before he used them."

Sutton asked, "Why weren't any jars found at the other scenes?"

Droplets of sweat trickled down the back of Mahoney's neck. "That's a really good question."

Quesnel walked up to the map. "If he used jars, they weren't found, or photos weren't taken. He may not have used jars. Let's step back. The scenes here, in the cave, were elaborate. He used a set of jars for each of those kills. He had a garden, at Doris'. Maybe he was planning on settling here. But it didn't work out. So, he migrates. He could have been practising while finding his way to the ultimate spot. The place that he would live out his fantasy to his best execution. He may have been saving the jars for that place."

A tingle crept through Mahoney's gut. He scratched his chin. "When he left here, he left behind a failed garden. Maybe he was severing his past. Looking for a fresh start. A place to grow his ultimate garden. California. Or the desert."

Quesnel nodded, examining the map. "We focus on California, then move into the desert. Amp up the profiling."

Mahoney walked over to the whiteboard where he'd scribbled bright-blue notes about what this guy would need to live out his convoluted fantasy. "Summer year-round. Library. Classes. Schools. Playgrounds. Garden. Maybe a plot of land."

Dara said, "Bug, I had done an initial filter on this. I moved south. Then I filtered on summer year-round. Then I layered on the others. It left me with a sizable list. There're just too many places that fit our criteria."

Mahoney responded, "We filter further. Focus on California. The desert. Where fruit trees thrive. Then add in the profiling we did before."

Quesnel nodded.

Sutton slipped his lips off the red straw poking out of his Big Gulp. "We should amplify the weirdest criteria."

"Sorry, I'm out of the loop. Which ones are those?" Hayes asked.

"We think this guy studied Thanatology. It's the science of the dead," Sutton said.

Hayes' eyes bulged. "Creepy."

Sutton continued, "Yeah. And he needs supplies to preserve these kids."

"Your idea here is good. But don't downplay his need to hunt. He needs the playgrounds and schools even more than he needs his knowledge of how to keep the bodies up to his standards," Quesnel said.

"So, schools and playgrounds are top priority," Dara said. "But libraries and post-secondary classes are a close second?"

"This isn't getting us anywhere," Mahoney said. "We're not eliminating anything. Look for sun, sand, and desert conditions."

Quesnel nodded. "He needs somewhere for his garden, his trees."

Sutton sipped his Big Gulp. Hayes nodded.

Mahoney said, "Yeah. All the other criteria can be met within a day trip. But having a garden of fruit trees...that requires a piece of land."

Hayes said, "A plot of land, a ways out, but within reasonable distance of a town."

"Dara. Focus on desert conditions. Plots of land. Towns within reach." The clock on the wall stared down at Mahoney. Sweat beaded on his forehead. A cold hand crawled up his back. The second hand on the white face clicked, faster and faster. Were they really getting anywhere? Were they going to be too late? Did this guy already have another kid? "Let's re-examine the evidence. Then get filtering. Sutton, Hayes, help Dara with the searches. Quesnel, can you continue your body hunt...look in the desert?"

Quesnel nodded. "You got it."

Sutton and Hayes started discussing searches with Dara. Quesnel stood close by, interjecting profiling suggestions. Mahoney swallowed hard, drowning out the chatter in the room, and stared at the list of criteria. *Playgrounds. Schools. Library. Garden. Plot. Land.* Something clicked in his mind. His black mug was back in his hand, he was sinking into the cavern worn into his couch, and a deep voice was half-speaking, half-singing to him. He walked over to the door, voices called after him, asking where he was going. Shuffling to his desk, he picked up his derby and tweed coat, then walked out to the parking lot.

Chapter Sixty-two

Severed Seth

The steel-barred door buzzed as it slid to the right. Mahoney followed the attendant into the room. Seth hadn't been walked in yet. The chair scraped against the concrete floor as Mahoney pulled it back. He sat down, set his briefcase on the floor and waited.

"Detective," a voice called from behind him.

He twisted in the steel chair, looking back through the bars.

An attendant stood. Her face was washed in worry. "Detective, it's seems there's been an issue with Seth."

Mahoney twisted in the chair and looked at the attendant. "Issue?"

"Yes. He's, well, why don't you come and see for yourself."

He stood, grabbed his briefcase, and followed the attendant down a maze of hallways. His shoes clicked against the floor, echoing off the white walls.

The attendant halted at a door, twisted her neck awkwardly, and motioned for Mahoney to step through a door. "Here."

Mahoney peered into the room.

Seth lay limp on a bed against the far wall, two attendants bent over him.

The taller attendant said, "He has no pulse."

Mahoney's mind whirled. *What? Seth? Gone?* It seemed impossible. He walked up to the bed and looked down at the lifeless form of the dark-haired fiend who had been his friend and his enemy. His head lulled back against the bed, dark strands of hair sticking to the sides of his face. A circular pattern of yellow and purple bruises wove around his neck.

The shorter attendant said, "We found him, hanging..." She looked up at the barred window. "Seems he tore his bedsheets, tied them together, stepped up on the nightstand, and, well..." She looked down at the lifeless Seth on the bed.

The taller attendant said, "We tried to revive him. It was too late. He had no pulse at all." His deep voice stuck over his last few words. "We called it in, they're on their way."

The short attendant shook her head. "I thought he was doing better."

The tall man reached out his hand, holding a folded paper. "He left this. It's addressed to you, Detective. Looks like it's been torn from a book. My guess is he wrote it during a session, and somehow snuck it out."

Mahoney took the paper and nodded. He looked back at Seth. His pale face and dark hair had become familiar. Mahoney thought he had more time. More time to get more from him, about Sid, about the hidden Glam Boy dolls. There was too much unfinished business. The ball of anger secretly swelling in the pit of his stomach, reaching it's hot tentacles through him, had to be for something. Now it seemed as though having Seth in his life was for nothing.

He forced his gaze away from Seth's face. Nodding at the attendants, whispering a thank-you, he exited the institute.

Chapter Sixty-three

Last Words From a Psycho Killer

Mahoney plunked down into the driver's seat and pulled the creaky door shut. He closed his eyes. *What the fuck just happened?* His mind whirled with new images. Seth lying limp, dark hair plastered to his cheeks. His glassy eyes glazed over. His face pale. Seth. The psycho killer. His alter ego, Simon, the smiling bartender.

A fire of rage broiled in Mahoney's belly. He snapped his eyes open and stared at the main doors of the psychiatric institution. The place where Mahoney had deposited Seth in a pair of handcuffs. The same place he'd been coming day after day to listen to Seth share whatever he was willing to about any of his human dolls that had yet to be discovered.

The fire burned hotter. Sweat slithered down Mahoney's cheeks. He'd been playing the game of a madman for weeks, trying to get answers. Trying to provide closure to the families that had lost their sons. And for what? Mahoney swallowed hard against the acid crawling up his throat.

He thrust his hand into the inside pocket of his tweed coat and pulled out the note. He unfolded the paper and stared at the handwriting of the psycho killer.

Detective,

It is my time.

I must go.

My dolls will never...

The words blurred on the page. He didn't give a fuck about Seth's love for his human dolls any longer. He pictured the bloodied, torn sheets lying on the floor in Seth's room. The black and purple remnants of the last breaths that left Seth's mouth crawled over pale flesh and into Mahoney's mind. He crumpled the paper in his hand. Why should he care about the death wish of a sick psycho who had left gruesome corpses? Dead faces wove their way into hellish nightmares threatening to haunt him for the rest of his life.

He loosened his fist and looked at the crumpled paper in his hand. He tossed it onto the passenger's seat, slid the key into the ignition and listened to the rumbling of the engine. Kicking the images of Seth from his mind, he peeled out of the driveway and sped through his city.

Chapter Sixty-Four

In Deep at Happy Hour

Sasha lifted the martini glass toward her candy-floss lips. Taking a slow sip, she looked directly at Mahoney. He lifted the heavy glass and tossed back half the bourbon on ice in one shot.

"You look tired." Sasha reached toward him, resting her hand on his arm. He tingled from her touch. A waft of strawberry floated over in a cloud, surrounding him.

He hunched over. "Yeah. Guess I am. This case is getting out of hand." Images of Seth floated across the shiny countertop, reminding him of what he wanted to forget.

"Well, I'm a lucky girl then, getting a few minutes of your precious time." She smiled her sweet candy-floss, sparkly-white-teeth smile. It pulled him in. He couldn't look away. "Thanks for the drink." Tipping the martini glass toward him, she took another sip. Resting her chin in the palm of her hand, her pink-polished nails drummed softly against her cheek. "Do you have time for dinner?"

Glass after glass of bourbon swam through his mind. Her creamy ass drifted along, black lace calling to him. Maybe another night of bourbon and strawberry would take his mind off everything. "Dinner?"

"Yeah. Dinner. When's the last time you ate?"

He chugged back the rest of the bourbon in the glass and looked at her. One more dip wouldn't hurt, would it?

"I could take you somewhere nice. We could talk."

He sat up straight. *Talk. Sounds serious.* He looked at his watch. "I can't. Gotta follow up on something right away."

Her mouth turned downward into a playful pout. She walked her fingers along his arm, up to his face. Gently grasping his gruff chin between her pointer and thumb, she turned his head to face her. "That's too bad. I've been dreaming of a replay of the other night."

Tingling migrated down his body. The image flashed into his mind against his will. She was standing in her bedroom doorway, scantily clad in black lace, blonde curls framing her face, lips darkened to a fuschia. Smiling back at her, he looked into her eyes, letting his bristly chin rest against the soft palm of her hand.

Something jolted him. *Bug. What the hell are you doing?* He pulled his face abruptly from her hand. He was playing with fire. He had to sever this, now. "Look, the other night, it was nice. Real nice." He paused, staring into the bourbon. "But..." *Oh hell.*

"But it was a mistake," she finished for him. Sitting back into the chair, she placed her hands in her lap, her eyes lingering on his face.

He turned to look at her. "Sasha. It wasn't a mistake. I think you and I both know what it was."

Her eyes glistening, the corners of her pink mouth turned down. She swallowed hard. "Listen, Mr. Detective, I don't know what you think. But I love being around you. Just cause I'm younger than you, just cause I serve at a bar, doesn't mean I'm not serious about my life. About being with someone who makes me feel like you do."

Her eyes pierced into him. He could feel her looking inside of him, searching his thoughts, feeling her way through him, looking for a reason. "I thought you wanted a good time. A little fun. Sasha, I didn't know you wanted more. I...I can't give you much." Shaking his head, he turned and looked at the bar. Running his hands through his hair, he rested them on the bar top.

"Can't. Or won't?" She took a sip of her drink, placed the glass on the bar, then slid off the high chair. Slipping her coat over her arm, she grabbed her purse. "For a smart guy, you don't see what's in front of you. You can't assume things about people based on their outer appearance. I thought you saw me." She turned, started walking away, then halted. Turning back toward him, her blonde curls slipping over her shoulders, she looked him in the eye. "You have a lot to offer. You're just the only one who can't see that. Good luck with your investigation." Turning, she slipped through the door, out of his life, just like that.

Bug. What did you do? Turning back to the bar, he stared at his empty glass. Contemplating another shot of bourbon, he shook his head. He needed to get back to hunting Sid. He pulled out his wallet, fishing for a bill or two. Catching a glimpse of a photo stuffed between wrinkled receipts, he pulled it out and stared at Stella. His only child. His stomach churning, he suddenly felt a wave of nausea. Trying to recall that last time he had seen her, his head started spinning. *It's on you, Bug. You don't see her, because of your choices. Now what? You drown yourself in corpses. You hop from girl to girl, refusing to get close to anyone. You use them. They're a drug. They numb your pain.* He thought of the tears in Sasha's eyes, the frown on her face. *You think you don't leave any damage in your wake?* A rock of darkness plunged to the pit of his stomach. He slipped a bill onto the bar, grabbed his tweed and derby, and snuck through the door.

CEREAL
AND
FLESH

Chapter Sixty-Five

Snitch

Bzzt. Bzzt.

Mahoney opened his eyes. His phone scuttled across the coffee table. *Bzzzt.* He sat up on the couch and answered the buzzing.

"Mahoney."

"Detective. It's Jake."

"Jake. What's up?" Soft, orange light glowed through the window. He looked at the clock on the stove. "Why are you up so early? It's not even six."

"I know. I wanted to beat Hammington into the office. I talked to Cunning."

"Cunning?"

"Yeah. Mike Cunning. The guy who has been writing the articles about you. Revealing those personal things."

"Right." He'd grilled Hammington about it. He couldn't get anything but a bunch of bullshit about protecting sources and uncovering the truth.

"Cunning always comes in early. I caught him this morning. I got something."

Mahoney sat up straighter, leaning on the edge of the couch. "Yeah?"

"Yeah. He said he didn't know the name of the guy—his source. But he had a detective badge. Says he was on your team. Real lean. Buzzcut."

Mahoney's neck burned. "What?"

"Yeah. Do you know who it is?"

Hayes' face popped up clear and bright, invading his thoughts. "Yeah. I suspect I do."

"Good. Do what you want with the info. But we didn't have this conversation."

Mahoney chuckled.

"I haven't found any subscriptions for a Sid or Sydney in the desert. I'll keep looking."

"Thanks, kid."

"No problem."

Mahoney clicked his cell phone shut and scanned the carnage of the night. A half-empty bottle of Maker's Mark sat open on the coffee table, surrounded by an empty glass, Seth's open journal, and photos of small corpses. A crumpled piece of paper lay on the floor. He picked it up and smoothed it out. The note, from Seth, that he'd read a million times while the darkness descended over his small apartment. He tossed it onto the couch. It would have to wait. He had a rat to deal with.

Chapter Sixty-six

Dukes Up

Mahoney stomped down the hallway, glaring at the rows of cubicles. He halted at the line of desks where Sutton and Hayes sat. Neither of them were at their desks. He clenched his fists and trudged toward the war room. About three feet before the door to the stuffy little room, he caught a glimpse of Hayes heading straight for him.

"Hayes," Mahoney barked. "War room. Now."

"What's up, boss?" Hayes smiled. His buzzcut stuck out in obnoxious strands.

Mahoney opened the war room door, walked into a cloud of hot, stuffy air, and waited for Hayes to follow. He slammed the door as soon as Hayes had stepped through.

"You've been talking to the Chronicle," Mahoney yelled. His temples pulsed.

"I don't know what you're talking about." Beads of sweat formed across Hayes' forehead.

"Don't freakin' lie to me." Heat flushed over Mahoney's face and down his neck. "Mike Cunning. The journalist writing all the articles about our case. You're the one who has been talking to him."

Hayes shook his head. "Boss, I don't know what you're talking about."

Mahoney stepped forward and plunged his face within an inch of Hayes'. Hot, loud breaths escaped his mouth as he gritted his teeth. "I know it was you. I talked to Cunning. Says he got his info from a detective, on my team, lean with a buzzcut. You telling me that isn't you?"

Hayes stared, eyes wide, frozen in place.

"Tell me the truth." Mahoney's nostrils flared, hot air seeping from them onto Hayes' face.

Hayes put up his hands and stepped back. "Fine. Yeah. I told him a few things about the case. Look, he's an old college buddy. He's trying to make it as a reporter. He pressured me. I didn't give him anything that wasn't public record."

"Is 'Bug' public record? And my lack of ability to conduct an investigation?"

"Well, no, I guess not," Hayes stammered. "Listen, he pressured me. I owed him a favor. And he twisted my words. He wrote stuff I didn't say." He looked at the ground.

Mahoney stomped over to the centre table and pounded it with his fist. "Dammit, Hayes."

"Listen, boss..."

"What the hell is going on in here?" Sergeant Jackson bellowed from the war room door.

Mahoney jolted. "Sarge. We have a problem."

"Oh yeah, what now?" Sergeant Jackson raised an eyebrow.

"Hayes has been leaking to an old buddy over at the press."

"What? Hayes, is this true?" The sergeant looked at Hayes.

"Well..." Hayes swallowed and frowned.

Sergeant Jackson shook his head. "What next? Hayes—get in my office. Now. Mahoney, I need you to go get Doris. Bring her in."

"What? Why?" Mahoney asked.

Hayes shuffled out of the room, avoiding Mahoney's gaze.

"The flesh you found on the hook, when you searched Doris' basement, it was bloody. Blood type doesn't match either of our bodies."

"What? It didn't belong to the Saskatchewan boy?"

"No." Sergeant Jackson put his hands on his hips. "We have no idea who the flesh belongs to."

"You think this is Doris' doing?"

"I need you to find out. She's the prime suspect. Go get her."

Mahoney's mind whirled. The note Seth had left him flashed through his mind. He was supposed to be finding Sid. "What about Sid?"

"We're not halting the hunt for Sid. Just go get Doris. Question her. Continue with Sid's investigation." He paused. "And enough with that patrol car. If this Sid was here, he's not coming back."

Fuck. Sid seemed real. Now this. I'm back to competing suspects. "Fine." Mahoney stomped over to the door and headed for his car before he could say anything he'd regret.

Chapter Sixty-seven

Flesh and Hook

Doris sat across the metal table, staring down at her hands. Her hair looked like it hadn't been washed in at least a week, sticking to her scalp in greasy clumps. She smelled like she'd been holed up in her house drinking Jim Beam and eating Cheetos.

"Doris." Mahoney pulled out the chair and sat across from her.

She continued to look at her hands, not responding.

"Doris," Mahoney tried again.

Doris glanced up. Her faced was streaked with dirt, salt and tears. "Yes," her raspy voice scratched across the table.

"Doris, I'll be straight with you, if you'll be straight with me."

She grunted. "About what?"

"We found human flesh on the hook hanging from the ceiling in your basement."

"So what? I know what Seth did. I know what Sid did. Those two fuckers used my basement."

"The flesh doesn't belong to any of Seth's or Sid's victims. The flesh wasn't there when we arrested Seth. Has anyone else been in your basement, other than Sid?"

"No. No one comes over."

"So, then, how did the flesh get on the hook?"

"Don't know." She glared at him.

"Doris." He slammed his lips together, suppressing his anger. "There has to be an explanation for the flesh. We think that Sid was in your basement, with the kid he took from Saskatchewan. We have the kid's eyes. The flesh doesn't belong to that kid. The only other person who has been in your basement is *you*, according to *you*. So, unless you tell us where that flesh came from, the only conclusion to be drawn is that *you* put it there. Which means you hurt someone. Which means you'll be locked up." He leaned over the table and glowered at her.

She looked right at him. "I don't know how the flesh got there. My son is dead. Because of you. You talked to him about Sid." She stood up and loomed across the table. "You upset him. Now he's dead." Without warning, she spit a good-sized gob across the table. The gooey glop landed on Mahoney's cheek with a splat. She sat back down in her chair and glared at him.

Veins pulsed in his temples. He forced himself to stay still when all he wanted was to reach across and strangle her. Pulling a white kerchief from his shirt pocket, he wiped the disgusting Doris saliva from his face. He stood up and peered down at her. "That is no way to behave, Doris. The only way I can help you is if you talk to me." He walked over to the door and into the hallway, securing the lock behind him.

He didn't have time for this. Yet he couldn't help wondering where the hell the flesh came from, and if all this time Doris had her own torturous routines. *Dammit.* He had to get back to the hunt for Sid. Doris wasn't going anywhere. He'd let her sit and stew for a while. Maybe she'd realize her only option was to spill her secrets about the hook and the flesh.

He headed to the war room. The handwritten note, crumpled and stuck in the cavern of his couch in his apartment, shot through his mind. He had to read Seth's last words again. First, he needed to beef up his resources. He needed anything that stuck out on this case, anything that could help him decipher the cryptic words of a psycho killer.

Chapter Sixty-eight

Disgusting Date

Jud stretched his arm out and rested it across the seat next to him. He hesitated, then positioned his arm over Evelyn's shoulders. He could almost feel his skin singe against the rot of her filthy skin. *Relax. It's all for the final plan. Make her pay. Save Jeremy.*

Evelyn smiled at him, her bright-red lipstick electrifying his eyes.

He smiled back. She returned her attention to the film playing on the big screen, resting her neck against his arm. Her dry, yellowish hair scratched his skin. He reminded himself again this was all for the climax of the years of work he'd put in. The final tree. The final sacrifice. And to save Jeremy. He pictured Jeremy's creamy skin and vanilla-bean hair. He took a deep breath and relaxed against the seat.

He reminisced about the moment he first saw Jeremy running across the playground. He'd hunted, carefully, planning his every move. He watched and recorded the schedule of a single mom and her innocent young boy. They kept a predictable schedule. Even their grocery trips were planned out for the same day every week. They were always alone. No friends. No family. No-one to notice if they went missing. He'd timed his own shopping to coincide with theirs, resulting in a serendipitous meeting of a fit, courteous man and a lonely, single mother. He offered to buy the Fruit Loops Jeremy wanted when his mother told them they weren't on the list, and thus not in the budget. He smiled, remembering the excitement in Jeremy's eyes.

Evelyn slid down in her seat, pressing her head against his arm. Locks of stiff hair scraped his skin. He fought against the flinch his arm wanted to make. She smiled up at him again. He forced a wide grin across his face.

A couple of plastic people with perfect smiles walked through a fake park on the massive screen, pretending to be in love. Evelyn seemed to buy it. She seemed to be having a good time. *Good.* He needed her to be happy. He was sick of feigning interest in her. It was time to get Jeremy involved in their happy outings.

Chapter Sixty-nine

Album Review

A strange trail of clues lined up across the cracked coffee table. Seth's journal, opened to the page capturing a young boy's thoughts about the sadistic man who tortured him. The symbol of innocence drawn crudely in soft graphite. A photo of a jar, a pair of eyeballs floating in clear liquid, staring. An album cover, holding dark poems of severed gardens.

The trail of a sadistic psycho, saving the innocence of young boys by taking their eyes. Severing a garden in a destructive climate. Following his passion along a migratory path, heading south, seeking year-round sunshine and sandy soil.

Mahoney snapped his gaze way from the trail of wild clues. Seth's handwritten note, crumpled in a ball, sat at the bottom of the crevice in the old couch. He picked it up, then plunked down into the cavern. He unfolded the letter. The words sprung off the page in a fury.

Detective,

It is my time.

I must go.

My dolls will never be mine again.

It is my time.

I must go.

I will go willingly.

Sid will not. He will not go. Unless you find him.

Sid saw himself through his own eyes.

He deemed himself the Lizard King.

Just as the real one declared so in a single poem,

Whilst screaming that he could do anything.

Sid has gone where he always wanted to be.

Where warmth engulfs his mansion.

Where he lives above the rest,
Under the shade of his prized possessions.
Sid has gone where he always wanted to be.
To where it all began for the one he looked up to.
For he hoped to follow the same path.
To find himself.
Seth

The words flung themselves off the page and swirled around in Mahoney's mind. He leaned back against the couch, letting them simmer.

The Lizard King. The voice of the very albums that he listened to in his car. Every day. Sid had declared these were his albums of choice when he'd left one of them in the coffin in the cave. Coincidence? Unlikely. Sid left that album. As for his own musical taste, Mahoney shook his head, wondering how fitting it was that he himself chose the same tracks as the psycho killer he was chasing into the belly of the desert.

Many had deemed the voice of their mutually chosen rock god as the Lizard King. The dark poet turned rock god only declared the title to himself once. On one track.

Mahoney walked over to a box filled with LPs. He shuffled through them, plucked one from the box, slid the black disc from the cardboard and placed it on the record player. A drop of the needle and a deep voice seethed through the small living space. The poet sung and his words slithered through the room, weaving through Mahoney's mind. The story unfolded, telling of a house on top of a hill, shaded by trees, yet warm.

Fine. A house up on a hill with trees and warmth. But where?

Mahoney searched his mind, looking back into Seth's eyes, asking him about the album Sid left in the coffin in the cave. *What did Seth say?* Mahoney dug into his briefcase, pulled out his notepad and sifted through the pages. *Sid's true god. Was the Lizard King, the rock god plastered on the album, Sid's true god?* He rubbed the bristle on his chin, staring at the notepad. *A symbol of what he wanted to build.* Symbol. Build. The album, the song about the garden, did it symbolize what Sid wanted to build? A house with trees in a warm place up on a hill. A garden. Running his hands through his hair, Mahoney implored his brain to put the pieces together.

Where are you, Sid?

He stood up, walked over to the record player, and sifted through the stack of LPs he'd dug out of his closet. The rock god was obsessed with the desert. It seemed Sid had gone to the desert. But where? He looked down at the turntable as the song came to an end. He picked it up and dropped it again at the beginning. The dark voice seeped through the room, haunting him. He'd listened to the lyrics dozens of times, but nothing concrete came of it.

He walked back over to the couch, plunked down, and picked up the handwritten note. He scanned the words, over and over.

A warmth sliced through his gut. A tingle crept over his skull. He stared at the last portion of the note. Words popped off the page.

Where it all began...the one he looked up to...find himself.

Mahoney pulled his tweed coat across the tattered couch and dug in the pocket. The smooth polished pink stone shone in his palm.

"To where it all began," Mahoney spoke to the empty room.

Of all moments in life, every man has one moment more profound than all others. That moment when he truly sees the world, the people around him, and himself—all for what they really are. The heart of the matter.

It hit him like a sucker punch.

He jumped from the couch, bolted across the room, sifted through the LPs and pulled one out. In a flash, the black disc was spinning, the needle throwing eerie notes through the room.

The real Lizard King, the rock god himself, had his own life-changing moment. On a highway, in the desert. He wrote about it in a poem, then sung about it later on one of the most famous tracks he would ever record. Mahoney listened to that track now, letting the words seep into his soul. The words were of the desert and death, for it was out in the desert where the Lizard King first witnessed death. He was just a young boy. He saw death, he saw spirits and he saw himself. From that moment on, he was on a path to his declared title.

Where was that highway? Mahoney implored his brain to produce the long-lost information. He walked over to the lightly populated bookshelf and grabbed the tattered paperback copy of "No One Here Gets Out Alive." Flipping through the pages, he found the scene describing the young boy's first experience with death and spirits. The highway was Number 30. In Santa Fe. He tossed the book onto the coffee table.

Digging into his briefcase, he pulled out a wrinkled map and smoothed it over the coffee table. He eyeballed the dots he had drawn on the map, marking the locations of the trail of child mummies Sid had left. Plunging his hand into the briefcase again, he fished out a bright-blue marker and snapped off the cap. He drew a large circle around Santa Fe. It fit the pattern. There it was at the tail end of the migration pattern the killer had taken through BC, Washington, Oregon, California, and landing in the heart of the hot desert in Santa Fe. Mahoney scanned back up the map, finding Morse, Saskatchewan, and drawing another bright-blue circle around it.

Dragging the blue tip across the map, he dotted a line straight up from Santa Fe to Morse. The path would have taken the killer straight across the Big Beaver broader crossing. A lightly used entry way where someone could slip under the radar. He stared back at the circle he'd drawn around Santa Fe. His gut vibrated. His brain tingled. This had to be it. Sid's final resting place to build his garden high on the hill.

A small area. How many houses on hills could there be?

He stared back along the line of clues, sitting on the cracked coffee table. Two fantasies. Psycho Sid was saving the innocence of young beings, the innocence he had lost. Psycho Sid was also seeking to build a garden in the warmth up on a hill. Did Sid think this was the answer to finding himself? In the depths of a new garden?

The thoughts materialized in Mahoney's brain, clear as a bright-blue sky. He grabbed his phone, punching in the numbers fast. He had to find Sid. Now. The phone rang. He waited. "C'mon, kid, pick up." He looked at the clock on the old stove across the room. It was the middle of the night. No one would be at the paper. Not even Jake. After at least a couple dozen rings, he snapped the phone shut and leaned back against the couch. *Dammit.* It would be hours before he could probe for answers. A location. The hiding place of Sid.

Mahoney paced the room. He poured a bourbon, holding it in one hand, his cell phone in the other. He paced. He called Jake. He paced some more. The hands on the clock over the stove ticked.

He poured another drink, sat on the couch, and leaned his head back against the cushion. His eyelids drooping, weariness taking over his entire body, inch by inch, he succumbed and closed his eyes.

DESERT
MIGRATION

Chapter Seventy

Desert Subscription

Bzzt. Bzzt.

Mahoney flipped his eyes open. Where was he?

Bzzzt. The phone rattled on the chipped coffee table.

Oh yeah. His living space. He looked at the line of clues along the coffee table. A scratching noise pulled his attention to the far wall. The needle bobbed along the edge of the record. The desert. Santa Fe. Up on a hill. He'd been trying to get a hold of Jake.

Bzzzt. He leaned over and snatched up the phone.

"Mahoney," he barked.

"Detective, it's Jake Jefferson," the young voice chirped over the phone.

"Jake. I've been calling you all night."

"You have? I just got in. I have something for you. I would've dug more last night, but Hammington was breathing down my neck. He refused to leave the office until we were all gone."

Mahoney rubbed his eyes with his free hand. He looked at the clock on the stove. Six o'clock in the morning.

"Detective? You still there?"

"Yeah."

"I found an article from 1962, about the Morrison Family funeral home. The family that owned the home, they lived in an attached residence. They leased out a two bedroom suite to a young woman. Evelyne Wright. She was an ill behaved tenant. She prostituted out of her rental suite, until she was caught."

Mahoney blinked his eyes hard, trying to clear the fog seeping through his brain. "And?"

"Get this. The mom had a kid. His name was Judson. Jeepers—what kind of name is that? Anyways, guess he saw her attending to one of her clients. An old guy. The kid, Judson, he lost it. Went crazy. Attacked the guy. Cut him open real good. Someone called the cops. Boom, mom's business was over."

Mahoney's eyes jolted open wide. His mind cleared. "What happened to the kid?"

"The kid split. They searched, never found him. The old man was slit, from neck to stomach. His privates were covered in red lipstick."

Prickles enflamed Mahoney's gut. "Was the kid's last name the same as his mom's?"

"Yeah. Judson Wright. There's a photo of him—along with the article."

Mahoney's mind buzzed. "You got any subscriptions for a Wright in Santa Fe?"

"Hang on."

Mahoney could hear Jake typing at Mach speed.

"Yeah. A PO Box. Santa Fe. Judson Wright."

"Well, I'll be dammed. He went back to his childhood name. Thought he'd slip through our fingers. Sucker ain't so slippery."

"Want me to fax you the details to your office?"

"Yeah. That'd be swell. And I'm gonna need a copy of that article."

"You got it."

"Hey, Jake..."

"Yeah?"

"Thanks."

"Anytime."

Chapter Seventy-one
Shampoo and Fruit Loops

With two coffee cups perched atop porcelain saucers, one in each palm, Jud walked away from the café counter. He stepped up onto the circular cobblestone patio, bordered by trees in full bloom. Pink and white blossoms dotted an apple tree, their aromatic fumes swirling through the air. Setting the cups down with a clink onto the metal table, foam art bobbed on top of the creamy coffees. A leaf for him, a heart for her.

"Oh, Jud, thank you. That looks delightful!" Evelyn's voice sung from across the table.

"I assure you, the pleasure is all mine." Jud's syrup-coated words slid from his mouth with ease. He forced a wide smile.

Jud pulled an ornately decorated chair away from the table. The metal legs scraped against the concrete. He sat down, crossed his heavy work boot over his knee and brushed stray strands of hair away from his face. Looking across the table at Evelyn's maroon, whore lips dipping into her coffee, he wondered how many cocks she had wrapped them around.

"What a lovely spot."

"Mommy! Can I go to the park?" Jeremy squealed. Sitting cross-legged on the chair next to Evelyn, he dipped a straw in and out of a child-sized milk carton.

"Honey. It was nice of Jud to invite us here. You need to sit still for a few minutes. Here, eat your cookie." She slid a plate toward Jeremy. Evelyn turned back to face Jud. "Sorry about that. Thank you for bringing us here. It's really great of you not to mind him tagging along. I need to find a more reliable sitter." She turned the corners of her harlot mouth into a pout.

"Ah, he's good. Hardly know he's here." Jud wiped his sticky palms on his jeans. The scent of Jeremy was sweet. Jud took a deep breath. His head was fuzzy. *I don't mind your kid joining us. Not one bit.*

"This is a lovely spot." Her eyes drifted over the lush green leaves waving in the breeze. "What beautiful trees."

"Mommy, I'm done." Jeremy stretched his short arms toward Evelyn, wet crumbs sticking to his fingers.

Evelyn picked up a napkin and wiped the cookie from Jeremy. "I need you to sit still a little longer, please."

Look at you, doting on Jeremy, as if you care. Devious bitch. Reaching into a bag hanging from the back of his chair, Jud retrieved a colouring book and some crayons. He placed the items in front of Jeremy. "Here you go, kid. Something fun for you to do." He smiled at Jeremy.

"Oh boy!" Jeremy opened the crayon box and flipped through the book.

"Oh, Jud. How nice of you." Her cheeks flushed as she smiled. "Jeremy, what do you say?"

Jeremy turned his bright-blue eyes toward Jud. "Thank you, Jud."

"You're welcome." Warmth washed through Jud. He turned to Evelyn. "You were noticing the trees. They've selected well. That's a cherry tree." He tipped his cup in the direction behind Evelyn.

She turned to look. "Cherry tree? Oh my. I didn't know they could grow here. What beautiful blossoms."

"Yes, the creamy-white flowers are quite nice. That one likely started blooming about three weeks ago. As you can see, it's shedding and starting to spring some fruit. It appears to be a dark cherry tree."

"Really? How interesting. Do you know what type of tree that one is?" She pointed.

"The one with the pink and white blossoms?"

"Yes."

"That's a Honeycrisp Apple. As you can see, it's in full bloom. It only bears fruit every two years. The apples are sweet and crisp, just as the name implies."

"I wish I was more of a green thumb."

"The tree to your left there, that's a Bubblegum Plum. The fruit actually smells and tastes just like Bubblicious."

Setting her cup down, she turned toward the plum. "Oh lovely." She turned back. "I had no idea you were such a horticulturalist."

"I have a rather extensive garden on my plot. It's somewhat of a sanctuary for me. I've planted a nice array of perennials. Mostly trees. Just planted one of those Bubblegum Plums myself." He took a sip of the frothy dark roast. Clinking his cup back into the saucer, he met her gaze.

"Oh my, that sounds beautiful. I would love to see it sometime."

Jud shifted in his seat. *The fruit from the trees would rot the minute you set your corrupt foot into my sanctuary.* "That would be nice."

"What about tomorrow?" Leaning back in her chair, long, dehydrated locks of hair slid over her shoulders, split ends fraying out.

He paused, wondering if he was ready. "I'll have to check. I have an order in for some plants at the garden centre."

"Sure, Jud." Her crimson, call-girl lips were moving again. Nodding his head, pretending to listen, he sipped his coffee. The reek of her cheap perfume seeped across the table, nauseating him. He kept nodding his head and sipped his coffee, smiling wide.

Her tacky fluorescent-pink scarf bounced around her neck as she babbled on. *Pretending to be high class. Pretending like you are a lady. I see you. Cheap slut.*

His scalp tightened, pulling his ears, wrenching his forehead. He narrowed his eyes, nodding away, sipping his coffee.

Staring into her fraudulent eyes, he forced himself to focus on her. *I see you. I know what you really are. Poor excuse for a mother. Hustler.* His fingers curled into his palm under the table. Stretching his fingers out, he repeatedly pumped and released a tight fist.

He snapped his gaze to Jeremy. A rush of relief washed over him. His shoulders lifted as he inhaled long and hard. The fresh scent of Johnson's Kids' Shampoo infused his nostrils. His eyes wandered over Jeremy's soft skin, as creamy as the whole milk poured over the kid's Fruit Loops that morning. Jeremy's pink lips, dotted with chocolate, parted as he chattered at Evelyn. A hazy cloud swirled around Jud's head, muffling the sound. A waft of Jeremy's sugary cereal breath floated across the table. Jud sniffed. He closed his eyes and breathed. His garden, his sanctuary, sprung vivid in his mind. He was there. Plucking a ripe piece of fruit.

"Jud. Are you OK?" Evelyn's voice punctured the delicious image of the ripe, red plum.

Jud jerked his eyes open. "Yes. Yes, I'm fine. I was just enjoying the aroma of those Honeycrisp blossoms." He smiled, pinching the cup handle between thumb and pointer. "How is your coffee?"

"Oh, it's delightful. Thank you." Taking a sip of her coffee, her tongue slid across her top lip, removing the froth.

What else do you do with that tongue? Sick slut.

"Mommy, can I have another cookie?"

Jeremy's candied breakfast breath drifted across the table. Jud breathed it in. Shifting in his seat, he uncrossed his legs and pulled his jacket over the hardening result of the sweet concoction emanating from little Jeremy. He forced his attention back to Evelyn. "Would another cookie hurt?"

Evelyn turned from Jeremy. "Oh, well. I suppose not. Normally, I would say no, but I guess dinner is still hours away."

Jud fished a few coins from his pocket, his fingers brushing against his stiffness. "Here you go, kid. My treat." Reaching his hand over the table, he dropped the coins into Jeremy's small palm. Jud's fingers brushed the silky skin of Jeremy's fingertips. *I need Jeremy in my garden. That bed, under my new plum tree would be the perfect spot for him.*

"Thank you, Jud. That was real nice. Jeremy, thank Jud." The hot-pink scarf slid sideways as Evelyn adjusted Jeremy's pants.

"Thank you, Jud," Jeremy's high-pitched voice trickled over the metal table. He pattered his way to the counter.

"Jud, it's nice of you to include him like this. He's my world. It's been the two of us for so long now, it seems that's how it's always been. It's such a treat to spend time with someone who doesn't find him a burden." She reached a hand over the table.

Her fingers grazed Jud's hand. Her touch singed his skin. His body jolted. He forced his hand to stay in place. "Of course. He's a nice kid."

"Well, thank you. This afternoon has been absolutely lovely." Crossing her legs, her cheap skirt slipped, exposing her sallow flesh.

"Mommy, they had chocolate chip!" Jeremy's high-pitched squeal rang through the air.

Evelyn winced. "Well, now, isn't that special."

"Oh, he's so cute with his treat," Jud chimed in.

Gobs of chocolate goo formed at the corners of Jeremy's mouth and caked around his fingertips as he devoured the treat. Jud stared. *Focus on Evelyn. Focus. On. Evelyn.* He forced his head to turn, and willed his eyes to find her face. Exhaling the chocolate aroma now oozing from Jeremy, Jud tried to clear the thoughts of unblemished skin, bright-blue eyes and locks of vanilla bean swirling through his mind. *It's time for them both to visit my garden.*

Staring at Evelyn's lips, moving again, he sipped his coffee and nodded.

I bet Jeremy tastes so sweet. Just like a Bubblegum Plum. A ripe, juicy, sweet fruit. Jud's mouth watered. His tongue tasted sweet. He could feel the juice running down the sides of his mouth, the sticky sugar water dripping from his hands, as he pictured himself taking a bite out of young, innocent, ripe Jeremy.

Chapter Seventy-two

Plan of Attack

The pale face of a young boy drifted through Mahoney's mind. The boy's blue eyes swirled into black nothing spheres. Blinking hard, Mahoney tried to will the boy out of his mind.

Sergeant Jackson stood at the front of the stuffy war room, delving out instructions for the big show. The takedown of Sid the gardener, high up on the hill, in the belly of the desert.

"Thanks to Mahoney, we got ourselves a PO Box and a name. Thanks to Agent Quesnel, we've got an exact address." Sergeant Jackson smiled and nodded first at Mahoney, then at Quesnel. "We've got triple photo identification. The driver's license issued to Sydney Smith, who apparently lived at Doris' address ten years ago when our first victim was killed. We've now got a second driver's license issued to a Judson Wright, who currently lives in Santa Fe. Both pictures appear to be of the same man. To put the third layer of icing on the cake, we've got a photo from a newspaper article from the Calgary Chronicle, about a murder at a funeral home, twenty-five years ago. The photo is of one Judson Wright, a teenager at the time, and has a striking resemblance to the Jusdon Wright now living in Santa Fe."

Quesnel leaned against the back wall, arms crossed. She nodded slightly in response to Sergeant Jackson, then went back to her frozen stance.

Mahoney didn't respond.

Sergeant Jackson continued, "We need to approach with the utmost caution. This guy—Sid, or Judson—he's slipped through the cracks for a long time. I suspect he won't go down easy. And we don't know what's he's been up to. We might be walking into quite the scene."

Heads nodded around the room. Sutton sucked on the red straw of a fresh Big Gulp. Hayes sat forward in a cheap plastic chair, elbows resting on his knees. Mahoney gritted his teeth against Sergeant Jackson's words still vibrating in his mind. *We need Hayes on this case. His issue with talking to the press has nothing to do with his tactical skills. We don't have any more manpower. He stays.* Mahoney shoved the sergeant's voice away and looked at the back corner of the room. Dara sat perched, typing away.

He closed his eyes and took a deep breath. Black nothing eyes creeped across his mind. *We have no idea what we're walking into.* How many boys were wrapped up, preserved at Sid's place? What kind of freak show did he have going on up there on the hill? *He'll die before he stops.* Mahoney pictured himself sliding a thick knife into Sid's guts, looking into the wild eyes of the sick psycho that killed kids and kept them.

"We'll be out of our own territory. Working across jurisdictions can be challenging. Agent Quesnel has co-ordinated the effort. Agent, can you walk us through the plan?" Sergeant Jackson stepped aside.

Quesnel uncrossed her arms and walked to the front of the room. The fluorescent lighting glared off her fire hair. She faced the room, her lips in a tight line. "Given the history of the killer—Sid, otherwise known as Judson—we were able to secure beefed-up resources. Normally a full FBI SWAT lends half a dozen personnel, a SWAT leader, an entry guy, and two snipers. We'll have a dozen SWAT, one of which will be the entry guy, command leader and three snipers. The command leader..."

Her crisp voice drifted away as Mahoney focused on the black nothing eyes that wouldn't leave him alone. A pale face materialized, the room faded away around him. The face belonged to a boy with dirty-blond hair and creamy skin. The same face had been drifting in and out of Mahoney's mind for a couple of days now. He didn't know who the boy was. His gut told him he didn't want to know. Somehow he knew he'd find out.

Quesnel's voice pierced the image. "I repeat, the command leader will be in charge at all times. It is imperative in this type of tactical takedown that we have one, and only one, main point of communication. All eyes will be on him for orders. When we touch down tomorrow, he'll debrief us on the final plan. He's been given absolutely all information we have on the case. I'll walk you through the tactics now. He'll give us the final..."

Her voice faded again. Mahoney thought of his wife, her strawberry hair, her soft curves hidden by flowing blue scarves. Since he left the first scene in the cave, he felt her forever slipping through his fingers. He'd realized he'd only been grasping at a memory he couldn't let go of. She'd moved on. He tried to turn his attention back to Quesnel.

"The layout of the property has been captured on some old surveillance photos from a few years back. It appears the house is at the front of the lot, through the gates. The gates could have been updated; they might be electronic. We'll be prepared with electric bypass and a wire-cutter kit. One of the SWAT guys has experience. It'll be quick. When we get through the main gates, we'll hit the house first, make sure it's clear..."

His mind drifted again. Mahoney pictured his daughter, her blonde curls floating through the warm air. Her giggles drifting into his ears. At the start of this case, he'd had hope he could go see her soon. Now, he doubted he should. The images of corpse after corpse cluttered his mind constantly. He was afraid he'd descend a dark cloak on the new life his daughter had.

"If the house is clear, we'll head to the back of the property. Appears there's a stretch of land. Looks empty in the photos, but we don't know what's there now."

Sid's garden. A stretch of land, behind the house. It had to be Sid's garden. Mahoney pictured himself walking behind the house, into the garden, and hunting down Sid.

"The SWAT leader will assess the situation upon clearance of the house. We will not proceed until he determines how to approach."

Mahoney drifted in and out of paying attention to the orders. He didn't care. He had a monster to hunt. If there were any more boys in that garden, he wouldn't let them die.

"Mahoney," Sergeant Jackson barked.

Mahoney's mind snapped back to the small room. The lights glared into his eyes. The stiff air caught his throat.

"Yeah."

"You'll lead your team as usual. Same protocol. Stay in line with the FBI SWAT leader, as Agent Quesnel indicated."

"Of course." He had no idea how Quesnel's debrief ended. It didn't matter. He had a deranged man to hunt, deep in the desert.

"You're all on the next flight to Santa Fe. Bright and early. Try to get some sleep. You'll need to be alert. That's it, folks," Sergeant Jackson concluded his instructions.

The room buzzed with chatter. Heat swelled in Mahoney's gut. Little faces with black nothing eyes stared through his thoughts. Sleep was out of his reach. If he was lucky, Sid wouldn't be.

THE
GARDEN

Chapter Seventy-three

Lemonade

With long, slow strides, Jud climbed the incline behind his house leading up to his favourite place in the world. His garden. His sanctuary. He stole a glance over at Evelyn, walking beside him, holding Jeremy's hand. Her red whore lips glared at him. *Red. In the middle of the afternoon.* Second guessing his decision to allow her through the gates into his sacred spot, his head started to spin. *She better not spoil my sanctuary. Her putrid core better not rot the pure soil my trees thrive in.*

His stomach seized at the vision pulsing in his mind, the bright-green leaves of his precious trees fading to a dull brown, the ripe fruit rotting, mould creeping over the plums, pears and peaches.

"Your plot is huge. This land, it's beautiful." Her glossy red lips taunted him.

He saw his mother's mouth, painted with a thick layer of bright red, wrapping around an old man's veiny, wrinkled, shrivelling manhood. The old man's head tilted back, locks of greasy hair escaping his slick combover, his thin lips trembling as he moaned. The old man muttered obscene words as those red lips slid up and down. Jud felt the tears trickling down his cheeks just as they had that day he hid in the closet, playing spy, piecing together the clues of what his mother did alone with all those men in the spare bedroom.

"Jud." Evelyn's shrill voice punctured his memory, jolting him back to the present. "Are you all right?" She put her filthy hand on his shoulder.

"Yes." *All right? I'm all right. You're just like her, you cheap slut. You're exceeding my expectations.* He found his sugar-coated voice and said, "I was just lost in the scenery. People say the desert is barren. I find a lot of beauty hidden in the brown soil and red rock. Just look at those cacti in full bloom." He waved his arm over the expanse of open land surrounding them. Pink, purple, and yellow blossoms atop green, prickly cacti dotted the hill like a rainbow quilt.

"I see the beauty." She smiled at him. He wanted to cut her lips off. "It's so nice of you to show us your garden. I can't wait," Evelyn's shrill voice pierced the peaceful desert.

"My pleasure," Jud's syrup-covered words slipped from his mouth.

"Jeremy, it's really nice of Jud to invite us here. What do you say?"

"Thank you, Jud."

Jud's insides melted. The sweetness of Jeremy's young voice washed over him. The thoughts whirling in his mind slowed. His head cleared. *It was the right thing to bring them here. For Jeremy. I won't let her ruin it.*

"Well, Jeremy, I just hope you like my garden."

"It's way up there?" Jeremy pointed his little finger up the hill, toward the iron gate.

"Yes. Way up there." Jud smiled.

"Why?"

"Well, I needed a special place to put my garden. Somewhere safe and quiet."

"Oh." Jeremy stared with wide eyes up at the iron gate, tilting his head back. His shiny vanilla-bean locks dangled over his shoulders.

Freshly washed. Oh Jeremy, you are going to make all this worth it. How many dates had he been on with Evelyn, a lot of them without Jeremy. Listening to her incessant chatter in that shrill voice of hers. Watching those cheap, slut lips babble on and on. Pretending to listen. Pretending to care. But a good plan requires time and patience.

Evelyn peered through the intricate curls of metal into the secret place. "Oh, Jud. I can't wait."

"I'm delighted you are so excited. Just let me open the gate." He slipped his hand into the pocket of his jeans and pulled out a ring of keys. Choosing one, he slid it into a keyhole at chest height in the wrought-iron gate and turned it. The locked clicked. The door whined as he pulled it open.

"I'll lead the way. Please stay on the pathway. We don't want to disturb any of the plants and flowers."

"Jeremy, did you hear Jud?"

"Yes. Don't step on flowers." Jeremy's bright-blue eyes looked up at Jud imploringly.

Jud chuckled. The door clanged as he shut it behind them. Locking it, he returned the ring to his pocket. He walked slowly along the cobblestone pathway, manoeuvring around a massive tree. A crisp wave of cool air hit his face as he moved through the shade of a canopy of branches stretching over his head.

Following the cobblestones, he emerged from the shelter of the grand tree. The bright sun hit his eyes. The afternoon desert heat warmed his core in a split second. He slipped his sunglasses from the top of his head into place. Moving his gaze in a full circle, from left to right, to scan his entire sanctuary, he smiled wide. His shoulders relaxed. His mind rested.

"Oh, Jud. It's amazing. I mean, you described it, but I didn't picture this." Evelyn covered her red lips with a pasty hand.

Jeremy stood quietly, in a trance. He dropped his mother's hand and stared at the trees.

Evelyn spun slowly on one heel, taking in the entire circle. "Your trees, they're lovely."

"That one"—Jud pointed to the right—"was the first. Crab Apple. It blooms every year. I get dozens of jars of jelly. That one"—he pointed to the left—"is a Honeycrisp. Like the one at the café. Not the kind of apples for jelly, but great for baking."

"Oh my. And that one?" She pointed straight across, to the apex of the circle.

"That's my newest tree. The Bubblegum Plum. Sweet, red fruit. Blossoms smell like Bubblicious. That tree is a real special one." *Jeremy's going to love it.*

"Is that why it's at the head of the garden?"

Perceptive for a stupid slut. "Yes. I have carefully laid out my garden. Each tree has a certain position."

She walked toward the Bubblegum Plum. "I've never seen such a precisely laid-out garden. You must spend a lot of time working up here. Everything is perfect." She paused, looking down at her feet. "You've even engraved the stones. 'I have not slaughtered with evil intent the cattle of God.' Oh my. Is that biblical?"

"Do you read the bible?"

She looked at him sheepishly. "No, I can't say I do."

"Yes. It's biblical. Why don't you and Jeremy have a seat?" He motioned to a table in the centre of the circle. "I'll get us some refreshments."

Evelyn led Jeremy over to the table. Jud walked to the apex of the cobblestone path, and followed an offshoot of the pathway into a corner. He approached the small garden house he had built when he started spending full days in his sanctuary. As he walked through the door, the cold air soothed his sweat-soaked skin. He pulled his sunglasses off and squinted into the dark room. The overhead fan whirred, sending wafts of cool air over his hot body.

His boots thudded against the wooden floor as he walked over to the small fridge in the corner of the room. He grasped the handle of an ice-cold glass pitcher and set it on the counter. Opening an overhead cupboard, he retrieved a silver tray and three glasses. He opened the freezer. Icy air soothed his face. Sliding a tray of ice cubes from the top shelf, he twisted the tray, removing several miniature blocks. They clinked as they hit the insides of the glasses.

As he filled each glass with summer-yellow liquid from the pitcher, a fresh lemon scent rose into his nostrils. Placing the pitcher onto the tray, he slipped his fingers into his back pocket. He held a vial up to the ray of sunshine piercing through the window, manoeuvring through the openings in the soft white curtains. He opened the vial, tilted it toward one of the glasses and knocked it with his pointer. Several drops plummeted into the yellow liquid, spreading long tendrils down to the bottom of the glass. He closed the vial and returned it to his pocket. He shifted the tainted glass to the front of the tray. Lifting the tray with both hands, he proceeded to serve his guests.

He returned to the table and placed the silver platter down. Jeremy's little hand reached for the glass at the front of the tray.

Jud plucked Jeremy's fingers from the glass. "A gentleman serves the ladies first. You want to be a gentleman, don't you?"

Bright-blue eyes looked back at him. "Yes."

Jud picked up the glass and handed it to Evelyn. She took a long sip. "Delicious. it's so refreshing. I didn't realize how thirsty I am."

Jud handed a glass to Jeremy. "The desert heat. At this time of day it's at it's peak."

Jeremy gulped and slurped his drink. Jud chuckled.

Jeremy plunked the glass onto the table and wiped his mouth with his arm. "Thank you, Jud."

"You're welcome. There's plenty more if you're still thirsty."

Jud took a swig from his own glass. The sweet, cold lemon liquid soothed his throat.

"This is a big garden," Jeremy chimed.

"I'm glad you like it. It took me a long time and a lot of hard work, but now it's my very special place to come." Jud ran a hand over Jeremy's soft, vanilla-bean hair.

Jeremy smiled. "Special?"

"Yes. A place that makes me happy."

"Oh, like the park?"

"Yes."

"Oooh," Evelyn moaned, resting her forehead on her hand.

Her glass was empty.

"Are you OK?" Jud asked.

"I'm...dizzy." She lifted her head, then lowered it again.

"Could be the heat. Maybe we've been out here too long. Do you want to go over to the garden house? It's cooler and you could lie down."

"Umm...OK. Jeremy should come with us."

"Sure thing." Jud reached out and Jeremy took his hand. He helped Evelyn up with his free arm. "Lean on me. It's not far."

Jud shuffled slowly over the cobblestone. Evelyn rested against his shoulder, sliding her feet along the pathway. Jeremy skipped along, swinging Jud's arm.

They reached the garden house. Jud shoved the door open and guided Evelyn to the couch. She sat down with a thump and slumped against the back of the sofa. "Jeremy..." she mumbled, then toppled over. Jud positioned a cushion under her head and lifted her legs onto the couch.

"Mommy?"

"It's OK. Your mommy just needs a rest. She'll wake up soon. We can play in the garden until she wakes up."

"Play?"

"Yes. I made a picnic for us."

"Picnic!" Jeremy squealed.

Jud opened the fridge and pulled out a small cooler. He took Jeremy's hand and led him out of the garden house. The door closed with a click. He pulled the ring of keys from his pocket, selected one, and locked the door to the garden house.

"C'mon, Jeremy. Let's go have our picnic in the garden."

"Picnic. Garden." Jeremy declared with delight.

Jud walked hand in hand with Jeremy to the table in the centre of the garden. Placing the cooler on the table, he guided Jeremy to sit down. He opened the cooler and laid out a lovely lunch spread. Sandwiches. Sliced Honeycrisp apples. Freshly picked Bubblegum Plums. Chocolate chip cookies.

Jeremy's eyes grew wide with delight. "Oh boy. Yummy."

Jud sat down across from Jeremy and handed him a plastic plate. "Here you go. You can have whatever you want."

"Thank you, Jud." Jeremy reached eagerly for the food.

"Oh, you're welcome, kid." Jud reached for a plum. Taking a large bite, the sugary juice drizzled down his chin. He licked his lips and watched Jeremy.

Chapter Seventy-Four

Wall of Eyes

Mahoney wandered off down a dimly lit hallway. As soon as the SWAT team leader had busted down the door of the house up on the hill in Santa Fe, Mahoney had tuned out the orders the towering six-foot-five leader barked to the rest of the team. The musty hallway called to him. He followed his instincts, slipped from the pack unnoticed, and explored.

Dust particles clung to the beads of sweat drizzling down his forehead. A cold trickled down his back. Something pulled at him, drawing him through a doorway into a dark room. He blinked several times, trying to see into the room. As his eyes adjusted, rough shapes became familiar. The room appeared to be some kind of workshop. A workbench sat along the far wall, several shelves lined each side of the room, and a black door loomed in a far corner. The chill increased and crept up his neck, tingling his skull. He walked toward the black door.

Pointing his Glock steady in his left hand, he reached out and turned the knob with his right hand. An eerie creaking vibrated through the quiet room. The door eased open on rusty hinges. Formaldehyde permeated his nostrils, clinging to the back of his throat. The outline of a tall shelf loomed over him. He looked to his right, saw a light switch, reached out and flicked it on.

He swallowed hard against the shock choking him. The scene before him was a first. Despite the horrific corpses cluttering his mind.

He stood at the head of a storage room. Tall shelves lined the walls on either side, towering over him, rows upon rows of glass jars, filled with clear liquid.

In each jar, a pair of eyeballs floated, their dark pupils peering through the liquid, through the glass, as if searching for answers.

He shook his head, grabbed his radio, and pushed a button. White noise crackled through a dense layer of silence as he searched for the words to describe the wall of eyes peering down at him.

Chapter Seventy-five

Cave Adventure

Taking Jeremy's hand in his own, Jud led the kid along the cobblestone path.

"Jeremy, do you like caves?" Jud's sugar-coated words dripped from his mouth.

"Caves? Yes. Do you have one?"

"You bet I do."

"Can we go in it?"

"Yes. Now, Jeremy, it will be dark in the cave. And we have to walk through some tunnels to get there. But you don't have to be afraid. I will hold your hand. OK?"

"OK. I can hold your hand." Jeremy pumped his little fingers against Jud's.

Jud led Jeremy toward a large Cypress, surrounded by a plethora of cacti.

Jeremy tugged on Jud's hand. "What if Mommy wants to see the cave?"

"Don't worry. Your mommy is still resting. We can go into the cave and then I will go check on her. If she wants to see the cave, then I will take her."

"OK. Let's go to the cave," Jeremy squealed.

Jud pushed a large branch aside. "You go under the tree. The cave door is hidden." He followed Jeremy under the canopy of green leaves.

"Is that a secret door? To the cave?" Jeremy pointed at a small, black wooden door, built into a circular rock.

"Yes. It is. Should we go inside?"

"Yes."

Jud retrieved his key ring from his pocket, unlocked the door, and pushed it open. Hunching over, he walked through. He turned back, reached his hand out and motioned for Jeremy to follow him. Jeremy grabbed his hand and jumped through the door.

Jud creaked the door closed, locking it behind him. The bright sunlight vanished. Blackness surrounded them. He gripped Jeremy's soft hand. "Don't be afraid. I'm right here. Your eyes will get used to the dark."

"OK." Jeremy's voice sounded weak.

Jud squeezed Jeremy's hand. He blinked hard several times until he could make out the walls of the tunnel.

"Can you see the walls of the tunnel now?"

"Yes." Jeremy's voice had steadied.

Jud walked slowly along the hard-packed ground. The moist, cool air soothed his hot skin. A sharp squeal pierced the silence. Jeremy jumped, a small gasp escaping his lips. A scuttling noise clicked through the tunnel. Jud crouched down and looked Jeremy in the eyes. "It's OK. That was just a nocturnal animal."

"Nack...toonal...animal?"

"Yes. Just a small animal that lives in the dark. They won't hurt you. They just like it in here because it's dark and cool. It's part of our adventure." Jud held both of Jeremy's hands.

Jeremy looked back at him with wide eyes. "OK."

Jud continued to lead through the downward slope of the winding tunnel.

"This is a special cave. I only bring my special friends down here."

"I'm your special friend?" Jeremy's grip relaxed.

"Yes, Jeremy, you are my most special friend."

"Wow." Jeremy skipped along, swinging Jud's arm.

"You see? It's fun in here when we are together. And you can see better in the dark now, can't you?"

"Yeah."

"I'm your most special friend," a whisper seeped through the cave wall.

Go back to sleep.

"Look. This tunnel will lead us to the cave. It's right up there." Jud pointed ahead. The tunnel forked. They continued down the straight offshoot.

"We're close to the cave," Jeremy chimed in.

A staircase weaved up and out of sight. "We just have a few stairs to climb."

"I love to climb," Jeremy piped in with enthusiasm.

"What about me? *Your most special friend,"* a thin, raspy voice seeped down the staircase.

Go back to sleep. Jud shook his head.

They trotted up the stairs, hand in hand. At the top of the single, winding flight, Jud stopped. He dangled his key ring, selected a golden key, and unlocked the final black door. He pushed it open.

Jeremy squeezed his hand. "Wow." Jeremy stood in awe, his wide eyes scrambling over the vast space.

"Do you like my cave?"

"Yeah."

"Now, you remember how I said I only bring special friends down here?"

"Yes. I'm your special friend."

Whispers wove through the space, echoing off the walls, *"What about usss?"*

Go back to sleep. All of you. I'm with Jeremy right now.

Jud looked at Jeremy. "You are. Most special. Would you like to meet my other special friends?"

"Maybe they could be my friends too?" Jeremy looked up at him with hopeful eyes.

"Maybe. C'mon."

Jud led Jeremy into the centre of the circle. The room was cool and dark. The perimeter was lined with perfectly spaced, long rectangular boxes. The top of each box aligned against the circular wall. The bottom of each box pointed into the centre of the underground sanctuary.

"My friends are all resting. These boxes are their beds. Which friend would you like to meet?"

Jeremy looked at the boxes in confusion. "They don't look like beds."

"They are special beds."

"Oh." Jeremy looked over Jud's shoulder toward one of the boxes.

Jud spun on his heel and followed Jeremy's gaze. "Johnny is sleeping there. Do you want to meet Johnny?"

"Um...OK," Jeremy's voice seethed with unsureness.

"It's all right. Trust me." Jud squeezed Jeremy's hand.

Jeremy looked up at him and smiled. "OK, Jud."

Jud led Jeremy over to Johnny's rectangular bed. He wheeled over his bed-opening contraption, aligned the hooks into place and cranked the handle.

The lid raised. "Jeremy, this is the cool part. If we pull this lever here, the machine will move the lid for us. Do you want to pull the lever?"

"Yes." Jeremy scuttled over to the machine.

Jud guided Jeremy's hand and helped him pull the lever. The machine whirred as the lid moved through the air.

"Now let go of the lever."

Jeremy pulled his hand away from the control panel.

"Now, push the orange button. This one." Jud pointed.

Jeremy pushed the button. The machine whirred again. The lid moved away from the concrete box.

"The last step is to push that green button," Jud instructed.

Jeremy pushed the green button. The lid lowered to the ground.

"You see. Isn't that cool?"

"Yes."

"Now, let's go meet Johnny."

Jeremy froze.

Jud grabbed Jeremy's hand and led him to the concrete bed. As they approached, Jeremy's hand pulled against Jud's. Jeremy resisted the forward motion.

Jud reassured him, "Johnny is nice. You will like him. I know this is different than what you have seen before. It's part of our adventure. New things."

Jeremy hesitated, then let Jud lead him the rest of the way.

Jud walked right up to the concrete bed, thumped a boot onto a small staircase positioned next to the box, and peered in. White-cloth-wrapped Johnny lay still in his bed. Jeremy pattered up behind Jud. Little feet clattered up the staircase, then Jeremy stood beside Jud.

Jeremy's body shook. He whimpered.

Jud looked at Jeremy. Jeremy's eyes glistened with tears. "Wha-wha-what's wrong with him?"

"Nothing. He is wrapped up for safekeeping. Johnny will be kept forever. The wrappings keep him so that he can be a young, happy boy forever."

"Forever?" Jeremy gulped.

"Yes. Forever. Don't you want to be a young, happy boy forever?"

Jeremy stood in silence, tremors shaking his body every few seconds. "I...I...don't know."

Jud jumped down from the staircase and looked up into Jeremy's eyes. "Jeremy. You are my special friend. I want you to be my special friend forever. I want you to be young and happy. I don't want anyone to hurt you. Ever."

A glaze washed over Jeremy's wide eyes, freezing them into a hazy state. Vinegar stung the air as the crotch of Jeremy's pants darkened. His little arms shook.

"Jeremy, come with me. We'll get you cleaned up. We're going to be special friends forever. I will take care of you."

In a trance, Jeremy's limp arms hung at his side. Jud took Jeremy's hand and pulled Jeremy by his little, limp arm across the room. Jud lifted Jeremy and laid him on the sacrificial table in the centre of the dark burial grounds. He secured Jeremy's small wrists in the metal circles attached to the table. *Click.* One wrist. *Click.* The other wrist.

"You stay here, I'll go get your mom." Jud looked down at Jeremy and wiped away the tears trickling down the little boy's cheeks. "Don't cry. It's all right. You are with me now. You are my most special friend. You will be happy here. No one can hurt you. No one can rot your innocence. You will remain pure. Forever."

Chapter Seventy-six

Sid's Sanctuary

The sun, perched high in the pastel-blue sky, shone brightly over the barren desert. An unending stretch of dry, brown earth reached out in every direction. Straight ahead, a smooth incline spattered with bright-green cacti led up to an elaborate metal gate. Sweat sprouting across his brow, pouring down both sides of his face, Mahoney paused and wiped his forehead, cheeks and neck with a white handkerchief. His heavy SWAT vest suffocated him, his shirt sticking to his back underneath. He tucked the white cloth into a pocket in his vest, slid his hand across the velcro opening, and continued to climb up the hill, toward the gate.

Sweat drenching his armpits and plastering his shirt sleeves to his arms, he plugged his way up the hill. A tall gate loomed over him. He reached the top. The sun belted down on him as he examined the latch. *Locked.*

Pulling his radio from the holster on his belt, he pushed a button.

"Sutton?" He released the button.

A crackle echoed. "Boss? Where are you?"

He pushed the button again. "Behind the house. Up the hill. Get up here, pronto. Bring backup."

"Can't. Order is to wait for clearance from SWAT commander." White noise faded to silence.

Mahoney gritted his teeth. He pushed the button hard. "Get Quesnel. Get up here. Now."

"Ten-four."

Ripping echoed over the barren hill as he tore open the velcro band across a pocket in his vest. He pulled out two small, silver tools—a tension wrench and a pick. Sliding the hooked end of the wrench into the bottom of the lock, he twisted it right. *No give.* He twisted it left. The tension gave against the tool. Holding the wrench in place, he slid the pick into the top of the lock. Hidden pins clicked against the pick as he raked it back and forth. Steadying his hand, he slid the pin in again in a smooth, slow motion. Clicking against the pick settled the pins into place. A final click and the lock released. *Bingo.* He slipped the tools back into his pocket and slid his hand across the velcro, closing the pocket. He grabbed his Glock from a holster hanging from his belt. Finger on frame, he slid the Glock into load. The gate squealed as he pulled it open.

He stepped through, into the enclosure. The bright sun vanished behind a tall tree with wide branches, stretching out, creating a roof of leaves. He wiped his arm across his forehead, his wet shirt sleeve absorbing a small amount of his sweat. Gun pointed straight ahead, he took slow steps around the thick trunk.

He stopped and scanned his surroundings. He was caged in by a large, circular enclosure. The crisscross pattern of a gigantic pergola traced over the ground. The area was partitioned into eight equal segments, each pie-shaped slice bordered by a cobblestone walkway. A circle of trees outlined the space. The still air swelled with heat. Silence cloaked his ears. Gripping his gun with both hands, he slowly moved his outstretched arms around the circle. Nothing. No one. No noise. He was alone. He lowered his arms, keeping the gun ready to go in his right hand.

Stepping onto the stone walkway directly in front of him, he made his way to the centre of the circle. Bright-green cacti dotted with fluorescent red and yellow flowers lined the sandy plots between the stone walkways. *Someone spent a lot of time on this. Sid, the gardener. I'm gonna find you.*

Reaching the centre, Mahoney halted. Spinning around slowly, he scanned the entire circle. Five perfectly placed trees bordered the edge of each pie-shaped segment of the garden. Bright-green leaves dangled from the tree branches. Pink and white blossoms wove thick blankets over the branches. A sweet aroma clung to the stifling air.

At the head of the circle, directly across from the entranceway, a tall tree with a vase-like trunk stood. He walked toward the tree. Looking down at the stones as he stepped over them, a series of letters were carved along the path. Reading the letters one at a time, he pieced together the words.

"I have not slaughtered with evil intent the cattle of God."

Mahoney twisted his face into a grimace. *Book of the Dead. Number forty-two.* A cold crawled through him as he contemplated that there could be forty-two bodies close by.

Mahoney walked up to the tree, staring into the blossoms. He moved a branch to reveal an oval-shaped, purple-red fruit. He reached out and plucked the fruit free. Bringing it to his nose, he inhaled. It smelled liked bubblegum. *Where's your gardener?*

Turning to face the centre of the circle, the plum tree at his back, he inspected each tree. The most massive of them all, placed directly to his left, at the end of the walkway slicing through the centre of the circle, stretched its grand branches high into the pastel-blue sky. Blankets of white blossoms blended with the dark-green leaves. Small yellow-pink apples dotted the blankets of white.

Hand gripping the Glock, he walked toward the massive tree, continuously scanning the circle. A mixture of sweet and tart emanated from the tree. *Crab Apples.* His foot sunk into soft soil. He looked down. Freshly dug, wet, dark dirt, formed a rectangular shape, from the base of the tree to the start of the path. A cold trickled up his hot, sweaty back. He shivered. *What you have been up to out here, psycho gardener? I'll find you.*

He scanned the garden again. The sun bounced off a silver tray set on a table in the middle, catching his eye. He strode up to the table. Three glasses, partially filled with lemon-coloured liquid, sat next to two plates housing the remnants of sandwiches and cookie crumbs. A cooler sat beside the abandoned lunch. The last bits of ice cubes floated atop the yellow liquid in a glass pitcher. *You sicko. You've brought another kid here. Or is it two? Not this time. Not. This. Time.*

Shoulders tensed, brow sweating, Mahoney lifted his gun and scanned the garden. *Where are you?* His eyes darted along the cobblestones, the trees, the cacti, searching for some indication of where this gardener was hiding. *Bingo.* His eyes caught a thread of cobblestones shooting off in the right, top segment of the circle.

He jogged over to the side trail and followed it. He slowed his pace. His eyes constantly darted along the path, looking for any sign of movement, any indication of his prey. The path came to a dead end at the base of another huge tree.

Dammit. Where are you? Images of white cloths, doll eyes, and little boys swirled through his mind. *I need to find you, kid.* Keeping his hands on his gun, he pictured the round pink stone tucked away in the top, right pocket of his vest. A rush of warm energy washed through him. He reached out a hand and pulled at the ample branches of the tree. There was something behind the plethora of green.

Pushing heavy branches aside, he made his way to the back of the trunk.

A small, black door stared at him.

What the hell? He hunched over and turned the knob. *Locked.*

He retrieved the two small silver tools again and worked at the lock. After securing the wrench, he worked the pick inside the top of the lock. He waited for the click. The lock wouldn't give.

Sweat stung his eyes. He ran the back of his arm over his brow. His shirt was too wet to sop up the salty pools forming around his eyes. He shook his head, spraying droplets. He fiddled with the pick, sliding it slowly inside the lock.

C'mon. Open.

Click. He sighed. His stomach unclenched. Securing the pick, he turned the knob. The door opened.

A wave of cold hit him. He peered inside. Darkness. He stood up and unholstered his radio from his belt.

He pushed a button. White noise crackled. "Sutton?" He released the button. Nothing. He pushed it again. "Sutton." He waited.

"Boss! We've been looking for you."

"Behind the house. Up the hill. I'm in a garden."

"You alone?"

"Yeah. Get up here. There's some sort of tunnel."

"Wait for us."

"No time. He's here. I think he's got a kid. There's a black door, behind the circle."

"It's protocol. Don't go in alone," Sutton said, his voice raising a few notches.

"Just get here."

"Wait, what circle?"

He switched the radio off and holstered it. Unhooking a flashlight from his belt, he flicked it on. He pointed the beam of light into the tunnel. He followed it.

Chapter Seventy-seven

High Throne

Boots thumping against the packed dirt floor, Jud walked over to the record player perched on a sturdy wooden table at the back end of his underground, circular sanctuary. He picked up an LP, the wild hair and piercing eyes of the Lizard King—his desert king—plastered over the cover. He'd let go of many things. All his ties to his old garden in the cold of Doris' backyard had been severed. His mourning over Timmy was over. This was a fresh start, a new garden with the forty-second tree—the beautiful Bubblegum Plum, and fresh, innocent Jeremy to pair it with.

His sanctuary felt new. It was time for new vibes. He put down the Lizard King and picked up a new album. A special release, the album only had one song, done three different ways. It had been written by the band, but not included on their debut album. He'd heard the track on the cassette he'd stolen from Seth's collection and listened to it when he first saw Jeremy on the playground.

Faking interest in the ongoing chatter of the scrawny kid that manned the counter at Leon's Records had paid off, and he'd been able to get his hands on a copy of the rare album. He slid the round black disc from the cardboard and set it on the player. Clicking the player on, the black disc spun. He lifted the arm and placed the needle onto the record. Words echoing from the record player seethed around him, telling him he'd built his utopia, the sanctuary of a crazy man.

Jud pulled a heavy gas mask over his head, lifted his thick ponytail, secured the tight elastic band at the nape of his neck and rested the mask against the top of his head. He rolled his shoulders a couple of times, picked up a long, thin knife, and walked over to the centre of the circular, underground sanctuary.

"Let the ritual begin," he declared in a deep voice.

His heavy work boots thumped along the hard-packed dirt. He walked up to Jeremy, lying right where he had left him, secured on the silver sacrificial table in the centre of his sanctuary.

He took long, slow steps. *Thud. Thud. Thud.* His boots pounded the floor. *This is it. The moment I've been working toward.* He relished in the unfolding ritual. *All my planning. All my patience.* He circled the silver table, like a lion inspecting his prey, and looked at Jeremy's face. Creamy-white skin. Vanilla-bean hair. *Delicious.*

A whimpering sound, interrupted with sharp, wet sobs, quivered through the quiet space. Jeremy's eyes bulged from their small sockets, tears streamed down his unblemished, white cheeks, and his body trembled beneath the tight binds holding him close to the stainless-steel slab. The rough voice sang from the record player, reminding Jud that all his friends were in his garden.

"Don't be afraid, Jeremy," Jud spoke softy. "I won't let you lose your innocence. Just like when I led you through the dark tunnel, trust me. I will lead you to your destiny."

Jeremy's head twitched. His eyes opened wider.

Jud leaned in closer. He removed one of his gloves and stroked Jeremy's shiny, golden locks with his hand. "Ssshh. It will be all right."

"M-m-mommy," Jeremy spouted sporadic pleas, sniffing in globs of wet mucous sliding from his nose in a thick, viscous drip.

Pulling his glove back over his hand, Jud walked up to Jeremy and positioned the knife over Jeremy's right eye.

"Mmmfff," a muffled noise came from across the room.

Jud stood up and looked over to the far wall. He admired the majestic throne, perched high at the top of the steps leading to the apex of the circle and adorned with sparkling gems.

"Mmmfff. Fff." Evelyn breathed heavy against the white cloth stretching across her mouth and around her head. Her eyes glared and her nostrils flared. She leaned forward in the throne, forcing the small amount of movement her wrists could make against the tight binds securing her to the chair.

"Well, look who has joined us. You have awoken from your sleep. You see what happens when you chug the lemonade your host has so generously offered to you, hmmm?" Jud slithered his way over to the throne.

Placing one gloved hand on each of the arms of the chair, he leaned in close to Evelyn. He took a long, loud breath in through his nose. "You smell like...a slut. You cheap whore. I know you. You are the woman who betrayed me. You are the woman who pretended to love me, to care about me. Then you wrapped your whore lips around an old man's cock. Again and again. You soul-sucking, venom-filled slut. You betrayed me. You took my innocence. I won't let you take Jeremy's innocence too."

He slid the tip of the long, silver knife across Evelyn's throat atop her putrid skin in a taunting gesture. Her body went rigid. She glared at him with a cold stare.

"Moommmy," Jeremy's faint voice interrupted them.

Evelyn's eyes darted toward Jeremy. Jud stood up. "You will get what you deserve. I will save Jeremy's innocence. Your rotten core will not corrupt him." He turned and walked back to Jeremy.

"MMMFF!" Evelyn protested. Her eyes were wild. Sweat dripped down the sides of her face.

Jud ignored her and focused on Jeremy.

Reaching the centre of the room, Jud stood behind a tall pedestal and flipped open a massive hardcover book. He turned the pages, settling on a spot identified with a bookmark. He cleared his throat and spoke to his audience of two as if addressing a full congregation.

"Jeremy. I declare your innocence. You shall be placed in the final position, in the sanctuary that will preserve you and your innocence forever. By the negative confessions, to protect you in the afterlife, I declare you have not slaughtered with evil intent the cattle of God."

Jud closed the book with a thud and looked at Jeremy. With long, slow strides, his work boots thumping against the hard ground, he approached Jeremy. He slid his gloved fingers into his jeans pocket and retrieved a small vial. Perching the vial on the steel slab about Jeremy's head, he looked down at Jeremy. "Time to preserve your innocence, kid."

Jud slid the bulky machine-like mask from the top of his head over his face, his sandy-blond locks dangling over the elastic. He lifted the knife and moved his gloved hand over to Jeremy's right eye. The knife hovered over Jeremy's eyeball. Jeremy's body shook, his lower lip trembled.

A muffled scream crawled through the air from the vicinity of the throne.

Jud loomed over Jeremy, the knife in his hand.

The muffled screaming from the throne grew louder and raspy.

A rattle snapped Jud from his dream-like focus on his ritual. He whipped his head in the direction of the noise, toward the black door at the entrance to the sanctuary.

The handle twisted. Something on the other side pushed against the door. *What the fuck is this?* He stood frozen, staring at the black door.

The knob twisted left then right. *Bang.* Something hit hard against the door.

How could this be? He remembered locking the door behind him when he carried Evelyn into the tunnel from the garden. *Impossible.* He saw his hand clicking the key in the lock at the front gate where he led Jeremy and Evelyn into the garden.

Bang. Bang. Someone was trying to break into his sanctuary. His mind whirled. He looked at Jeremy. *Bang. Bang. Bang.*

He snapped his gaze to the door. *No time.* He spun and ran to the wall furthest from the black door. He slid into a dark opening, concealing himself and peering a watchful eye.

Chapter Seventy-eight

Gardener Hunt

Mahoney squinted into blackness.

He was blinded by the instant transformation of bright sunshine to darkness. Misshaped multicoloured forms disintegrating slowly, the walls around him came into focus. Pointing his gun steady with one hand, his flashlight with the other, he looked straight down a long, dark tunnel. Packed dirt walls closed in around him from either side.

He inched his way along, his shoes sinking into the wet soil. His shirt stuck to his back, cold and wet. A chill ran through him. His breath formed clouds as he exhaled. Something brushed along his head, tickling his ear. He jerked his shoulder. Tucking the flashlight under his arm, he ran his fingers over his head. His fingers pulled thick strands of cobweb from his hair. He shook his hand hard. The wisps of white floated to the ground.

He paused and took a deep breath.

Repointing his flashlight, he inched forward, following the beam. A fork formed in the dark tunnel. One tunnel continued straight ahead. Two more tunnels opened up, one on his right and one on his left. Each of them plunged straight ahead into nothing. The pink stone sat nestled in his vest pocket. A warmth surged through him. He continued down the straight path.

A squeal pierced his ears. He snapped his arm, pointing his gun toward the sound. A flapping noise closed in on him. A swoosh clipped his ears. A black bat came into focus as it swooped over his head then flew away. Shaking his head, he composed himself. *Bloody bat.* He refocused on the tunnel ahead.

Reaching the end of the tunnel, he was faced with a concrete staircase. Stepping up on the first stair, his shoe slid on a coating of slimy moss. Digging his foot into the green goo, he launched himself up, one step at a time.

Reaching the top of the stairs, he faced another black door. A muffled scream from behind the door jolted him. His shoulders clenched hard. His brain buzzed.

Get the fuck in there, Bug. Shoving his flashlight into the holster on his belt, he turned the knob. The door was locked. In a tight two-handed grip, he raised his gun.

He kicked the door hard with his boot. *Bang.* Standing tall, he repositioned himself. *Bang. Bang.* His boot hit the door, harder. *Not hard enough.* He shifted his weight to his left leg, crouching, then snapped his right leg into a series of kicks. *Bang. Bang. Bang.*

The door shattered. Splinters of wood crackled, flying through the air. He crept through the opening, gun raised.

Chapter Seventy-nine

Sid's Cemetery

Mahoney froze. A large, circular enclosure formed a dark cave over him. The ground was covered in packed dirt, a series of stone pathways carving out eight perfectly measured, pie-shaped wedges. Rectangular, concrete boxes circled around him, bordering the entire cave. The boxes were raised, up on stands, each with a small staircase leading to the base of the box. Cold surged through his insides, devouring every bit of warmth. He swallowed hard. The boxes loomed over him. The room swirled around him.

"MMMFFFF!"

Mahoney snapped his gaze in the direction of the muffled scream and lunged his way up the path. A women sat, high on an elaborate throne. Her hands were secured to the arms. A glint caught his eye. Red rubies gleamed at him. The woman's eyes were bulging from their sockets. Tremors shook her shoulders as sweat and tears poured over her dirty face.

"MMMFFF!" she forced the stifled scream through a gag.

He scanned the entire space, moving his gun slowly, probing his eyes into the dark space. He jolted. His body froze. A small figure lay in the centre of the circular cave, on a silver slab. Sandy-blond locks of hair spread around the kid's head. *Sandy blond.* Just like the locks framing the creamy-white face that had been floating through his mind for days.

White mummy faces popped up, crowding his mind. Black, glassy, vacant eyes stared into his soul. He shook his head and focused on the steel slab in the centre of the dark cave.

Picnic's over, you sick psycho.

Glock pointed, he crept along the dirt floor, toward the child.

Sutton's voice rang through his mind, *"Wait for us."*

Fuck it. Be alive, kid. Be alive.

He took another step, scanning the room, pointing his gun in a death grip. The kid whimpered.

You're not taking this one, you monster.

He walked up to the kid. "It's OK. I'm the police." He lowered his hands, keeping his Glock ready to go in his right hand. A silver clasp held each of the boy's hands close to the silver slab. He reached for one and pulled at it.

A flash came from the far end of the cave, opposite the door Mahoney had entered through. A man lunged through the air, tangled hair flailing wildly, a heavy-machine-like mask perched on his head, an evil, crazed look in his eyes.

Mahoney whipped around, turning his back on the steel slab and the boy. He faced the wild man as he lifted his arms straight out, raising his Glock. He pressed his fingers hard against the trigger. *Bang.* The bullet flew through the air.

Blood and flesh flung from the crazed man's muscular arm. *Gotcha, Sid.* Sid landed hard on his boot, lunging high into the air again.

Mahoney took two larges steps further into the cave as he pressed the trigger once more. *Bang.* Another bullet pierced the air, flying toward Sid. Fresh meat ripped from Sid's shin, blood spurting. Sid landed. Sid lunged again. *You motherfucker.*

Mahoney pointed his gun straight at Sid's head. Sid's arm flung out in a wild gesture. Sid, high in the air, lurched over him, a shiny, silver knife held in his hand. Mahoney pointed and pressed.

The weight of Sid came down onto him. His arm jerked. *Bang.*

He couldn't see the bullet. Pain pierced his left eye, erupting through his brain. Blood burst from his eyeball, trickling down his face.

Thump. His back hit the ground hard, his bones rattling. *Thump.* His head hit the cold dirt. A high-pitched ring deafened him. He could no longer feel his gun in his hand.

A sharp, cold blade slid deep into his gut. Pain sliced through him, reaching up inside of him. A thick, warm goo oozed from his stomach, drenching his shirt and seeping into his vest. His limbs convulsed.

This is it. Blue scarves drifted through his clouded mind. *The boy.* He wrenched his skull, forcing his eyes open. A pool of thick black-red clouded his vision on one side. Through his one functioning eye, he looked the crazed sick psycho right in the eyes. *Fight, Bug. Hold him off. Just till...*

Bang. Sid's crazed eyes bulged, then rolled back in his head. Smoke drifted from a red hole in the centre of his head. A mist of blood and brains floated behind Sid's head.

Thud. Sid flopped on top of him. The weight suffocated him. The machine mask scraped at his cheek, ripping at his mangled, bloody eye. Pain pierced his brain. He tried to scream. His mouth opened. Nothing escaped, only scratches along his parched throat. *Gotcha. Sick psycho.*

The kid was alive. Sid was done for. Purple almond eyes danced through his mind. A cloud of lavender wafted over him. *Blackwood.*

Blonde curls and giggles erupted in the back of his brain. A blue dolphin coasted over ocean waves, pulling Stella along. *Stella.* He closed his eyes. He moved his lips in a whisper. "Stella." He followed the darkness.

SINKING
PIRATE

Chapter Eighty

Purple Almonds and Lavender

Detective Mahoney leaned his weight into the heavy door. *Swoosh.* It opened. Cool air brushed his face. The Santa Fe morgue looked like a smaller version of the one back home. Blackwood perched in a corner, cleaning equipment. Her hands were gloved in plastic. Her almond eyes were encased in thick, square plastic goggles. Just the way he liked her.

Maybe it wasn't too late for him. He might be able to put a halt to his string of one-night stands, mixing sex with booze to numb everything else out of his life.

Get on with it, Bug. He swallowed against the nervous mix of bile, saliva, and cold coffee gurgling up his throat.

He removed his derby, holding it at his side, and strode toward her.

Blackwood turned and smiled. Warmth pulsed inside of him, in his heart, through his gut.

"Mahoney. They released you." A slight pout tugged her lips downward. "Your eye. How long do you have to wear that? You look like..."

"A fucking pirate. I know."

She giggled. "I'm sorry."

"It's OK. I look ridiculous." He smiled. Tingles surged through his stomach.

Her face turned grim. "You're lucky. You shouldn't have gone in there alone."

"Yeah. That's what I've been told about a thousand times. It was me or Jeremy. The kid has a more promising future ahead of him than I do."

Her purple almond eyes oozed concern. "Yeah." She sighed. "But people are...concerned, you know."

"I know." He stepped closer to her. A lavender cloud engulfed him.

"The bodies, they're all here. I'll be staying here with them until all the processing is done. I assume you're flying home now that you're out of the hospital?"

"Yeah." He paused. "So, are there really forty-one bodies here? And Sid."

"Yeah. Judson, otherwise known as Sid. And the forty-one boys he killed and buried in his underground sanctuary. Doctor Sabin flew down. She's worked non-stop trying to get everything processed."

"I'm sure you did too."

She looked down sheepishly. "Well, sure. I guess so."

"A lot of bodies in a short time. You're quite a team."

She looked back up, meeting his gaze. "Yeah, I guess we are." Her cheeks flushed a light pink. "You could take a look, at the bodies, if you want."

More little bodies. More faces. "Maybe."

"I just know how you get. You want to see."

He swallowed hard, rubbing the back of his neck. "Yeah."

She looked at him. Her expression softened.

He reached out and took her gloved hand. He slid the plastic away, touching her soft skin. Surges of tingles invaded his gut. His heart thumped. "Listen, I..." He swallowed. *Spit it out, old man.* "How about dinner?" He looked into her eyes. His insides melted.

She smiled. She turned his hand over in hers, facing his palm up. Circling her finger over his exposed palm, she looked into his eyes. "Mahoney. I like you. We connect. Deeper than solving a murder case."

"Then have dinner with me."

"I can't."

He sighed. "You don't mix murder and pleasure."

"Oh, I do."

A swoosh jolted them. Doctor Sabin glided through the door, smiling at them.

Blackwood squeezed his hand, then released it. Her eyes wandered over to the doctor walking toward them. The outline of the doctor's thighs swung back and forth against her white lab coat.

Mahoney could almost hear the clicking sound as the gears in his brain kicked in. "You do. Just not with me."

"I'm sorry, Detective. You're not my type."

He snorted a laugh.

Doctor Sabin slid up beside Blackwood. Her white lab coat slipped open as she placed a hand on her hip. A black dress hugged her thighs, stopping at her knees. "Detective. Nice to see you. Stand-up work on that case."

"Thanks. You're the first person not to hassle me."

"Well, the pirate look is good on you." She winked at him. Looking at Blackwood, her voice turned sultry. "You ready?"

"Yeah. Just let me slip out of my gear."

Mahoney asked, "You two headed somewhere special?"

"Just drinks. Maybe dinner," Doctor Sabin responded.

He snuffed a laugh. "Lucky girl."

"I am." Doctor Sabin shot him another wink.

Blackwood said, "I can show you to the room, where the bodies are."

Mahoney responded. "Sure."

Blackwood looked at Doctor Sabin. "I'll be right back. Mahoney, this way."

"Have a nice time, Doctor." He tipped his hat at Doctor Sabin, placed it on his head and followed Blackwood across the room.

Chapter Eighty-one

Horror Flick

Blackwood closed the door behind her. A rush of cold air hit Mahoney's face. He stood in the middle of a room in the Santa Fe morgue, preparing himself to see the carnage that had been recovered from Sid's underground sanctuary.

Blackwood pulled out all forty-one of the little corpses. Forty-two with Sid. He knew the demented monster's true identify was Judson, but he would always see him as Sid. Slippery Sid—the psycho killer who nearly slipped through his fingers.

Why he wanted to see them, he didn't know. He also knew that if he went home without a final look then a slew of questions would thrash his thoughts through the night.

He exhaled loud and hard, then walked up to the first small body. If he hadn't saved Jeremy, then he'd be looking at his corpse too. According to Quesnel, Jeremy suffered more psychological trauma than physical damage. Both his eyes were still in tact. One of them had a thin cut across the top which was stitched up without permanent damage. Evelyn, Jeremy's mother, also escaped physical injury. Evelyn coddled Jeremy all the way through the dark tunnels as they were escorted out of Sid's sanctuary.

A series of steel-slab beds were lined up along the room, creating a movie reel of little corpses. The FBI in conjunction with Sutton, Hayes and Quesnel had stayed on Sid's land for over a week, discovering and extracting the remains of the forty-one boys. Forty of them were in the underground tombs. One of them was in the plot above ground under a massive Crab Apple tree. Doctor Sabin was in the process of reconstructing forty-one faces and matching them to missing children reports over the last ten years. Jeremy would have been victim number forty-two. *Would have been.*

Mahoney didn't regret bursting into Sid's underground sanctuary without backup. Jeremy might be dead if he hadn't. Jeremy's life was more important than his. Looking now at so many small corpses, he wondered if he'd really done anything. What about all the other boys lying here now?

Mahoney walked down the line of small, motionless figures. Skeletons covered in a layer of persevered skin. White, waxy faces and empty eye sockets. His mind was forced back to the black door in the back corner of Sid's workshop. A wall of forty-one pairs of eyeballs stared at him. He shook off the chill crawling up his spine.

As Mahoney approached each dead child, he flipped over the tag attached and read the name aloud. One at a time, he silently apologized to the children he hadn't saved.

Finally, he approached a full-sized corpse. Sid. Sid's eyes were closed. His long, thick, reddish blond hair spilled over the steel slab, framing his face. The red hue reminded Mahoney of the Lizard King's mane on the LP cover left in the coffin in the cave. An empty circle pierced Sid's forehead. Quesnel had put a bullet right through his head. Mahoney gasped as he felt Sid's dead weight squishing against him, pressing him into the hard ground. He touched his eyepatch. Pain sliced through his skull as he relived the moment when crazed Sid plunged a knife into his eye.

Sid. Judson. The child who had witnessed his mother performing how many obscene acts on old men until one day he snapped. Most teenagers wouldn't have reacted by slicing his mother's client from neck to navel and watching him bleed out. Judson hadn't been like most teenagers.

What had happened to Jud between the day of his first gutting and the day he showed up on Doris' doorstep, they'd never know. He stared hard at Sid, lying on the shiny steel slab, a red circle burned into his flesh, between his eyes.

Sid had left in his wake forty-one boys, plus the six scattered across the states, the three in BC, the two in the cave in K-Country, and the unfortunate kid from Morse, Saskatchewan. Would they ever know if there were more?

Mahoney turned away from the bodies. He grabbed his tattered derby from where he'd perched it on an empty slab, and set it on his head. Slowly he walked toward the door. The corpses followed him. He'd saved Jeremy, yet pain sliced through him as he thought of all those other faces. White faces with black nothing eyes, staring into his soul. The movie reel clicked into motion, frame by frame replaying a gruesome flick he didn't want to see. He used to be able to walk away and the body would vanish from his mind. Not anymore. The horror flick played, it was on repeat, and it wasn't stopping.

Chapter Eighty-two

Pirate

Mahoney stared at the golden nameplate on the door, *Sergeant Jackson* etched in black lettering. He closed his right eye, matching the eternal darkness his left eye was cloaked in beneath the black eyepatch secured to his face. He couldn't remember the last time he was summoned like this. He'd maintained a long-time-running good rapport with his boss. *Dammit.* Better get this over with. He popped his right eye open and rapped on the door.

"Come in," the sergeant barked.

Mahoney swung through the door. "Sarge. You wanted to see me?"

Sergeant looked up from his paperwork and motioned him in. "Close the door behind you. Have a seat."

Mahoney followed his instructions. Queasiness swirled through his stomach.

"Mahoney. What were you thinking? You shouldn't have gone in there."

Mahoney pictured the shards of wood flying through the air as his boot busted through the door. "Jeremy could've died."

"You could have died. You directly violated protocol."

Sweat sprouted across his forehead. "Jeremy didn't die."

"You might not care if you die. But I do. Look what you've done. We caught Seth because of you." He ran his fingers through his thick hair, pulling short strands from his head. "And this psycho, Sid, or Judson, or whoever the fuck he was, you figured out how to find him. I don't know why these sickos have decided to hunt in our town. But they have. And I need you, here, leading your team."

"Fine. But if I'd waited, Jeremy could be dead."

Sergeant Jackson sighed long and loud. "Fine. I'm not arguing with you anymore." He shot his hands up in the air, then slapped his palms on the desk. "Look at you. You're a mess. And that goddamn eye patch. You look like a pirate."

"I don't feel like a pirate." Mahoney scowled.

Sergeant Jackson chuckled.

Mahoney rubbed the bristle on his chin. "What happened with Doris?"

The sergeant leaned back in his chair. "Doris. We had to release her."

A vein pulsed in the side of Mahoney's head. "What?"

"We have no match for the blood on the hook. No body—alive or dead. We stretched her stay, but after forty-eight hours we couldn't keep her."

"That blood, and the *flesh,* it got there somehow."

The sergeant leaned toward the desk. "I know. That's why we opened a new case. I'll have Sutton take it, for now."

Mahoney clenched his teeth. "What about Queen's park? The body that Seth left there."

The sergeant slipped his glasses off his face and narrowed his eyes. "We don't have enough to warrant a dig in a public park."

Mahoney's face reddened. "There is a body there. In the scattering grounds."

"That's speculation. Based on something a psychotic killer told you. Seth is dead. He can't kill anyone else. You need to move on."

Mahoney's hands balled into fists.

"You look ragged." The sergeant shook his head. "Listen. You're here. Sit in on the post review. Then take some time."

"Time for what?"

"Rest. Relax. Go see your daughter."

Blonde curls flashed through his mind followed by a giggle, then ran away. He was no good for her.

Sergeant Jackson sat down and rested his palms on the desk. "After the review, go see Doctor Sherry. Then go home."

His arms hung, pulling his shoulders toward the floor. He could hear the eerie quiet of his empty apartment. He could see the corpses of the past creeping into his mind.

"Mahoney. Did you hear me?"

He nodded. "Yeah. Sure, Sarge." He turned and shuffled out of the office.

Chapter Eighty-three

Dive Bar Awakening

Mahoney's black dress shoes clicked across the pavement. A buzzing broke the silence as the neon-blue *LiveWire* sign pulsed on and off. Reaching the black door, he paused, rolling his shoulders a couple of times, easing the tension in his back. *Well, Bug, you know what you have to do.* He pushed the door open.

The joint was nearly empty. A couple guys sat in the far-right corner, solving the world's problems over a pitcher of beer and a pack of smokes. A rock ballad hummed through the room. Sasha was at her station, scrubbing the shiny black bar top with a white rag, smacking her bubblegum and swaying to the beat.

Walking toward the bar, he caught her eye. She froze. Tossing the rag into the sink, she stood. Her candy-floss lips pursed into a straight line, her eyes glistened. As he approached the bar, she threw him the professional opening, "What can I get ya." *She used to tag me as sweetie at the end of that line.*

"Nothing. I'm here to see you." He swallowed against the doubt clawing up his throat. He had to smooth over the mess he'd made.

Leaning against the back of the bar, she crossed her arms. She raised her gaze, finding his. Her gum chewing halted. "What happened to your eye?" Worry washed over her face.

"Collateral damage. Perks of the job." He smirked.

Her face turned stern. "What do you want with me, Mr. Detective?"

Placing both palms on the shiny black bar, spreading his fingers open, he stood tall and looked her directly in the eyes. "To apologize."

She rubbed her shoulders with her hands. Her pink nails slid over her milky skin and her candy-floss lips turned slightly downwards. "Oh yeah?"

"Yeah. Listen. I was married. Seems like a lifetime ago. I'm not anymore. Has a lot to do with my job. Has a lot to do with me as well." His eyes glued to hers, he pushed hard against the bar.

Taking a few steps toward the bar, she rested her hands close to his.

He continued, "You were right. I thought you were young, fun and free. Didn't consider that you might want something more. Didn't want to."

Her eyes swelling with little salty pools, she slid one hand over his.

"I'll be straight with you," he said. "I don't allow anything serious into my life, on a personal note. I block it out. You called me on my shit. And you were right. I just wanted to say I'm sorry. I don't expect anything from you. You don't need an old man like me in your life."

Dabbing at the bottom of her eyes with her finger, she looked at him. "You think you have nothing to offer. You think you can't let someone in...Mr. Detective." Her eyes pleaded with him. "You have a lot to offer. You don't give yourself any credit."

He lowered his eyes to the bar. He sighed, then looked back at her. "Well, this old guy can only take one step at a time."

A smile stretched her lips wide, revealing her sparkly whites. She chewed her gum. "You want a drink?"

"No. I've gotta run. Need to try and get a little sleep."

"So, your case is over?" She stared at his eye.

"Yeah." He tapped the bar with his fingers. "Sasha, it was lovely meeting you."

"You too."

He turned and starting walking away.

"Hey, Mr. Detective."

He paused and looked back at her, blonde curls framing her face, candy-floss lips smiling at him.

"You take care of yourself, you hear? And we always got a hot dinner here for you when you need it."

"Thanks." He tipped his hat, turned, and walked out of the bar.

Chapter Eighty-Four

Dinner in a Box

Mahoney sunk into the cavern in the middle of the tattered couch. Removing his derby, he placed it on the cushion next to him. The paper bag crinkled as he opened it. He retrieved plastic cutlery and thin napkins, placing them on the cracked coffee table. Staring into the paper bag at the Styrofoam box, his stomach churned. He pulled the dinner in a box from the bag and placed it next to the fake fork and knife. The silence of his empty apartment weighed down on him like a heavy cloak. His heart sagged. Nausea revolted in the pit of his stomach.

He tossed the paper bag aside and watched it drift to the rug. Leaning his head back against the couch, he closed his eyes. Images of the past crawled through his brain. A cherry-wood table surrounded by sunny-yellow walls, classical music drifting through his ears, and them. Stella, her blonde pigtails bobbing as she pranced down the stairs, taking her favourite seat across from him. The aroma of roasted meat and vegetables wafting from the kitchen. Bea—walking into the room, strawberry-streaked hair dancing on her shoulders, a platter piled high with a homemade dinner in her hands. A warmth rushed through him, followed by a slice of cold. He opened his eyes and moved them across the contents of his present-day dinner. A Styrofoam box. Plastic cutlery. An unopened bottle of Maker's Mark. A crystal glass.

He sat up and leaned toward the coffee table. "Well, Bug. Looks like it's just you tonight." He tried to summon up a chuckle, but it stuck in his throat.

He stood and walked over to the record player against the wall. Shuffling through the dusty box of LPs that had become part of his investigation. *Not tonight.* He needed to move away from the music of a dark poet, the very music that Sid had woven into his twisted fantasy. Mahoney scanned the collection again. He settled on a rock god from his past, back when he was younger and cooler. He slipped a case out and pulled the record from it. He set the record on the player, picked up the handle and dropped the needle. A mad guitar riff echoed through the room, sending electric vibes through the pit of Mahoney's gut. The wails of Robert Plant echoed through the small living space, warning that the levee might break. Mahoney chuckled. His levee had burst wide open long ago. The dark gloom hovering over him lifted.

He made his way back to the couch, sat down on the plump cushion next to the cavern, and reached over to his Styrofoam-boxed dinner. Opening the lid, he scanned the fancy contents. Lasagna for one. Garlic toast for one. He had passed on the salad. He had no one to tell him to eat his vegetables. *Wish I did.*

Picking up the plastic fork, he dug out an ample square from the cheesy layers of pasta and meat sauce. It wasn't bad. The comfort food wrapped his stomach in a warm hug. After eating half the square of pasta, he removed a shoe by pressing his toes against his heel, then repeated with the other foot.

Sweet alcohol tantalized his nostrils as he poured caramel liquid into a crystal glass. He drank it down in one smooth shot. Sweetness lingered over his tongue. A slight burn drizzled down his throat. He poured another, picked up the glass, then leaned back against the couch.

He took a long, slow sip of the drink, then rested his head back against the cushion. As soon as he closed his eyes, the flashes began.

Flash. A shiny black cloak and pale face. *Flash.* A mummy and black nothing eyes. *Flash.* An arctic-ice pendant. *Flash.* Jars full of organs. *Flash.* A wall of forty-one pairs of eyes staring into his soul. Asking him why they weren't saved. He snapped his eyes open and sat up straight. Swallowing back the rest of his drink, he placed the glass on the table with a clink. *What the fuck is happening to my mind?*

He could feel the corpses lining up in his brain. *No.* He shook his head. *No more.* He stood up.

Heat flushed through him. He was still wearing his tweed coat. He pulled it off and tossed it over the arm of the couch. Something fell from the pocket and fluttered to the floor. The plane ticket. The one he hadn't used. The one he was supposed to reschedule. He leaned over, picked it up, and stared at it. Stella's face materialized in his mind. A warmth rushed through him. He sat down on the plump cushion on the couch, reached over and grabbed his phone off the coffee table. He flipped it open, then flipped it closed again. Was he just a dark cloud in her life?

Leaning over, he reached into the pocket of his tweed coat, and pulled out the pink, polished stone. He set it on the coffee table and stared at it. Holding the expired ticket in his hand, staring at the gem, his mind buzzed. He pictured a shiny, blue dolphin dancing over ocean waves. His spirit animal, as declared by a woman in a gem store. What had she said? Her trickling stream of a voice rang though his mind. The dolphin was a symbol of breath. Check your life's blueprint. Still your inner chatter and self-doubt.

He picked up the pink stone, placed the ticket on the table, then sat up straight. He flipped his phone open, punched in the numbers, and took a deep breath.

"Hello?" Her voice was like a songbird.

"Stella. It's dad." His stomach churned. Would she talk to him?

"Dad. Is your case over? Are you coming to see me?"

"Yes, it's over. And, would you like that? For me to come and see you?" He bit down on his bottom lip.

"More than anything. I've been wishing every night that you would catch the bad guy so you could come and see me. It's nice here, Dad. You would like it."

Mahoney squeezed his eyes shut. A tear trickled from beneath the eyepatch. "How about tomorrow?"

Acknowledgments

The writing of every book is a journey with highs and lows. This book would not have flourished into existence without the love and support of family, friends, and fellow authors. Thank you to everyone who inspired me, encouraged me, and supported me along the way.

Dave Sweet – Thank you for answering my gruesome questions night and day, and for the seedlings of ideas that came to life on these pages.

Sarah L Johnson – Thank you for continuing to share your creative passion with me. You are always there for a writing sprint, a warm hug, a winter stroll, or to devour a wheel of cheese and polish off a bottle of wine. Your devotion to the craft of writing inspires me.

Taija Morgan – Thank you for continuing to challenge me with your above and beyond editing magic. Your knowledge and attention to detail is vast. Your support and encouragement have been a critical component in my journey as an author. Your last minute availability to devour a dark horror movie is outstanding.

Sylvia Nunweiler, Cami Schulte, Holly Marinelli – Thank you for finding the time to read this book in its ragged beta state. The long hours you put in scouring the words and providing detailed input shaped the story into what it is today. Without you, this book would not be what it is.

Chris Aune – Thank you for capturing the essence of Bon Julie / Demon Julie and Detective Mahoney. The photos are brilliant.

To the Boot Camp Babies, who have pushed my limits, encouraged me, and been there to remind me of who I really am, just when I needed it.

About Author

Julie Hiner spent endless hours during her childhood lost in the pages of books. The only thing that took precedence over a book was her Walkman. To this day, Julie is a hardcore 80s rocker at heart.

After securing a solid education in computer science at the University of Calgary, Julie spent over a decade working on large scale network systems. On a break between contracts, Julie followed her longing to finish a book she had started, a work of non-fiction portraying her personal story of facing fear and anxiety on a bicycle in the European mountains. After some deep soul searching, she decided to write a novel.

Following her fascination of the dark mind of the serial killer, and finding inspiration at a talk given by a local homicide detective, Julie surged down her new path to writing a dark, serial killer novel. She now writes dark crime and horror. She loves detailed research, creating in depth character, and unleashing her inner artist on photos to create the cover and marketing material.

Also By

Final Track – Detective Mahoney Series, Book 1: books2read.com/finaltrack

Soil Solo – Detective Mahoney Newsletter Exclusive: killersanddemons.com

Owen's Terrarium – books2read.com/owen

The Omens Call – Horror Anthology, Edited by Hiner and Willcocks, Featuring 'Room Thirteen' by Julie Hiner, DevilsRockPublishing.com
'Hallowed Killer', featured in Pulp Harvest – BloodRitesHorror.com
'Corpse Forest', featured in The Other Side: Horror Anthology – DevilsRockPublishing.com
'Tuny', featured in Terrace VI: Forbidden Fruit - TheSeventhTerrace.com

If you enjoyed Acid Track, please consider leaving a review Goodreads(.com), or Bookbub(.com), or your retailer of choice. A review is worth a lot to an author.
Come visit @ KillersAndDemons.com

ACID TRACK

9 781778 142451